April's words chilled Ali. If the killer had been some-where nearby when the crash occurred, then he was probably still there when the emergency vehicles were dispatched to the scene as well—at the same time Ali herself was driving past on the freeway. That meant they'd come after Ali—with a vengeance.

As someone with the three necessary ingredients—motive, opportunity, and an unidentified accomplice—Ali would be exactly what the detectives wanted and needed, a prime suspect.

RAVE REVIEWS FOR THE FICTION OF NEW YORK TIMES AND USA TODAY BESTSELLING AUTHOR J.A. JANCE

"Jance delivers a devilish page-turner."

—*People*

"Heart-stopping. . . . Jance deftly brings the desert, people, and towns of Southeastern Arizona to life."

—*Publishers Weekly*

"An intriguing plot, colorful characters."

—*San Diego Union-Tribune*

"Characters so real you want to reach out and hug—or strangle—them. Her dialogue always rings true."

—*Cleveland Plain Dealer*

ALSO BY J.A. JANCE

ALI REYNOLDS MYSTERIES

JOANNA BRADY MYSTERIES

J.P. BEAUMONT MYSTERIES

WALKER FAMILY MYSTERIES

POETRY

J. A. JANCE

WEB OF EVIL

AN ALI REYNOLDS MYSTERY

POCKET BOOKS

NEW YORK   LONDON   TORONTO   SYDNEY   NEW DELHI

Pocket Books
An Imprint of Simon & Schuster, Inc.
1230 Avenue of the Americas
New York, NY 10020

This book is a work of fiction. Any references to historical events, real people, or real places are used fictitiously. Other names, characters, places, and events are products of the author's imagination, and any resemblance to actual events or places or persons, living or dead, is entirely coincidental.

First Pocket Books paperback edition January 2019

POCKET and colophon are registered trademarks of Simon & Schuster, Inc.

For information about special discounts for bulk purchases, please contact Simon & Schuster Special Sales at 1-866-506-1949 or business@simonandschuster.com.

The Simon & Schuster Speakers Bureau can bring authors to your live event. For more information or to book an event, contact the Simon & Schuster Speakers Bureau at 1-866-248-3049 or visit our website at www.simonspeakers.com.

Manufactured in the United States of America

10 9 8 7 6 5 4 3 2 1

ISBN 978-1-9821-0469-6
ISBN 978-1-4165-4519-4 (ebook)

For Donna A., the last missing piece of my childhood.
I've been looking for you for years.

{ PROLOGUE }

When the man opened his eyes, it was so dark that at first he thought they were still closed. So he tried again, but nothing changed. It was dark—a hot, black, stifling darkness that seemed to suck the breath out of him. He sensed movement, heard the whine of tires on pavement, but he had no idea where he was or how he'd gotten there. He tried to move his legs but couldn't. They were jammed up under his belly in a space that was far too small, and they seemed to be tied together somehow.

His hands were stuck behind him, shoved up against something hard. After several minutes of struggling he was finally able to shift his body enough to free them. He was stunned to discover that they, too, had been bound together in the same manner his legs were. The combination of their being tied too tight and being stuck under his body had cut off the circulation. At first his hands were nothing more than a pair of useless and inextricably connected deadweight cudgels. After a few moments the blood returned to his fingers in a rush of needle-and-pin agony.

As his senses gradually reasserted themselves, he realized that the rough surface under his cheek was carpet of some kind, and from somewhere nearby came the distinctive smell of new rubber—a spare tire. That meant he was in the trunk of someone's vehicle being taken God knows where. He tried to shout, but of course he couldn't do that, either. His mouth was taped shut. All that emerged from his throat was a guttural groan.

What was it you were supposed to do if you found yourself trapped in a vehicle like that? Kick out the taillights, hang an arm out the hole, and signal for help? But he couldn't kick anything. He couldn't move his legs, and his bound hands were still useless.

As the man gradually understood the seriousness of his predicament, his heart beat faster while his breath quickened to short panicky gasps. For a while he was afraid he was going to pass out again, but he fought it—fought to bring his breathing back under control. Fought to concentrate. What the hell was happening? Where was he? Who was doing this? And why?

He tried to remember something about what had gone on before. He had a dim recollection of something like a party. Lots of lights and laughter, lots of girls, lots of liquor. So had he gotten drunk and pissed someone off? Was that what was going on? He knew that given enough scotch he wasn't anyone's idea of Mr. Congeniality, but still . . .

Sweat trickled down the side of his face and dribbled into one eye, burning like fire. Without the use of his hands, there was no way to brush it away.

The vehicle slowed suddenly and swerved to the

right, rolling him back onto his hands. Outside he heard the roar of a semi going past followed immediately by another and another. So they were on a busy freeway somewhere—or had just left one. But where? As hot as it was, it had to be somewhere over the mountains—somewhere in the desert. Palm Springs, maybe? Or maybe farther north, up toward Needles and Parker.

Why can't I remember where I was or what happened? he wondered. He had always prided himself on being able to hold his liquor. He wasn't like some of the guys he knew, high-powered wheeler-dealers who would have to call around after a wild night on the town, checking with valets at local watering holes to see where they had left their favorite Porsche or Ferrari. He usually knew exactly where he'd been. He also knew when he'd had enough. But now, his mind was fuzzy. He couldn't quite pull things together—not just tonight, but what had gone on in the days before that, either.

The vehicle slowed again. He braced himself, expecting another right-hand turn. Instead, the vehicle turned sharply to the left and bounced off the pavement and onto a much rougher surface. Fine dust swirled inside the small space, filling his eyes and nostrils, making his eyes water and his nose run. Definitely the desert somewhere.

There was another hard jolting bump, then the vehicle came to a sudden halt. What must have been the driver's door opened and shut. And then there was nothing. No sound at all. At first he hoped and dreaded that the trunk lid would click open and his captor would free him, but that didn't happen. He strained his ears, hoping to establish if the freeway was still near enough that he'd be able to hear semis speeding past, but for the longest time, he heard nothing at all. He felt only the oppressive heat and wondered how long it would be before the oxygen ran out and he suffocated.

He felt it first. The car trembled as if it were alive, as if it were being racked by a bad case of the chills. Then he heard it—a distant rumble growing louder and louder until it turned into an unmistakable roar. The car rocked in concert with the sound until the terrible roar and the shaking were one. It was then the man heard the shrill, earth-shattering screech of a fast-approaching freight train. The whistle sounded once, in a single, long, warning wail. Only then did he realize that whoever had locked him in the trunk had left him on the train tracks—left him there to die.

He struggled desperately against his restraints, but it was no use. He couldn't free himself. The engine of the speeding eastbound train plowed into the stationary vehicle, peeling it open like an empty tin can and then dragging the wreckage along underneath the engine for the additional mile it took for the shaken engineer to finally bring the fully loaded train to a stop. As the engineer spoke to the 911 operator in Palm Springs, he reported having seen something fly up and out of the shattered vehicle, something that had looked more like a rag doll than it did a human being.

{ CHAPTER 1 }

CUTLOOSEBLOG.COM
Thursday, September 15, 2005

For all you cutloose fans out there who've been following my story from the beginning, tomorrow is the day the D-I-V-O-R-C-E becomes final. For those of you who may be new to the site, the last few months have been a bit of a bumpy ride since both my husband and my former employer simultaneously sent me packing in hopes of landing a younger model.

My soon-to-be-ex—aka Fang, as he's known in the blogosphere—called me yesterday. It was the first time I'd heard from him directly in several months. What surprised me more than anything was how much I DIDN'T feel when I heard his voice. That, I believe, is a good sign. It turns out Fang was calling, in his own imperious way, to make sure I'd be in court tomorrow so the divorce decree can be finalized. I could have given him grief about it. Could have claimed I was sick or maimed or just too annoyed to bother driving eight hours plus from Sedona over to L.A. And, had I done so, it would have sent him up a wall. You see, Fang needs this divorce right about now a whole lot more than I do. Our court appearance is scheduled for Friday. Saturday is Fang's wedding day.

I've heard rumors that he and his blushing bride, aka Twink, are planning a big-deal celebration, a catered affair with all the right people in attendance at what used to be our joint domicile on Robert Lane. In view of the fact that Twink is expecting Fang's baby within weeks of the scheduled nuptials, you might think a little more discretion was called for, but discretion has never been Fang's long suit. For that matter, it must not be Twink's, either, since the baby was conceived some time prior to my abandoning our marriage bed.

For those of you who are concerned about my state of mind as I approach this change in marital status, don't be. I'm fine. I'm ready to make a clean break of it; glad to have what was clearly my sham of a marriage—as far as Fang was concerned anyway—over and done with. I'm moving on with my new life. When you're doing that, hanging on to the old one doesn't help. Neither does bitterness. As my mother is prone to point out, bitterness destroys the container it's in.

If I do say so myself, this particular

container is going to be in pretty fine shape tomorrow when I show up in court. With my son's help, I've been working out. My personal shopper at Nordstrom down in Scottsdale has set aside a couple of new outfits for me. I plan on picking up one of them on my way through the Phoenix area later on this afternoon.

In other words, for today anyway, I'm a rolling stone, and rolling stones gather no moss—and do no blogging.

Posted 7:23 A.M., September 15, 2005 by Babe

As soon as Ali Reynolds hauled her suitcase out of the closet, Samantha, Ali's now-permanent refugee cat, disappeared. Completely. Ali found it hard to believe that a sixteen-pound, one-eyed, one-eared cat could pull off that kind of magicianship, but she could.

Six months earlier, a series of forced moves had left Sam in a new, unfamiliar home with a new owner who wasn't exactly enamored of cats. Over time, Ali and Sam had developed a grudging respect for each other. With the unwelcome appearance of a suitcase, however, all bets were off. For Sam, the sight of a suitcase and/or the dreaded cat crate brought back all those bad old times and sent the panicky kitty scrambling for someplace to hide.

It took Ali a good two hours—two hours she didn't have—to find the animal again, scrunched in beside the drainpipe behind the washing machine in the laundry room. And finding Sam was only part of the problem. Extricating the cat from her snug little hidey-hole and into the cat crate for a trip to Ali's parents' place was a whole other issue. Had it been any other weekend, Sam could have remained at home and been looked after by Ali's son, Christopher, but it happened that Chris was due at a two-day seminar in Phoenix starting early Saturday morning.

"Off to Grandma's with you," Ali said, retrieving the indignant cat and stuffing her into the waiting crate. "And you'd better behave yourself, too."

And so, hours later than she had intended, Ali finally finished packing. With Sam yowling in bitter protest, Ali left her hilltop mobile home digs and drove her lapis blue Porsche Cayenne down to the highway, where she parked under the shady weeping willow tree outside her parents' family-owned diner, Sedona's fabled Sugar Loaf Café.

Inside, the lunch hour rush was just beginning. Edie Larson, Ali's mother, was working the cash register and lunch counter while Ali's father, Bob, held sway in the kitchen. Edie picked up an empty coffeepot and headed for the back counter to refill it, glancing reflexively at her watch as she did so.

"You call this an early start?" Edie asked.

Since Edie rose every morning at o-dark-thirty to prepare the Sugar Loaf's daily supply of signature sweet rolls, she considered any departure that happened after 6 A.M. to be tardy. She had thought Ali's initial estimated departure of nine to be close to slothful. Now it was coming up on noon.

"Unfortunately, Sam had other ideas," Ali said. "She saw the suitcase and went into hiding. I found her, though, finally."

"Good," Edie said reassuringly. "Cats usually don't

like change, but by the time your father gets finished spoiling Sam, that ugly cat of yours won't even want to go back home. Where is she, by the way?"

"Out in the car in the shade."

Edie poured Ali a cup of coffee. "I'll call Kip to come get the crate and take Sam back to the house."

Kip Hogan was a formerly homeless Vietnam War vet Bob Larson had dragged home about the same time his daughter had adopted Sam. Originally Kip had been hired to help look after Bob in the aftermath of an unfortunate snowboarding accident that had left Ali's father temporarily wheelchair-bound. Bob had since recovered and was back at work, but Kip continued to hang around, living in an old Lazy Daze motor home parked in the Larsons' backyard, helping out with odd jobs around both the house and the restaurant, and gradually becoming more and more indispensable.

"Want some lunch before you go?" Edie asked. "Or should I have Dad make up one of the coolers to take along with you?"

"What would go in the cooler?" Ali asked.

"Fried chicken," Bob Larson answered from the kitchen service window. "Biscuits. Some homemade applesauce."

Having been raised on her father's crisp fried chicken and her mother's lighter-than-air biscuits, there was really no contest. "I'll have coffee now and take the cooler option," Ali answered.

Edie took a brief jaunt down the counter, delivering coffee as she went, then she returned to Ali. "Are you all right?" she asked.

"I'm perfectly fine," Ali said. "It'll be good to have this whole mess behind me."

"Yes," Edie agreed. "I'm sure it will be."

Ali had retreated to Sedona, her hometown, to find her bearings in the initial aftermath of both losing her job and learning about her husband's infidelity. She hadn't expected to like it; hadn't expected to be comfortable there, but she was. The double-wide mobile home her aunt Evelyn had left her may have seemed like a big comedown from the gated mansion on Robert Lane, but it suited Ali's needs, everything from the Jacuzzi soaking tub to the basement wine cellar. And having her son, Chris, for a roommate didn't hurt, either.

Chris had graduated from UCLA and was in his first year of teaching welding and American history at Sedona High School. Ali enjoyed her son's company. He never left a mess in the kitchen, didn't stay out all that late, and spent much of his spare time working on his metal sculpting projects down in the basement. From what Ali could tell, she and Chris got along better than did many parents and their newly adult children.

All in all, she felt at ease being back home in Sedona—at ease and at peace.

"I wish Chris were going over with you," Edie added, seeming to read Ali's mind. "Driving to L.A. is a long trip to do all by yourself."

"Chris is busy with a seminar this weekend," Ali replied. "I don't mind driving. In fact, I enjoy being on the open road. Besides, I've got Aunt Evelyn's library of musicals along to keep me company."

"Well, be sure you take plenty of breaks," Edie cautioned. "They say tired drivers are as bad as drunk drivers."

Bob rang the bell, letting Edie know that an order was ready. While she left to deliver it, Kip Hogan turned up at Ali's elbow. "Keys?" he asked.

When Kip had first appeared, six months earlier, he had come from a snowy, outdoor homeless encampment up on the Mogollan Rim. After years of living rough, he had been gaunt and grubby, with long, filthy hair, dirty clothes, missing teeth, and a much-broken nose. Kip's missing teeth and crooked nose were still at issue, but months of eating decent food had allowed him to fill out some. And dressed in respectable if secondhand clothing and with ready access to running water, the man looked far less scary than he had initially.

Without a word, Ali handed over her car keys.

"Leave the cat in her crate in the living room," Edie told Kip as he started for the door. "That way she'll have a chance to get used to her new digs before we let her out to explore."

"Yes, ma'am," Kip replied. "Will do."

"When will you be back?" Edie asked her daughter.

"Tuesday or Wednesday," Ali replied. "The divorce hearing is tomorrow. Then on Monday or Tuesday there's supposed to be a deposition in the wrongful dismissal suit. It didn't make sense to do two trips when one would work. So I'll stay over however long it takes to give the deposition."

"Good," Edie agreed. "It's always better to kill two birds with one stone. More coffee?"

Ali let her mother refill her cup. Initially she had blamed her tardy departure on Sam. Now Ali realized that she was stalling even more all on her own—and she knew why. Months after the fact, there was part of her that dreaded getting on I-17 and heading down to Phoenix. Ali Reynolds had almost died on one particularly dangerous stretch of that freeway when someone had tried to push her off the highway and over the edge of a sheer cliff. Being the target of an attempted murder is something that lingers, and even though Ali had driven that same route several times between then and now, she was still skittish. Just thinking about driving past the Sunset Point rest area and heading down the steep grade into the valley was enough to make her hands go clammy.

Her face must have betrayed some of the concern she was feeling.

"Are you sure you wouldn't like some company?" Edie Larson asked solicitously. "And some moral support once you get there and have to go to court? I'm sure your father could manage without me for a day or two. He wouldn't like it, but having to get up early enough to make the rolls wouldn't kill him."

Touched by the offer, Ali smiled. "Thanks, Mom," she said. "I'll be fine. Really."

"And you'll call and let us know how it's going?"

"I promise."

Kip returned with her car keys, and Ali took her leave. She stopped by the bank and picked up some cash. She had a particular pet charity that she wanted to help along while she was in L.A., and she knew a cash gift would be most welcome.

A little less than an hour after leaving the bank, Ali was past the most worrisome stretch of the Black Canyon Freeway and headed into Scottsdale. At the time she had left her evening news gig in L.A., she had ditched her old newscasting wardrobe and her California persona like a snake shedding a cast-off skin. For as long as she'd been in Sedona, she'd worn her hair in a less-than-stylish ponytail and limited her wardrobe to what was comfortable—mostly sweatshirts and worn jeans. Now, though, facing courtroom appointments and the prospect of more than a little public notoriety, Ali understood that she needed to dress and look the part. Not only did she pick up several outfits, she stopped by one of Scottsdale's upscale salons for some much-needed pampering, including a haircut along with a spa-style mani/pedi.

Properly attired, coiffed, and accessorized, Ali felt ready to face what she had come to think of as her California ordeal. She headed west in late-afternoon rush-hour traffic and soon found herself stuck in a jam of speeding eighteen-wheelers, all of them driving blindly but hell-bent-for-election into the setting sun. Tired of trying to stay out of their way, Ali pulled off at the first rest area she saw. There, sitting at a shaded picnic table, she opened her cooler. Not only was her father's carefully prepared food there, so was a collection of plastic utensils. With noisy traffic rushing by in the background, Ali savored her combination lunch/dinner of fried chicken and honey-slathered biscuits. Then, feeling fatigued and still not wanting to face into the glaring sunset, she returned to the Cayenne, locked the doors, lowered her seat back, and allowed herself the luxury of a nap.

She slept far longer than she expected. It was dark when she woke up, but she felt refreshed. Once back on the road, Ali was relieved to realize that traffic was noticeably lighter, and she was grateful she'd had the good sense to wait out the setting sun rather than driving into it.

Ali realized that that was one of the wonderful things about traveling on her own. She could eat when she was hungry, sleep when she was tired. It wasn't necessary to take anyone else's needs, wants, or opinions into consideration. Yes, being back on her own was definitely growing on Ali Reynolds.

She took her mother's advice to heart. When she stopped for gas in Blythe, she stopped at a roadside restaurant for coffee as well. She was halfway through the second cup when her phone rang.

"Well," Helga Myerhoff said in her distinctly gruff and smoky voice. "Have we girded our loins?"

Helga, sometimes called Rottweiler Myerhoff, had a not-undeserved reputation for being one of the Hollywood elite's premier divorce attorneys. With Helga's help and with the added impetus of Paul wanting a fast divorce as opposed to a cheap one, Ali had a generous divorce settlement coming to her, one that gave her pretty much everything she wanted. Between them Helga and Ali had, in fact, taken Fang to the cleaners.

Ali laughed. "They're girded, all right. New duds, new haircut, killer nails. Believe me, I'm ready."

"Good," Helga said. "And you're staying at the Westwood on Wilshire?"

"That's right," Ali answered. "I'm booked there through Tuesday. Marcella has a wrongful dismissal deposition coming up on either Monday or Tuesday. I'm staying over for that as well."

Marcella Johnson and Helga both worked for the same high-end legal firm, Weldon, Davis, and Reed, but the two women had wildly divergent styles and areas of expertise. Helga specialized in divorce cases.

Marcella focused on employment issues. Ali counted herself fortunate to have not one but two dynamic attorneys on her team.

"Don't worry about tomorrow," Helga said. "We're in good shape on this and I'm pretty sure it'll go through without a hitch. Still, though, until everything's signed, sealed, and delivered, our agreement in principle could conceivably go south."

"Paul won't let that happen," Ali said with a laugh. "Not with his shotgun wedding set for Saturday. If something goes wrong with his walking April Gaddis down the aisle, there'll be hell to pay."

"You're all right then?" Helga asked.

Everyone seemed to be concerned about how Ali was holding up through all this. Why didn't anyone believe her when she said she was fine? She said it again, one more time and for the record.

"I'm fine, Helga. I wish people would stop worrying about me."

"Getting a divorce is stressful," Helga said.

"No," Ali corrected. "Compared to being married to a jerk, getting a divorce is easy."

"All right," Helga said. "See you in court, ten A.M. sharp. Judge Alice Tennant is very old-fashioned. She doesn't brook tardiness from anybody—attorneys or plaintiffs."

"Ten sharp," Ali repeated. "I'll be there."

Leaving Blythe, Ali turned up the volume on her MP3 player and sang along with the tunes from one musical comedy after another, from *A Connecticut Yankee* to *A Chorus Line*. As she drove, only a bare sliver of rising moon was visible in the rearview mirror behind her, but the nighttime sky was clear enough that even by starlight she could see the hulking forms of distant mountain ranges jutting up out of the silvery desert floor.

Crossing through California, Ali felt a strange disconnect. She had gone there years earlier with a new husband and a new job, following what had seemed then to be an American dream. Now, coming back to L.A. for the first time since that dream had exploded in her face, she realized that she was, literally, yesterday's news. Her job and her connection to her prominent network-exec husband had made her part of the L.A. in-crowd. This trip was the exact opposite. As an antidote, she turned up the music even louder.

Sometime around midnight, shortly after passing the exit to Twentynine Palms, Ali saw a whole phalanx of emergency vehicles surging eastbound and toward her on the freeway. Worried that debris from some unseen accident might litter the road ahead, Ali slowed, but then, one by one, the approaching vehicles veered off on what she knew to be the Highway 111 exit angling toward Palm Springs.

The emergency response was so massive that Ali found it worrisome. Wondering if maybe a plane had gone down, Ali turned off her original cast recording of *Camelot* and scanned through the radio dial until she found one of L.A.'s twenty-four-hour all-news channels. It was another ten minutes, after bits about Iraq and the latest riots in France, before the announcer cut in with a local news flash.

"The Riverside Sheriff's Department is investigating a possible train/vehicle collision on the eastbound tracks approaching Palm Springs. Emergency vehicles have been dispatched to the area and a CALTrans spokesman is suggesting that the area be avoided until further notice."

Relieved to hear that whatever was wrong didn't involve a problem on the freeway, Ali punched the "resume" button on her cruise control and took the Cayenne back up to speed. Then she switched off the news and went back to listening to King Arthur's bored and disaffected knights singing their rousing rendition of "Fie on Goodness."

As she drove past the Highway 111 interchange, the emergency vehicles had mostly stopped, forming a long, unbroken string of flashing red and yellow lights that erased the starlight and cast an eerie pulsing glow on the surrounding desert.

Ali drove on, thinking about trains and cars and what happens when one crashes into the other. In her days as a newbie television reporter, Ali had seen plenty of incidents like that, ones where people seemingly determined to opt out of the gene pool had decided, for one incredibly stupid reason or another, to try to outrun a speeding train, leaving behind a trail of bloody carnage and shattered metal. Sometimes the incidents included groups of teenagers playing a deadly game of chicken. Others drove onto the tracks deliberately and with the full intention of ending it all. Regardless of their motivation, the people in the vehicles usually didn't survive. Sometimes the engineers on the trains didn't make it out alive, either. The ones who did often lived out their days with a lifelong burden of guilt.

"At least this time it's got nothing to do with me," Ali breathed aloud as she headed west toward Banning and Beaumont and the sprawling city of Los Angeles glowing far in the distance. "And thank God I don't have to report on it, either."

{ CHAPTER 2 }

Helga called the next morning at eight. "So you know where you're going?" she asked.

Ali had lived in California for years. She knew her way around Beverly Hills. "The West District Courthouse, right?"

"Close, but no cigar," Helga said. "Your husband wanted this divorce in a hell of a hurry. In California, if you don't want to wait in line for court time, you can hire a private judge. I told him fine, as long as I got to choose the judge, which I did. Judge Alice Tennant's court is a few blocks away from there in what used to be a private residence."

"I didn't know there was any such thing as a private judge," Ali muttered.

"You do now," Helga returned.

Helga had referred to Alice Tennant's courtroom as a private residence, but the term hadn't done the place justice. *Mansion's more like it,* Ali thought an hour and a half later when she pulled up in front of the two-story porticoed edifice with lions guarding either side of a gated entrance complete with a circular drive.

Helga was waiting on the front porch, pacing back and forth in front of a pair of Art Deco doors radiant with what looked like genuine Tiffany stained glass. Beyond the glass doors was a marbled foyer, its old-fashioned elegant ambience marred by the mundane and thoroughly modern presence of a wand-holding uniformed security guard and a metal detector.

They were directed into an ornate room that had probably once served as a formal dining room. A magnificent, hand-carved sideboard at the far end was covered with a silver coffee service, plates, cups, saucers, and silverware, and a collection of breakfast pastries that would have put most self-respecting hotel buffets to shame. The display came complete with a uniformed butler who handled the pouring.

Ali was sipping freshly squeezed orange juice and nibbling on a deliciously flaky croissant when Paul's attorney, Ted Grantham, came rushing into the room.

"Paul's still not here?" Grantham demanded of Helga.

"Not so far," Helga returned with a tight smile.

Ted Grantham was someone Ali knew slightly. He had been a guest at their Robert Lane home on several occasions, and he was a regular attendee at Paul's daylong Super Bowl extravaganzas. Now, though, Ted barely acknowledged her. Refusing offers of coffee, he paced back and forth in the entryway, making one brief cell phone call after another. By five to ten, when Paul had yet to arrive, Ted was downright frantic.

"So where's his bad boy?" Helga muttered under

her breath. "Hope he's not planning on keeping the judge waiting."

But it turned out that was exactly what Paul seemed to have in mind. At three minutes after ten, a bailiff summoned all three of them into the judge's chambers.

Judge Alice Tennant was seated behind an immense partner desk that reminded Ali of one she'd seen in an antiques shop in the idyllic Cotswold town of Stow-on-the-Wold. Dwarfed by the desk, Judge Tennant was a sixty-something with flaming red hair and a temper to match.

"My time's very valuable, and you know I don't like being kept waiting, Mr. Grantham," she snapped as they filed into the room. "So where exactly is your client? Was he aware that he was expected here at ten this morning?"

"Yes, of course he knew," Grantham said hurriedly. "I've been trying to reach him all morning. He isn't answering any of his phones. The calls keep going straight to voice mail, and he hasn't called me back, either."

"I was given to understand there was some urgency about our doing this today," Judge Tennant observed. "About Mr. Grayson wanting to have his divorce final-ized in a timely fashion."

Grantham looked uncomfortable. "Yes," he said. "There is something of a deadline."

"Because?"

Grantham glanced briefly in Ali's direction before he answered. "Well," he said reluctantly. "Actually, Mr. Grayson is due to be married tomorrow."

"I presume that would be to someone other than the wife who happens to be here right at the moment?" Judge Tennant asked. Her sharp blue eyes focused fully on the squirming attorney, whose forehead, by then, had popped out in a very unlawyerly sweat.

"Yes," Grantham muttered. "That would be correct. To someone else. I'm sure I'll be able to locate my client in the next little while. If you could find a spot for us in this afternoon's calendar—"

Alice Tennant's reply was brisk. "There is no afternoon calendar. As it happens, I'm leaving town right after lunch," she said with a cold smile. "You'll have to check with my clerk to see if it's possible to reschedule for sometime next week—if that's all right with you, Ms. Reynolds. I understand you've driven all the way over from Arizona."

"Of course," Ali said quickly. "Next week will be fine. I want to stay on until this is sorted out."

"Excellent," Judge Tennant said.

"Perhaps you could see your way clear to hand this off to another judge—" Grantham began.

Helga started to object, but Judge Tennant silenced both attorneys with a single wave of her hand. "I was contracted to deal with this case," she said severely. "I have no intention of handing it off to anyone. Once the next court date is set, I trust you'll notify your client that he will be present on the appointed day and at the appointed hour. Please remind him that I may be a private judge, but I can nonetheless cite him for contempt of court. Is that clear, Mr. Grantham?"

"Yes, ma'am," Grantham replied contritely. "Quite clear."

"Just for the record," she added. "If I hear that any

kind of marriage ceremony is performed tomorrow without your client being properly divorced from Ms. Reynolds beforehand, I'll see to it that he's charged with bigamy, which happens to be a criminal offense. Is that also clear?"

"Yes," Grantham said. "Very."

"All right then. See my clerk."

Ali couldn't help feeling a bit giddy at the idea that Paul's absence at the hearing had left Twink's lavish plans for her wedding day in utter shambles. Hurrying out into the corridor to wait while Helga Myerhoff and Ted Grantham dealt with the court clerk, she almost collided with a man rushing toward her from the security checkpoint.

"Ali!" he exclaimed. "Don't tell me the hearing's finished already."

Ali recognized the new arrival as Jake Maxwell, one of Paul's fellow network execs. She was surprised to see him there; surprised to think he'd squander some of his precious time on Paul's legal issues. Jake and his ditzy wife, Roseanne, weren't high on Ali's list of social acquaintances any more than Ted Grantham was.

"Hi, Jake," she said. "We're done for today. What brings you here?"

At least he had the good grace to look sheepish. "You know, moral support and all that."

"Well, you missed on that one," Ali said. "Paul didn't show."

Helga emerged from the courtroom wearing a grim smile. "Thursday morning. Ten A.M. again." Then, looking at Jake, she added derisively, "Oh, Mr. Maxwell, you must be Mr. Grayson's cheering section.

I'm afraid the match has been rescheduled for next week—same time, same station. See you then." Dismissing Jake, Helga turned back to Ali. "Is that all right with you?"

"Thursday is fine," Ali said. "I can stay that long if I have to."

Ted Grantham entered the hallway. Jake quickly gravitated in his direction.

"Why isn't Paul here?" he asked.

"Beats the hell out of me," Grantham replied heatedly. "He blew off our court appearance, and now the judge is pissed at me."

"Did you check with April?"

"Of course I checked with April. She has no idea where Paul is. He never came home last night."

The glass doors closed behind the two men, taking the rest of the conversation outside with them.

"So he didn't come home last night," Helga observed. "Not good. Not good."

"It sounds amazingly familiar to me," Ali said.

"Well," Helga said, "if Paul Grayson knows what's good for him, he'll cancel his wedding and make the cancellation a media event all its own."

"Why? The bigamy thing? Would Judge Tennant really put him in jail for going through with the wedding?"

"Absolutely," Helga replied. "Alice Tennant takes a dim view of those kinds of marital shenanigans. Her ex, Jack, did the same thing, you see. Got married while the divorce decree was still warm to the touch—the same day, in fact. It's lucky for Paul—and for Ted Grantham, too—that we've already hammered out a property settlement."

Ali was astounded. "Why on earth did Paul agree to use her as a judge?"

"Because he was in a hurry," Helga answered. "Like I told you, I got to choose."

Just then, the glass entry doors swung open and a very tall black woman, clad in sweats and tennis shoes, entered the building. She paused briefly while going through the security checkpoint, then came trotting down the hall toward Ali and Helga.

"Am I too late?" the newcomer asked breathlessly, smothering Ali in a bone-crushing hug. "Sorry. I went to the courthouse and looked everywhere for the right courtroom before someone finally pointed me in this direction. Is it over already?"

"Not *over* over," Ali replied. "But it's over for today."

"Who's this?" Helga wanted to know.

"*My* cheering section," Ali replied with a smile. "My friend Sister Anne. And Sister Anne, this is my attorney, Helga Myerhoff."

At six foot seven, Sister Anne towered over both Ali and the diminutive Helga. She was dressed in blue-and-white UCLA insignia sweats and high-end Nikes and looked far more like the NCAA championship basketball player she had once been than the Sister of Charity she was now. Jamalla Kareem Williams had left college with a degree in business administration, plenty of basketball trophies, and a permanently damaged knee. Rather than going into business, she had become a nun. For years now, she had managed My Sister's Closet, a Pasadena-based clothing recycling program that helped provide appropriate, low-cost attire for impoverished women hoping to get into the job market. That was where Ali had dropped off her newscaster duds when she had left town months earlier.

Sister Anne held out her hand in Helga's direction. "Glad to meet you," she said with a gap-toothed smile while her beaded cornrows clicked and clattered around her head.

"Sister Anne and I met years ago at a charity fundraiser and just hit it off," Ali explained. "In fact, if it weren't for her, I probably wouldn't know about you. Marcella Johnson was one of Sister Anne's basketball teammates at UCLA. When I was looking at filing a wrongful dismissal suit against the station, Sister Anne pointed me at Marcella, and when I needed a divorce attorney, Marcella sent me to you."

Sister Anne turned back to Ali. "What do you mean it's not *over* over?"

"My not-quite-ex didn't bother showing up for the hearing," Ali told her. "The new court date is set for Thursday of next week."

"Well, then," Sister Anne said briskly. "Let's go have some lunch."

Helga begged off, so Ali and Sister Anne drove to Beverly Center and had lunch in a Mexican restaurant where one of Sister Anne's recent clients from My Sister's Closet had hired on as the hostess. Over a shared plate of fajitas, Ali reached into her purse and pulled out an envelope, which she handed to Sister Anne.

"What's this?"

"Money," Ali said. "It's one thing to donate clothing, but this time I decided to give you something that would help pay the rent and keep the lights on."

Sister Anne counted through the bills, then looked up. "You can afford this?"

"Helga's a very good attorney. I'm going to be fine."

Smiling, Sister Anne slipped the envelope into a zippered pocket on her pants. "This couldn't come at a better time," she said. "We've been right on the edge of having to close the place down. You have no idea how much we needed this."

The hostess, a young Hispanic woman dressed in a stylish black dress and sling-back high heels—clothing that had been someone else's castoffs—smiled shyly at Sister Anne and Ali as she led a group of diners to a table.

"Glad I could help," Ali said. And she was.

After lunch, feeling a strange sense of letdown, Ali returned to her hotel. First she called her mother, who was still at the Sugar Loaf.

"Well?" Edie Larson said. "Are you free as a bird now?"

"Not exactly," Ali said, and then went on to explain the situation.

"My word," Edie said. "If that doesn't take the cake! After you had to drive all that way! It's inexcusable for him to not show up like that. Did you try calling him?"

"No," Ali admitted. "Under the circumstances, that didn't seem like a good idea. His attorney called, though. From what he was saying, it sounded like Paul stayed out all night."

"And he hasn't even married the poor girl yet?" Edie demanded. "Seems like it's a little early for him to be up to his old tricks."

Ali didn't exactly agree with the "poor girl" part. But the "old tricks" reference worked. "Yes," Ali said. "It does seem early."

"You stay there as long as necessary in order to get this all straightened out," Edie said. "Everything here is under control. Chris stopped by last night before he headed for his seminar in Phoenix tomorrow. We invited him to come to dinner Sunday night when he gets home, so he won't starve to death. As for Sam? She's fine. She took to your father the way most strays do. In other words—love at first sight. What are you going to do with this extra time, hook up with some old friends?"

What old friends? Ali wondered. Other than Sister Anne, she didn't seem to have any real friends waiting for her. The ones she did have were people who were primarily friends of Paul's. In the aftermath of her blowup with Paul and the abrupt ending to her television career, Ali had been surprised and hurt by the number of people who had simply vanished from her life the moment her face had disappeared from the evening news. It had been hard to accept that people she had considered close friends had been drawn by her celebrity rather than anything else. Coming to terms with the reality of those lost relationships still hurt, but Edie Larson didn't need to know that.

"Already handled, Mom," Ali said as airily as she could manage. "Not to worry."

But it wasn't. When Ali got off the phone with her mother, she slipped out of her new Nordy's "court dress" and changed into a T-shirt and jeans. There were, of course, people she could have called, some of whom were bound to be in town. But she didn't call any of them. There was something so trite and Hollywoody—so whiny and pathetic—about gathering a group of pals around to hold your hand during stalled divorce proceedings that she couldn't bring herself to do it. Instead, Ali pulled out her computer and turned to Babe of Yavapai's new friends—the ones who were only a mouse click away.

CUTLOOSEBLOG.COM
Friday, September 16, 2005

Surprisingly enough it's more difficult to be cut loose legally than one would think. The divorce that was supposed to be finalized today isn't because my soon-to-be-former husband was a no-show in court, and our rent-a-judge refused to issue a decree without his being present and accounted for. So here I am stuck in limbo for a little longer. This should all be brought to a conclusion next week, but for now I'm here with time on my hands and not much to do.

In the past I've always had work to fall back on. And family responsibilities. But my son is raised now. I no longer have to look after him, and although I'm not entirely finished with him yet, I no longer have a husband to look after, either.

So I've decided to treat this like an extended vacation—a vacation in a place where I used to live, but where I was always too busy working to do the things tourists from around the world come here to do.

Starting with the Getty. And the La Brea Tar
Pits. Who knows? I may even throw over the
traces completely and go for a walk on the
beach or spend a day at Disneyland.

In other words, blogging will be light for
a while for the very good reason that I'm out
having fun.

*Posted 2:16 P.M., September 16, 2005 by
Babe*

After that, Ali read through and posted some of the
comments that had come in from her readers while
she'd been otherwise engaged.

Dear Babe,
I know you're lawyer said your divorce would be
final, but don't you believe him. Divorces ain't
never final. They can give you a hundred pieces
of paper that say your single, but being married
don't just go away because of a piece of paper,
especially if you have kids. And I should know.
My husband can still drive me crazy even though
we've been divorced for fifteen years and hes
been dead for ten. If I end up still being married
to him when I get to heaven, I may just turn
around and walk right back out.

LILY

The next comment came from one of Ali's regulars, a widowed longtime fan from California, who
wrote cheery little notes every other day or so. Over
the months, Ali had come to think of the woman as

a friend, despite the fact that they had never met in person.

> *Dear Babe,*
> *I know this is a tough time for you. I just*
> *wanted you to know my thoughts and prayers*
> *are with you.*
>
> VELMA T IN LAGUNA

Then there was Fred.

> *What happened to "Whosoever God has joined*
> *together let no man put asunder"? No wonder*
> *the world is going to hell in a handbasket. First*
> *women wanted the Equal Rights Amendment*
> *and now they don't even want to bother with*
> *having husbands. And did you ever give any*
> *thought as to how you treated your husband*
> *and what might have driven him into the arms*
> *of another woman? I'm glad I only have sons*
> *and no daughters.*
>
> FRED

So am I, Ali thought. She decided not to post Fred's comment. Then she changed her mind. She suspected there were a lot of people in the world who shared his opinion and regarded independent women as a direct threat to their manhood and to their very existence. Maybe that was something cut-looseblog needed to bring up as a topic of discussion.

Dear Babe,
My husband did the same thing, married his little
cutie two days after our divorce. It didn't last.
Two months later he was back, knocking on my
door because she'd thrown him out and begging
me to take him back, which I did. He stayed for
three more years after that then he left again and
now I don't know where he is. But I know you're
smarter than I am, so if your cheating husband
asks you to take him back, whatever you do,
don't.

WISER NOW

Ali's phone rang. She recognized the number—
the Flagstaff branch of the YWCA. "Hi, Andrea," Ali
said.

Andrea was Andrea Rogers. A year ago, Andrea had
been second in command in what was essentially a
two-woman nonprofit spearheaded by Ali's girlhood
best friend, Reenie Bernard. Reenie had been the out-
going, fund-raising brains of the outfit, while Andrea
had functioned as office manager, keeping the place
running smoothly in Reenie's absence. After Reenie's
tragic murder, it had been Andrea who had tracked
down Reenie's personal effects and, for the benefit of
Reenie's orphaned children, rescued them from the
thrift shop where they'd been shipped by Reenie's
less-than-grief-stricken husband.

For Andrea, that one act of kindness on behalf of
Reenie's kids had been the beginning of a new sense
of self-confidence and independence. The Flagstaff
YWCA had been so much Reenie Bernard's baby that,

in the initial aftermath of her murder, there had been serious talk of shutting the place down, but Andrea in particular had been determined that Reenie's dream wouldn't perish with her. Over a period of several months, Andrea had managed to keep the doors open while Ali worked to convince the board of directors that, with a little assistance and encouragement from them, Andrea could be groomed to take over the executive director's position.

Her official promotion had happened three months ago. The board had hired a new assistant for Andrea, but Andrea had yet to catch on to the fact that she no longer needed to answer the phone herself—which she did most of the time.

Andrea was a plugger. She was dependable. She didn't have the finesse or the vision of a Reenie Bernard. What she had instead was an absolute devotion to her murdered boss and unbridled enthusiasm about carrying Reenie's life's work forward. One way or another, Andrea managed to get things done.

"Is it over then?" Andrea asked.

" 'It' being the divorce?" Ali asked.

"Of course, the divorce," Andrea returned. "What else would I be asking about?"

"I'm beginning to wonder if my divorce will ever be over," Ali replied and went on to repeat the gory details one more time.

"But what if you're not home in time for the board meeting next Friday?" Andrea asked, as a hint of her old reticence crept into her voice. "I've never handled one of those by myself. I've always had you there to backstop me."

"I'll do what I can to be home by then," Ali said.

"But if I'm not, you'll be fine. You know more about what's going on at the YWCA than anyone. You'll be able to handle it."

"I hope so," Andrea said, but she didn't sound convinced.

Ali was talking on her cell phone. It surprised her when the room phone began to ring. "Sorry, Andrea," Ali said. "I need to take that."

"Ms. Reynolds?" a woman's voice asked.

"Yes."

"My name is Detective Carolyn Little," she said. "I'm with the LAPD's Missing Persons Unit. Mr. Ted Grantham said you were staying at the Westwood, and I took the liberty of calling."

"About?" Ali asked.

"About your husband."

"My soon-to-be-former husband," Ali corrected.

"Are you aware he's missing?"

"I know he failed to show up in court this morning for our divorce hearing," Ali answered. "That's all I know."

"He's been reported missing by one April Gaddis."

"His fiancée," Ali supplied.

"Yes," Detective Little answered. "She did mention that she and Mr. Grayson are engaged. It seems he went to a bachelor party last evening and never came home."

Ali felt like mentioning that for Paul to declare himself a bachelor prior to his divorce being finalized was a bit like putting the cart before the horse, but Detective Little didn't sound like she had much of a sense of humor.

"When was the last time you saw your husband?" Detective Little asked.

"That would be Friday, March eleventh of this year," Ali answered at once.

There was a slight pause. "March eleventh? That's a long time ago—six months, but you still remember the exact date?"

"And the exact time," Ali responded. "I had just lost my job. I came home, expecting some sympathy from my husband, but in our house, you find sympathy in the dictionary between 'shit' and 'syphilis.' He took off with his girlfriend bright and early the next morning before I even woke up."

The "shit and syphilis" reference was one of her father's more colorful expressions, one that was guaranteed to send Bob Larson's wife into a spasm. Even Carolyn Little chuckled a little at that, so the woman wasn't entirely devoid of humor.

"This same girlfriend?" the detective added. "The fiancée?"

"Yes," Ali agreed. "That would be the one—the same one who's expecting his baby."

"And you came to town when?"

"Last night," Ali said. "I drove over from Sedona yesterday afternoon. I got a late start. It was almost two in the morning before I finished checking in."

"And you're here until . . . ?"

"Paul and I have another court date scheduled for next week."

"On Thursday," Little said. Obviously she had already acquired the information from Ted Grantham. "And you'll be staying at the Westwood? And is there another number in case I need to reach you again?"

It had been six months since Ali had seen Paul

Grayson, and she didn't see why the Missing Persons Unit would need to speak to her again, but she gave the detective her cell phone number all the same.

As Ali ended the call with Detective Little, she was already groping for the television remote. Within minutes of turning on the set she located a news tease from Annette Carrera, Ali Reynolds's blond, blue-eyed, surgically enhanced news anchor successor. The promo was already in progress when Ali tuned in: ". . . network executive who disappeared from his bachelor party last night. We'll have the story for you live on the evening news."

Carrera! Ali had to give credit to whoever had dreamed up that name. It was calculated to be high-toned enough to appeal to L.A.'s Porsche-craving yuppies, but it also sounded vaguely Hispanic—if you didn't look too closely at the blond hair, blue eyes, and fair skin. In Ali's not-unbiased opinion, Annette was far too young and far too perky. Her hair looked as if she had stuck her finger in an electrical outlet and then moussed the resulting hairdo into a froth of permanent peaks—like whipped cream beaten to a turn.

Disgusted at the idea of having to wait another two hours to glean any additional details, Ali reached for her computer, intent on surfing the Net to track down a breaking-news Web site. As she touched the keyboard, though, she heard a new-mail alert. She paused long enough to read the message.

Dear Babe,
I just saw a news blurb on your old channel.
I've gone back to watching them even though I

*hate that new Annette person. Anyway, it said a
man named Paul Grayson, some network bigwig,
is missing. I seem to remember that was your
husband's name. So is this your Paul Grayson or
is it just someone with the same name?*

VELMA T IN LAGUNA

No matter who he is, he isn't my *Paul Grayson,* Ali
thought, but she sent Velma an immediate response.

*Dear Velma,
Thanks for bringing this to my attention. The
missing man most likely is "my" Paul Grayson.
Once I have more details on the situation, I'll try
to let you know.*

BABE

{ CHAPTER 3 }

For the next while, Ali surfed the Net. Her years in L.A. had taught her that Southern California news outlets had an insatiable appetite for anything involving the entertainment industry—movies or television. Paul Grayson was high enough up the network food chain that it wasn't long before Ali found what she was looking for, even though it offered little more information than she had gleaned from the earlier news promo.

NBC EXEC MISSING

Paul Grayson, long considered NBC's West Coast go-to guy, has gone missing after an early and abrupt departure from his own bachelor party at the stylish Pink Swan on Santa Monica Boulevard in West Hollywood. His red Porsche Carrera was found stripped and abandoned in an apartment parking lot in Banning early this afternoon.

There it was again. Everybody seemed free to refer to Paul as a bachelor, despite the inconvenient fact that he was still legally married—to Ali. And what exactly was this "stylish" Pink Swan? Probably some cheesy strip joint or pole-dancing outfit. Whatever it was, the name sounded suitably sleazy. The next paragraph, however, shook her.

A spokesman for LAPD's Missing Persons Unit said they have reason to believe that Mr. Grayson has been the victim of foul play.

"Foul play." Ali repeated the words aloud. The very possibility that Paul had been victimized made Ali's earlier conversation with Detective Little seem much more ominous.

Jake Maxwell, who co-hosted the bachelor party, said the guest of honor departed early on in the proceedings. "Somewhere around ten or so, Paul went outside to take a phone call and didn't come back. Everyone was having a good time. It was a while before anyone noticed that he hadn't returned."

Because everyone was too blasted to notice, Ali thought. The news item ended. For several long minutes afterward, Ali wondered what, if anything, she should do. Finally, however, it seemed reasonable to let her divorce attorney know that Paul had now been declared a missing person. Ali picked up her cell phone and dialed Helga Myerhoff's number.

"What's up?" Helga asked.

"I thought you should know Paul didn't just miss his court appearance this morning," Ali told her attorney. "He disappeared from what they're calling his 'bachelor party' last night. There's some suspicion that foul play may be involved. His Carrera was found abandoned in an apartment house parking lot in Banning this afternoon."

Helga was all business. "How did you find this out?"

"Part of it I learned just now from reading a breaking-news Web site. The rest of it, though, came from a phone call from Detective Carolyn Little of the LAPD Missing Persons Unit."

"Why did she call *you*?" Helga asked. "And, beyond that, how did she even know to call you?"

"Since I hadn't seen Paul in more than six months, I thought it was odd that she'd be asking me for information, but Ted Grantham evidently told the detective I was in town and where I was staying."

Ali heard a slight rustling on the phone and could picture Helga standing behind her desk and squaring her shoulders, bristling to her diminutive but tough-as-nails five foot two. "What exactly did this detective say? And what's her name again?"

"Detective Carolyn Little, LAPD Missing Persons. She asked when I had arrived, why I was here, where I was staying, when did I last see Paul. All the usual stuff, I guess."

"Did she mention the possibility that you might be under any kind of suspicion?"

The severity of Helga's tone put Ali on edge and made her wonder if perhaps Detective Little's questions weren't quite so "usual" after all.

"Me?" Ali demanded, dumbfounded. "Why on earth would I be a suspect?"

"Has Paul changed his will?" Helga asked.

"I have no idea about that," Ali said. "We're getting a divorce, remember? I've rewritten my will so Chris is my primary beneficiary in case anything happens to me. I would assume Paul has done the same thing in favor of April and her baby."

"Not necessarily," Helga mused. "In my experience, men often put off handling those pesky little details."

"What are you saying?" Ali asked.

"Let's assume the worst," Helga said. "Let's say Paul Grayson turns up dead, a victim of some kind of foul play. If you and he aren't divorced—and you're not—and if, by some chance, his will hasn't been rewritten, it's likely you'll make out far better as a widow than you would have as a divorcée. From an investigative point of view and considering the dollar amounts involved, that might well put you at the top of the suspect list in a murder-for-profit scheme."

"Me?" Ali asked. "How is that possible? I had nothing to do with any of this—nothing at all. Besides, at the time Paul disappeared from his so-called bachelor party, I was out in the middle of the desert, somewhere this side of Blythe."

"Let's don't push panic buttons then," Helga reassured her. "We'll just sit back and see what happens. But, in the meantime, don't talk to any more detectives without having your attorney present."

"My attorney," Ali repeated. "You mean you?"

"No. Not me. I do divorces. I don't do criminal law," Helga continued. "That's a whole other can of worms. Not to worry, though. Weldon, Davis, and Reed has several top-drawer criminal attorneys on staff. I'll get a recommendation and have one of them be in touch with you."

Great, Ali thought. *Just what I need. Another frigging attorney!*

Once she was off the phone, Ali paced for a while. Finally, she lay down on the floor and forced herself to do some relaxation exercises. After settling some of her agitation, she climbed up on the bed. She never expected to fall asleep, but she did, waking just in time to switch on the local news. Out of force of habit, she turned once again to her old station.

Of course, the amazingly perky and spike-haired Annette Carrera was front and center, but so was the rest of the old news gang. The foppish Randall James, still wearing his appallingly awful wig, continued on as co-anchor. There, too, was Axel Rodbury, who, false teeth and all, had to be older than God. If Ali was considered over the hill, why wasn't he? And there was Bill Nickels, too, the leering and always overly enthusiastic sportscaster. Ali had wanted to smack the smug grin off his face for years, especially after hearing rumors that, when it came to student interns, Mr. Sports Guy had a tendency to try for a home run.

Ali had steeled herself for the ordeal, expecting that seeing her old colleagues gathered in the familiar confines of the newsroom set would hit her with some sense of loss. But as the quartet yucked it up in the required and supposedly unscripted pre-newscast lead-in, Ali wasn't at all surprised to see that Bill Nickels and Annette seemed to have an especially chummy relationship.

Don't you have brains enough to aim a little higher

than that? Ali thought. *Not that aiming higher did* me *any good.*

Beyond that, though, she felt nothing at all. Nothing. Her leaving may not have been of Ali Reynolds's own volition, but as it turned out, she really had moved on. Whatever had happened, she was over it—except for her wrongful dismissal lawsuit. She wasn't over that—not by a long shot.

The lead story, introduced by Annette herself, had to do with Paul Grayson's disappearance. This was, after all, the NBC affiliate, and Grayson was a high-profile NBC bigwig. A young female reporter—one Ali had never seen before—delivered a brief story filmed in front of the gated entrance to the house on Robert Lane. That, Ali knew, would send Paul utterly ballistic once he got wind of it. Having your front gate identified on television news for all the world to see was not good from a security standpoint.

The second, related segment, done by a roving reporter, was filmed in the paved parking lot of a less-than-desirable apartment complex somewhere in Banning. Of course, by the time the filming occurred, Paul's Arena Red 911 had already been towed away. Yellow crime scene tape was still visible but the vehicle wasn't, as the reporter earnestly let viewers know that this was where Paul Grayson's abandoned Porsche had been found early in the afternoon.

By the time the two segments were over almost three minutes of news time had elapsed and Ali had learned almost nothing she hadn't known before from simply surfing the Net.

"Useless," Ali muttered under her breath. She was close to changing the channel when part of a story

Randall James was relating penetrated her consciousness. This one concerned an unidentified man found dead in the desert late Thursday night in the aftermath of a fatal train/vehicle collision that had occurred northwest of Palm Springs. Since Ali had been in such close proximity to the incident when it happened, she stayed tuned to see the remainder of the piece.

The smiling faces on the tube, reading blandly from their teleprompters, didn't seem to make any connection between that case and the one they had reported on two stories before, and why should they? After all, they were paid to read what was given to them—stories that had already been written and edited by someone else. Connecting dots was never a required part of the news desk equation.

But Ali's life had undergone a fundamental change months earlier when she had started trying to piece together the details that would explain the sudden death of her friend Reenie Bernard. And now, this newly reconstituted Ali Reynolds was incapable of *not* connecting dots, especially when they were this obvious.

The body of an unidentified man found outside Palm Springs? Paul's abandoned vehicle located in a parking lot somewhere in Banning, ten or fifteen miles away? Without knowing how, Ali understood immediately that the two incidents were connected. She knew in her bones that the dead man found near Palm Springs had to be Paul. The only remaining question was, how long would it take for someone else to figure it out?

The answer to that question wasn't long in coming. Before Axel could launch into his weather report, there was a sharp rap on Ali's door.

"Who is it?" she asked, peering out through the security peephole. Two men wearing white shirts, ties, and sports jackets stood in the hall. One was white and older—mid-fifties—with a bad comb-over and the thick neck of an aging football player. The other was younger—mid-thirties, black, with a shaved head and the straight-shouldered bearing of an ex-Marine.

"Police," the older one said, holding up a wallet that contained a badge and photo ID. "Detectives Sims and Taylor, Riverside Sheriff's Department. We need to speak to you about your husband."

Helga Myerhoff's warning should have been upper-most in Ali's head, but it wasn't. Shaken by her sudden realization that Paul really was dead, she unfastened the security chain and opened the door.

"Is he dead?" she asked.

"He may be," Detective Sims, the older one, said. "That's why we need to speak with you. May we come in?"

Ali opened the door and allowed the two men into her room. Their looming presence combined with the weight of the news they carried filled what had previously seemed to be a spacious area. Ali retreated to a nearby chair. The detectives remained standing.

Ali's mind raced. She remembered the desolate desert, the darkness, the flashing emergency lights. She had driven Highway 111 into Palm Springs numerous times. She remembered the tracks running alongside the roadway. On the other side of the tracks was nothing—only desert. There was no reason to cross the tracks there, unless . . .

"This is about that car that got run over by the train

last night, isn't it?" she said. "What happened? Did Paul commit suicide?"

The two detectives exchanged glances. "You're aware of the incident then?" Detective Sims asked.

"The incident with the train?" Ali asked. "Sure. It was on the news just now. So was the story about Paul. When I saw that his Porsche had been found stripped and abandoned in a parking lot in Banning, I put two and two together."

"That's what we're doing, too," Detective Taylor said, "putting two and two together. We have an unidentified victim we *believe* to be your husband, but we're not sure. Detective Little from LAPD told us where to find you. We need someone to do a positive ID."

"I'll get my purse," Ali said, standing up. "Where do you want me to go?"

"To the morgue," Sims said quickly. "In Indio."

"But that's hours from here, on the far side of Palm Springs."

"Riverside is a big county," Taylor returned. "That's where they've taken the body. But don't worry about how far it is. We'll be glad to take you over and bring you back. It's the least we can do."

Ali's purse was on the desk. Her Glock 26 was locked away in her room safe. She had left it there that morning when she was on her way to court, and she was glad it was still there. Even though she had a properly issued license to carry, it was probably not a good idea to show up in a cop car with a loaded hand-gun in her possession. Ali collected her purse and her cell phone.

"Let's go then," she said.

People glanced warily at the trio as they walked through the Westwood's well-appointed lobby. Ali was in the middle with the two cops flanking her on either side. Detectives Sims and Taylor may not have been in uniform, but they were still clearly cops. Outside, the real giveaway was the plain, white, well-used Crown Victoria parked directly in front of the hotel entrance. Sporting a rack of two-way-radio antennas and black-wall tires, the Crown Victoria stuck out like a sore thumb next to its nearest neighbors—a silver Maserati Quattroporte and a gleaming black Bentley GT.

Sims opened the back door of the sedan to let Ali inside. When she saw there was no door handle, she felt a moment of concern. She realized belatedly that she probably should have called Helga before agreeing to come along with Sims and Taylor. Presumably Helga would have warned her against getting into a vehicle with them.

On the other hand, why not? Ali thought. *All they need is for me to identify the body. What's wrong with that?*

Ali remembered times in the past when she'd been assigned to cover ongoing police investigations. She remembered instances where some of the people involved refused to cooperate or to give statements of any kind to investigating officers without having an attorney present. And even though at the time Ali had known full well that was everyone's legal right, she had still harbored a sneaking suspicion that people who hid behind their attorneys had something else to hide as well.

Well, I don't, Ali told herself firmly. Settling into the backseat, she fastened her seat belt. While Detective Taylor drove, Sims rode shotgun and chatted her up.

"I understand from Detective Little that you and your husband are in the process of getting a divorce?"

Are getting *a divorce?* Ali wondered. The use of the present tense was telling. Until the detectives had a positive identification of their victim, they were going to hold firm to the fiction that Paul Grayson was still alive.

"Yes," Ali answered. "It was supposed to be finalized today. That was probably the first time anyone besides April noticed Paul was missing—when he didn't show up for the hearing."

"Friendly?" Sims asked.

At first Ali wasn't sure what Sims meant. "I beg your pardon?"

"You know," he responded. "Your divorce. Is it amicable and all that?"

"As amicable as can be expected considering my husband's girlfriend—his fiancée—is eight and a half months pregnant."

"With his baby?" Sims asked.

"So I've been told," Ali said. "They were supposed to get married tomorrow. Speaking of which, why am I doing the identification? Why not April?"

"You're still married to him," Sims said. "From our point of view, you're a surviving relative. She's not."

Ali thought about that for a few moments. It was rush hour. Traffic was painfully slow. As they inched along, Ali realized that she and the two detectives were in the same situation. They wanted information from her; she wanted the same from them.

"This man who's dead," she said, "this man who may be Paul. What was he doing on the railroad tracks? Did he go there on purpose? Was he trying to commit suicide or something? Maybe he and April had a fight and it pushed Paul over the edge."

"It wasn't suicide," Sims replied.

"An accident then?"

Sims said nothing.

Ali thought about what Jake had reportedly said about Paul bailing on his own bachelor party without bothering to tell his host or anyone else that he was leaving. Unless . . . Paul Grayson had never had a good track record where women were concerned. Ali could well imagine him picking up one of the strippers or the pole dancers or whatever brand of feminine charm the Pink Swan had available and taking her somewhere for a little private tête-à-tête.

"Was he alone or was he with someone?" Ali asked.

"We're not sure," Sims said. "We have people doing a grid search, but so far no other victims have been found."

There was a short pause before Detective Taylor piped up. "When exactly did you get to town, Ms. Reynolds? And did you drive over or fly?"

Taylor's questions activated a blinking caution light in Ali's head. She considered her words carefully before she answered. The very fact that she'd been close enough to see the flashing lights on the emergency vehicles might give the cops reason to think she was somehow involved. If she told them about driving past Palm Springs at midnight and seeing the lights, Sims and Taylor could well turn Ali's coincidental proximity into criminal opportunity. Still, she'd already given the same information to Detective Little. It seemed foolhardy to withhold it a second time, and there was even less point to not being truthful.

"I drove over yesterday," Ali said. "Last night. I left Phoenix late in the afternoon. Got to the hotel around two in the morning."

"Which means you were driving through the Palm Springs area around . . . ?"

"Midnight," Ali answered without waiting for Detective Taylor to finish posing his question. "And you're right. I did see the cop cars and ambulances and other emergency vehicles showing up at the scene of the wreck. It's dark in the desert. You could see those lights for miles. Later on, I heard on the radio that a train had crashed into a car."

Ali's cell phone rang just then. The phone number wasn't one she recognized. "Hello?"

"Ali Reynolds?"

"Yes."

"My name is Victor, Victor Angeleri. My colleague Helga Myerhoff asked me to call you. Sorry I couldn't get back to you earlier. I've been tied up in a meeting. I thought maybe it would be a good idea for us to get together so I could have a little better feel for what's happening. Helga gave me a brief overview, but I'd like a few more details from you. Since the office is just down the street from your hotel, I thought maybe I could drop by in a little while before I head home."

"Sorry," Ali said. "That won't be possible." She was aware that the cops in the front seat were listening avidly to everything she said and to every nuance of her side of the conversation. Their interest gave Ali a hint about how badly she had screwed up by not heeding Helga's advice.

"Why not?" Angeleri wanted to know. "What's more important than meeting with me?"

"It's just that I'm not at the hotel right now," she said. "I'm actually on my way to Indio. Two detectives from the Riverside Sheriff's Department picked me up and asked me to come with them. They need someone to identify a dead man—the man they think is my husband."

Angeleri uttered a string of very unlawyerlike words, ones Edie Larson would have deemed unprintable. "Are you nuts or what? You mean you just got in the car with them?" he demanded. "And now they're taking you all the way to Indio?"

Ali didn't know Victor Angeleri, but he sounded upset—furious, even—as though he couldn't quite believe he'd been stuck with such a numbskull for a client. Ali couldn't believe it, either.

"That's where the body is," Ali said.

"You're going to the coroner's office there?" Victor wanted to know.

"Evidently," Ali answered meekly.

"All right!" Victor shouted into her ear. "Where are you now?"

"Merging onto the Ten."

"I'm leaving the office right now. I'll meet you there. In the meantime, keep your mouth shut."

"Where did you say we're going?" Ali asked, directing her question at Sims.

"The Riverside County Morgue," he answered. "The address is—"

"I know the address!" Angeleri interrupted, bellowing the words loud enough to break Ali's eardrum. "I'll be there as soon as I can. Until you and I have a chance to talk in private, you're to say nothing more. Nothing! You can talk about the weather. You can talk about the World Series, but that's it. Understand?"

"Got it," Ali answered. "I hear you loud and clear."

That was actually something of an understatement since Sims and Taylor must have heard him, too. The two detectives exchanged a raised-eyebrow look, and Sims heaved a resigned sigh. Clearly they had been having their way with her. Now the game was up. Ali's only hope was that Victor Angeleri would be smart enough to dig her out of the hole she had dug herself into before she made it any deeper.

Ali glanced at her watch. At the rate traffic was moving, it would be another two hours before they made it to Indio. And with Victor leaving the office on Wilshire that much behind them, Ali calculated that it would be hours before the attorney could catch up with them. That meant she was in for several uncomfortable hours of keeping her mouth shut.

Gradually traffic began to thin. The car sped up, but clearly Taylor and Sims had gotten the message. They made no further attempt to ask her questions about anything—including the run-up to the World Series. Left to her own devices, Ali spent the time trying to figure out how, in the course of one short day, she had gone from being an almost divorced woman to being a homicide suspect.

Ali checked her watch when they pulled up outside the coroner's office in Indio. She expected they'd have to wait another hour at least before Victor could possibly catch up with them. Then, after however long it took to do the identification and conduct any additional interviews, there would be another three-hour car ride back to the hotel.

Resigned to the idea that it was going to be a very long night, Ali was astonished when an immense man rose from a small waiting room sofa and hurried toward them.

"Ali Reynolds?" he asked.

Assuming this was yet another cop of some kind, Ali nodded.

"Good," the newcomer said, turning to the detectives. "If you don't mind, I'd like a word in private with my client."

"We'll be right outside," Detective Sims replied before he and Taylor returned the way they had come.

"You're Victor?" Ali asked. "My attorney?"

He nodded. Victor may have served as the attorney to some of Hollywood's "beautiful people," but beautiful he was not. Victor was a wide-load kind of guy—John Candy wide—with droopy jowls and a receding hairline. His suit may have been expensive, but it didn't quite meet around his considerable girth. In one hand he carried a scarred, much-used leather satchel–style briefcase that was crammed to overflowing with papers.

"We left long before you did," Ali said. "How did you manage to get here first?"

"I chartered a plane from Santa Monica," he answered. He led her back to the sofa and placed his briefcase on the floor beside it. "Flew from Santa Monica Municipal to Jacqueline Cochran Regional here in Palm Springs. Believe me, at my hourly rate, it would be a total waste of your money for me to spend six billable hours driving back and forth to Indio. Now sit down here," Victor continued, indicating a place next to him on the sofa. "I need to know what's going on."

Too tired to object, Ali sat. She had been through

enough emotional upheaval in the course of the day that she was feeling frayed and close to tears. When Victor reached for his briefcase, she expected him to extract either a hanky for her or else a laptop computer for him. Instead, he removed a dog-eared tablet of blue-lined paper. Reaching into his shirt pocket, he retrieved a black and white Montblanc fountain pen.

Over the past few years, Ali had come to rely on computers more and more. Somehow, though, she found it strangely reassuring to see that Victor Angeleri was not a high-tech kind of guy—that when it came time to do a job, he relied on brainpower and old-fashioned pen and paper. That was exactly what Ali Reynolds needed right then—not someone blessed with good looks or glitz or style, but someone with substance—someone who would be big enough and tough enough to take on the combined girth of Detectives Sims and Taylor and win.

"All right then," Victor said, removing the cap from his pen. "Tell me everything—from the beginning."

{ CHAPTER 4 }

It's after one. I should be sleeping, but I can't. I didn't expect yesterday to be a good day. You know before it starts that the day you go to court to get a divorce isn't going to be a red-letter day or a time for celebration. But I didn't expect it to be a disaster, either. I didn't expect it to end with a trip to the morgue.

Because, although my divorce wasn't finalized yesterday, my marriage ended anyway. My husband is dead. He didn't show up for our ten A.M. court appearance because he died the night before—died after taking an early powder from his own bachelor party and departing the premises without telling anyone else he was leaving.

After spending hours in the company of a pair of homicide detectives, I now know how Fang died. His hands and feet were bound with duct tape. His mouth was taped shut.

He was placed in the trunk of a stolen car that was left parked on the railroad tracks near Palm Springs. The vehicle with him in it was subsequently struck and demolished by a speeding freight train. He was ejected upon impact and thrown into the desert, where his body was found hours later. The autopsy won't be done until much later today. My hope is that he died upon impact.

And so, since the divorce was never finalized, the authorities consider me to be his "next of kin." For the first time in my life, I had to go to a county morgue to make a positive ID.

I expected the place to be dingy and cold inside. It wasn't, but the chill I felt had nothing to do with an overly active air-conditioning unit because the air-conditioning unit was barely functioning. As I stood there in the viewing room, waiting for an attendant to wheel out the loaded gurney, my blood turned to ice. And when I had to look down into that scratched and battered but oh-so-familiar face, it was all I could do to remain upright. I didn't exactly faint when I saw him lying there, but my knees went weak. Fortunately, someone helped me to a chair.

I didn't cry, couldn't cry. Mostly because I didn't know what I was feeling or what I was supposed to feel. Fang and I were divorcing if not divorced. Our relationship was over if not ended. And yet, this was a man I had loved once—someone vital and strong with whom

I had hoped to share the rest of my life. It makes my heart ache to know that he is gone. And yes, it makes me sick to think that his unborn child—a baby due within the next few weeks—will never know him at all, will grow up without ever once seeing him. That's wrong. Leaving a child fatherless is WRONG! WRONG! WRONG!

After I'd done the ID, someone—a clerk—gave me a paper to sign—a form that says what's supposed to happen to Fang's remains once the authorities are finished with them. It seemed inappropriate for me to be the one deciding which mortuary should be brought in to do that job. I've been out of Fang's life for a long time—longer, it turns out, than the six months I've been out of the house. It seemed to me that Twink . . . No, correction. Make that, it seemed to me that his fiancée—the woman who's expecting his child—should be making those decisions, but it turns out the very fact that we were still legally married automatically puts me in charge. So I looked in the phone book, tracked down the name of the mortuary that handled Fang's mother's services six years ago, and called them.

Two days ago—was it just two days?—I told you about my plan to pick up some new clothing on my way through Scottsdale so I could go to court looking like a bit of a fashion plate in something more sophisticated than what I wear hanging around home in Sedona. I even splurged

on a haircut, a manicure, and a pedicure. I
wanted to be able to put my best foot (and
toes) forward when Fang and I stood in
front of the judge to disavow our vows.

The irony is, when I came back to the hotel,
I took off my courtroom duds and slipped into
something comfortable—a T-shirt, a pair of
jeans, comfy tennis shoes. I took off my makeup
and pulled my hair back into a ponytail. That's
how I was dressed when two homicide cops
came to ask me to ride along and see if I could
positively identify the body of their dead victim.
And that's how I looked hours later when the
identification ordeal was finally over and I
stepped back outside the Riverside County
Sheriff's Substation in Indio to return to the
hotel.

I have no idea who alerted the media to
what was going on. I know for sure someone
had already leaked Fang's name. As cameras
flashed and reporters yelled questions,
someone recognized me and called me by
name as well. I'm sure my photo will be all
over the news tomorrow, and I'll look as
bedraggled as some of those awful mug shots
that turn up when some celebrity gets booked
for drunk driving.

It's one thing to stand outside the
emotional box and report on someone's
untimely death for whatever reason. It's
something else to be living it—to be inside
that awful box and trying to make sense of it.
Now, because of the way the media works, I'll

no longer be reporting on events—I'll be part
of the story.

So this is an early warning for all my
cutlooseblog.com fans. I'm sure all kinds of
crap is going to hit the fan first thing in the
morning. I just want you to know that I'm fine.
And I'll keep you posted as we go.

Posted 1:07 A.M., September 17, 2005 by
Babe

Scrolling through her e-mail list, Ali could see more
than a dozen comments lined up and waiting to be
read, but she was too drained to face them.

Go to bed, she told herself, switching off her computer. *Tomorrow's another day.*

Ali did go to bed then. Not only that, she surprised
herself by falling asleep almost immediately. After
what seemed like only a matter of minutes, the ringing
phone awakened her.

"What in the world is going on?" Edie Larson
demanded.

"What are you talking about?" Ali grumbled groggily.
"And what time is it?" The room's blackout curtains
were pulled shut. In the pitch-black room she had to
turn over to see the clock, which read 5:35 A.M.

"Why didn't you call me?" Edie continued. "What
happened to Paul? And why did you have to do the
identification? What about his bride-to-be who isn't?"

"Who told you all this?" Ali asked.

"You did," Edie answered. "In cutloose."

Ali was astonished. It had never occurred to her
that her mother might join the Internet world. "You
read my blog?" she asked.

"Of course I do," Edie said. "Why wouldn't I? Every morning while I'm waiting for the sweet rolls to rise and when there's no one here in the restaurant to keep me company, I read the whole thing. When Dad and I got Chris that new Mac, he gave us his old one. Hooked it up here in the office, got me an Internet account, the whole nine yards. My Internet handle is sugarloafmama, by the way, but I didn't call to talk about me. I want to know what's going on with *you*. Tell me everything, and hurry it up. We open in a few minutes."

So Ali told her mother as much as she could remember—the parts she had put in the blog as well as the parts she'd left out. The truth is, after sitting through the statement she'd given to Detectives Sims and Taylor, Victor had advised her to say nothing in her blog about any of it—nothing at all. Feeling a certain loyalty to her readers, Ali had written her blog entry anyway, saying only what she thought would pass muster. She never came right out and said that she had ridden to Indio in the company of the two homicide detectives. And she never breathed a word about hitching a ride back from Jacqueline Cochran Airport with the newest member of Ali's burgeoning troop of attorneys.

In talking to Edie, however, Ali corrected this deliberate oversight by mentioning Victor Angeleri by name, while at the same time somehow glossing over the criminal defense portion of his curriculum vitae.

"You say his name's Victor, Victor Angeleri? What kind of a name is that?" Edie wanted to know.

"Italian, I suppose," Ali answered.

"And he flies his own plane?"

"No. He chartered one." *And on the way home, to take my mind off my troubles, gave me an in-depth lesson on Jacqueline Cochran, the lady the airport is named after, and on the Women Airforce Service Pilots of World War II,* Ali thought.

"What's he like?" Edie asked. "Old? Young? What?"

"About the same age as Dad, I suppose," Ali said. "And big. He had to use a seat belt extender in the airplane."

"I don't care one whit about his size," Edie declared. "What I want to know is whether or not he's any good. Now what kind of attorney is he again? Not your divorce attorney," she added. "That's Myra somebody."

Ali wondered how it was Edie Larson could somehow play dumb while simultaneously and unerringly sniffing out Ali's every attempt at subterfuge.

"Not Myra, Helga Myerhoff," Ali corrected. "She was the one handling the divorce proceedings. Victor specializes in criminal defense."

"But why on earth would you need a criminal defense attorney?" Edie wanted to know. "Do the cops think you had something to do with Paul's death—that you're somehow responsible? How could you be? You were miles away at the time."

Ali remembered the pulsing, telltale glow from that long line of emergency lights that had lit up the desert floor as they streamed through the night toward the scene of the wreck.

Not nearly as many miles away as I should have been, Ali thought.

Victor hadn't wanted her to mention seeing those

flashing lights in the course of giving Detectives Sims and Taylor her taped statement, but since they already knew what time she'd left Phoenix and since they already knew what time she'd checked into the hotel, that meant they also knew the approximate time she would have been passing Palm Springs. Consequently, it seemed pointless to skip over that part. The truth was, she *had* seen the flashing lights. She would have had to be blind not to, and lying about that in an official statement seemed both pointless and stupid.

"The cops probably do suspect me," Ali said, trying to deliver the words in a casual, offhand manner that she hoped would throw Edie off course. "But Victor says not to worry. It's just routine. That's what homicide detectives do. To begin with, they look at everyone. Then gradually they eliminate the ones who didn't do it until they arrive at whoever did."

"So you're saying for sure that Paul was murdered?" Edie asked.

Ali sighed. "Yes. When Victor and I left Indio, they hadn't yet released any details about the case because April hadn't been notified, but I'm sure she has been by now. If that's the case, the story is probably all over the airwaves. I was asleep, though, so I haven't had a chance to check."

The idea that the questioning was routine did nothing to calm Edie's outrage. "This is unbelievable!" she announced. "I should never have let you drive over there on your own. Never. The subject came up before you left. Dad said I should probably pack up and go along, but then I let you talk me out of it. Big mistake. There are times women need their mothers with them, Alison. This turns out to be one of them."

In the background Ali heard a door open and close. "Speak of the devil," Edie said. "Here's your father now. I'm in the office, Bob," she called to her husband. "Ali's on the phone. Come listen to this. You're not going to believe it."

Briefly Edie began to recount everything Ali had told her. Halfway through, though, the story came to an abrupt stop.

"My word!" Edie exclaimed. "I completely lost track of time. The first customers just pulled up, Ali. We have to go now. I'll call again later, but you take care of yourself. Don't let those turkeys push you around."

Once Ali put down the phone, she dozed for a little while, but by seven when she was wide awake, she called room service and ordered breakfast and newspapers. She managed to jump in and out of the shower before her breakfast tray showed up.

Sipping coffee, she went through the newspapers, where the homicide—yes, a Riverside Sheriff's Department spokesman actually used the H-word—of prominent television news executive Paul Grayson was front-page news. So, unfortunately, was Ali's picture, which turned out to be every bit as bad as Ali had predicted it would be. The caption stated: "Former L.A.-area newscaster Alison Reynolds, accompanied by noted defense attorney Victor Angeleri, leaves the Riverside County Sheriff's Substation in Indio after identifying the body of her slain husband, Paul Grayson."

Trying not to look at the tabloid-worthy photo, Ali turned her attention to the accompanying article. Despite the use of a banner headline and the expenditure of lots of front-page column inches, there was surprisingly little content, and hardly anything Ali hadn't already gleaned on her own.

Today was supposed to be Paul Grayson's wedding day. Instead, the prospective groom is now a murder victim, having fallen victim to a bizarre kidnapping/murder scheme in which he was left bound and gagged in the trunk of a stolen vehicle that was abandoned on a railroad track near Palm Springs. The stolen vehicle was subsequently struck by a speeding freight train, killing Grayson on impact. An autopsy has been scheduled for later today.

A joint homicide investigation by the Los Angeles Police Department and the Riverside County Sheriff's Department is attempting to establish the exact chain of events from the time Grayson abruptly departed a posh bachelor party being held in his honor to the time an eastbound Burlington Northern freight train slammed into the vehicle in which he had been imprisoned.

Ali scanned the next several paragraphs, which mostly contained information she had already learned. She slowed and read more carefully when she reached the part that discussed the ill-fated bachelor party at the Pink Swan.

"We were all at the Pink Swan having a good time," said bachelor party host and former NBC executive Jake Maxwell. "I remember someone saying there was a call for Paul. I believe he went outside to take it, and he never came back. I finally went outside looking for him and noticed his Porsche was missing from the parking lot. I just assumed he'd decided he'd had enough and gone home."

Early yesterday afternoon, Mr. Grayson's Porsche Carrera was found stripped and abandoned in an apartment parking lot in Banning. The Camry destroyed by the speeding train had been reported stolen earlier in the day from a vacant-lot private-vehicle sales location in Ventura. The Riverside Sheriff's Department is asking that anyone with information on either vehicle contact them immediately.

Mr. Grayson was in the process of divorcing his wife, former local television news personality Alison Reynolds. He was due at a hearing to finalize their divorce at 10 A.M. yesterday morning. It was his failure to appear in court that prompted his fiancée, April Gaddis, to contact LAPD's Missing Persons Unit, which immediately began conducting an investigation.

The story continued on page two, but Ali didn't bother following it. There was nothing new here. She tried two other papers with similar results—much the same story with no additional information and with equally bad photos of Alison Reynolds. Disgusted, Ali gave up, poured another cup of coffee, and turned on her computer. Once it booted up, she logged on and went to check out her new mail. Scanning the subject lines, she saw that three of them were addressed to Fred, the guy who had objected to the fact that Ali was divorcing her husband.

Dear Fred,
You are an ignorant asshole. I hope you die.

So much for reasoned discussion. That one was unsigned, and Ali simply deleted it.

Dear Fred,
You sound just like my first husband, and you know what? It's been years now and he still hasn't figured out how come I took the kids and left him. I tried to tell him his actions were pulling us apart, but he didn't want to hear it—so he didn't hear it. It was a struggle, but money isn't everything. I know the kids and I— two daughters and a son—are all better off.

CONNIE IN MI

Dear Fred,
Let no man put asunder? God must have heard what Fang did to Babe, and She smacked him a good one. Maybe She'll smack you, too. Sounds like you deserve it.

CASEY THE OLD BAT

Casey was someone who wrote in often. Usually Ali posted her comments, but this time they were a little too close to the "hope you die" one. Ali deleted Casey instead. As she was about to move on, a click announced a new e-mail, this one also addressed to Fred. But what caught Ali's attention was the sender's address, sugarloafmama.

Dear Fred,
I agree with you. Marriage vows are sacred, but
they need to be kept by both parties involved.
It reminds me of that old song, about Frankie
and Johnny. "He was her man but he done her
wrong." All I can say is, good riddance!

SUGARLOAFMAMA

Laughing, Ali posted Edie's comment. Anyone who lived in or around Sedona would know exactly who Sugarloafmama was. And the fact that Edie Larson held some reasonably strong opinions on any given subject, especially her former son-in-law, wouldn't be news, either.

Google sent me here. I thought this was a health
care site. If I wanted advice to the lovelorn, I'd
go to Dear Abby. You guys should get a life.

That one was unsigned and it went away. After that Ali read a whole series of comments that were essentially notes of condolence to her. One in particular stood out.

Dear Babe,
I understood exactly what you meant when
you said you didn't know what to feel and that
you couldn't cry. My divorce had been final for
only two weeks when my husband committed
suicide. He always said he would but I didn't
believe him. I needed him out of my life. He
was into meth and gambling both, and watching

him destroy himself was killing me. But I didn't mean for him to die. For a long time I thought his death was my fault. It took three years of therapy for me to come to terms with what happened.

So please accept my condolences. I'm sure you loved Fang once. According to my therapist, I had to grieve not only for the man who was gone but also for the man who never was—and for the dream I once had about how our life together would be. Grieving for the dream is as hard as grieving for the person. Don't be afraid to seek help if you think you need it. But it's hard work. Harder than anything I've ever done.

I've been a cutloose fan for a long time. Through the months I know you've focused a lot of your anger on Twink even more so than on Fang. I understand that, as far as you're concerned, Twink is "the other woman," but I also suspect that she's much younger than you are and not nearly as smart. She isn't going to have the emotional resources you have to deal with this tragedy. Try to remember that her dreams are in ashes today, too, right along with yours.

Since your divorce from Fang wasn't final when his death occurred, I expect that you and Twink will find your lives intertwined in unexpected ways. I hope you can find it in your heart to be kind to her and to her innocent baby as well.

Remember, God will see to it that you reap what you sow.

PHYLLIS IN KNOXVILLE

Ali was in tears by the time she finished reading Phyllis's note. There was so much hard-won wisdom in the words and so much caring that it took Ali's breath away. She posted the note in the comments section and then sent Phyllis a personal response.

> Dear Phyllis,
> Thank you for writing. Thank you for your kindness—for knowing what I was feeling and giving me comfort; for giving me much needed guidance when I was in danger of losing my way.

> BABE

Several of the other notes were in the same vein. Ali responded to them all, but the one from Phyllis was the only one she posted. That was the one that said it all and said it best. When her cell phone rang a little later, she expected the caller to be one of her parents or maybe even Chris. She didn't expect to hear the voice of Dave Holman—Yavapai County homicide detective Dave Holman.

"I just talked to your mom," Dave said grimly. "Is it true? Do the cops out in L.A. think you're involved in Paul's murder?"

In the years before Sedona had built its own high school, kids from Sedona had been bused to Mingus Mountain High School in Cottonwood. Dave Holman had been a tall skinny kid a year ahead of Ali in school. After graduation, he had joined the Marines. He went to college later, studying criminal justice. He was both a detective in the sheriff's department and a captain in the Marine Reserves who had served two tours of duty in Iraq. He was also a much-valued breakfast regular at Bob and Edie Larson's Sugar Loaf Café.

Ali felt an initial stab of resentment that her parents had spilled the beans about what was going on in her life. Then she remembered her blog. Maybe Dave read cutlooseblog.com the same way Ali's mother did. Maybe that was where he was getting his information—everything but her phone number, that is.

Why was it I wanted to have a blog? Ali asked herself.

"They didn't come right out and say so," Ali replied. "Not in so many words."

"What words?" Dave asked. "Tell me exactly what was said."

"They took my statement," Ali said.

"With your attorney present, this Angel guy?"

Obviously Edie had given Dave a complete briefing on Ali's conversation with her.

"Angeleri," Ali corrected. "Victor Angeleri, and yes, he was there."

"Edie says you told them about driving past the crash site, seeing the emergency vehicles, all that?"

"I had to," Ali said. "It's the truth. I could see those lights from miles away. Coming past Palm Springs at that time of night, I couldn't not see them."

"Great," Dave muttered. "What else did they have to say?"

"I don't know. They asked a bunch of questions. I answered them. End of story."

"What did they say when the interview was over?"

"What do you mean?" Ali asked. "You mean, like, did they say good-bye?"

"No, I mean like, 'Don't leave the state without letting us know.'"

Ali paused. "Well, yes," she said at length. "I suppose they did mention something to that effect. They told me they'd be pursuing all possible leads but it might be best if I stayed around L.A. for a while. I told them that was fine. That I had planned to be here several more days. They hinted it might take a little longer than that for them to get all their ducks in a row."

"I'll just bet," Dave said. "Well, it doesn't matter. I'm glad your mother is on her way."

"Mom is coming here—to L.A.?"

"Yes. Edie Larson is riding to the rescue. Didn't she tell you?"

"No," Ali said. "As a matter of fact she didn't. I'll call and tell her not to come."

"That's probably why she didn't mention it to you, and by now it's too late, because she's already on her way. I may show up, too," Dave added. "I came to Lake Havasu to see the kids this weekend, which means I'm only four and a half hours away."

Ali knew that since Dave's ex-wife and her new husband had taken the children and moved to Lake Havasu City, Dave had spent at least one weekend a month going there to see them.

"Really, Dave," she told him. "That's not necessary. What about your kids?"

"What about them? I already did what Rich wanted me to do this weekend—which was to get him signed up for his learner's permit. As for Cassie and Crystal? They'll be glad to have me out of their hair. Spending weekends with me is more of a hassle for my daughters than it is anything else. I'm not nearly cool enough to suit them."

"But it makes no sense for both you and Mom to

drop everything and come running to California," Ali argued. "I'm sure this is no big deal."

"No big deal?" Dave repeated. "Are you kidding? Being accused of murder is always a big deal, even if you end up getting off. Ask O. J. Simpson. Ask Robert Blake. And since you obviously don't want me to do this for you, let's just say I'm doing it for your folks—for your mom. This is my cell phone, by the way," he added. "Feel free to call me on it anytime if you need to."

The truth of the matter was, Ali still had Dave's cell phone number stored in her phone. She had needed his help once, desperately, when the abusive husband of one of her cutloose fans had come looking for Ali. But there was no way she was going to admit that to him, especially not right then.

"I still think this is silly," she said.

"Everybody's entitled to his or her opinion," Dave returned. "I don't have enough available cell phone minutes to waste time arguing about it."

"All right," Ali said, capitulating. "You know where to come?"

"Edie gave me the address. Rich is putting it into MapQuest right now. Unfortunately my Nissan Sentra doesn't come equipped with the fancy-schmancy GPS you have in your Cayenne. I can't leave until a little later, but I'll be there."

He hung up. Ali was still holding the phone in her hand when it rang again. "Ali?"

Helga's near-baritone usually made people think they were talking to a man. Ali knew better. "What's up?" Ali asked.

"Are you decent?"

"Not exactly."

"Get that way," Helga ordered, "and then meet us downstairs."

"Us?"

"Victor and me," Helga said. "We have an appointment with Ted Grantham half an hour from now."

"With Ted?" Ali asked. "What for?"

"With Ted and with Les Jordan," Helga replied.

"Who's Les Jordan?"

"Paul Grayson's estate planning attorney."

Far be it for Paul to have one attorney when he could have two, Ali thought. Then she realized she had no room to talk.

"Why are we meeting him?" she asked.

"For a reading of the will."

"Now?" Ali wanted to know. "Don't people usually read wills after funerals instead of before?"

"Under normal circumstances that's true," Helga said. "But these circumstances are far from normal. Meet us downstairs in fifteen minutes."

{ CHAPTER 5 }

Victor and Helga arrived together in Victor's silver Lincoln Town Car. When Ali looked inside the vehicle, she could see that Victor took up more than half of the front seat, with the steering wheel grazing his ample belly. Helga, on the other hand, was so tiny that once Ali settled into the backseat, the top of the diminutive attorney's hairdo didn't clear the headrest.

"I'm not sure why we're doing this in such an unseemly hurry," Ali said, once her seat belt was fastened. "Yesterday we found out Paul was dead. Today's the day he and April were supposed to get married. Couldn't we wait a day or two and give the poor woman a chance to adjust?"

"We're doing it now because we need to," Victor said. "Because if the cops are going to pin a murder-for-profit motive on you, we need to know whether or not it will fly, and it may, especially if you're still a beneficiary under the will. The cops will naturally expect that the will won't be read until after the funeral, and they know the funeral can't take place until after the coroner releases the body—sometime next week. In other words, reading the will now gives us an investigational leg up for at least the next several days."

"We're also reading it now because Ted Grantham is a spineless wuss," Helga observed. "When I called and suggested reading the will today, he practically fell all over himself saying yes. He even suggested we go to the house to do it. He said he'd call Les Jordan and April and set it up."

Ali was dismayed. "We're going to the house on Robert Lane?" she asked. "Couldn't we do this somewhere else—anywhere else? Why would Grantham suggest such a thing? Why would you agree to it?"

"Because evidently he doesn't think April's in any condition to go elsewhere," Helga said. "I think he also agreed to reading the will today because he's nervous. His divorce case is in the toilet, but he still wants to be paid. Grantham may not have drafted the new will, but I'm guessing he knows the terms. He hasn't come right out and said so—that would be a breach of client privilege—but from the way he's acting, I'm guessing the new will has been drafted without being put into effect."

"And I'm still the main beneficiary?"

"Right," Helga answered. "So Grantham is making nice with us because he thinks you'll be the one settling Paul's estate—as well as paying any outstanding bills."

"He's doing this because he's buttering us up?"

"Buttering *you* up," Helga corrected. "He also said something about preserving community assets. I think he's worried about handing things off to you before any of those assets has a chance to disappear. If that were to happen, he's concerned he might somehow end up being held responsible."

"What do you mean disappear?" Ali asked.

"You've never had the pleasure of meeting April Gaddis," Helga said with a disdainful sniff. "Ted has met her, and so have I. Prior to meeting your husband and signing on for what she thought would be a very luxurious free ride, her greatest ambition was to become a Pilates instructor someday. She's gorgeous but not exactly the brightest bulb I ever met. The same goes for some of the bodybuilding pals she likes to hang out with. I wouldn't call them the salt of the earth, either. April's bachelorette party the other night was wild enough that the cops had to be summoned to quiet things down—and that's with her about to give birth.

"Ted's worried that when some of the more disreputable wedding guests who've been staying at the house pack up to go home, some of Paul's precious objets d'art might end up going home with them. Grantham is lobbying for you to demand a full inventory of the contents of the Robert Lane house—an immediate full inventory."

"In other words," Ali said, "Ted's rooting for the old will over the new one because he expects to hand the whole mess over to me and maybe get paid faster besides. But if the old will is still in effect and I'm the primary beneficiary, doesn't that give me a clear motive for wanting Paul dead? Doesn't it make me look that much worse to the cops?"

"That just about covers it," Victor agreed. "What's good for Ted could be bad for us."

"I still don't like the fact that we're having the will read now," Ali said after a pause. "It seems rude and pushy."

They had come to a stop at a light on Sunset. Victor sought Ali's eyes in the rearview mirror. "It probably is rude and pushy," he agreed. "But let me remind you, this is a homicide investigation, Ali—possibly even capital murder. With your life at stake, you by God better believe we're going to be pushy."

"All right," Ali conceded finally. "Fair enough."

Robert Lane was only a few blocks long and sat on top of a steep hill just up from Sunset Boulevard; it was a winding, narrow, and supposedly two-way street. Whenever Paul and Ali had thrown parties—which they had done often—they had rented the parking lot from a neighboring church down on Sunset and then hired one of the local parking valet firms to ferry guests' cars up and down the hill.

Since the wedding and reception had both been scheduled to take place at the house, Ali assumed the parking arrangements would have been canceled once the wedding was called off. The sides of the street were full of illegally parked vehicles, most of them bearing media insignia. When Victor pulled up to the gate, Ali was surprised to see that it was wide open. She was even more surprised to see the parking valets very much in evidence although most of the newsies had chosen to disregard the valet parking option. So did Victor.

"Keep your cool, Ali," he advised as he turned in at the gate. He maneuvered his Lincoln into a narrow parking place between a catering truck—if the wedding had been canceled, why a catering truck?—and an enormous RV garishly painted an overall red and blue plaid pattern. On the side was a picture of a muscle-bound, bare-chested man wearing little more than a kilt. Beside him, printed in huge gold letters, were the words TEAM MCLAUGHLIN. SUMO SUDOKU.

Ali had a passing knowledge of sudoku. In fact, the waitresses at the Sugar Loaf had become sudoku addicts and experts, spending their break times working the puzzles in discarded newspapers left behind by customers who weren't so afflicted.

Puzzles of any kind had never really appealed to Ali, but she had learned enough to understand that sudoku was a game of logic played on a square containing eighty-one boxes divided into nine smaller squares. It was similar to a crossword puzzle only with numbers rather than words. The object was to fill in all horizontal and vertical lines with the numbers one through nine without ever having the same number appear twice in any of the lines. Each of the smaller boxes was also supposed to contain the numbers one through nine with no repetition. Ali assumed that Sumo Sudoku was more of the same, only bigger.

"Your husband's death is a big story, and everybody is covering it," Victor cautioned. "That means there may be reporters outside the door. So when we get out of the vehicle to go inside, try to keep quiet. I don't want any off-the-cuff remarks from anybody, you included, Helga," he added.

With Ali's attention focused on the garishly painted truck, she almost missed the group of reporters bearing down on them as Ted Grantham hustled out of the house to usher them inside. "Right this way," he said hurriedly. "Les isn't here yet. He called to say he's tied up in traffic. April should be down in a few minutes."

Down from what used to be my *room,* Ali thought, but she said nothing.

"Sorry about all the uproar," Ted commented, leading them toward the front door, where a hand-lettered DO NOT DISTURB sign had been posted over the doorbell. "But the film crew was already scheduled to be here today as part of the festivities," he continued. "Since this is the only day they *can* be here, April decided to go ahead with the shoot after all. Even with Paul gone, she thinks once the program is in the can there's a chance they'll still be able to get it on the air—maybe on one of those reality shows."

"What shoot?" Helga asked.

"The Sumo Sudoku shoot," Ted answered. "Surely you've heard of Sumo Sudoku. It's Paul's latest brainchild. April's, too, for that matter. It's all the rage around here and supposedly the next big thing. You play it with rocks. When Tracy McLaughlin of Team McLaughlin takes the RV down to the beach and sets up a match there, it's amazing. People line up to play; they're even willing to fork over good money for the privilege."

Only half listening to Ted, Ali stepped through the double doors with their elegant frosted glass and into the spacious foyer. It was a strange experience. This light-washed entryway with its hardwood floor and antique credenza had once been part of her home. Most of the house had been decorated in accordance with Paul's unrelentingly modern sensibility. In the face of all that brass and glass, Ali had gravitated to the one exception—a beautifully wrought, bird's-eye maple credenza that had occupied the place of honor in the entryway. She had loved the slightly curved lines of the piece and complex patterns in the grain of the wood. In a way, the credenza had seemed almost as much of an interloper in Paul's house as Ali herself had been.

Now the credenza was covered with a collection of fragrant condolence bouquets, all of them complete with unopened envelopes from various senders. At least one of the vases had been carelessly deposited on the polished wood, leaving behind a distinct and indelible water mark. Seeing the stain saddened Ali. She made a halfhearted effort to rub it out but it didn't go away. It would take someone wiser in the ways of cleaning to make the offending moisture ring disappear.

With no one paying any attention to her, Ali ventured a few steps into the living room. In anticipation of the wedding, most of the furniture had been removed—replaced by a dozen or so rows of cloth-covered banquet-style chairs arranged so they faced a wooden arch at one end of the room. On either side of the arch stood ranks of candles and immense baskets of flowers—an avant-garde mix of traditional and fragrant lilies punctuated with an occasional bird-of-paradise.

Ali wasn't the least bit surprised by this somewhat odd combination. Bird-of-paradise wasn't exactly commonplace in bridal floral arrangements, but Paul had always preferred it to any other flower. He would insist on sending it on occasions when other people—Ali included—would have preferred roses or gladiolas or even snapdragons. The oddly angular buds with their comical topknots and brilliant colors had never spoken to Ali the way they had to him.

The same could be said of Paul's choices in furniture—unabashedly modern and not especially comfortable—and art. On this early Saturday morning, with most of the furniture removed in honor of a wedding that would never happen, only the artwork remained. The big splashy original oil canvases had bold colors and plenty of panache. Ali knew the paintings came with top gallery pedigrees and spectacular price tags. What they lacked was heart.

Just like the rest of the house, Ali thought. No wonder she had never felt at home here. If it hadn't been for Elvira Jimenez doing her cooking magic in the kitchen, the house on Robert Lane could just as well have been a museum of modern art.

The far wall of the living room was lined with French doors that led out onto a spacious terrace. Through the open doors, Ali saw the terrace was stocked with a dozen or so linen-covered cocktail tables and even more chairs. Empty buffet tables, chafing dishes at the ready, were situated at both ends of the terrace. Again, Ali wasn't surprised that Paul would have selected this spot as the site of his now-canceled wedding reception. Paul had always loved entertaining on the lavish terrace with its unobstructed if sometimes smog-obscured view of the city. Ali had usually gravitated toward the smaller and more private tree-and-bougainvillea-lined patio out back by the pool house.

With the three attorneys settled in the library in a low-voiced huddle, Ali wandered out onto the terrace. The grassy lawn below the stone balustrade was a beehive of activity. Someone was using a handheld dispenser to lay out a complicated pattern of white chalk lines on Paul's carefully tended grass. Ali looked around for Jesus Sanchez, Paul's longtime gardener. He had always taken great pride in the fact that his grass could have been plunked down on the eighteenth green of any self-respecting golf course without anyone knowing the difference. Ali more than half expected Jesus to appear out of nowhere, bellowing a loud objection to the chalk-spreader's desecration.

Moments later Jesus did in fact appear around the corner of the house above and behind Ali, but he wasn't making any kind of fuss about the chalk on his grass lawn. Instead, he was totally occupied by two young men who were pushing a pair of heavily laden wheelbarrows loaded with perfectly round rocks down the steep path that led from the back of the house to the lawn below.

As one of the men made the corner, the wheelbarrow wobbled in his hands. The next thing Ali knew, the load of rocks came spilling down the hill and onto the flagstone terrace. Some of them bounced almost head high while one of them smashed to pieces, sending shards of granite flying in every direction. One needlelike piece seemed headed directly for Ali's throat. It missed her by an inch. Seconds later, a man vaulted off the path and over the rail, landing on the terrace next to her.

"Are you all right?"

Ali was shaken but unhurt. "I'm fine," she said.

Nodding, the angry man turned back to the frightened workman who was still clinging to the handles of his empty wheelbarrow.

"You stupid jerk! Don't you know how to do anything? You could have killed this poor woman!"

Only then did Ali recognize him. The man doing the yelling had to be Tracy McLaughlin, the same tall blond guy pictured on the RV. The big difference was that now he wore regular khakis rather than a kilt.

"Are you sure you're all right?" he asked Ali again. "It's a good thing that eight broke into a million pieces. Otherwise it might have taken your head right off. I'm not surprised, though. The kind of piss-poor help we're having to put up with here today . . ." He shook his head in disgust. "Come get these, will you?" he shouted up at the men waiting on the path. "And then go back to the truck. Thank God I have a spare eight there. It's got a crack in it, but it'll have to do."

As the one man came to collect his scattered load, the other made his way down to the grass. "Don't put them there, you stupid asshole," Tracy shouted at him. "Don't you know anything? Those are the fours. They belong on this side."

As the man hefted the rocks out of another wheelbarrow and onto the ground, the truth about Sumo Sudoku finally came home to Ali. When Ted had said it was played with rocks, Ali had envisioned something the size of marbles. These smooth, round hunks of granite were more like boulders, with large numbers chiseled into the surface. From the size and obvious weight of the "fours," Ali could only guess how much damage the stray eight might have done had it hit her full-on.

Ali was still shaken from her near miss when she saw a young woman, blond and very pregnant, emerge from the living room. She walked over to the debris field left by the broken rock and kicked at some of it. "What's this?" she wanted to know.

Helga had said April Gaddis was gorgeous, and that was true. Even without makeup and with her hair in disarray, she was a fine-featured beauty except for her eyes. They were red and puffy from a combination of weeping and lack of sleep. And she was pregnant enough that the silk robe she wore didn't quite cover her expanded middle. She was beautiful but utterly distraught and very, very young.

"One of my rocks," Tracy explained. "That cretin up there didn't know how to work a friggin' wheelbarrow. He lost his whole load and it came crashing down on the terrace here. It's a wonder he didn't kill this lady. A miracle really."

As the workman in question scurried to load the remaining rocks back into his wheelbarrow, April looked at Ali uncertainly.

"What are you doing here?" April asked. At least she didn't try to pretend that she didn't know who Ali was.

"The lawyers," Ali said, quickly forgetting her near miss with the exploding rock. "We're supposed to be meeting with the lawyers this morning in the library."

April shrugged. "I'm not in any condition to deal with this stuff right now. All I was trying to do was sneak down and get some breakfast from the buffet, but there are way too many workmen here already. I had no idea the crew would be this big."

Ali had sometimes imagined how she would react in what she had thought was the unlikely event she would ever come face-to-face with April Gaddis, her rival. Ali had scripted any number of biting remarks, but faced with the young woman and seeing her obvious desolation, Ali forgot all of them. Instead, Ali tried to focus on the homespun wisdom passed along to her in the e-mail from Phyllis in Knoxville.

"I'm sorry we're meeting like this, April," Ali said kindly. "I'm sorry for your loss."

Ali's words seemed to sap all of the young woman's strength. April staggered over to a nearby table, where she sank onto a chair and made a halfhearted attempt to smooth her hair.

"No one told me *you'd* be coming," she said accusingly.

"Ted Grantham is the one who set up the meeting," Ali returned. "He should have told you."

"He didn't." April seemed close to tears.

"I'm sorry," Ali said.

April probably could have handled a fight, but she was unable to cope with kindness. Her lips trembled, her face crumpled. Burying her head in her hands, she began to sob.

"I can't believe any of this is happening," she said despondently. "This was supposed to be my wedding day. I can't believe Paul is gone, just like that—with no warning at all. Instead of our wedding guests, the house is full of lawyers who are here about his will. Paul's *will,* for God's sake! What am I going to do without him? How will I manage? What'll happen to me? What'll happen to my baby?"

April's unbridled grief over losing Paul struck Ali as utterly raw and real—and refreshingly different from her own conflicted emotions. Learning about Paul's death—seeing him dead—had left Ali more empty than sad. Having him dead made her own life far less complicated. She hadn't cried. In fact, she hadn't shed a single tear, not even in the coroner's office. For that she felt guilty. In a way, being a party to April Gaddis's uncompromising despair made Ali feel better. She was relieved to know that Paul's sudden death meant something to someone—even if that person was the one who had unceremoniously booted Ali out of her home and out of her marriage.

And where were April's friends? Why was she here all alone? Without thinking about it, Ali sat down next to the grieving woman, laying a compassionate hand on her shoulder. What this very pregnant twenty-five-year-old was facing now was territory Ali Reynolds knew all too well. She had been there once, too, only she had been a few years younger than April when it had happened to her.

Ali had been a happily married twenty-two-year-old and pregnant with Chris when her first husband, Dean Reynolds, had been diagnosed with glioblastoma and died within months. Ali knew what it meant to be expecting a baby who would most likely be and indeed was a fatherless child on the day he was born. She remembered lying awake at night, pregnant, with her back hurting, and with the baby hurtling around inside her womb, and asking those very same questions over and over: What will become of us? How can I raise this baby on my own? Why is this happening to me?

During those dark, sleepless nights she hadn't known that she would be able to make it; that despite being a single mother she'd somehow manage to go back to school to finish her education and then go on to have a life and career that most people would have thought of as charmed. Back in that terrible time, there had been no easy answers for her, and she didn't try to pass along any easy answers to April Gaddis, either.

"You'll manage," Ali said, patting the weeping woman on the shoulder. "Being a single mother is tough. There are times when the baby is crying and the responsibility is all on your shoulders and you'll think you won't be able to live through one more day, but you will. There are times you'll question God and times when you'll rail at Him. But someday, on a bright fall after-noon, you'll be standing on the sidelines of a soccer field cheering like mad when that baby of yours kicks his first goal. That's when you'll know God was right; that's when you'll know everything you went through was worth it."

April raised her head. Her bleak eyes met Ali's. "But the divorce didn't go through," she said. "Paul and I weren't even married. What if he left me out of his will? He said he was going to rewrite it. He told me he had, but what if he didn't? Where will the baby and I live? What am I going to *do*? What?"

Ali could see that April's grief had her operating on a very short loop. "That's why we both have attorneys," Ali counseled gently. "I'm sure that's what they're doing right now—they're inside sorting things out."

"But I don't even have an attorney," April said. "I never thought I needed one."

Oh, honey lamb, Ali thought, *if you were messing around with Paul Grayson, how wrong you were!*

"It's going to be okay," Ali said with more conviction than she felt.

"Are you sure?" April asked.

Ali nodded. "Now what about you? You look a little queasy. You said you were looking for something to eat?"

Faced with a crisis, Ali automatically reverted to the coping skills she had learned at her mother's knee. In the Edie Larson school of crisis management there was nothing so bad that it couldn't be improved by the application of some well-prepared food served with equal amounts of tender loving care and judicious advice.

April nodded. "I called down to the kitchen, but no

one answered. The cook's probably out overseeing the caterers for the film crew."

Ali stood up. "Someone in your condition shouldn't be running on empty. Let me go ask Elvira to fix you something. An omelet, maybe? Elvira's huevos rancheros are wonderful, but probably not for someone as pregnant as you are."

"Elvira doesn't work here anymore," April said. "She quit, or else Paul fired her. I'm not sure which."

Ali was surprised to hear Elvira was gone— surprised and sorry, both. "But you do have a cook," Ali confirmed.

April nodded.

"Why don't I go find her," Ali offered. "What's her name?"

"We've gone through half a dozen cooks since that first one left," April said. "Sorry. I don't know her name."

"What would you like then?"

"Toast," April said uncertainly. "And maybe some orange juice."

"How about some bacon?"

"Oh, no. I don't eat anything that had a face. I'm a vegan."

That was, of course, utterly predictable. "Whole wheat?" Ali asked.

"Yes, please. With marmalade. And coffee. Have her make me a latte—a vanilla latte."

Ali wasn't sure a dose of caffeine was in the baby's best interests, but she set off for the kitchen without saying anything. On the way she caught a glimpse of Ted Grantham, Victor Angeleri, and Helga Myerhoff still huddled in the library, still conferring. In the spacious kitchen, Ali found a heavyset black woman standing in front of the stainless steel sinks and working her way through a mountain of dirty dishes.

"The breakfast buffet's out by the pool house," she said impatiently. "That's where the film crew is. There's food and coffee out there. Help yourself."

She sounded exasperated, overworked, and under-appreciated if not underpaid. Having another stranger wander into her kitchen was more than she could handle.

"This is for April—for Ms. Gaddis," Ali explained. "She asked me if you could make her some toast—whole wheat toast with marmalade, orange juice, and a vanilla latte."

The woman shook excess water off her hands and then dried them on a tea towel. "Very well," she said with a curt nod. "Do you want to wait here for it or should I bring it to her?"

"It might be best if you brought it," Ali said. "We're out on the terrace."

"You want some coffee, too?"

"Yes, thank you," Ali said. "That would be nice."

Ali returned to the terrace to find April sitting exactly where Ali had left her. She seemed to be absorbed in watching the ongoing rock-hauling and arranging process down below, but when Ali sat down next to her, she realized April was really staring off into space, seeing nothing.

"Breakfast's on its way," Ali said.

April nodded without answering.

"So when's the baby due?" Ali asked. She hoped that drawing April into a conversation might help shake her out of her solitary reverie and back into the present.

"Two weeks," she said. "Paul wanted to go to the

condo in Aspen on our honeymoon, but my ob-gyn said I shouldn't fly this close to my due date. We were going to drive over to Vegas instead."

"Do you know if it's a boy or a girl?"

"A girl. Paul wanted to name her Sonia Marie. I don't like that name much," April added, "but I guess I'll use it anyway. I wanted something a little more modern. You know—like Hermione from Harry Potter."

To Ali's way of thinking, Sonia Marie was a better bet than Hermione any day, but Paul was gone now. Soon enough April would realize that, when it came to her child, she was the one who would be making the decisions—all of them. By virtue of being run over by a freight train, Paul Grayson no longer had any effective say in the matter.

"Breakfast is coming," Ali said. "It'll be right out."

"Thank you," April said. Then, after a pause she added, "Thank you for being so nice to me."

You have a lady named Phyllis to thank for that, Ali thought. *Someone you've never met and most likely never will.*

She said, "This is a very tough situation, and we'll probably have to work together to sort it all out. It'll be better for all concerned if we can be civil to each other."

April nodded. "Did the cops tell you Paul was murdered?"

"Yes."

"Who would do such a thing?" April asked as the tears started up again. "I just can't imagine it. How could they be so cold-blooded as to put him on the train tracks and just leave him there to die?"

"I can't imagine that, either," Ali said. And it was

true. The idea was as unfathomable for her as it was for April.

"They think whoever did it left him there and then escaped by walking down the train tracks," April continued. "That's why they didn't find any footprints at the scene. They must have planned it that way so there wouldn't be any evidence. They think the killer had an accomplice who met him somewhere down the tracks, and that's how he got away. They said he was probably still in the area when Paul died. I guess the engine on the Camry was still warm when the cops got there. Can you imagine doing something like that and then standing around waiting for it to happen?"

April's words chilled Ali. If the killer had been somewhere nearby when the crash occurred, then he was probably still there when the emergency vehicles were dispatched to the scene as well—at the same time Ali herself was driving past on the freeway.

That meant the cops would go looking for someone who might have given the escaping killer a ride. That also meant Detectives Sims and Taylor wouldn't have far to look, especially if the old will was still in effect. They'd come after Ali—with a vengeance.

As someone with the three necessary ingredients—motive, opportunity, and an unidentified accomplice—Ali would be exactly what the detectives wanted and needed, a prime suspect.

{ CHAPTER 6 }

It turned out April was hungry enough that one order of toast and marmalade wasn't enough to do the job. Ali went back to the kitchen for a second helping. When she returned with it, she was surprised to find a camera crew had arrived. Someone was sweeping up the broken rock, and others were setting up cameras on the side of the terrace, where the city of L.A. would serve as a backdrop. She returned to the table just as Tracy McLaughlin came jogging up the stairs and back onto the terrace.

Earlier, when he'd been giving grief to the groundskeepers, he'd been clad in a T-shirt and a pair of khaki Bermuda shorts. Now he was dressed in what looked like the same kilt he'd worn for the RV mural. Tucked under one arm, like a football, was a ball of granite—a four, Ali estimated. Nodding briefly in April's direction, he marched over to the camera crew. He put the ball down on the flagstone terrace. When he straightened, he brushed a long lock of blond hair off his forehead and then stopped to confer with a member of the crew. Meanwhile, the ball of granite set off on its own and rolled drunkenly across the terrace. It came to rest near the leg of Ali's chair. A five-inch-tall numeral 3 had been sandblasted into its otherwise smooth surface. Having it roll in her direction seemed far less dangerous than having it bounce.

Leaving the camera crew, McLaughlin hurried over to retrieve it. "Sorry about that," he said.

"This is Tracy," April said to Ali. To Tracy she added, "And this is Ali."

No last names were mentioned or seemed to be necessary.

"Glad to meet you," Ali said.

He nodded. "Same here."

Just then a sweet young thing, a Hispanic woman in a very short skirt and very high heels, came through the French doors from the living room. Ali recognized her as a former intern from the station, although she couldn't remember the name. She wore a lapel mic and was dressed in a business suit— interviewer rather than intern attire. Obviously her career had taken an upward swing since Ali had last seen her. As she headed for the camera crew, so did Tracy.

"Now, if you'll excuse me," he said. Grabbing his ball, he hurried after her, smoothing his unruly hair as he went. Something about seeing the woman seemed to penetrate April's fog and she suddenly realized that, of all the people on the terrace, she was the only one wearing a robe.

Abruptly, she pushed her chair away from the table. "I've got to go get dressed," she said.

Since no one had come to summon Ali, she stayed where she was. A few seconds later, Tracy McLaugh-

lin, still holding his granite ball, and Sandy Quijada—
she announced her name at the beginning of the
interview—stepped in front of the camera for an old-
fashioned stand-up.

"This is Tracy McLaughlin," Sandy said, smiling
engagingly into the camera. "You're generally credited
with inventing Sumo Sudoku. Do you mind telling us
how that all came about?"

"Just because someone is strong doesn't mean he's
stupid," Tracy told her. "It's one of the oldest clichés in
the book. I mean, how many times have you heard the
words 'dumb as an ox'? If you're a jock, people automatically assume you're also a dolt. Sumo Sudoku is a
game that mixes brains and brawn."

"How?" Sandy asked.

Not exactly insightful, Ali thought.

"Sudoku is a game of logic," Tracy replied. "Regular
sudoku is usually played with a paper and pencil. Or a
pen if you're very good."

"Like a crossword puzzle," Sandy supplied.

"Right," Tracy said. "Only with numbers instead
of words. It's done on a square layout of eighty-one
squares arranged in a nine-by-nine matrix. Numbers
from one to nine are placed in the squares so that all
values occur without repetition in each horizontal line,
in each vertical line, and in each of the nine three-
by-three submatrices that fit within the nine-by-nine
square."

Sandy frowned slightly, as though the word "submatrices" was leaving her in the dust. "So how is Sumo
Sudoku different?"

Not a dumb blonde, Ali thought. *But dumb never-
theless.*

"For one thing, it's played outdoors," Tracy explained patiently. "Instead of using paper, we use grass or sand or even gravel. It has to be played on level ground so the numbers stay wherever they're placed. And instead of using a pencil to fill in the numbers, we use rocks like this." He hefted the granite ball into the air and held it up to the camera so that the sandblasted number 3 was showing.

"This is a number three rock. It weighs thirty pounds. The number one rocks weigh ten pounds. The number nine rocks weigh ninety pounds."

"That's a lot of rocks," Sandy marveled.

Tracy nodded. "It is," he agreed. "The total weight of the playing pieces is four thousand fifty pounds. Not exactly your grandfather's game of checkers."

"I'll say." Sandy beamed.

"So when we set up for a game, the grid is made up of individual squares that are two feet on each side, so a full layout is eighteen feet per side. As I said, the terrain should be flat enough to prevent placed markers from rolling on their own, but it may be flat or sloped, grassy or sandy—slightly damp sand is better than dry. Like golf, you must play the terrain as well as the basic game."

"Here you're going to play on grass?" Sandy asked.

If Tracy McLaughlin had a sense of humor, it wasn't apparent in the dead seriousness of his responses. "That's right. The game is prepared by placing all the markers ten feet from the edge of the grid. The judges will place the starting pieces in position. They are marked with an International Orange adhesive tag and may not be moved for the duration of the round. The remainder of the pieces will remain untouched and on the sidelines until the starter's signal. Markers may be moved at will during the round, but doing so more than once will slow the competitor. Markers may be carried or rolled. Speed is essential. So is accuracy."

Listening to him drone on, outlining the rules, it occurred to Ali that she was listening to an engineer masquerading as a bodybuilder. Sandy's attention seemed to be wandering, too.

"So how will today's match work?"

"What's all this?" Victor Angeleri demanded. His sotto voce greeting to Ali provoked an angry frown and a shushing motion from a woman on the sidelines, one with more tattoos and piercings than clothing.

Ali rose to her feet and hurried inside with her attorney on her heels. "Mr. McLaughlin is outlining the rules for Sumo Sudoku," she said, once in the living room. "It's supposed to be the next big thing."

Victor stopped and looked back out on the terrace. "Really? Next to what?"

"Beach volleyball, for all I know," Ali answered. "But from what I'm hearing, I'm guessing the world is safe from Sumo Sudoku. What about the will?"

"Les just got here," Victor told her. "It's time."

Victor ushered her into Paul's study—what used to be Paul's study. An unfamiliar man was seated behind Paul's ultramodern mirrored glass and stainless steel desk. He rose when Ali entered the room. "Les Jordan," he said. "You must be Ms. Reynolds."

Ali nodded.

"Sorry to be meeting under such unfortunate circumstances."

Ali nodded again. She looked around. Usually there were only three extra chairs in the room—two captain's chairs and a leather sling-backed contraption that was supposedly ergonomically superior to any other chair in the house. It was also Ali's least favorite. Helga was seated next to the wall in that one. It would probably soon be Helga's least favorite as well since her feet barely touched the floor. But today, with four lawyers already present, three extra swivel chairs from the game table in the family room had been crammed into the study as well.

Ali took one of those while Victor and Ted Grantham settled into the two captain's chairs. "I expect Ms. Gaddis should be joining us any moment," Mr. Jordan said seriously. "If you don't mind waiting . . ."

It wasn't lost on Ali that, while they waited for April to put in her appearance, Ali was sitting in a roomful of attorneys, all of them chalking up billable hours at an astonishing rate.

And it's all Paul's fault, she thought. *If he hadn't gone and gotten himself killed, if he'd tended to business, if he'd kept his pants zipped . . .*

"Would you care for some coffee?" Mr. Jordan asked.

There was something about being in her former home and being offered coffee by a visitor, especially a visiting attorney, that rubbed Ali the wrong way. "No thanks," she said. "April and I had coffee together out on the terrace a few minutes ago."

It was worth the price of admission—whatever that might be—to see four attorneys watching her in drop-jawed amazement. Before any of them replied, however, two newcomers showed up in the library doorway. One was a relatively attractive woman of indeterminate age. Her face was a tight-skinned mask that spoke of too many dollars spent on a high-priced plastic sur-

geon. Ali recognized the type—a Hollywood socialite
wife—or more likely ex-wife—with more nerve than
money. The bow tie–wearing man at the woman's side
was, Ali realized at once, yet another attorney—making
the grand total five in all. Five too many.

"Good morning, Mrs. Ragsdale," Les Jordan said
smoothly, rising to his feet. "Come in, please. I didn't
realize you would be here or that you'd be bringing
someone with you. I'll send out for more chairs."

"We'll only need one," the woman said. "My daughter won't be attending this meeting after all. She's not
feeling up to it."

"Well then," Les said, "with all due respect, you
probably shouldn't be here, either, Mrs. Ragsdale.
Client confidentiality rules and all that."

Dismissing him with a look, Mrs. Ragsdale turned
away from Les Jordan and addressed the other people
in the room. "My name's Monique Ragsdale," she said.
"April Gaddis is my daughter. And this," she added,
indicating the man beside her, "is Harlan Anderson.
I've retained him to be here on the baby's behalf—
on Sonia Marie's behalf. Regardless of whether or
not we're dealing with an old will or a new one, Mr.
Anderson and I are here to make sure that my granddaughter's interests are protected."

Leaving Harlan standing, she strode into the room,
settled her designer-clad self into one of the game
room chairs, crossed her long high-heeled legs, and
then gave Les a cool appraisal. "Shall we get started
then?" she asked.

Ali knew at once that Monique was one tough
cookie. Short of someone bodily throwing her out of
the room, she and her attorney weren't leaving.

Les looked questioningly at Ali. "By all means," Ali said. "Let's get on with it."

Les Jordan sighed. First he went around the room, making all the necessary introductions, saving Ali for last.

"I know who she is," Monique said shortly. "I've seen her before. On TV. Now tell us about the will."

"The truth is, a new will was prepared," Jordan continued. "It's been drawn up, but it was never signed. We expected to finalize this after the divorce hearing yesterday. Obviously that didn't happen, so the most recent last will and testament, the one that's still in effect, is the one that was drawn up eight years ago shortly after Paul's marriage to Ms. Reynolds here."

A file folder had been lying on the table in front of him. He opened it now and began to read. Ali only half listened. She was familiar with the provisions. Shortly after the wedding, she and Paul had signed similar documents. Ali had left behind a trust for Chris. Paul had named some charitable bequests. Other than those, they had left everything to each other. Ali remembered that they had signed the wills in some other attorney's office. At the time, it had seemed that Paul was going out of his way to protect Ali's interests. Now, though, under these changed circumstances, being Paul's sole beneficiary opened several cans of worms, not the least of which, Ali realized, would be Monique Ragsdale.

As Les Jordan read through the provisions—the charitable bequests as well as the personal ones— Monique became more and more agitated. The bottom line was clear. Ali Reynolds was still Paul Grayson's wife, and since much of what they owned was community property, it went to Ali.

"You mean to tell me that April and her baby get nothing?" Monique demanded. "How can that be? You drew up the new will. Why wasn't it signed?"

Les Jordan was exceedingly patient. "Paul and I had an appointment to sign the will yesterday afternoon after the divorce was final. He wanted to do it that way. Thought it would be cleaner somehow. We were scheduled to meet here at the house so he and April could both sign new documents."

"I knew Paul Grayson," Monique declared. "He was an honorable man. I can't believe he meant to leave either his intended bride or his child unprovided for."

Honorable? Ali thought to herself. With Paul Grayson's legal widow sitting right there in the room and with his pregnant not-bride sitting somewhere upstairs, that seemed an odd thing to say. You could call Paul any number of things, but honorable certainly wasn't one of them.

"Intended and legally married are two different things," Jordan pointed out.

"But still," Monique continued. "The only thing that prevented him from marrying April was his tragic and untimely death. In fact, I happen to believe that's the whole reason he's dead. That whoever killed him did so just to make sure the marriage between my daughter and Paul Grayson never happened." The pointed look she cast in Ali's direction at the end of that little speech spoke volumes.

Ali's cheeks flushed. It was galling to have to sit in the room and have your husband's mistress's mother come right out and accuse you of murder. Ali was about to open her mouth to defend herself when

Victor touched her arm. With a slight warning shake of his head he admonished her to keep quiet.

"We're all dealing with a good deal of emotional upheaval at the moment, Ms. Ragsdale," he said soothingly. "For right now, though, I think it would be best if we all refrained from tossing around unfounded allegations."

Les Jordan nodded in agreement. "Mr. Angeleri is right," he said. "We need to keep from being drawn into making any kind of accusations. As for the baby, there are laws on the books in the state of California that are specifically designed to deal with cases like this—laws that protect the interests of in utero or omitted offspring. No doubt some funds would be made available from the estate to support the child and monies held in trust until he or she—"

"She," Monique supplied.

Jordan nodded. "Until she reaches her majority. Most likely a guardian *ad litem* would be appointed to protect the child's interests in the meantime."

"That's fine and good for the baby," Monique Ragsdale objected. "But what about my daughter? What happens to her? Does that mean she could be evicted and put out on the street?"

"No one here is suggesting any such thing, certainly not at this time," Les Jordan said. "But the truth is, as I told you earlier, your daughter is merely an intended wife as opposed to a wife in fact. Unless Mr. Grayson has made some kind of specific provisions for her, through the purchase of life insurance or something of that nature, I don't know of any legal remedies that would come into play that would allow your daughter to go against the will.

That's not to say there aren't any, but none come readily to mind."

"What if you went ahead and finalized the divorce?" Monique's question was addressed to Ted Grantham.

"Excuse me?" he asked.

Monique was undaunted. "Harlan here has found a similar case in New Jersey where the divorce was finalized after the husband's death. That cleared the way for the property agreement to stand in court and made for simplified estate planning. The divorce also automatically negated the old will. In this case, that might work to Sonia's benefit."

"But not to mine," Ali said sharply.

"This isn't about you," Monique said firmly. "It's all about the baby."

"And what about me?" April asked. "Divorce or no, it sounds like I'm left with nothing."

Until April spoke, no one else gathered in the room had noticed her unannounced arrival. How long she had been outside the library door listening was anyone's guess. She clearly had changed her mind about going upstairs to dress since she stood in the doorway still wearing her nightgown and robe.

Monique leaped to her feet and hurried to her daughter. "You shouldn't be here," Monique said. "You should be upstairs resting."

"I don't need to rest," April protested. "I deserve to be part of this discussion. After all, it's my life, too. I need to know what's going on instead of the bunch of you talking about it behind my back. Besides, I already heard what he said. According to Paul's will everything goes to her." She nodded in Ali's direction. "It's so not fair. How can this be happening? It's like a nightmare or something. And where are all my friends? Who sent them away?"

"I did," Monique said. "And I'm sure others have called, but I sent them all to the answering service. And I posted a 'Do Not Disturb' sign out at the front door. I didn't want people bothering you at a time like this. And having too many people running around would just get in the way of the filming."

"But I *need* my friends," April returned. "I *need* the company more than I need the rest. You had no right to send my friends away."

All of which answered one of Ali's earlier questions as to the whereabouts of April's friends. And Ali noticed something else. Out on the terrace April had been grieving, but she had been a grieving grown-up. Now, with her mother in the room, April seemed to have reverted to some childhood script. She sounded even younger than she was—more like a petulant, demanding teenager than an adult.

Ignoring her mother's advice, April made her way into the crowded room, where she sank into one of the swivel chairs. Pulling the gaping robe more tightly around her, she stared at Ali. "You were nice to me before," she said flatly, "but I guess this means things have changed. When do I have to leave, before the baby's born or after?"

"No one has said a word about your having to leave," Ali said. "And certainly not right now. With a baby due in a matter of days, you need to stay where you are until the lawyers can help us get things sorted out."

"How long does sorting-out take?" April asked. "And what's there to sort?"

Since Les Jordan had been effectively chairing the meeting, Ali looked at him for guidance.

He shrugged. "Uncomplicated estates can be set-tled in a matter of months," he said. "Complicated ones can take much longer than that, especially if other matters arise—like needing to liquidate prop-erty, for example. And there are always other legal issues that can cause indefinite delays."

He didn't spell out exactly what kind of "legal issues" he meant, but Ali had a pretty clear idea he was thinking about criminal proceedings. She guessed that everyone else in the room, with the possible exception of April herself, was making a similar assumption. Ali might be Paul's widow and the major beneficiary of his will, but she also knew that she wouldn't be allowed to inherit a dime as long as she was considered a suspect in his death. Until she was cleared, settling the estate would be stuck in neutral—and accumulating legal fees like crazy.

"What about the funeral?" April asked.

"What about it?"

"I'm twenty-five years old," April said. "I don't know anything about planning funerals." *I didn't either*, Ali thought, *but I figured it out*.

"You don't need to worry about any of that," Monique told her daughter. "I'll handle it all."

"No, you won't," April said. Her reply was forceful enough that it took everyone by surprise, most espe-cially her mother. "Since I wasn't Paul's wife and since I'm not his widow, it isn't my place to handle it. And it isn't yours, either."

April looked at Ali as she spoke. Monique, on the other hand, seemed utterly astonished by this small but dry-eyed and very determined rebellion. Monique was so surprised, in fact, that Ali wondered if there had ever been another instance in which April had drawn a line in the sand and told her mother no in such unequivocal terms. Before Monique had a chance to say anything more, Ali stepped into the breach.

"My first husband died of cancer when I was about your age," she told April. "My son was born two months after his father died, so I do know a little of what you're going through. Planning Dean's funeral was hard work, but I needed to do it. And you'll need to do it, too. Funerals are really for the living, but they're also a major part of the grieving process. I'll be glad to help you plan it, if you want me to."

"Wait a minute," Monique objected. "April is my daughter. You can't just come horning in like this—"

"Mother," April said. "Stop." And then, to Ali she added, "Yes, I'd like you to help me. How long does planning a funeral take?"

"Not that long. Other than choosing a casket or an urn and deciding on cremation or not, you really can't do much until after the coroner releases the body. In the case of a homicide, that could take several days. Only after the body is released can you establish a time for the services, arrange for flowers, get the announcements into the paper, and all of that."

"I've never even been to a funeral," April said. "Where do people hold them? At a church somewhere? Here at the house?"

"Not at the house," Ali said quickly. "And Paul wasn't someone I'd call a churchgoing kind of guy. So maybe the funeral home would be best for the service itself with a catered reception here at the house afterward."

"Do you send out invitations or something?" April asked.

She really is young, Ali thought.

"No, someone writes an obituary with an announcement at the end telling the time and place of the services and whether or not they're open to the public. That goes into the *Times.* Then whoever wants to come shows up."

April nodded. "You said funeral home. Which one?"

Ali remembered the form she had signed, the one the clerk in the coroner's office had handed her.

"When I went to Indio to do the identification, I signed a form in the Riverside County Coroner's Office. Once they're done with the body, it authorizes them to release it to the Three Palms Mortuary here in Beverly Hills," Ali answered. "I chose them because, years ago, they handled the services for Paul's mother. They did a good job. The facility is lovely, the chapel is spacious, and I remember the people were nice to deal with. And the funeral chapel is relatively close—only a mile or so away, on Sunset. But if you'd rather use someone else . . ."

"No," April said. "I'm sure they'll be fine."

"Wait a minute, April," Monique interjected. "This is ridiculous. You can't just let her walk in and take over everything. For God's sake, stand up for yourself, April. Take charge!"

"I am standing up for myself," April returned. "I'm going to do this my way, and Ali is going to help." She looked around at the faces of the legal eagles gathered there. "Is there anything else?"

Les Jordan shook his head. "Not that I know of," he said. "Not at this time."

"Good. I'm going back upstairs," April said. "And now I really am going to get dressed. I want to go out and check on the sudoku shoot."

The arms on the game chair were low. With April's bulging belly throwing her center of gravity off-kilter, it was a struggle for her to rise to her feet. Victor stood and gave her a hand up. Ali expected Monique to get up and follow her daughter out of the room, but she didn't. She stayed right where she was.

"April is my daughter," she said. "I'm not going to stand by and let you walk all over her and control the purse strings."

"No one is walking all over her," Les Jordan pointed out. "We're simply apprising her of the legal ramifications of her situation."

But Ali understood at once that Monique wasn't addressing the attorneys. She was talking to Ali directly, telling her to back off.

"Are we done here?" Victor asked.

"As far as I know," Les said.

"Good. We'll be going then. Come on, Ali. Helga."

Ali rose to her feet, aware of Monique's glare fastened on her. She walked past Monique toward the doorway, then turned and came back. "Your daughter's going through a terrible time right now," Ali said. "I have no intention of walking all over her. I'm trying to help."

"She doesn't need your help," Monique insisted. "Why would she? She has me."

Exactly, Ali thought as she followed Victor and Helga out the door. *Poor baby. Why would April need anyone else?*

{ CHAPTER 7 }

When Victor, Ali, and Helga emerged from the house, they discovered that Victor's Lincoln was blocked by a second huge RV, this one with the logo SUMO SUDOKU DRAGONSLAYER TEAM. In the process of shoehorning the second RV into the circular drive, the driver had taken out one of the gateposts and one side of the RV as well. Jesus, the gardener, and the guy who was apparently the driver were involved in a heated conversation about the incident with the entire discussion taking place in high-volume Spanish.

As the newly reinstalled mistress of Robert Lane, Ali supposed she should take a hand in the discussion, but since Jesus appeared to have the situation under control, she didn't. Ali had concerns that were far more compelling than fixing a broken gate.

She and Helga got into the Lincoln, and Victor waited outside until the damaged RV had been moved out of the way. Off to one side of the house, in the yard outside the pool house, Ali caught a glimpse of people looking on as a film crew followed the action of a bare-chested man who bent over, reached down, picked up one of the sudoku rocks, and then lugged it off. So the Sumo Sudoku contest was under way.

"Have you ever heard of a postmortem divorce?" Ali asked.

"It'll never happen," Helga replied. "For one thing, we'd be stupid to sign off on it. Just losing the marital deduction would cost a fortune in estate taxes. Besides, April's smarter than that—smarter than I gave her credit for, anyway."

"What do you mean?"

"I mean she looked around that room full of lawyers, figured out you were the softest touch in the place, and snuggled right up to you, driving her mother crazy in the process."

"Aren't you being a little cynical?" Ali asked. "April's in a tough position. I happen to know from firsthand experience what she's going through about now."

"Don't fall for it," Helga insisted. "She's just buttering you up because she figures you're the one who'll be doling out the money for her baby."

"What's wrong with that?" Ali asked. "Wasn't Ted Grantham trying to do the same thing—buttering me up—in order to be sure that his bill gets paid?"

"That's different," Helga returned. "April has a way better hand than Ted Grantham does. He isn't eight and a half months pregnant, and she is. Believe me, April is going to use that as a club. She'll play on your sympathy for all she's worth. She's got you pegged as being too nice to throw her out in the cold. Besides, she won the first round fair and square."

"What first round?" Ali asked.

"When you said you'd let her stay on in the house until after the baby is born. When it comes time for her to actually leave, I predict you'll have to evict her. And I agree with Ted, by the way. While settling the estate is in limbo, you need to request an inventory and appraisal of everything in the house. I've known plenty of women like April Gaddis in my time. She'll figure out what's worth stealing and what isn't and she'll make off with anything that isn't nailed down. And requiring a paternity test wouldn't be out of line, either."

It was ironic for Ali to find herself in the position of having to defend her dead husband's pregnant girlfriend to Helga Myerhoff, Ali's own divorce attorney. She was relieved and glad to change the subject when Victor opened the door and clambered into his seat.

He looked over at Ali and shook his head in seeming disgust. "What part of 'whatever you say may be held against you' don't you understand?"

"Excuse me?" Ali asked.

"Your blog," Victor said. "My assistant just called. She's been reading your blog on the Web—reading all about it, as they say. You have to understand it's not just what you say to the cops that can be held against you, Ali. It's what you say anywhere to anyone. Fang? You really called Paul Grayson Fang?"

"He's been Fang in my blog for a long time," Ali protested. "Since long before somebody killed him."

"Believe me, Detectives Sims and Taylor are going to love that. For right now, you're to say nothing more in your blog about this case, understood? For as long as this is an active investigation, commentary from you is off the table."

"Yes," Ali said. She felt stupid and chagrined. "And about Sims and Taylor . . ."

"What about them?" Victor asked sharply.

"They've evidently been in touch with April," Ali said. "She told me about it earlier, when we were out on the terrace."

"What did she say?"

"That they think Paul's killer escaped by leaving the car on the railroad tracks and then walking down the ties far enough so he was able to exit the tracks without being detected. They're speculating that he met up with an accomplice somewhere in the vicinity and they took off from there," Ali said.

Victor expelled a long sigh. "Which explains why they didn't find any footprints at the scene."

Ali nodded. "Yes," she said.

"That would also mean that the killer or killers were still in the general area at the time Paul died. Which, according to the receipts from the gas station and the restaurant in Blythe, would have placed you in the area as well."

Ali nodded again. She liked the way Victor immediately connected the dots even if she didn't like the dots he was connecting. "Yes," she said.

"My guess is, they're already going after your phone records then," Victor mused. "Trying to see who all you've contacted recently, to see if they can get a handle on who you might have enlisted as an accomplice."

"My phone records?" Ali demanded. "Isn't that illegal?"

"It's illegal to listen in on your phone calls without a warrant, but it's perfectly legal to look at your billing information to see who you called and who called you, as well as where you were and what cell phone towers were in use when those calls occurred."

"They can look at my phone records until they're blue in the face," Ali said. "They're not going to find anything. They're going to have to look elsewhere."

"If they look elsewhere," Victor responded.

"What do you mean, 'if'?"

"Sims and Taylor have a high-profile case on their hands, one their bosses are going to want cleared in a hell of a hurry. They also have a likely suspect—you. I think there's a good chance that they'll work like crazy to make whatever evidence they have fit what they think happened, rather than looking very hard for what else might have happened or who else might have been involved."

"What other suspects are there?" Ali asked.

"You tell me," Victor returned. "April would have to be dumb as a stump to knock Paul Grayson off without knowing in advance that she was going to inherit."

"What about April's mother?" Ali asked.

"Ms. Ragsdale may bear looking into," Victor conceded.

"I think so, too," Helga agreed. "That woman is a piece of work. The very idea of our agreeing to a post-mortem divorce is ridiculous."

A few minutes later, Victor dropped Ali off at her hotel. A glance at her watch told her that, depending on traffic, her mother would probably be arriving within the next hour or so. She went upstairs to await Edie's arrival. While Ali waited, she logged on and found her in-box once again brimming with messages. Before she read any of them, however, she wrote a post of her own.

CUTLOOSEBLOG.COM
Saturday, September 17, 2005

Ali's first instinct was to begin her post with the words "On the advice of my attorney . . ." but then she remembered what Victor had said: "Anything you say can and will be held against you." So she went for something much less descriptive and also, to her way of thinking, much less real.

> For the time being commentary from Babe
> will be suspended due to my involvement in a
> complex personal matter. As time allows, I will
> continue to post appropriate or interesting
> comments from readers. In the meantime,
> thank you for your loyalty and your interest.
> *Posted 11:12 A.M., September 17, 2005 by Babe*

When she began reading through the e-mails, most of them had to do with the posting from Phyllis in Knoxville. Some correspondents seemed to agree that Phyllis had the right idea.

Dear Babe,
Phyllis is right. Be nice to Twink and be nice to yourself. As ye sow so shall ye reap.

ANNA

Dear Babe,
You suffered a terrible loss, too. More than one.
Please know that you're in my thoughts and prayers.

LESLIE IN IOWA

Surprised by the number of people offering their condolences, Ali replied to all of them without necessarily posting them. Not all of the notes were kind, however.

Oh, great. Another Southern California celebrity murder by another "abused" media wife. The gossip columnists will go nuts. No doubt you'll hire yourself some high-priced attorney and get off scot-free. You people all make me sick. I hope you rot in hell.

That one wasn't signed and didn't merit a response.

Dear Babe,
When I read the part about the homicide detectives interviewing you, I couldn't believe it, but then the cops always suspect the spouse, although usually the killer is the husband instead of the wife. Does that mean they think you did it? Are they going to arrest you or are you just a person of interest? If they do arrest you, my nephew, Richard Dahlgood, is an attorney in L.A. I don't know what he charges, but if you want to get in touch with him, let me know and I'll give you his numbers.

VELMA T IN LAGUNA

Ali wanted to tell Velma that she had all the legal assistance she could handle about then. She had no doubt that Velma's nephew was probably far more affordable than the hulking Victor Angeleri. But she was paying the man too much to disregard his advice. She replied to Velma with a carefully noncommittal thank-you.

Dear Velma,
Thank you for your concern. Please don't worry about me. I have the situation well in hand.

BABE

The next e-mail stunned her.

Dear Ms. Reynolds,
Please forgive me for contacting you through your blog. I tried calling your home number in Arizona. I left a message there, but it seems likely you're here in California at the moment. My name is Sheila Rosenburg. I'm a local (L.A.-area) producer for Court TV. We would like to be in touch with you whenever it might be convenient for you regarding a possible interview. My contact information is listed below.

SHEILA ROSENBURG

The very idea that Paul's death had now become fodder for the "true crime" network was nothing short of chilling. If Court TV was on the job, could Fox's Greta Van Susteren be far behind? And in that fanatical crowd, Ali knew producers and commentators could make as much of a story about what wasn't said as they did about what was.

Dear Ms. Rosenburg,
Thank you for your interest. I'm not granting any
interviews at this time. Should that change, I'll let
you know.

REGARDS,
ALI REYNOLDS

The next one was a stunner.

Hey, Ali,
How's it going. Long time no see. I have a line
on a possible job offer for you that'll put you
back where you belong—on live TV. If you're
going to be in L.A. anytime soon, let me know
and I'll see what I can do to set up an interview.

JACKY

Jacky was short for Jack Jackson, Ali's agent—at least he had been her agent. The words that came to mind now were: more nerve than a bad tooth. In actual fact, Jacky had been Ali's agent for a long time—from her first on-air job out of college in Milwaukee to her move from Fox News in New York to the L.A. anchor desk. Ali had gotten the L.A. job on her own and without any help from Jacky, but he had been glad to take his cut of the action. Then. But once she'd been let go—once she'd been booted off the air and once she'd made it clear that she wasn't going to take her age-based firing lying down—Jacky had disappeared off the face of the planet. He had stopped taking Ali's calls, hadn't returned her e-mails, either.

She had understood what was going on well enough. In television circles, network executives counted for something. Paul Grayson had been the four-hundred-pound gorilla, and no one had wanted to piss him off. No doubt Jacky had read about what was going on and had decided to distance himself, leaving Ali and her stymied career to her own devices. Now, with Paul gone, Jacky must have reached the sudden conclusion that Ali Reynolds was bankable again. No doubt he expected to be welcomed back with open arms. And his assumption that she'd want to have him back rankled worse than anything.

Screw you, Ali thought. *No vultures allowed.* With that she deleted Jacky's message.

The phone rang a few seconds later—the room phone. "There's someone down in the lobby who would like to see you, Ms. Reynolds," the smooth voice of the concierge said. "She says she's your mother. Would you like me to send her up?"

"Yes," Ali said. "Please do."

Ali stood in the open doorway of her room to greet Edie Larson when she arrived a few minutes later, dragging an immense roll-aboard bag behind her.

"I hope it's okay if I bunk with you," Edie said uncertainly.

"It's fine," Ali said, gesturing toward the king-sized bed.

"Did you know Dave Holman was coming?" Edie asked. "I ran into him down in the lobby. He was going to rent a room here, but then he found out how much they cost and almost had a heart attack, so he's gone to find someplace else to stay." Edie stopped in the middle of the room and turned around, slowly examining the plush surroundings. "Are you sure you can afford this?"

"Yes," Ali said, thinking back to her lawyer-filled morning and the news that over time she was bound to inherit a good deal of Paul Grayson's considerable fortune. In fact, she could afford to stay here now far more easily than she could have before. She closed the hallway door and turned to face her mother.

"So how are things?" Edie Larson asked. "And how are you?"

For some reason, those two questions, coming from Edie, were enough to cause Ali's emotional dam to break. All the tears she hadn't shed in the coroner's office—all the tears she had put on hold and hadn't shed during her visit to the house on Robert Lane—burst through now. Sobbing, she let herself be pulled into her mother's arms—held and comforted—while Edie patted her shoulder and crooned soothing words.

"Shush now," Edie murmured. "It's going to be all right. You'll see. Now then, have you had any lunch?"

This was so typically Edie Larson that Ali had to smile through her tears. Edie's daughter might be a crazed killer on her way to the slammer, but Edie would move heaven and earth to be sure Ali was properly fed beforehand.

"Not yet," Ali said.

Edie heaved her oversized suitcase up onto the bed and unzipped it. "Now then," she said. "Let me hang up my clothes and put things away. I'll be able to think better once I get organized."

"When you finish, maybe we can go downstairs and have something to eat."

"Bad idea," Edie said. "We'd probably be better off ordering from room service."

"How come?" Ali asked.

"Because there are a lot of people milling around down in the lobby who looked like news people to me. I asked one of the helper guys, a doorman, I think, what they were doing. He said they were looking for you."

"For me?" echoed Ali.

"Not by name," Edie answered. "He said they were here because there's a 'murder suspect' reportedly staying at the hotel right now. He said they're trying to get a glimpse of her. This may be California," Edie added, "but I'm assuming that even in L.A. there's not more than one murder suspect at a time staying in a place like this."

When Ali had worked the news desk, one of the rules had been that suspects weren't mentioned by name until they'd actually been charged with a crime. But that wouldn't help her. Her face had already turned up on camera the night before as she and Victor were leaving the coroner's office. And people had noticed. People had recognized her. She didn't know how they had managed to trace her to the hotel. Most likely someone had followed Victor's Lincoln when they left Robert Lane. Now, knowing they were here, Ali felt besieged.

"Room service sounds good to me," she said.

Half an hour later, Ali's cell phone rang. "How do people stand this traffic day in and day out?" Dave Holman wanted to know. "And it's not just during rush hour, either. It lasts all day long."

"Where are you?" Ali asked.

"Motel 6. That's a little more my speed than the place you're staying."

"Where?"

"Highway 101 and some other freeway, I-210, I think. The good thing is, I should be able to make my way back there from here on surface streets. The people driving on the freeways are nuts."

Ali had come to L.A. from New York. The metro area had seemed different to her but not entirely alien. Dave hailed from Sedona. She could see how foreign the city must seem to someone accustomed to living in small-town Arizona.

"Our room number is 703," she told him. "When you get back here to the hotel, come directly up to the room. Whatever you do, don't ask for me by name. Mom says there are reporters down in the lobby. One of them might be listening."

"No kidding," Dave returned. "I may be a hick, but when I met up with Edie a while ago down in the lobby, I did notice one or two reporters had been added to the mix."

"So we'll have lunch up here," Ali said. "From room service. What do you want?"

"A burger. Medium rare. No tofu!"

Ali laughed at that. "No tofu it is."

She called room service and ordered a burger for Dave and tortilla soup for Edie and herself. When she put down the phone, she found Edie studying her daughter's reflection in the mirror.

"Have you met her?" Edie asked.

"Met who?"

"April Gaddis," Edie replied. "Paul's fiancée."

"How do you know her name?" Ali asked.

Edie reached into a capacious purse and pulled out a handful of newspapers. "I stopped for coffee at that truck stop on the far side of Palm Springs and picked up a couple of newspapers," she replied. "I wanted to know what we were up against before I got here."

Edie laid the papers on the desk and then pulled out a brand-new spiral notebook. She opened the notebook to the first page, which was blank. "When Dave Holman is working a homicide, I know he always keeps a casebook," Edie added, picking up a pen. "I think we should do the same thing. I'm going to write down everything so we don't forget details. So tell me. What's April like?"

Under any other circumstance, Ali might have found her mother's businesslike approach amusing, but this wasn't funny. As Edie sat with her pen poised over paper, it was clear she wanted answers.

"Very young, very pretty, very pregnant," Ali said finally.

"And she was supposed to get married today," Edie said.

Ali nodded.

"Is she considered a suspect in Paul's murder?" Edie wanted to know.

"Probably not," Ali said. "No motive. Had the divorce been finalized and the wedding ceremony performed, it might be a different story, but when the will was read this morning, I was still Paul's legal wife and primary beneficiary. If April was going to knock him off, surely she would have been smart enough to wait until they were actually married."

"Is she that smart?" Edie asked.

Ali thought about what Helga had said—about April being smart enough to throw herself on Ali's mercy. "I think so," Ali responded.

WEB OF EVIL   125

"Who else would have a motive then?" Edie asked. She was approaching the problem in her accustomed manner—with no nonsense and plenty of common sense. "Is there a chance there's another man in the picture?" she added. "If money isn't the motivating factor, maybe something else is—like jealousy, for example. From what I see on TV, jealousy works."

Ali had thought about April Gaddis and Paul Grayson primarily in terms of the two of them cheating on her. The idea that they might have been cheating on each other had never crossed her mind.

"It's possible, I suppose," Ali said dubiously. She wasn't entirely convinced.

"Of course it is," Edie declared. "If Paul would cheat on you, he'd cheat on her, too. That's what your father says: Once a cheat, always a cheat. So the first thing we have to do is find out everything there is to know about April Gaddis."

"We should ask Christopher about that," Ali said. "He knew about April long before I did. She's related to some friend of his. April was working for Paul as his administrative assistant, but I don't know which came first, the chicken or the egg—the job or the affair. I think it's likely that he got her the job so she could earn enough money to support herself. That way there wouldn't be a paper trail linking money from him to her."

"Right, a little prenuptial nepotism never hurt anybody," Edie observed. "So I'll ask Christopher about April."

"I met her mother," Ali supplied.

"April's mother?" Edie asked. "You have?"

"Her name's Monique Ragsdale. She came to the house this morning to meet with the attorneys. She claims she's looking out for the interests of the baby. I suspect she's mostly looking out for herself. She came hoping we'd agree to a postmortem divorce decree."

"You can't divorce someone after they're dead, can you?"

"Helga doesn't think so," Ali said.

There was a knock on the door. When Ali opened it, the room service trolley was waiting out in the hallway, and so was Dave Holman. His broad-shouldered, military bearing was something Ali really needed about then—something she welcomed. Reaching past the waiter, she gave Dave a brief but heartfelt hug.

"Thanks for coming," she said.

"Wouldn't have missed it," he said.

While the waiter set up a table out on the deck, Dave prowled the room. "This one's a little nicer than mine," he said. "There's no room service at Motel 6, but there's a Denny's up the block, so I'll live." He peered over Edie's shoulder at the notebook.

"Just trying to get an idea of who all's involved," she explained.

"Good work," he said.

All through lunch, Edie and Dave continued to pepper Ali with questions while Edie took copious notes. Once again Ali recalled what Victor had told her: "Anything you say . . ." But surely what she told her own mother and her good friend Dave couldn't hurt her, could it? Especially since everything she said was the truth.

They were just finishing lunch when the phone rang. "Ted Grantham here," he said. "This is a bit awkward, but . . ."

"What is it?"

"April called while Les and I were having lunch," he said. "I didn't get the message until I came back to the office. She said she was having a problem with her mother about planning the funeral. She wanted to talk to you about it if you wouldn't mind coming back up to the house to see her."

"Of course," Ali said. "I'll be glad to."

"Glad to what?" Edie asked when Ali got off the phone.

"April wants me to come back up to the house and talk about funeral arrangements."

"With you?" Dave demanded.

"Yes. With me." Ali was already searching the room for her purse and her keys.

"How come?" Dave wanted to know.

"Because she's twenty-five years old and doesn't know how to go about handling all those details."

"Shouldn't her mother help her with that?" Dave asked.

"April doesn't want her mother involved."

"Wait a minute," Dave said. "Your dead ex-husband's girlfriend is arguing with her own mother about Paul Grayson's funeral arrangements, and she expects you to walk right into the middle of it? What's wrong with this picture?"

"You don't understand," Ali said. "You haven't met Monique Ragsdale. I have."

"I do understand," Dave said. "All too well. Stay out of it, Ali. Run, do not walk, in the opposite direction."

Ali looked at Dave. He was a nice enough man, but he had no idea what it was like to be pregnant with someone's baby and to have that person snatched out of your life. No matter who April Gaddis was or whose baby she was carrying, at this point it was impossible for Ali to feel anything but compassion for her.

"April asked for my help. I'm going to give it to her," Ali said.

"Well then," Edie declared. "If you're going, so are we."

"All right," Dave said glumly. "But when it all goes to hell, just remember—I told you so."

Ali called down to the desk for her car. "This is Ali Reynolds," she added after relaying her valet parking ticket number to the bell captain. "Are there still reporters down there looking for me?"

"Yes," he replied. "I'm afraid there are."

"Is there a chance you could smuggle me out of the building without my being seen?"

"Sure. I could come up and get you in the service elevator and take you out the back way, through the kitchen."

"Would you?"

"Of course."

Dave shook his head the whole way down in the service elevator and raised a disapproving eyebrow at the size of the tip Ali handed over to the bellman, but the ploy worked. Ali was relieved that in the paparazzi bidding wars, her tip was large enough to allow them to exit the hotel without meeting up with even one of the waiting reporters.

With Edie in the backseat of the Cayenne, Ali drove back up the hill to Robert Lane. The broken front gate was still open, but filming had ended for the day. The Sumo Sudoku RVs were nowhere in evidence. The film crews had pulled up stakes and gone home, too. Leading the way to the front door, Ali was surprised to find it ajar. The DO NOT DISTURB sign had been removed. She paused long enough to ring the bell, but no one answered.

The entire entryway was awash in banks of floral bouquets, even more than had been there earlier.

"Hello?" Ali called. "April? Anybody home?"

There was no answer.

With Dave and Edie trailing behind, Ali ventured farther into the house. They found Monique Ragsdale lying sprawled at the bottom of the stairway. While Dave bent over the stricken woman and checked for a pulse, Ali dialed 911.

"Is she still breathing?" Ali demanded.

"Barely."

"Nine-one-one," the operator responded. "What are you reporting?"

"Someone's fallen," Ali found herself yelling into the phone. "She's fallen down a flight of stairs."

"Is she conscious?" the operator asked.

"No! She's barely breathing. Send someone. Hurry."

"Units are on the way," the operator said. "They'll be there soon."

Not soon enough, Ali thought. *Not nearly soon enough.*

"And your name is?"

"Ali," she answered. "Alison Reynolds."

"You just stay on the line with me, Ms. Reynolds. Help is on the way."

{ CHAPTER 8 }

Ali remained on the phone with the emergency operators while Dave stayed with Monique. Edie was dispatched to the upstairs bedrooms for a blanket to cover the injured woman. While she was at it, she searched through the rest of the house to see if anyone else was home.

"No one's here," she reported. "No one at all."

"Not even the cook?" Ali asked. "Did you check the kitchen?"

"I looked everywhere," Edie replied. "The whole house is empty."

The EMTs arrived within minutes. As they worked to shift Monique onto a board in order to load her onto a gurney, Ali spotted a cell phone and a key ring lying on the floor. She grabbed the phone, opened it, and hit the "redial" button. The words "April Cell" appeared on the screen.

"Where will you take her?" Ali asked one of the EMTs.

"The ER at Cedars-Sinai," he said.

Ali pressed the "talk" button and was disappointed

when, instead of being answered, her call to April went straight to voice mail.

"April," Ali said urgently. "It's Ali Reynolds. Call me back as soon as you get this message. Your mother has fallen down the stairs. The EMTs are taking her to Cedars-Sinai. You may want to meet us there."

When she finished the call, Ali slipped the phone into her pocket.

"You shouldn't have touched that," Dave observed.

"Why not?" Ali asked. "I needed to get hold of April to let her know what's happened."

"If this turns out to be a crime scene, you've contaminated some of the evidence."

"A crime scene?" Ali repeated. "What crime scene? She fell."

"After she and her daughter quarreled," Dave pointed out. "You should put it back."

Ali looked around at the field of debris being left behind by the EMTs. The crime scene was contaminated, all right, and not just by her.

"I'm not putting it back," Ali insisted. "I told April to call me back on this number when she gets the message."

Dave shot her an exasperated look and then went to greet the pair of uniformed police officers who had arrived on the scene as the gurney was being wheeled out the front door.

Ali was still holding her car keys. She thrust them into her mother's hands. "I'm going to the hospital," Ali said. "Once Dave finishes with the cops, the two of you can come to the hospital in my car."

"But how do we get there?" Edie wanted to know.

"Don't worry," she said. "Use the GPS. You should

be able to key Cedars-Sinai into it, and it'll lead you straight there."

"But—"

"No buts, Mom," Ali returned. "I'm going."

By the time she got outside, the doors on the ambulance had already slammed shut. Knowing she wouldn't be allowed to ride in that anyway, Ali went looking for an alternative. By then a fire department supervisor had arrived on the scene. After some persuading, Ali managed to convince the driver to take her along to the hospital.

"You're a relative?" he asked.

Mentally Ali thought through her actual connection to Monique Ragsdale: *the mother of my murdered husband's pregnant girlfriend.*

That would sound more than slightly suspect. "Yes," Ali said. And let it go at that.

By the time Ali arrived at the entrance to the ER, Monique had already been wheeled inside and out of sight. Ali started toward the registration desk and then stopped. There was no point in even talking to those people. She knew nothing—no social security numbers, no insurance information. Saying she was a relative might have been enough to bum a ride to the hospital, but it wasn't going to wash with some sharp-eyed receptionist whose main purpose in life was to ascertain who would be responsible for authorizing lifesaving treatment and/or paying the bill.

Walking to one of the few unoccupied chairs in the room, Ali took Monique's phone out of her pocket and once again hit "redial." Still April didn't answer.

Where the hell are you? Ali wondered in frustration. *Why don't you answer?*

Gradually, the sights, sounds, and, even more, the

smells of the waiting room assailed her. She had been pregnant the whole time Dean was sick. While he struggled with cancer, she had struggled with morning sickness, sitting in ER and hospital waiting rooms and clutching her own barf bucket. Being there brought all the memories back with awful clarity.

Around the room people sat huddled in their own private miseries. An older woman, in a wheelchair and on oxygen, sat with her eyes closed while the old man next to her periodically patted her hand. A few feet away from Ali, a feverish-looking toddler wailed inconsolably while his young mother, speaking in Spanish, tried in vain to comfort him. Then, with no warning, the anguished wail suddenly devolved into a spasm of projectile vomiting.

Ali knew that active puking or bleeding was the key to getting ER attention, and this was no exception. A nurse appeared from behind a curtained doorway, collected the sick baby and his mother, and then disappeared again. In less than a minute, a janitor, wearing gloves and a face mask, was there to clean up the mess. Meantime, a hugely pregnant young woman, also Hispanic, walked into the lobby on her own. At the receptionist desk, though, she was hit by a contraction that brought her to her knees. Someone grabbed a nearby wheelchair and whisked her away as well.

Living and dying, Ali thought. *Coming and going. That's what hospitals are all about.*

She tried April's number again, with the same result, then Ali closed her eyes and tried to shut all this out; tried to make it go away. But it didn't work. She was back in Chicago, lost in that awful time more than twenty years ago. Back in her own peculiar version of hell.

"Ms. Reynolds." A voice from far away pierced her reverie. "Ms. Alison Reynolds. Would you please come to the registration desk?"

As Ali rose to answer the summons, a phone rang. It wasn't her ring and so at first she didn't realize it was for her. Then Monique's phone began to vibrate as well as ring.

"Mom?" April asked.

"It's not your mother," Ali interjected. "It's me. Ali. Where are you? Did you get my messages?"

"I went for a drive. I had to get away for a while. The walls were closing in on me. I couldn't stand to be in the house a minute longer. But what are you doing on my mother's phone? I saw that she had called three times. I didn't bother listening to the messages. There's no point. She's always bossing me around and saying the same thing, over and over."

"The messages weren't from your mother," Ali said firmly. "They're from me, April, all of them. Your mother's been hurt. She's in the ER at Cedars-Sinai. You need to get here as soon as you can. Where are you?"

"Hurt? What do you mean, hurt?"

"She fell down the stairs at the house. She must have hit her head, either on the way down or on the tile floor at the bottom of the staircase."

There was a pause—a long pause. "Is it like, you know, bad?" April asked.

"I don't know how bad it is," Ali returned. "Since I'm not a blood relative, the people here at the hospital won't tell me anything."

By now Ali had reached the registration desk, where a woman seated in front of a computer terminal glared at Ali impatiently, waiting for her to finish the call.

"You brought Ms. Ragsdale in?" the receptionist asked. "We're going to need some information."

Ali thrust Monique's cell phone in the woman's direction. "There's no point in talking to me because I don't know anything. This is April Gaddis, Monique Ragsdale's daughter," she added. "You should probably talk to her."

The receptionist took the cell phone and handed it over to the same nurse who had come to collect the puking toddler. About that time two uniformed LAPD officers—a man and a woman—made their way into the ER. Ali recognized them at once. They were the same officers Ali had passed as she sprinted out of the house on Robert Lane intent on hitching a ride to the hospital. Unfortunately, three other people followed the two cops. Two of them carried cameras—one still and one video. The reporters were still on the hunt, and this trio had just gotten lucky.

The officers spotted Ali standing near the reception desk and hurried toward her. "Ms. Reynolds?" the female officer asked. "Could we speak to you for a moment, please?"

The flurry of activity that marked the arrival of the cops and the cameras caused every head in the waiting room to swivel curiously in Ali's direction. The room went totally silent as everyone strained to hear her answer.

"Yes, of course," she said. "How can I help?"

"I'm Officer Oliveras. We understand you're the person who found Ms. Ragsdale at the bottom of the stairs?" she asked.

"Yes," Ali answered. "That's correct."

"Can you tell us how you came to be there?" That question came from Officer Oliveras's partner, one Dale Ramsey.

"Monique's . . . that is, Ms. Ragsdale's daughter, April Gaddis, sent a message to me and asked me to come there—to the house. April said she needed my help."

"With what?" Ramsey asked.

"With making funeral arrangements," Ali began, then she paused and looked around the room. All ears seemed to be cocked in her direction. "It's all rather complicated," she added.

Officer Oliveras didn't smile. "Maybe you'd rather speak to us in a somewhat more private setting," she offered. "Our squad car is right outside."

The idea of being closeted in a vehicle with two more inquisitive cops didn't sound all that appealing, especially if there were photographers here ready to capture each and every vivid detail on film.

"No," Ali said quickly. "This is fine. I was sitting over there in the corner. Maybe we could do this there."

She led the cops into an area where the distinct odor of puke, barely covered by some astringent cleaning solution, still lingered in the air. Officer Oliveras followed Ali while Officer Ramsey rounded on the reporters.

"All right, you bozos," he said. "Enough! Get the hell out of here. Can't you see there are sick people here? You're botherin' 'em."

"So," Officer Oliveras said to Ali. "We're given to understand that the house where this happened, the house on Robert Lane, actually belongs to you?"

"Supposedly," Ali said. "But all that's pretty much

in a state of confusion right now. You see, my husband died the night before last. Because our divorce hadn't been finalized and because his will hadn't been changed, the house evidently comes to me."

"And Ms. Ragsdale is the mother of your ex-husband's intended bride."

"Yes," Ali said. "That's correct."

"And you know her?"

"We've met," Ali admitted. "Only this morning. We were at a meeting together there at the house—a meeting with our several attorneys."

"Where you discussed this will situation—where your husband left everything to you and nothing to Ms. Ragsdale's daughter, the mother of your husband's baby?"

"Yes," Ali said, although her answer was barely audible. It was difficult to speak when what she was hearing loud and clear in her head were Victor Angeleri's words: "What part of 'whatever you say' don't you understand?"

"Should I have an attorney with me when I'm answering these questions?" Ali asked.

Officer Oliveras's face darkened. "It's up to you," she said. "If you feel you need one, that's fine, but at this point, all we're trying to do is get a handle on who all was there at the house this morning and why."

"We gathered there for a reading of my husband's will," Ali answered after a pause. "I was there along with April Gaddis, my husband's fiancée; Ms. Ragsdale; and then four attorneys. No, wait. There were five attorneys actually, counting Ms. Ragsdale's."

Ali reeled off each of the several attorneys' names while Officer Oliveras took notes.

"You say this last one, Mr. Anderson, is Ms. Ragsdale's attorney?" Oliveras asked. "Why would she need one? Is she a beneficiary under the will?"

It didn't seem wise to mention the possibility of a postmortem divorce. That wasn't necessarily lying. "No," Ali said finally. "Mr. Anderson was there ostensibly to protect the rights of the unborn baby. My understanding is, however, that regardless of whether or not the baby is named in the will, she'll still benefit from it."

"The baby?" Oliveras asked.

Ali nodded.

"You already know the baby's a girl then?"

"Yes."

Officer Ramsey sighed and shook his head impatiently, as though all the marital back-and-forthing was boring him to tears.

"If you and Ms. Ragsdale met just this morning, it's fair to assume you didn't have any particular bone of contention with her?"

"No. None at all."

"Was anyone else there?"

Ali did her best to recall everyone else—the cook; Jesus, the gardener; Tracy McLaughlin and the Sumo Sudoku people along with the accompanying film crew. Of those the only name she knew for sure was that of the interviewer, Sandy Quijada.

"All right now," Oliveras said. "Tell me again why was it you went back to the house this afternoon."

"April called and invited me over. Or rather, she called Ted Grantham's office and left a message asking me to come over and help her work on making funeral arrangements."

"For your ex-husband?"

"Yes."

"You must have a pretty cordial relationship with your husband's fiancée," Oliveras observed. "It seems to me she would have asked someone else for help with that kind of thing—her mother, for example."

This was exactly what Dave had said when he had warned Ali to stay away. And, as he had predicted, things were indeed going to hell.

At that moment April herself came charging through the ER's automatic doors. Her eyes were wide, her skin deathly pale. Panting, she raced up to the receptionist, who, after only a few murmured words of conversation, immediately summoned the nurse who was still holding Monique's cell phone. With no more formalities than that, April was handed the phone and then ushered through the curtains and back into the treatment rooms.

Across the crowded waiting room another baby started to cry. An ambulance arrived, sirens blaring, and discharged a new gurney adding a new set of stricken relatives into the mix. But Ali paid almost no attention to any of that. She knew without having to be told that Monique Ragsdale's condition had to be grave at best. The only thing that rushed anyone past loyal ER gate-keepers was the reality that someone in one of the back rooms was hanging by a thread between life and death.

"I guess," Ali said vaguely. "She was probably just feeling overwhelmed. That was April, by the way—the woman they just took back into the treatment rooms."

Officer Oliveras exhibited no interest in April, however. She was still focused on Ali, until there was yet another flurry of activity near the front door. To Ali's immense relief, Victor Angeleri barged into the room and stopped just inside the door. With a graceful pivot that belied his size, he took in the entire room at a glance and then strode toward the corner where Ali was huddled with the two cops.

"What's going on here?" Victor Angeleri demanded.

Once again the accidental audience in the ER subsided into a spellbound silence.

"How did you get here?" Ali wanted to know. "Who called you?"

"That's immaterial. The point is, what's going on with these officers? What kinds of questions are they asking you, and did they read you your rights?"

"You're Ms. Reynolds's attorney, I assume?" Officer Ramsey inquired. The two men were about the same height, but Victor outweighed the younger man by a good third.

"Yes, I'm her attorney," Victor declared forcefully. "And until I have a chance to confer with my client, this discussion is over."

Somewhere a flash went off. Ali had no doubt that every word of the conversation was being recorded for posterity—or, more likely, for the evening news.

Edie Larson and Dave Holman rushed through the ER doors and joined the mix. "Sorry it took us so long to get here," Edie said. "I just couldn't figure out how to make the GSP thingy work."

But seeing her mother's face answered at least one of Ali's questions. No doubt Edie Larson had been the one who called Victor Angeleri into the fray. Some other time, Ali might have reacted badly to this kind of parental interference. This time she was simply grateful.

April staggered through the curtains and reentered

the waiting room. She seemed dazed and uncomprehending. Excusing herself, Ali hurried over to her. "Are you all right?"

"They're taking her to surgery," April managed. "The doctor said she hit her head. Her brain's swelling. If they can't relieve the pressure, she may die."

With that, April buried her head in Ali's shoulder and began to weep. "How can this be happening on top of everything else?" she sobbed. "I can't believe it!"

"This would be Ms. Gaddis then?" Officer Ramsey asked, sidling over to them.

Ali simply looked at him. "Yes," she said, "but as you can see, this is not the time to speak to her. What do you want to do, April? Go to the surgical floor waiting room? Go home? What?"

"The surgery will take hours," April managed. "I think I need to go home."

"You can't go home," Officer Ramsey interjected. "It's a crime scene."

"Crime scene?" April repeated. "My home is a crime scene? What are you talking about?"

"One of our forensics teams is going over it right now. We think it's possible that what happened to your mother is actually a case of attempted homicide."

"But they told me she fell," April objected.

"She may have been pushed. Until we complete our investigation, that house is off-limits and no one goes there."

"What am I going to do then?" April wailed. "Where do I go?"

"Call your hotel, Ali," Victor ordered, taking charge. "See if they have a room available where she can stay." Then he rounded on Officer Ramsey. "As far as asking questions of Ms. Gaddis? Right now that's off the table. She's in no condition to be interviewed by anyone. She's pregnant, her fiancé has been murdered, and her mother is undergoing emergency surgery. If you ask her even one question, buddy-boy, I'll have you and your partner up on charges of police brutality so fast it'll make your head swim."

Officer Ramsey seemed ready to object, but Oliveras silenced him with a single but definitive shake of her head. "All right," she said. "We can talk to her later. Just call and let us know where she ends up."

The cops disappeared shortly thereafter. Their departure removed a lot of the drama from the room. With their attention lagging, the other occupants turned to their own, more pressing physical ailments and bodily concerns.

Ali and company made the return trip to their hotel room in much the same way they had exited hours before—through the back door and, with the help of the bell captain, up the service elevator. An hour later April was wrapped in a thick terry-cloth robe and tucked into a bed in the darkened bedroom of a two-room suite—the only room available on that floor—just down the hall from the one Ali was sharing with her mother. Once April was settled in, Ali went out into the living room, closing the bedroom door behind her.

"Is she asleep?" Victor asked.

"Resting," Ali said. "Not asleep. She asked the hospital to call my cell once her mother's in the recovery room. Then we'll take April back to the hospital."

Victor Angeleri was seated at the desk in the corner, staring morosely at the telephone. He nodded absently.

"You were talking to someone on the phone?" Ali asked.

He nodded again.

"Did you find out why those cops are so interested in talking to me?"

"Unfortunately, yes. Somebody's leaked the contents of Grayson's will to the press," Victor replied. "That means that now the whole world knows that despite your marital difficulties, you're still your husband's primary beneficiary. As far as John Q. Public is concerned, that makes you a prime suspect in Paul Grayson's murder. And the cops are going to be operating on that same wavelength. I expect we'll be hearing from Detectives Sims and Taylor again real soon."

"How can information about the will be out in public?" Ali demanded. "The will hasn't been filed in court, so it isn't a matter of public record. Who would have leaked it?"

"Good question. Presumably one of my erstwhile colleagues from this morning's meeting. I think I can make a fairly educated guess as to which one."

"But isn't that illegal?" Ali objected. "Doesn't it violate attorney-client privilege?"

"Of course it does," Victor returned. "And once I figure out who's responsible, you can bet I'll have his *cojones*, but for right now we have to live with the consequences of those revelations and with the fact that you're now a suspect in two incidents rather than just the one."

"Two?" Ali asked.

"One homicide and one attempted homicide."

"So now I'm supposedly responsible for what happened to Monique Ragsdale, too? How come? I barely know the woman."

"By showing up this morning armed with that cock-amamie postmortem divorce attorney, Monique Rags-dale as good as declared war on you. That's certainly how it's going to look—as though the two of you were in some kind of a turf dispute. I can see exactly how it'll play out in court, a David and Goliath routine. Monique will be portrayed as a sympathetic character, selflessly trying to protect the welfare of her daughter and her unborn grandchild. You'll be depicted as the greedy ex-wife defending her territory and her pock-etbook by taking the bothersome grandma out of the picture."

"But Monique fell down the stairs," Ali objected. "That's not my fault."

"What if she was pushed?" Victor returned. "I know how cops think. You're already on their radar as a sus-pect in Paul's death. They're going to operate on the premise that if you're good for one homicide, you're good for another."

"But I have an ironclad alibi," Ali objected. "I left the house at the same time you did. You and Helga brought me back here to the hotel. I was here in my room all afternoon, first with my mother and later with Dave Hol-man. How could I possibly be responsible?"

Victor shrugged. "The cops have already decided that at least two people were involved in what hap-pened to your husband. If you had an accomplice in that case, you'd be likely to have an accomplice for this one as well."

"But I didn't *do* it," Ali insisted. "Mom, Dave, and I went to the house together. That's when we found her."

"Do you know how many people who 'discover' bod-ies end up being the doers?" Victor asked. "And tell me this. If you went to the house and no one was home, how did you get inside?"

"Through the front door. I rang the bell, but no one answered. Then, since the door was open, we went in."

"Didn't that strike you as unusual, that the door would be left open like that?"

"I didn't think about it at the time because I thought April was home. With the big crew involved in the shoot, there had been people coming and going all day long."

"Do you still have keys to the house?"

"Probably," Ali answered. "Back home in Sedona somewhere, but I certainly didn't bring them along, and I doubt they'd work anyway. I expect Paul would have changed the locks as soon as I moved out. I'm sure I would have."

"All right," Victor said. "Now tell me about the telephone."

"What telephone?" Ali asked.

"Come on. Don't play dumb. Monique's cell phone—the one you lifted from the crime scene. That's called evidence tampering. When the cops find out about it—if they find out about it—they're going to go nuts."

"The EMTs were busy hauling Monique off to the hospital when I noticed the phone was lying there on the floor," Ali explained. "By then I knew April wasn't home. I needed to reach her so I could let her know what was happening. I was sure her cell phone number would be in her mother's call records, and it was. How else was I supposed to find her number?"

"You could have called Ted Grantham back," Victor pointed out. "But you didn't. For right now the cops haven't noticed the phone issue. If they end up figuring out you took it, then we'll have to decide how to handle it. Now, what's the deal with Dave Holman?"

"What about him?"

"Are you an item or what?"

"Dave's good friends with my parents, and he's a friend of mine, too—a homicide detective for Yavapai County over in Arizona. But we aren't an 'item.'"

"What's he doing here then?"

"He drove over from Lake Havasu to help out."

"He should go home," Victor said simply. "So should your mother. I have my own team of investigators working on this case. What I don't need is a bunch of people—amateurs or otherwise—blundering around and muddying the waters. Having your mother and Dave here is going to be more of a hindrance than a help. Anything you say to them is going to be fair game for whatever detectives are doing follow-up on either one of these two cases. They'll ask Dave or your mother what you've said, and they'll end up being required to answer truthfully. So you can't confide in them—not at all. Understand?"

"It's too late," Ali said bleakly. "I already did."

And for the first time in all this, she actually felt afraid.

{ CHAPTER 9 }

Victor finally left. For a long time afterward, Ali sat alone in the living room area of April's suite mulling over her situation. What if Monique Ragsdale didn't survive? Would Ali really be a suspect in her death as well? Could the cops turn Monique's mere threat of litigation into a motive for murder?

From what Ali had seen, Monique's fall had looked like an accident, but was it really? And speaking of accidents, what about the Sumo Sudoku boulder that had come flying in Ali's own direction? That, too, had appeared to be nothing more than an accident caused by an overloaded wheelbarrow, but what if it wasn't?

Pushing away that worrisome thought, Ali decided to track down how much of the story had surfaced in the media. Rather than switching on the television and possibly waking April, Ali did as she had so often done in the months since she had fled L.A., her former job, and her foundering marriage—she turned to her computer and to her blog and to the cyber support network from cutlooseblog.com that had sustained her through some pretty dark times.

> *Dear Ali, or I suppose I should say, Dear Babe,*
> *When they booted you off the air months ago, I*
> *always knew you'd be back on TV here in L.A.*
> *eventually. I just didn't think it would be like this.*
>   *I saw what they showed on the news the other*
> *night when you were leaving the coroner's office*
> *in Indio. That young woman they replaced you*
> *with was so damned smug as she was reading the*
> *story. I wanted to slap her. She didn't come right*
> *out and mention you by name and say you were*
> *a suspect in whatever had happened to your ex,*
> *but people recognized you. I recognized you, even*
> *though you weren't wearing makeup or anything.*
> *And that big guy, Victor, was there with you.*
> *Anybody who follows criminal cases in Southern*
> *California knows what he's all about. Why would*
> *you need a big-time defense attorney if you weren't*
> *a defendant?*
>   *All I'm trying to say is there are lots of us*
> *out here who are still real fans of yours and who*
> *think you're being sold down the river. Again.*
> *So be strong. Know that people—people you*
> *don't even know—are praying for you every day.*
> *I'm one of them.*
>
> CRYSTAL RYAN,
> SHERMAN OAKS, CA

She didn't post Crystal's note, but wanting to say something in reply—something that wouldn't get her in trouble with Victor Angeleri—Ali penned a simple response that said nothing yet covered all the bases.

Dear Crystal,
Thank you for your support.

ALI REYNOLDS

Dear Babe,
Have you called my nephew yet? From what
they're saying on the news, I think you'd better.
It sounds like things are getting more compli-
cated all the time.

VELMA T IN LAGUNA

Yes, Ali thought. *Things are getting more complicated.*
No, I haven't called your nephew, and I probably won't.

She sent Velma the same note she had sent to Crystal. That was Ali's best bet for the moment—respond but do not engage. Keep a low profile.

Dear Ms. Reynolds,
After what happened to you, I can't believe you'd do
the same thing to my uncle. You should be ashamed.

ANDREA MORALES

Ali studied that one for a very long time. She had no idea who Andrea Morales was, much less who the woman's uncle might be or what Ali could possibly have done to him. In the end, she felt she had to defend herself by sending a response.

Dear Andrea,
I'm sorry, but I'm unaware of who your uncle is
or what it is you believe I may have done to him.
If it's something for which I should offer an apol-
ogy, please let me know. I would appreciate it if
you could supply some additional information
which would allow me to be more knowledge-
able about this situation.
Thank you.

ALISON REYNOLDS

The next one was even more disturbing.

Hmmmm. Let me get this straight. Your soon-to-
be-ex-husband died unexpectedly without having
a chance to unload you by slipping loose from
that little gold tie that binds? Too bad somebody
didn't warn the poor guy about black widows.
I think he was married to one. RIP, Fang. You
deserved better. As for you, "Babe"? I hope you
get what you deserve.

LANCE-A-LOT

Black widow, Ali thought. *Thanks-a-lot. Let's hope*
this one doesn't hit the blogosphere. If it does, it'll go like
wildfire.

She didn't reply to that one.

Ali's cell phone rang just then. She hurried to answer it, thinking it would be the hospital. It wasn't.

"Aunt Ali?"

She recognized the voice of ten-year-old Matt Bernard. Months earlier, Matt's mother, Ali's childhood friend Reenie Bernard, had been murdered. In the messy aftermath of Reenie's death, her husband, a professor at Northern Arizona University, had taken off on sabbatical with a new wife in tow and had left his two children, Matt and his younger sister, Julie, in the care of their maternal grandparents in Cottonwood. Ali had stayed in touch with Reenie's two kids as much as possible. Thanks to their grandfather's pet allergies, Ali was also looking after their cat, the plug-ugly, one-eared, sixteen-pound wonder, Samantha.

"Hi, Matt."

"How's Sam?"

"Sam's fine," Ali said. She didn't know that with absolute certainty, but she felt confident in saying so.

"Grandpa and Grandma are driving to Sedona tomorrow afternoon after church," Matt went on. "I was wondering if Julie and I could come by your house for a while to visit and play with Sam."

That was the weird thing about cell phones. Callers dial numbers with a complete mental image of where the other person is and what he or she is doing. No doubt Matt was envisioning Ali in her spacious mobile home in Sedona, curled up on her living room sofa with Sam right there beside her. Instead, Ali was several hundred miles away, sitting in a hotel room, and embroiled in a set of circumstances that might well keep her from returning to Sedona for some time. Ali didn't want to go into any of those messy details with Matthew Bernard right then. Or ever.

"Oh, Matt," she said. "I'm so sorry. I've been called out of town. I won't be there tomorrow."

"Who's taking care of Sam then?" he asked.

"My dad," Ali said. "He loves cats, and they love him. If you're coming up in the afternoon, after the Sugar Loaf is closed for the day, maybe you could visit with Sam at my parents' house."

Matt sounded dubious. "Wouldn't your father mind?"

Ali thought about Bob Larson, a man who adored animals and little kids. "As long as it's after hours, I'm sure he'd be thrilled to have you, but why don't you call him and ask?"

"I think that would be weird." Suddenly Matt seemed stricken with an uncharacteristic case of shyness. "I mean, I don't really know him."

"By the time you and Julie spend Sunday afternoon with him, you will know him," Ali countered. "He may be my father, but he's also a really nice guy."

The call waiting signal beeped in Ali's ear. She glanced at the readout—Chris's cell phone. As soon as she saw the number, she felt guilty. She hadn't called her son—deliberately hadn't called him—when things started going bad. She had considered the mess to be her problem. With Chris starting a new job and a new life, she hadn't wanted to embroil him in her difficulties. But then, she hadn't much wanted Edie Larson and Dave Holman to be dragged into the situation, either.

Ali ended the call with Matt as soon as possible, but by then, Chris had left an irate voice mail message: "Mom. What the hell is going on out there? Call me."

"I knew you were busy," she said, once she had Chris on the phone. "I didn't want you to worry. How much have you heard?"

"I just got off the phone with Gramps, who had talked to Grandma. I know Paul is dead. I know April's mother fell down a flight of stairs and could very well die, and that the cops think you're a suspect in both cases."

"That just about covers it then," Ali said as lightly as she could manage. "Sounds like you're completely up to date."

"Mother!" Chris exclaimed accusingly.

Chris hardly ever called her "Mother." It usually meant that the two of them were on the outs. And the reverse was true when Ali called him Christopher. This time she was the one who had crossed their invisible line.

"Tell me now," Chris ordered. "I want to hear it from you."

And so Ali did—she told him everything.

"I'm guessing April's mom is the one who came up with the idea of pushing for a postmortem divorce," Chris said when she finished.

"Either she did or her lawyer did," Ali said. "I'm not sure which."

"If anybody would know the ins and outs of divorce, Monique Ragsdale would probably be it," Chris said.

"What do you mean?"

"Monique's had several," Chris replied. "Divorces, that is. Scott Dumphey, one of the guys I used to play basketball with in college, is good friends with Jason Ragsdale, April's stepbrother. That's how I found out about Paul and April in the first place—through Scott."

The comment made it clear to Ali that there was a whole lot she didn't know about April Gaddis's family situation.

"April has a stepbrother?" Ali asked.

"'Had' is the operative word," Chris corrected. "Jason is a former stepbrother. From what I remember of the story, Jason's dad was a widower, an optometrist with a fairly decent nest egg, when April's mother arrived on the scene with April in tow. When Monique dumped the poor guy a couple of years later, his nest egg was a whole lot smaller."

Ali had no way of knowing if any of this information would prove useful or not. Nonetheless, she used a piece of hotel notepaper to jot down all the relevant names.

"What about April's dad?" Ali asked.

"What about him?" Chris returned. "I'm assuming he was several husbands ago."

That little tidbit of information made April's way of dealing with the world much more understandable. She had been raised by an often-married gold digger of a mother. That kind of background made it entirely reasonable for her to grow up thinking someone else's husband—anyone else's husband—was fair game. If that was how Monique had gotten ahead in the world, why wouldn't her daughter try doing the same thing? In that context, April's involvement with Paul Grayson must have seemed like business as usual.

"Anything else you can tell me about April?"

"Dropped out of college after only a semester or two," Chris replied. "According to Scott, she's not all that bright. At least he didn't think so."

Even with the door to April's room pulled shut, Ali wasn't prepared to comment on that either way.

"What's going to happen now?" Chris asked. "And should I call in to work and have them get me a substitute teacher so I can drive over to help out?"

"No," Ali said. "Absolutely not. Mom's here. So's Dave Holman."

"He is? What's Dave doing there?"

"Grandma called him and he came."

"She called him, but she didn't call me."

Chris sounded understandably hurt.

"I'm sure she was thinking the same thing I was—that we didn't want to bother you or take you away from what you're doing."

"Thanks a lot," Chris said. "To both of you. Like mother like daughter, I guess, but I'm a grown-up now. I get to choose, remember?"

Ali would have said more, but call waiting buzzed again. The readout said Cedars-Sinai Medical Center. At the same time, her phone was telling her she was running out of battery power.

"Sorry, Chris," Ali told her son. "There's another call. I have to take it." She switched over.

"April Gaddis?" a male voice asked.

"No. April's in the other room, lying down."

"This is the contact number we were given, and it's about her mother. Can you put her on the line, please?"

The caller's voice sounded so distant, so impersonal, that Ali knew without hearing another word that the guy wasn't calling with good news.

"Just a moment," Ali said quickly. "She's resting, but I'll get her for you."

With the low-battery alarm still sounding, Ali hurried into April's darkened room. The young woman lay on her side, snoring softly. Ali shook her awake. "April," she said. "There's a call for you."

April took the phone. "Yes," she said. "What is it? Is my mother all right?

But of course Monique Ragsdale was anything but

all right. She had died on the operating table, most likely as a result of the brain injury. With a slight whimper, April dropped the phone. As soon as it fell, Ali Reynolds knew she was now a suspect in two separate homicides.

Sobbing, April buried her face in the pillow. "Mom's gone," she wailed. "So's Paul. I'm all alone now. What's going to happen to me? What's going to happen to the baby?"

Ali reached down and patted April's shoulder. "I'm so sorry," she said. "But you'll be all right. We'll figure it out."

Then Ali picked up the phone, took it into the other room, plugged it into the charger, and called Victor Angeleri at home. "You need to know what's happened."

In the end, Ali stayed behind at the hotel for yet another meeting with Victor. Her mother and Dave were the ones who volunteered to take April back to the hospital to handle whatever paperwork needed signing. After several phone calls, Victor managed to locate Detectives Tim Hubbard and Rosalie Martin, the two L.A. homicide cops who were now in charge of the Monique Ragsdale investigation.

"Look," Victor said once he had Detective Hubbard on the phone. "I don't like the circus atmosphere any more than you do, and it's going to get a lot worse before it gets better. My client is willing to cooperate and give you a voluntary statement, but it needs to be done on our terms. I'd rather do it here at the hotel, where we have some control over the media. How about if you come to us?"

In the end, that's what happened—the detectives agreed to come there. For the next two hours, and with a tape recorder running, they went over the whole story again, in great detail. They wanted to know who was at the morning meeting at the house on Robert Lane. Both detectives seemed intrigued by the pre-funeral reading of Paul Grayson's will, and they seemed especially interested in the fact that Paul Grayson's murder had left Ali holding a bagful of monetary goodies.

"What was Ms. Gaddis's reaction to that?" Rosalie Martin wanted to know.

Ali shrugged. "What you'd expect. She was upset."

"What about her mother, Ms. Ragsdale?" Detective Hubbard asked. "Was she upset, too?"

"I'm sure she was worried about her daughter—and the baby," Ali told her.

"Which put the two of you on opposite sides of the fence."

Ali glanced in Victor's direction. He gave a slight shake of his head, and Ali said nothing more.

With the topic of the will pretty much exhausted, Hubbard moved on to other issues. The two cops seemed to have missed the Sumo Sudoku craze entirely and had to have the concept explained to them. When it came to the names of the players and the film crew, however, Ali wasn't able to offer much detail.

"What about workmen?" Detective Hubbard asked.

"Jesus Sanchez is the gardener," Ali said.

"What can you tell us about him?"

Ali shrugged. "Not much. He more or less came with the house. He was working there long before Paul and I bought the place. Most of the time he works alone, but today he had a crew working with him. I didn't know any of them."

Was this the time Ali should mention her near-encounter with the falling boulder, or would the cops see that as nothing more than a lame attempt on her part to deflect their suspicions away from her? She decided to let it go.

"What about the cook?" Detective Hubbard asked.

"I met her, but she's new. I don't know her name."

"What about address information or contact numbers for the two of them?"

"Jesus and the cook? I'm sure Paul had the information, probably in his office somewhere, but I don't. We were getting a divorce, remember?"

"We'll see what we can find," Hubbard said. "Now about the house. Does it have a security system?"

"Of course," Ali told him.

"But it wasn't alarming when you got there this afternoon and found Ms. Ragsdale at the bottom of the stairs?"

"No. The front door was half open but the alarm wasn't sounding. I assumed someone must have switched it off."

"Why would that be?"

"Maybe with so many people coming and going throughout the day, it was easier to turn it off."

"Isn't that unusual?"

"It would have been for me," Ali said. "But I'm not sure about how April runs the house."

"Your house," Hubbard added.

Ali didn't like it that Hubbard seemed so eager to come back to the idea that the house on Robert Lane ultimately belonged to Ali.

"April Gaddis is the one who's been living there most recently," Ali returned. "Maybe she's not all that worried about security."

"Maybe not," Hubbard agreed. "And no one else was there at the house when you arrived?"

"No one. Not the cook. Not the gardener."

"What time did you get there?"

"Four or so. I don't remember exactly."

"The nine-one-one call came in at four-fifteen."

"So around four."

"The people who were with you at the time you found Ms. Ragsdale were your mother and this friend, one Dave Holman."

"Yes," Ali said. "That's correct."

"And he's a police officer?"

Ali nodded. "Dave's a homicide detective with the Yavapai County Sheriff's Department in Sedona."

"I've heard about Sedona," Hubbard said. "The crystal place. So he drove all the way over here from there?"

"From Lake Havasu, actually," Ali replied. "He's divorced. He was there visiting his kids."

"When did he arrive?"

Ali was a little puzzled by this segue into questions about Dave Holman. "Early afternoon," she answered. "In time to have lunch."

"And he was with you most of the afternoon?"

"Yes."

All this time, Detective Rosalie Martin had been sitting back and letting her partner do most of the questioning. Now she leaned forward once more.

"You mentioned that you came and went from the hotel via the service elevator?"

"Yes," Ali said.

"Why was that?"

"Because the lobby was full of reporters. I wanted to avoid them if at all possible."

"Couldn't it also be because you didn't want to be observed, period?" Rosalie asked. "Not just by the reporters but by anyone?"

Her not-too-subtle implication was clear and Victor balked. "This interview is over," he announced. "My client has been more than cooperative. She's answered all your questions. If you want to know whether or not she left the hotel in the course of the afternoon, I suggest you avail yourselves of the hotel's security tapes. I'm sure those cover the service elevator as well as the public ones."

The cops left shortly thereafter. Victor turned to Ali. "Has anyone ever told you you're a hell of a lot of trouble?"

"Yes," she answered. "I'm pretty sure several people have mentioned it."

"By the way," Victor said. "My assistant did a Lexis-Nexis search on you. We need to talk about the man you shot last March."

Having already been questioned by the cops for more than an hour, Ali was surprised when Victor began grilling her as well.

"What about him? Ben Witherspoon was a vicious man who broke into my house and attacked me. I shot him, all right, but since he attacked me in my own home, the shooting was ruled self-defense, and I'd do it again in a minute."

"What about the lady who tried to force you off the highway? She's dead, too, isn't she?"

"Yes, but—"

"Do you happen to see a pattern here?" Victor asked.

"I do see a pattern," Ali said, her temper rising. "You seem to be giving me hell about all kinds of things that have nothing whatsoever to do with what's going on here. Why? Aren't you supposed to be my attorney?"

"I am your attorney. It's my job to look down the road, see what's coming in our direction, and do what I can to mitigate it. All those reporters down in the lobby—the ones who aren't getting a chance to interview you—are doing exactly the same thing I did. They're checking out every available bit of Ali Reynolds's history they can, including every archived posting on cutlooseblog.com. By the time you wake up tomorrow morning, regardless of whether or not you've been officially charged with a crime, you're going to be on trial in the media for everything you've ever said or done. They're going to turn you into this year's big story. You'll be cast as a former media elite who considers herself above the law and is probably getting away with murder."

"All I did was defend myself. Bringing up those old cases isn't fair."

"No, it's not," Victor agreed. "But that's how it's going to play out, especially if charges are brought in either one of these new cases."

"What about innocent until proven guilty?"

"Don't be naive, Ali," Victor said. "You know as well as I do, perception is everything, and the media are the ones who control that. Even if we prove you innocent in a court of law, dodging the criminal charge will only be the start of your problems. Next on the agenda will be a wrongful death suit where the burden of proof will be far less stringent. As Paul Grayson's primary heir, you'll make a very inviting target. Where's your gun, by the way?"

"My Glock? It's in the safe in Mom's and my room, but it's also legal. I have a valid license to carry."

"Valid or not, leave your gun in the safe," Victor advised.

"If you end up being questioned again, you'll be way better off if the cops don't find a weapon on your person."

Before Ali could reply, the door opened and Dave Holman ushered April into the room. She looked ghastly. "I think she needs to lie down," Dave said.

As Ali rose to relieve Dave of his charge, Victor gathered his briefcase and stood as well. "I'll be going then," he said. "Hopefully for the last time today."

Ali led April into the other room, where she flopped down onto the bed without even stripping off her clothes. "Are you all right?" Ali asked.

"I'm tired," April said. "My back hurts. I need some sleep."

Ali left her there and returned to the other room, closing the door behind her. She found Dave standing by the window. "I don't think your attorney likes me," Dave said.

"That's fair enough," Ali said, "since I'm not so sure I like him very much at the moment, either. How was it?"

"The hospital?" Dave shook his head. "Not a good scene," he replied. "I felt sorry for April. It's a lot for someone her age to handle."

Ali nodded and looked around the suite, realizing for the first time that Edie hadn't returned with Dave. "What about Mom?" she asked.

"Said she was dead on her feet," Dave replied. "Told me to tell you she was going to bed and not to worry about waking her when you come in. She said she'll take out her hearing aids and won't hear a thing."

"Why wouldn't she be tired?" Ali returned. "I'm sure she got up at the usual time this morning and drove all the way here. Now it's way past her bedtime."

"What about your bedtime?" Dave asked. "And what about dinner? Did you have anything to eat?"

"Not since lunch."

"I'll take you to dinner then."

"What about the reporters?"

Dave grinned. "Don't worry. I'm not stupid. I've learned the drill. You call the bellman, go up and down in the service elevator, and hand over the tip. How do you think I got April in and out without being seen? And then there's my secret transportation device."

"What's that?"

"I'm sure the reporters have spotters keeping an eye on your Cayenne. And I don't doubt there was a huge flap when Victor took off in that enormous Lincoln of his. But it turns out nobody pays the least bit of attention to a beat-out Nissan Sentra. It's right up there with one of Harry Potter's invisibility cloaks."

Ali was genuinely surprised. In the months since she'd stopped working, she had returned to her long-neglected habit of reading for pleasure. She had allowed herself the guilty indulgence of reading the entire Harry Potter series and had enjoyed it far more than she had expected.

"You read Harry Potter?" she asked.

Dave rolled his eyes. "I've got kids, don't I? Now, are you coming to dinner or not?"

"Where are you taking me?"

"Somewhere no one will expect to find you," he said. "Denny's. And don't give me any grief about it. After forking over a fortune in tips this afternoon, it's the best I can do."

"Are you kidding?" Ali asked. "If you're offering a Grand Slam, I'm there."

{ CHAPTER 10 }

In the months Ali had been back home in Sedona, she had become reacquainted with the small-town intimacy of the Sugar Loaf Café. Now she found herself disappearing in the bustling anonymity of a corporate-run restaurant. The colorful, multipage plastic menus were the same everywhere. So was the food. The meal Ali ordered was good, but it didn't come close to measuring up to one of Bob Larson's.

"Victor thinks you should leave," Ali told Dave over dinner. "You and Mom both. He's afraid that having you poking around will somehow 'muddy the waters.'"

"Tough," Dave Holman replied. "I don't like Victor. Victor doesn't like me. That makes us even. I have three weeks of vacation coming. I called the office this afternoon and told Sheriff Maxwell I'm taking 'em. I'm here for the duration. And if things get settled sooner than that, I'll camp out over at Lake Havasu and visit with my kids."

"How are they doing?" Ali asked.

While Dave had been off serving in Iraq with his reserve unit, Roxanne, his now-former wife, had taken up with a sleazy time-share salesman. Months earlier, when the new husband had been transferred to Lake Havasu, Roxanne had moved, taking Dave's kids with her. He had been devastated.

"Medium," Dave replied glumly. "Gary, the cretin, lost his job. Got caught in some kind of corporate hanky-panky. Roxie didn't tell me any of the gory details, and I'm probably better off not knowing. The thing is, Gary is currently unemployed, and they may end up having to move again. I'm not sure where—Vegas, maybe. The kids are sick about it. So am I."

"Have you thought about taking Roxie back to court and trying to get custody?" Ali asked.

Dave shook his head. "Are you kidding? I'm a man. I've got about as much chance of winning a custody fight as I do of winning at Powerball. And since I never buy a lotto ticket, that's not likely to happen. But let's not talk about that. Let's talk about you."

"What about me?"

"This is serious, Ali. Really serious."

"Victor has already pointed that out," Ali responded. "Several different times. And it could be serious for you, too. Earlier the LAPD cops were asking a lot of questions about you. So was Victor, for that matter."

"Screw Victor," Dave said. "But it makes sense. If the cops are looking for you to have an accomplice, then I could be a likely subject. Who better than a renegade homicide detective to figure out a way to cover up a murder?"

"So what do we do?" Ali asked.

"We fight back."

"But you can't do that, can you? You're a cop."

He smiled grimly. "You'd be surprised at what I can do. What did you tell the two homicide dicks?"

"I told them exactly what happened, that you and Mom and I were all together at the hotel this afternoon, right up until we went over to the house and found Monique at the bottom of the staircase. I got the impression that they were going to go check out the hotel's security tapes to see whether or not I was telling the truth about my comings and goings."

"Did they tell you what time Monique took her header?" Dave asked.

"No. Why?"

"Because she may have been on the floor for a long time before we found her. If she fell before I got to the hotel, we could still have a problem on that score."

"Is there any way to find out?" Ali asked.

"Officially, no," Dave replied. "Unofficially, maybe. I'm assuming they asked you who all was at the house today."

Ali nodded.

"You'd better tell me, too, then," he said. "Give me the whole list. As far as I'm concerned, it's time we started running our own parallel investigation."

"But—" Ali began.

"Victor Angeleri is looking out for you," Dave said, "but the man is being paid good money to look out for you. Nobody's paying my freight. I'm the one who has to look out for me. If you don't want to have anything to do with this, fine. I'll do it on my own."

"What do you need exactly?"

"I need you to tell me whatever you told them. In detail."

Knowing she had been leaving April's room for the

night, Ali had dragged her computer along with her when she headed out. Now, at Ali's request, Dave went out to his Nissan and retrieved her laptop. For the next hour or so, Ali told the story one more time, using her air-card network to pluck appropriate telephone numbers and addresses off the Internet. Dave's method was far more low-tech. He jotted his notes expertly on a series of paper napkins, including the part about her close encounter with the boulder.

"You're sure it was an accident?" Dave wanted to know.

"I think it was an accident," Ali told him. "It *looked* like an accident, but with everything else that's gone on . . ."

"We'd better check it out," Dave said.

When they finally finished the grueling process, Ali was a rag. "I've got to go back to the hotel," she said. "It's time."

By then it was late enough and the lobby deserted enough that Ali risked venturing in through the front door. Upstairs, walking toward her room on what was posted as a nonsmoking floor, she was surprised to find the corridor reeking of cigarette smoke. She was tempted to call back down to the lobby to complain, but then she thought better of it. The last thing April or Edie needed was someone from hotel security pounding on doors and waking everybody up.

Inside the room, Ali found that her mother hadn't bothered to close the blackout curtains. Even without turning on a light, there was plenty of illumination for Ali to find her way around the room. Her mother was sound asleep, clinging to the far side of the single king-sized bed. Ali undressed and climbed in on the other side. By the time her head hit the pillow, she was asleep. She awakened to the click of the door lock and the smell of coffee as Edie let herself back into the room. A glance at the clock told Ali it was past seven.

"Sorry to wake you," her mother apologized. "I've been up since four, and I finally couldn't stand it anymore. I had to go downstairs to get some coffee and the newspapers."

She unloaded two paper cups and a stack of newspapers onto the coffee table while Ali got up and staggered into the bathroom.

"You must have gotten home late," Edie observed over the top of a newspaper when Ali emerged.

"Dave took me to Denny's for dinner," Ali answered. "And you're right. It was late when I got home. Anything in the paper?"

"Lots," Edie replied. "Help yourself."

Ali settled onto the couch and picked up one of the other papers where Monique Ragsdale's death, under suspicious circumstances, was front-page news. Her relationship to network executive Paul Grayson, who had been murdered two days earlier, was laid out in tabloid-worthy detail. The cops were cagey. The public information officer mentioned that detectives had identified several people of interest in the case but that no arrests had been made at this time.

Edie was evidently reading something similar. "I'm assuming you're one of the 'persons of interest'?"

"Who else?" Ali responded. She said nothing more.

When the first cup of coffee was gone, she called room service and ordered breakfast for two along with more coffee—a full pot this time. Then, with Edie still preoccupied with the hard-copy newspapers, Ali booted up her computer.

Dear Babe,

My name is Adele Richardson. I used to watch you when you were on the news here in L.A. and I've been a fan of cutlooseblog.com from the time you started it. And I'm sure you know the reason. Something very similar happened to me. Not the job thing but a very similar marriage disaster. Over the months I've admired the way you've picked yourself up and gone on, reaching out to help others along the way. In fact, I think it's safe to say that you're one of my heroes. And, because of you, I've started reading other blogs as well. Who knows? Maybe you've turned me into an addict. Are there twelve-step programs for people addicted to reading blogs?

Anyway, I read your last post and I'm smart enough to read between the lines. As long as you're caught up in any kind of legal proceedings, I'm sure your attorney won't let you do any posting. But I'm also selfish enough to miss having cutloose as part of my morning routine. So I'm writing to you today with a proposition. Maybe you'll think I'm being too forward. If so, all you have to do is press the delete button.

I was a journalism major in college. Then, during my senior year, I got engaged and realized that for me, marriage and kids and a career in journalism just wasn't going to work, so I switched over to elementary education. I've

been teaching third grade in Escondido for the
past fifteen years. It turns out that marriage and
elementary education didn't work out very well,
either, but how was I to know?

So here's the nervy part. Unlike you, I'm not
famous, but I am a survivor. My husband ended
up getting caught up in online gambling. We
lost everything, including the house, our savings,
and most of my retirement account as well. I'm
divorced now. Slowly but surely I'm rebuilding
my life—just as you're rebuilding yours.

Sometimes one of the bloggers I read needs to
take a break to go on vacation or to have a baby
or even because there's some kind of health crisis. A lot of the time, they just put their blog on
hiatus for a while and then go back to writing it
when they're good and ready. Others invite guest
bloggers to sit in and take over for them in the
meantime. That way, regular readers don't get
out of the habit of checking the site every day.

And that's why I'm writing to you today—to
see if you'd like me to be your guest blogger for
the next little while—until you're able to come
back. Yes, I suppose I could just kick over the
traces and start my own blog, but I've followed
what you do on cutloose, and I'd really like to
make a contribution and help you.

I'm assuming you can see from this that I'm
not exactly illiterate. From reading your blogs, I
know we share similar opinions on many issues,
although you probably can't tell that from what
I've written here. (I do have an unfair advantage,
since, through reading your columns, I know you
far better than you know me.)

You don't have to answer right now. In fact,

you don't have to answer at all, but if you'd
like to have me do a couple of sample blog
postings for you, I'd be glad to audition. Let me
know.

ADELE RICHARDSON, AKA LEDA

Ali was touched by Adele's offer. She was also
provoked by it. Based on Victor's advice, she had
announced she was putting cutloose aside for the
time being, and Adele was responding to that in a
kind and supportive fashion. But included in that
kindness was an implicit agreement with Victor's
take on things—that Ali Reynolds needed to sit
down and shut up. This morning that didn't seem
likely.

Dear Adele/Leda,
Thank you for your kind offer. I've been
rethinking my position. In the past I've used
cutloose as a way of responding to and dealing
with events that were going on in my life at
the time. As you so correctly pointed out, the
legal ramifications occurring in my life right
now make that difficult since there are things
happening—the things that are most important
to me—that I won't be able to discuss. But I don't
think I can walk away from cutloose entirely.

From your note, I see you have an interesting
perspective about having had your life blow up
and figuring out a way to move on afterward.
And that's the whole point of cutlooseblog.com—
to support women who find themselves in those

difficult circumstances. So do send me your comments, and I'll be glad to post them, but for right now, cutloose is back in business, and I'd better go to work.

BABE

About then room service showed up. Edie let the waiter and his serving cart into the room. "Shall I see if April's ready for breakfast?" Edie asked.

Ali had ordered a fruit plate along with a basket of pastries. "I'm sure there'll be plenty," she said.

Edie bustled off down the hall. She returned a few minutes later with a puffy-eyed April in tow. Her hair was in disarray, and she was wrapped in a terry-cloth robe that once again didn't quite cover her middle. The faint odor of cigarette smoke entered the room when April did.

"Thanks for waking me," she said, helping herself to a coffee cup and a plate of pastries. "The baby was jumping around all night. I hardly got any sleep at all, but now I'm starving."

April had been starving the day before, too. Ali remembered how, while she was pregnant with Chris, she'd also been hungry all the time. "Help yourself," she said.

Settling into the room's only armchair, April set her coffee on a nearby end table and perched a loaded plate on her belly. "The cops said I won't be able to go back to the house until they're done with it," she announced, buttering a blueberry muffin. "They say it's a crime scene. I thought Mom just fell down the stairs, but they're thinking she was pushed."

Ali simply nodded.

"One of my friends, Cindy, runs a shop called Motherhood in Bloom," April continued. "I thought I'd call her later this morning to see if she can bring some stuff by here—underwear, bras, and some new maternity clothes. I've got to have something to wear. And what about colors? I don't have anything in black. Or should I wear navy? Would that be better?"

Ali and her mother exchanged glances. As far as Ali was concerned, April's preoccupation with her wardrobe seemed very cold-blooded. Edie was the one who answered. "For the services, you mean?" she asked.

April nodded. "And for interviews, too," she said. "Last night at the hospital I happened to run into someone named Sheila Rosenburg. She wants to set up an interview with me."

Happened to run into her? Ali thought. *That was no accident.* "An interview for Court TV?" she asked.

April nodded again. "You know Sheila then?"

Ali had flat-out refused Sheila Rosenburg's offer of an interview, and she hoped April would do the same, but it wasn't Ali's place to tell her so. *It's April's decision, not mine,* she reminded herself.

"I know of Sheila Rosenburg," Ali answered aloud, "but I don't know her personally. I'm concerned that she'll try to turn your mother's death and Paul's into some kind of media circus."

April seemed unconcerned. "Some people pay for interviews," April replied, reaching for another pastry. "And she said she knew of an author who might be able to get me a book contract—you know, so I can write about all this while it's going on, sort of like a diary or a journal. She said people are really interested in true crime. It might even end up being a best-seller. I wouldn't have to do the actual writing, either, since I'm not that good at it. My name would be on the cover of the book, but the publisher would hire somebody else to do that part of it, a ghostwriter, she called it."

Ali was appalled. Shocked and appalled, but her mother was the one who spoke up.

"Are you sure you want to do that?" Edie asked. "I know this is all happening to you, April, but it's also happening to your baby. It's going to be part of Sonia Marie's history, too. Do you want to bring a child into the world with that kind of notoriety?"

It's also happening to me, Ali thought, but there didn't seem to be any point in mentioning it. April was totally absorbed in her own concerns.

"Maybe not," April agreed, "but I think I'm going to need the money."

"Surely we'll be able to work something out so you won't have to lay all our lives bare for the world to see," Ali said.

"I hope so," April said. She stood up. "I'd better go make that call. Those detectives said they'd be by to see me later this morning, too. I'd like to have some clean clothes to wear before they get here."

April went out and closed the door behind her.

"Whoa!" Edie Larson said. "That girl is a lot tougher than she looks."

Ali nodded. "Maybe she's a chip off her mother's block."

"And smoking while she's pregnant?" Edie shook her head.

At that juncture Edie's cell phone rang with a call from

Bob Larson back in Sedona. While Edie brought her husband up to date, Ali's phone rang, too. It was Chris.

"Sorry I was so cranky last night," he said. "I felt like you were leaving me out of everything."

"I'm sorry, too," she said.

"So do you want me to come out there or not?"

"Not right now," she said. "I'll probably need you to come over later, but for now I think Grandma and I have things under control."

"All right then," he said. "But remember, keep me posted."

Edie was still chatting on the phone, so Ali returned to her computer.

Ms. Reynolds,
You fired my uncle yesterday without giving him even so much as a day's notice much less two weeks. And then you have the gall to say you have no idea what you could have done or whether or not you should apologize? How dare you?

ANDREA MORALES

But I didn't fire anyone, Ali thought. *What the hell is this woman raving about?*

Then, sitting staring at the words on the computer screen, Ali had a sudden flash of memory. She remembered coming home late one night to find the house alive with the smells of cooking meat and masa. Following her nose and the sound of voices and laughter to the brightly lit kitchen, Ali had found Elvira and several others, women and girls both, clustered in the kitchen busily making dozens of tamales in advance of Paul's annual

Cinco de Mayo celebration. One of the women had been Jesus Sanchez's wife, Clemencia. Had one of those girls been his niece, perhaps? Ali had a dim memory that one of them had been named Andrea, but she wasn't sure.

Still puzzled, Ali sent off a four-word reply:

Dear Andrea,
Who is your uncle?

REGARDS,
ALI REYNOLDS

Ali worked her way through a long list of well-wishing e-mails, most of them begging her not to abandon her blog. Because many of the notes touched on Paul Grayson's death, she didn't post any of them but answered each one directly with the same kind of non-engagement strategy she had employed earlier. It was gratifying to know that her readers were as reluctant to give up on her as she was on them. Finally, she turned to write her response.

CUTLOOSEBLOG.COM
Sunday, September 18, 2005

In my last post I said I was going to step away from cutloose for a time, but it turns out that was a lie. I don't want to step away. I've heard from many of you this morning. Most have wished me well and urged me not to abandon ship. So I'm not going to.

I've been doing this for more than six months now—yes, last week was my half-year blogiversary. In the past, there has always been a sense of immediacy to what I've written. My posts have offered me a way to examine things that were going on in my life. I've been amazed to learn that what I've written has resonated with so many people, some of whom have shared similar experiences.

This morning one of my fans wrote and offered to stand in for me for as long as necessary. While I appreciate Leda's kind offer, hearing from her brought me up short and made me realize I'm unwilling to give up my forum. So cutlooseblog is back. For right now, there are things I simply won't be able to discuss. I probably won't be able to post comments from you regarding those issues, either, and I beg your understanding in that regard.

But there is something I can say. My mother is sitting right here beside me as I write this. We're in a hotel room several hundred miles away from both our homes, away from her business and from her husband, my father, who is working two jobs—his and hers—to keep their restaurant afloat while she's here backstopping me—her daughter. Their daughter.

So this post is for parents—for my parents and for all those other parents out there—the ones who stick with their offspring through

thick and thin; who don't turn their backs on
their children no matter what; who realize
that regardless of how old their kids may be,
their children are still their children.

Thanks, Mom and Dad. You're the greatest.
*Posted 11:10 A.M., September 18, 2005 by
Babe*

By the time she finished writing her post, there
were several new e-mails. The third one of those was
from her old fan Velma.

*Dear Babe,
When I first started reading cutloose, I didn't
even know what a blog was. Now I read several
of them. One of the ones I read daily, besides
yours, is called socalcopshop. It talks about stuff
going on here in the L.A. area that hardly ever
makes it into the regular papers. You might want
to check out this morning's post. Do you know
this guy? Can you sue him?*

VELMA T IN LAGUNA

Even as Ali searched for the Web site, she had an
inkling of what she would find there, and she wasn't
disappointed. The moment she saw the headline, her
heart sank.

BLACK WIDOW OF ROBERT LANE RIDES AGAIN

Alison Reynolds, already a person of interest in
the grisly homicide of her estranged network
executive husband, Paul Grayson, is now the

target of a new police investigation as police look into the mysterious death of the woman who, had she and he both lived, would have become Paul Grayson's new mother-in-law. Monique Ragsdale, now deceased, was the mother of April Anne Gaddis, Mr. Grayson's intended bride, whom he was scheduled to marry in a ceremony at his Robert Lane mansion early yesterday afternoon.

Sources close to the investigation state that the two women may have clashed during a meeting earlier in the day, prior to Ms. Ragsdale's fatal plunge down the stairway of the house formerly owned by Ms. Reynolds and her husband. Rather than the site of a joyous celebration, the house is now surrounded by crime scene tape as investigators attempt to get to the bottom of what happened.

Mr. Grayson disappeared from a pre-wedding bachelor party on Thursday night. His bound body was found later near the wreckage of a vehicle that had been left on the train tracks west of Palm Springs.

At least one anonymous source claimed that because divorce proceedings between Mr. Grayson and Ms. Reynolds were never finalized, she is allegedly her husband's sole heir, leaving his pregnant fiancée unprovided for. This was supposedly the basis for the alleged confrontation between Ms. Reynolds and Ms. Ragsdale.

Messy divorce proceedings between Ms. Reynolds and her estranged husband have played out in a very public fashion after she was fired from her position as an evening newscaster by the local affiliate of her husband's network. For the past six months she has vented her side of the story as an ongoing saga in posts to a feminist-leaning Web blog called cutlooseblog.com.

In that same six-month period, Ms. Reynolds has been questioned as part of four separate homicide investigations. In two of those she has been exonerated and the cases are considered closed. The other two are still under active investigation, one by the LAPD and the other by the Riverside County Sheriff's Department.

In view of Ms. Reynolds's mounting legal difficulties, her blog has reportedly gone on hiatus.

Posted 7:55 A.M., LMB

No, it hasn't, Ali thought to herself. *Cutloose is definitely back.*

Ali scanned back through the post. There were enough journalistic weasel words—"alleged," "supposed," "reportedly"—along with the ever-so-useful anonymous sources routine, that the article probably wasn't actionable. So, no, Velma, I probably can't sue this guy. As for the signature? LMB. There was no additional information about him available, but Ali had a suspicion that he and the guy who had sent her the poison-pen note earlier, Lance-a-lot, were one and the same.

She looked back through her discarded mail. Sure enough, his address was still there. She started to send him a terse note about publishing unfounded speculation, then she changed her mind. Instead, Ali deleted her half-written e-mail and permanently deleted his e-mail address as well. If Lance-a-lot wanted attention, he sure as hell wasn't going to get it from her.

Ali was disheartened to know, however, that his cutesy pet name for her, Black Widow, was out. Even though the man's allegations were groundless, she understood that other media outlets would most likely pick up on Lance's lead and run with it.

Ali was about to turn off the computer to go shower and dress when another e-mail popped up. Ali recognized the address—Andrea Morales.

There were only two words in Andrea's message:

Jesus Sanchez.

So she was right, this Andrea was that Andrea—the one from the kitchen tamale-making project. But what was this about someone firing Jesus? It made no sense. It was his TLC that kept the grounds of the Robert Lane mansion in pristine order. Why would anyone fire him? Ali sent off yet another immediate reply.

Dear Andrea,
Please believe me that I know nothing about
this. Your uncle's work for us has always been
more than satisfactory.
*   Below you'll find my relevant contact*
information.
*   Give me a call at your earliest convenience so*
we can discuss this and sort it out. Thank you.

REGARDS,
ALI REYNOLDS

Ali slammed shut her computer and started into the bathroom. "What's going on?" Edie asked.

"I'm going to shower and get dressed," Ali said. "Somebody fired the gardener yesterday, and Jesus's niece thinks it's my fault."

"I'm not surprised," Edie replied. "You're as bad as George Bush. It looks like everything is your fault."

Yes, Ali thought. *Isn't that the truth.*

A few minutes later, dressed but with a towel wrapped around her wet hair, Ali hurried down the hall to April's room and knocked on the door. A young woman Ali had never met before opened the door. The room was strewn with a collection of clothing and garment bags. April stood in front of a mirror wearing a full-length navy blue maternity smock complete with wide pleats, a white Peter Pan collar, and matching white cuffs.

"This is my friend Cindy Durbin," April explained. "Even though it's Sunday and she's supposed to be off work, she brought over some clothes for me to try on. What do you think?" April turned in front of the mirror. "Is this too retro?"

Ali nodded curtly in Cindy's direction. The outfit was retro, all right. It looked like it could have stepped right out of Lucille Ball's 1950s costume closet for the old *I Love Lucy* shows that were still in perpetual reruns on TV Land.

"It's fine," Ali said.

April turned from the mirror and studied Ali's face, which must have betrayed some of her roiling feelings. "What's wrong?" April asked.

"Someone fired Jesus Sanchez, the gardener, yesterday," Ali said. "Did you do it?"

"No," April responded. "Mom did. His salary and the cook's both came out of what Paul kept in petty cash. Other than my credit cards, that's the only real money I have right now. Mother said I couldn't afford to keep paying them because I'd run out of money that much sooner. She said she'd take care of getting rid of them for me so I wouldn't have to do it. Why, did we do something wrong?"

Yes, you did something wrong, Ali thought, but there didn't seem much point in discussing it.

"Never mind," she said. "I'll fix it. What's the cook's name?"

"Henrietta, I think," April said. "Henrietta Jackson."

"Where does she live? How long had she worked for you? Do you have a phone number for her?"

"No. Paul probably had that information, but I don't. It would be in his office."

And that's locked up behind a wall of crime scene tape, Ali thought. *How convenient.*

"That's all right," she said. "I'll find her."

"Why?" April asked. "What are you going to do?"

"I'm going to hire them back," Ali replied. "Or, if nothing else, I'll at least offer them severance pay."

"But who's going to pay it?" April objected. "I can't."

"Then I guess I will," Ali said.

With that, she stalked out of the room and slammed the door shut behind her.

{ CHAPTER 11 }

With her temper flaring, Ali stormed back into the room she was sharing with her mother, where she was surprised to find Edie seated at the desk in front of Ali's open laptop. Dave Holman had arrived and taken over the easy chair. He was also finishing up the leavings from their breakfast cart.

"No breakfast buffet at Motel 6," he explained, polishing off the last remaining croissant. "Who lit a fire under you?"

"Monique Ragsdale fired both the cook and the gardener yesterday to keep April from spending some of her precious stash of cash. She sent them packing and blamed it all on me."

"So?" Dave said.

"We're going to find them and hire them back."

"But they can't go back to the house," Dave objected. "The place is a crime scene."

"The fact that it's a crime scene isn't their fault," Ali replied. "If nothing else, I can offer them severance pay. Did anyone call?"

Edie nodded and handed Ali her cell phone.

"Andrea Morales," Edie said. "She wants you to call her back."

"The gardener's niece," Ali explained as she scrolled through her received calls and punched the appropriate number.

"Andrea?" Ali asked.

"Yes."

"This is all a terrible misunderstanding. Your uncle never should have been fired in the first place. Is it possible for you to put me in touch with him?"

"Why?" Andrea asked bluntly.

"Because I want to offer him severance pay at least and possibly his job back," Ali answered. "There's some confusion with my husband's estate at the moment. The right hand doesn't necessarily know what the left hand is doing."

"The woman who fired him knew perfectly well what she was doing," Andrea countered. "She told him he should get his stuff together and get the hell out. She said you were the boss now, and that you didn't want to pay him anymore."

"But I will pay him," Ali insisted. "Can you put me in touch with him?"

"My uncle's English isn't so good," Andrea said. "He'll need someone to translate."

"Would you?"

"I guess," Andrea agreed.

"So where is he?"

"Here," she said. "Well, a few blocks away."

"Where's here?" Ali asked.

Andrea didn't answer the question directly. "Let me ask him if he wants to talk to you. I'll call you back."

Ali hung up and turned to face Dave. "Now how do I find Henrietta Jackson?"

"Who's she? The cook?" Dave asked.

Ali nodded.

"And that's all the information you have on her—just her name? No address? No phone number?"

"Paul probably had more information than that, but it would be in his office and—"

"And the house is a crime scene," Dave finished for her.

"Exactly."

Dave busied himself with making phone calls, but Ali didn't listen to what he was doing. She was thinking about Paul Grayson. She had always had her own money, but Paul had handled the bill paying for everything, including the household accounts. She had never realized until today that the help had been paid in cash. Despite the fact that they had been in this country for years, it probably meant that either Jesus or his wife, Clemencia Sanchez, or both of them were illegals, living and working beneath the INS radar.

For the first time Ali wondered about Elvira Jimenez, Paul's former cook. Was the same true for her? Was she, too, working without proper papers? And what had happened to her? After years of working in the household, why had she been let go? And what about Henrietta? The woman's distinctive accent placed her as being from somewhere in the southern United States. She certainly wasn't an undocumented immigrant, so was she working in an underground economy simply to avoid paying taxes? And if Ali did manage to find Jesus and Henrietta and offer them their jobs back, what kind of liability would she be incurring?

"Your cook has no driver's license as far as I can find," Dave announced a few minutes later. "At least, she doesn't have a California driver's license."

"How did you do that?"

"I know people who know people," he said.

"What about Jesus Sanchez? Could you find him?"

"I thought his niece was going to put you in touch with him."

"What if she doesn't? What if I need to find him on my own?"

A moment later, when Ali's phone rang, her concern about locating Jesus Sanchez proved entirely accurate. "My uncle doesn't want to see you," Andrea Morales announced.

"I just want to talk to him," Ali began.

"He doesn't want to talk to you," Andrea returned forcefully. "He said no, and that means no." With that, she hung up.

Ali was stunned. Because of Jesus's limited English skills and because Ali spoke only rudimentary Spanish, communications between the two of them had always been minimal at best. As far as Ali knew, however, there had never been any kind of ill will.

"Andrea Morales," Dave was saying into his phone as Ali put down hers. "You've dozens? Give me the addresses."

Minutes later, though, armed with a phone book and the list of addresses, Dave was able to match one specific Andrea Morales with the received call number logged into Ali's cell phone. "There you are," he said triumphantly. "Andrea and Miguel Morales, two-twenty-four South Sixth, Pico Gardens."

Ali knew from her days on the news desk that Pico

Gardens had a reputation for being a center of gang-related activities. It was also known as a haven for newly arrived illegal aliens.

"Let's go," Ali said. She went over to the wall safe, opened it, and removed both her Glock and the small-of-back holster she had purchased to carry it.

"Go where?" Dave asked. He eyed her weapon uneasily. "And is that really necessary?"

"In Pico Gardens?" Ali returned. "Yes. If a couple of gringos are going there, being armed is probably the only sensible idea. Andrea told me that Jesus lives somewhere nearby—within a few blocks of where she and her husband live. Jesus drives an old blue van. If it's parked on the street, I'll recognize it."

"It didn't sound as though Jesus is eager to talk to you," Dave pointed out.

"Doesn't matter," Ali said. "I want to talk to him." Ali turned to her mother. "Are you coming along?" she asked.

"I don't think so," Edie said. "If you don't mind, I think I'll hang around here. I'll use your computer to surf the Net."

The idea of her mother, Edie Larson, "surfing the Net" was still strange to Ali. Amazing even. "Be my guest," she said.

"I'll also look in on April from time to time," Edie added. "Just to make sure she's okay."

When Dave and Ali left the hotel, they attempted the back door exit that had worked flawlessly for them the day before, but the media folks had wised up. A reporter, one lowly enough to be relegated to hanging around by the reeking kitchen Dumpster, and her equally low-on-the-totem-pole photographer were lying in wait just outside the door.

"Hey, Ms. Reynolds," the reporter called, holding her microphone aloft and rushing up to the car. "Is it true you've been brought in for questioning in two homicide cases? Do you have any comment?"

Of course I don't have a comment, Ali thought. She said nothing as Dave opened the door on his Nissan. It was too bad they hadn't taken her Cayenne on this trip. Now the media would have information on what had previously been their stealth vehicle.

The photographer focused his camera on Dave. "Out of my way," he said with a snarl, but the photographer didn't take the hint. He was still snapping away as Dave scrambled into the driver's seat and slammed the door shut behind him.

"What jackasses!" he exclaimed. "Were you ever that bad?"

"I don't think so," Ali said. *I hope not,* she thought.

The reporter and photographer were legging it for the front of the building and, presumably, some vehicle, when Dave peeled out of the back driveway and bounced over the edge of the curb into the street.

"Are they going to catch us?" Ali asked.

"Not if I can help it," Dave returned. "Now which way?"

Without her GPS or a detailed map to rely on, Ali had to think for a moment before she was able to get her bearings and direct him onto the southbound ramp of the 405 and from there onto the 10.

"How's your Spanish?" Ali asked as they sped down the freeway.

"I speak menu Spanish fairly well. Why?"

"Because Jesus speaks almost no English and I speak almost no Spanish."

"Maybe his niece, Andrea Whatever, would translate for us."

"I doubt that," Ali said. She picked up her cell phone and scrolled through her phone book until she located the name Duarte.

During her time as a newscaster in L.A., one of Ali's PR roles had been serving as the station's goodwill ambassador to the cancer community. Because of her own tragic history with Dean's death from cancer, she had been a likely and willing candidate. She had served on boards and walked in Races for the Cure and Relays for Life. But she had also done a lot of hands-on caregiving, work that had nothing to do with public relations and never made it into the news. One such case had been a three-year-old leukemia patient named Alonso Duarte.

Lonso's father, Eduardo, had worked at Ali's television station in the capacity of janitor. His wife, Rosa, had worked as a maid for a series of hotels. Once Lonso was diagnosed, the station had broadcast a series of stories about his battle and about his family's plight as well. They had helped raise money to fill in the gap between the bills and what medical insurance actually paid. The station's official involvement had eventually ended, but Ali had remained a part of the family's support system during Lonso's many hospitalizations and chemo treatments. The last Ali had heard, the boy had been in remission for four years.

Eddie Duarte had been working at the station the night Ali had been let go. He, of all people, had been drafted to carry her box of personal possessions out to her car. At the time he had offered to testify on her behalf in any wrongful dismissal suit. Since negotiations on that score were still pending, Eddie's testimony in the matter had so far been unnecessary. As far as Ali knew he was still on the station's payroll, but since he was a nighttime janitor, she worried about calling during the morning hours and waking him. But she did it anyway—called him and woke him.

"Ali," he said, when he finally realized who she was. "So good to hear from you. How are you? I heard about your husband. I'm so sorry."

Sorry for what? Ali wondered. *Sorry because Paul's dead or sorry because he was such a jerk?*

"Thank you," she said. "How is Rosa? How's Lonso?"

"Rosa's fine and Lonso's great. He even got to play peewee league this year—second base."

For a child who had been hovering at death's door five years earlier, this seemed like nothing short of a miracle.

"But what about you?" he asked. "I don't work for the station anymore. I got hired on with another company. If you need me to testify . . ."

"We may still need you to do that, but right now, I need something else," Ali said.

"Name it," Eddie said.

"I'm trying to find my old gardener," Ali said. "There's been a misunderstanding. I need to hire him back, but I don't speak enough Spanish."

"You need me to translate?" Eddie asked.

"Yes," Ali said. "Please."

"Where? When?"

"Soon," Ali said. "As soon as possible. But I'm not sure where. He lives somewhere in Pico Gardens, but we're not there yet, and I don't have an address."

"The only place I know there is that old Linda Vista

Hospital, the abandoned hospital they use for movies and TV shows," Eddie said. "I could meet you there— out front in the parking lot. It'll take me about forty- five minutes to get there."

"Great," Ali said. "Maybe by then we'll have found him."

"Who's Eddie?" Dave asked.

"Long story," Ali returned. "A very long story."

With Ali on the phone and Dave preoccupied with dodging other drivers, they were in the wrong lane and had missed the fork onto I-10 East. Half an hour after leaving the tony environs of Wilshire Boulevard, they were driving around the desolate, graffiti-marred streets of Boyle Heights. It was a neighborhood of houses that had been built in the early part of the twentieth century and were somehow still holding together. Some of them appeared to be in reasonably decent shape. Others were little more than crumbling wrecks.

They started by locating the Morales household on Sixth and then circled out from there, searching for Jesus Sanchez's van. As they turned up South Chicago, Ali pointed. "There it is," she announced. "That's his van."

The aging, much-dented Aerostar was parked in the driveway of a decrepit duplex.

"Now that we know where to find Jesus, let's go back to the hospital parking lot and wait for my inter- preter to show up."

"What if he doesn't?"

"Don't worry. Eddie will be here."

Once they were parked and waiting, Ali told Dave the Eddie Duarte story from beginning to end. She was just finishing when her phone rang.

"You're not going to believe this," Edie Larson said. "If I weren't down here in the lobby seeing it with my own eyes, I wouldn't believe it myself."

Ali switched her phone to "speaker" so Dave could hear both sides of the conversation. "Seeing what?" she asked. "What's going on?"

"Lights, camera, action," Edie replied grimly. "April is down here in the lobby in a blue and white maternity outfit with perfect makeup and perfect hair. She's doing a sit-down interview with some young woman with very long blond hair and an astonishingly short skirt. I saw the logo on one of the cameras. It said Court TV."

"The blonde would be Sheila Rosenburg," Ali said. "So April is doing the interview after all."

"And against our advice," Edie added. "But there's more. I told you when you left that I was going to go check on her and see if she needed anything. Only when I opened my door, there was a man coming out of her room, so I ducked back inside ours. He was a young man, by the way, a very good-looking young man."

"Probably one of her friends," Ali said.

"That's what I thought right up until he kissed her good-bye," Edie returned. "Believe me, it was a lot more than a 'just friends' kiss. But when he turned away from her, I recognized him. I had seen him before."

"Where?" Ali asked.

"On his Web site."

Ali felt like she was bumbling around in the dark. "What Web site?" she asked.

"Ever since you told me about all that Sumo Sudoku

nonsense, I've been curious about it," Edie answered. "I mean, why would Paul and April want to have a bunch of supposedly brainy bodybuilders cluttering up their wedding day? In my experience, weddings are stressful enough without having a film crew and extra people mucking around under hand and foot at the same time. So this morning, I looked up some Sumo Sudoku Web sites and that's where I found him. The guy's name is Tracy McLaughlin."

Ali was stunned. "You're saying you think April has been messing around with Tracy McLaughlin? Are you kidding?"

"I'm not kidding," Edie replied. "Do you know if there's been a paternity test?"

Ali remembered how pleased Paul had been when he learned April was pregnant—pleased and excited.

"I have no idea," Ali said.

"If there hasn't been one, there probably should be," Edie said. "As Paul's executor, if you're going to be forced into setting up a trust fund for Paul's supposed catch colt, you'd best be sure the baby is really his."

Edie Larson had always been a keen observer of human behavior. One of the spooky things about Ali's mother, something that had always left her daughter more than slightly mystified, was her innate ability to see through things that went over other people's heads. Aunt Evelyn, Edie's twin sister, had always claimed that Edie had eyes in the back of her head. As a child, Ali had believed it was true. Maybe it still was, but this seemed like too much.

"Based on seeing the man in a hotel hallway, you're

convinced Sonia Marie is really Tracy McLaughlin's baby rather than Paul's?" Ali asked.

"I'd bet money on it," Edie declared. "You should have seen the little love tap and the kiss the man laid on April's tummy as he was saying good-bye. That was a daddy-style maneuver if I've ever seen one."

That meant Paul was cheating on Ali with April, and April was cheating on Paul with Tracy McLaughlin. This was, Ali supposed, entirely predictable.

"What goes around comes around," she said. "So what do we know about Tracy McLaughlin?"

"Only what was on his Web site, and I've got his bio right here," Edie replied. "Says he came to Hollywood from Des Moines, Iowa, determined to be a stuntman. He ended up in a stunt that went bad and spent the next six months in a full body cast. When he got out of the cast, he went into bodybuilding to regain his strength. He worked puzzles while he was laid up and invented Sumo Sudoku once he got better as a way of proving to people that he had recovered completely. But that's not all."

"What's not all?" Ali asked.

"You'll never guess who put up a major part of the capital to get Sumo Sudoku off the ground."

"Paul?"

"You've got it. He's one of the original investors in the organization. There are ten people who put up big bucks to get it started. I don't recognize any of the other names, but you may. I think that's why they were holding the Sumo Sudoku tournament at the house on the same day as the wedding. I'm sure Paul knew there would be lots of media coverage. That way the tournament would generate lots of interest . . ."

"And lots of buzz," Ali finished. "In this town, buzz is everything. Once something is the current 'in' thing, then it's everybody's 'in' thing. Get one appearance on *Jay Leno* and you're on your way."

A gray Chevrolet Impala pulled up and stopped beside Dave's Nissan. "I've gotta go, Mom," Ali said. "My translator is here."

Leaving the Chevy idling, Eddie Duarte hurried over to Ali's door, reached in, and gave her a swift hug.

"Thank you for coming," she said.

"No problem," Eddie returned. "Now, where's this guy you need me to talk to?"

With Eddie following in his Chevy, Dave and Ali drove back to South Chicago Street, where Jesus Sanchez's distinctive blue van was still parked in the driveway. Dave drove half a block beyond the Sanchez house and then stopped in a parking spot that was large enough for both his Nissan and Eddie's Impala. Before they could open their doors, however, a big unmarked Crown Victoria came careening around the corner and grabbed the spot just behind Eddie. Dave watched in his mirror as two people exited the vehicle and hurried past the van and into the fenced yard.

"Hey," Dave began. "I think I know them. Aren't they the two homicide detectives who came to the hospital to talk to April last night?"

Ali turned and looked. Sure enough, Detectives Tim Hubbard and Rosalie Martin hurried up onto the duplex's shaded front porch and rang the bell. "They talked to me, too," Ali said. "What are they doing here?"

"Same thing we are," Dave replied. "Looking for answers."

"Which means we're too late then," Ali said.

"Looks like," Dave agreed. "They'll recognize you. You stay where you are, and I'll let your friend Eddie know what's going on."

While Ali watched, the two detectives tried ringing a doorbell. Then they knocked—and knocked some more. Finally a woman Ali recognized to be Jesus's wife, Clemencia, came to the door and slipped out onto the porch. She stood there talking to the two detectives for several long minutes, alternately shaking her head and gesturing. A little later, an LAPD patrol car pulled up as well. A young Hispanic officer exited the vehicle and hurried up onto the porch, where he joined in the conversation.

By then Dave had returned. "The new guy is probably here to translate," Dave muttered. "That means they have the same language problem we do."

They waited and watched for another fifteen minutes. Finally, the clearly frustrated detectives and the patrolman stepped off the porch and returned to their two separate vehicles. As they drove away, Dave let out a sigh of relief.

"If Jesus is there, he refused to come out and talk to them, and they didn't go in after him. That means Hubbard and Martin were only here on a fishing expedition, and they went away empty-handed. If they'd had enough for a search warrant, it would have been a different story."

"Let's go then," Ali said, opening her door. "I know Clemencia. At least I've met her. Maybe she'll talk to me."

Dave Holman didn't budge. "Are you coming or not?" Ali asked.

"You and Eddie go on ahead," Dave said. "And you'd better make it quick. If Hubbard and Martin come back with a warrant, this may be your only chance."

"And what are you going to do?" Ali asked.

"I'll let you know if it works," Dave replied.

Ali scrambled out of the Nissan and motioned for Eddie Duarte to join her. A moment later, they were standing on the porch in front of a sun-bleached mahogany door. Ali pressed the doorbell, but there was no answering ring from inside. While she waited, Ali edged over to one of the windows. The curtains had been pulled shut, but there was enough of a space left between them that Ali was able to see into the living room, where a stack of taped cardboard boxes and a collection of mismatched luggage gave evidence of hurried packing. Apparently Jesus and Clemencia Sanchez were headed out of Dodge.

Convinced the doorbell wasn't in working order, Ali tried knocking instead. Nothing happened then, either.

"Her name is Clemencia," Ali told Eddie. "Call out to her. Tell her we know she's inside. Tell her I'm here. Say I need to talk to her and that we aren't going away until I do—that we'll stay here all afternoon if necessary. Tell her that the neighbors already saw the cops come and go, and they're watching us now."

It was several long minutes before Clemencia Sanchez finally came to the door. She pulled it open slightly and then slipped outside. The look she leveled in Ali's direction was nothing short of venomous.

"What do you want?" she demanded.

"Where's Jesus?" Ali returned. "I need to talk to him."

Ali knew for sure that Clemencia understood that much English, but the woman deliberately turned away from her, looking instead to Eddie as though she expected understanding from him rather than a translation, which he nonetheless provided.

"He's gone," Clemencia answered. "He went away."

"Gone where?" Ali asked.

Clemencia shrugged. "It doesn't matter. He isn't coming back."

"But I want to give him his job back," Ali said. "He should never have been fired in the first place. It was a mistake."

Unimpressed, Clemencia shrugged again. Ali tried another tack.

"The cops that were here before. What did they want?"

Clemencia's dark eyes sparked with sudden fury. Her nostrils flared. "Jesus knew they would come for him, and they did. That's why he left, thank God. He went away before they got here."

"But why would they come for him?" Ali asked.

"Because that awful woman fired him," Clemencia said in a barrage of angry Spanish. "You wanted him gone, but she was the one who did the dirty work for you. And when he was ready to leave and went to turn in his keys, there she was—at the bottom of the stairs."

"Monique had already fallen before Jesus left? Why didn't he call for help?"

"Because he thought she was already dead," Clemencia answered. "It looked to him like she was dead.

And Jesus knew what the cops would think—that since she fired him, he killed her. He dropped his key ring, and he's sure they found it. They'll find his fingerprints there, too, and they'll blame him." For the first time, Clemencia's fury seemed to dissolve into something closer to despair. She stopped speaking and blinked back tears.

At the time the EMTs had been moving Monique to the gurney, Ali had been too busy to pay any attention to the key ring. She had been focused instead on the phone. But she remembered it now. And she knew, just as the detectives had, that the keys had belonged to Jesus Sanchez because his name had been on the ring as well. Paul Grayson had been a great one for wielding his P-Touch labeler. Everyone who had access to the house or the grounds, Ali included, had been issued appropriate sets of keys with their names clearly visible.

She also understood why Jesus had chosen to disappear. She knew full well that the U.S. Constitution aside, all men are *not* created equal. Hispanics or blacks accused of crimes often found themselves on an entirely different legal track than Anglos did—one with an automatic presumption of guilt rather than innocence. In fact, she thought wryly, the same thing held true when media babes ended up accused of crimes they may not have committed.

"I'd like to help," Ali said quietly.

Without needing or waiting for Eddie to translate, Clemencia replied, "Why?"

"Because I know what it feels like to be suspected of doing something you haven't done," Ali said. She scrounged in her purse until she found one of Victor's cards. She handed it over. "If Jesus wants an attorney, have him call this man."

Clemencia studied the gold-embossed card, then handed it back. "We could not afford someone like this," she said.

Just then Ali remembered Velma T's nephew. Maybe Jesus and Clemencia wouldn't find him quite as daunting. "There's another man I could recommend then," Ali said. "I'll forward his information to your niece, Andrea."

"But still . . ." Clemencia objected. "We can't afford to pay for any attorney."

"I can afford it," Ali said. "And I will. Be sure to tell Jesus that when you talk to him. And be sure he knows that if he wants it, he still has a job."

With that, she turned and walked away.

CHAPTER 12

Eddie Duarte stayed on the porch for several minutes after Ali returned to the car and while she was giving Dave a brief summary of what had transpired.

"You gave Jesus Sanchez Victor Angeleri's card?" he asked incredulously. "Who's going to pay the bill? I'd hate to think what his hourly billable rate is."

"She didn't take it," Ali said. "But I'll pay for whatever attorney they do hire."

"So now you're setting out to save the world?"

"Only the parts of it I've screwed up," Ali responded.

"Excuse me," Dave returned. "As far as I can tell, you had nothing at all to do with the fact that Monique Ragsdale took a header down those stairs."

"No, but if it turns out she was pushed—"

"She was," Dave interjected.

"You know that for sure?" Ali asked.

Dave nodded. "I have a source who confirmed it as a suspected homicide while you were busy with Clemencia."

"Then whoever's responsible is probably connected

to me as well," Ali asserted. "And if Jesus is being wrongly blamed for what happened to her? Well, I'm connected to him, too."

"I hope your husband left you a ton of money then," Dave said. "It sounds like you're going to need it."

Eddie Duarte approached Ali's side of the car and tapped on the window. She rolled it down.

"What did Clemencia say after I left?" Ali asked.

Eddie frowned. "She told me that you're as evil as your husband."

That revelation hurt Ali's feelings. Personally, she had to agree about Paul—he was evil—but Ali didn't like being tarred with the same brush.

"I told her I knew you were a good person," Eddie continued. "And that if you said you would do something, you would do it. I'm not sure she believed me, though."

Why would she? Ali thought. "Thank you for saying that, Eddie, and thank you for coming," she added. "I really appreciate your help."

"Not that it did much good," Eddie said dejectedly and, offering a good-bye wave, returned to his car.

"Where to now?" Dave asked. "Back to the hotel?"

Ali nodded.

"How did you find out Monique's death is now classified as a homicide?" Ali asked. "Who told you?"

"Ken Nickerson is one of my good old buddies from the Marines. We served together in Iraq. Now he works for LAPD."

"Ken's the one who got you Andrea Morales's address information?" Ali asked.

"That's right. While you were talking to Clemencia, I called him up and asked him straight out if they had autopsy results back on Monique Ragsdale, and they did."

"Already?" Ali asked.

Dave nodded. "Preliminary," he said. "It may be Sunday, but since it's a high-profile case, the guys over on North Mission Road really got their rears in gear on this one."

"And?" Ali asked.

"Bruising on her arms and on her back. Defensive wounds and definite signs of a struggle. No sexual assault. They took scrapings from under her nails. There could be identifiable DNA found in those. The real problem for Jesus Sanchez is that the cops found something at the crime scene that links him to Monique's death."

"I know," Ali said. "Keys with his name on them. I saw them, too. According to what Jesus told Clemencia, after he was let go, he came to the house to turn in his keys. That's when he found Monique at the bottom of the stairs. I'm sure he was upset at seeing her like that, and I don't blame him. I know how I felt when we found her later on. He must have panicked and dropped his keys. Later on, when he realized what had happened, he knew the cops would find them and come looking for him—which they did. That's probably why he took off."

"The big question is, were the keys under the victim or were they beside her?" Dave asked. "If they were under, it means the keys and Jesus were probably there either before she fell or at the same time. In that case, things are looking pretty grim for poor old Jesus. If the keys were found nearby, they could have been dropped at the same time or either before or after the fact."

Ali thought about that. "I don't know," she said finally. "I don't remember seeing them until after the EMTs put Monique on the stretcher. It could be they were right there in plain sight the whole time, and we just didn't notice them."

"One way or the other, why is it you think it's your responsibility to hire a defense attorney for Mr. Sanchez?"

"Shut up and drive," Ali returned.

The fact that Dave Holman did so made Ali like him better.

"And that's not all," he said a few minutes later.

"There's more?"

"Actually, yes. It turns out your Sumo Sudoku pal's Web site bio didn't tell the whole story."

"What did he leave out?"

"That when he was eighteen he went to prison for grand theft auto. It's not the kind of thing somebody puts on a résumé when he's out trolling for well-heeled investors."

"What if Paul suspected something was going on between April and Tracy? What if he started looking into McLaughlin's background and found out some of this stuff?" Ali asked.

"Sounds like possible motive to me," Dave said.

"Except the cops aren't looking in that direction."

"Not yet," Dave said. "But there's no reason we can't point them that way."

Without missing the critical merge, it didn't take nearly as long to get back to the hotel as it had taken to drive to Pico Gardens. "Are you coming up?" Ali asked, as they drove up to the entrance.

"I think I'll take a pass," Dave said. "I want to go

back to my place and call my kids. I try to talk to them on Sunday afternoons."

"Just drop me at the front door then," Ali said. "At this point I don't care if the lobby is teeming with reporters. I'm tired of sneaking around. I'll just brazen it out."

"Good girl," Dave said. "I'm glad to hear it. Maybe you can afford to keep handing over those terrific tips. I can't."

The hotel lobby was completely devoid of reporters as Ali made her way upstairs, leading her to conclude that something more interesting must have turned up as fodder for that evening's news broadcasts. Back in the room she was surprised to find her mother wasn't there. Ali tried calling Edie's cell phone. When the call went to voice mail, Ali hung up. Maybe Edie had decided to take advantage of being in L.A. by going to a movie. Edie preferred what her husband called "arty" films to his shoot-'em-ups, but the former seldom made it to the screens of Sedona's single multiplex.

Kicking off her tennies, Ali returned her Glock to the safe and raided the honor bar for a Diet Sprite. While there she noticed something odd. Her mother carried her daily allocation of vitamins in a series of ziplock sandwich bags, which she carefully saved each day, packing them away for future use. One of those plastic bags lay in the armoire next to the TV remote. It contained a single cigarette butt.

Ali picked up the bag and examined the contents. The filtered stub was unremarkable in every way. There was no lipstick residue that might indicate that whoever had smoked it was a female. For Edie, a lifelong vociferous nonsmoker, to see fit to keep the remains of a cigarette in what was a clearly designated nonsmoking room could only mean Edie was playing detective in her own right.

Replacing the bag, Ali took her soda to the couch, sat down, picked up her computer, logged on, and googled Richard Dahlgood, Velma T's nephew. There were several hits, all of them concerning appearances in state and federal courts on behalf of various clients. From everything Ali was able to glean from those reports, Dahlgood seemed like the real deal.

The first e-mail she sent was to Velma T in Laguna.

Dear Velma,
A friend of mine may well be in need of your
nephew's services. Please let him know that if
he is contacted in regard to defending someone
named Jesus Sanchez, he should be in touch
with me so arrangements can be made for han-
dling any necessary retainer. My contact phone
number is listed below.

ALI

Next Ali wrote to Andrea Morales.

Dear Andrea,
I spoke to your aunt, Clemencia Sanchez, earlier
today. It seems likely that your uncle, Jesus,
may require the services of a defense attorney.
A friend of mine has recommended someone
named Richard Dahlgood. Although I don't
know the man personally, he does appear to have

*a considerable defense practice here in the L.A.
area. His contact information is listed below.*

*If your aunt and uncle are interested in
engaging Mr. Dahlgood's services, please let me
know so I can make arrangements for payment
of any required retainer. Also, please let your
uncle know that he is back on my payroll at the
moment regardless of whether or not he is able to
return to work. Also tell him the house on Robert
Lane is currently off-limits to all of us due to the
ongoing police investigation. I will need to know
where his pay envelopes should be delivered.*

*Also, if he has any information concern-
ing the whereabouts of Henrietta Jackson, the
cook who was fired along with him, or of my
former cook, Elvira Jimenez, I would appreciate
knowing how to reach them. I'm concerned that
Elvira may have been let go under circumstances
similar to what happened to your uncle.*

REGARDS,
ALI REYNOLDS

Several readers weighed in on Ali's legal issues.
Those she responded to briefly and let go. Several others addressed her earlier post about her mother.

*Dear Babe,
I read several blogs a day and have been a fan
of yours for some time. Not all mothers are
created equal. You're lucky. Your mother sounds
wonderful. Mine was poison. I'm glad she's dead.*

ALMA

That one Ali posted. As she kept reading, she found that the people who had written in were divided almost fifty-fifty on either side of the good mother/bad mother spectrum. By the time she had worked her way through that set of correspondence and added several more posts, Ali found herself agreeing with Alma's assessment. Ali Reynolds really was lucky.

As the afternoon waned, Ali realized she was hungry. Edie had not yet returned. Ali tried calling her mother's cell again—to no avail. Once again the call went straight to voice mail. Just to be sure, Ali checked her own phone to see if she had missed receiving a message. She hadn't. She checked the room phone for messages as well. No luck. Finally she called down to the desk. Edie hadn't left a note there, either. And then, just to cover all the bases, she tried April's phones, too, both her room and her cell. Again, no answer.

Feeling the first inkling of concern, Ali transferred over to the bell captain. "This is Ali Reynolds," she said.

Her reputation for generous tipping had preceded her. For Ali Reynolds no ticket number was required. "Right, Ms. Reynolds," the bell captain said at once. "Would you like me to have your vehicle brought around to the back?"

"No," she said. "I'm actually calling about my mother's vehicle. Is it there?"

"Do you have the valet number for that one?"

"No," Ali replied. "It's a white Oldsmobile Alero with Arizona plates."

"Oh, that one," he said. "It was self-parked. She left like she was headed to a fire sometime right around one. It was busy, and we were totally backed up here.

She was in such a hurry that she almost ran down one of my guys."

"Was she alone?"

"As far as I know."

Off the phone, Ali tried to imagine where Edie would have been going in such a hurry. As an out-of-town driver, she wasn't familiar with the L.A. area. Wherever it was, it was likely she would have needed detailed directions. If she hadn't asked one of the parking valets for help, maybe she had done so online.

Ali returned to her computer and checked out the search page, looking for the most recent searches. She expected to find a listing for MapQuest or one of the other online map providers. What she found instead was a list of several Iowa-based searches, including one for the *Des Moines Register*. Iowa. Tracy McLaughlin had been sent up for grand theft auto in Iowa.

Ali grabbed her phone and dialed Dave.

"What's up?" he asked.

"We may have a problem," Ali said. "I can't find my mother, and I'm pretty sure she's been playing detective. While I was gone, she was looking up something in the *Des Moines Register*."

"Smart woman," Dave said. "She must have been tracking Tracy McLaughlin, too."

"She may be smart, but she's also not here," Ali said. "At the hotel."

"Where'd she go?"

"That's what I'm trying to tell you. I have no idea. The parking valet said she left in a hell of a hurry, but she didn't leave a note, and she's not answering her cell."

"How long has she been gone?"

"She left the hotel a little after one," Ali replied.

"Have you called your dad?" Dave asked. "Maybe she's called him."

"I can check," Ali said.

"Good. You do that," Dave said. "In the meantime, I'm on my way. I'll be there as soon as I can."

Ali was waiting at the hotel entrance when Dave pulled into the driveway in his Nissan. "Well?" he asked as she settled into the passenger seat.

"Dad hasn't heard from her," Ali reported. "His first thought was that she'd probably gone to see a bargain matinee. That was my idea, too, but the movie would be over by now. Dad's worried, and so am I. Should I call the cops and report her missing?"

Dave shook his head. "It won't make any difference. They're not going to go looking for her right now anyway. We're better off looking ourselves. Where do you think she might have gone?"

"Mom's from out of town," Ali replied. "She doesn't really know her way around L.A. The only map she has in the Alero is that big atlas. I know she used MapQuest directions to get to the hotel, but there were no MapQuest searches on my computer."

"So wherever she went, if she drove herself, she must have known where she was going," Dave concluded.

Ali nodded. "Right. And the only two familiar places I know about for sure are the hospital and the house on Robert Lane. If April went into labor, she could have gone to Cedars-Sinai. I'm pretty sure that's where Mom said April plans to deliver. But it's possible she might have gone to the house for some strange reason, too."

Dave put the Nissan in gear. "The hospital isn't going to tell us anything. Let's try the house first. Have you tried calling April?"

"I did," Ali told him. "Both her room and her cell. No answer."

"Try again, just in case."

Once again both of April's phones went to voice mail. Ali tried Edie's phone again with the same result. By then Ali was feeling the first tinge of real panic.

When they reached the house on Robert Lane, they found it deserted. Crime scene tape was still draped across the front door, warning people not to enter. There was no sign of Edie's Oldsmobile anywhere and no sign of any other vehicles, either.

"She's not here," Ali concluded. "And I'm beginning to get a bad feeling about this—a really bad feeling."

"Don't worry," Dave said. "Not yet. I'm sure she's fine. Let's try the hospital next."

At Cedars-Sinai, Dave drove through the parking garages, prowling the stalls and searching for the Alero, while Ali went inside to the patient information desk and tried to bluff her way into finding out whether or not a patient named April Gaddis had been admitted. It was like banging her head on a brick wall. No one would tell her anything. Period. When Ali caught up with Dave again, she learned that his garage search had been equally fruitless.

"Back to the hotel then?" Dave asked.

"I guess," Ali said. "Is it time?"

"Time for what?" Dave returned.

"To call Missing Persons?"

"After less than five hours?" Dave responded. "Believe me, they'll laugh you off the phone. At this point they probably wouldn't even bother taking a report. Your mother's an adult. Adults are allowed to disappear whenever they want to. They can and do. Let's go back to the hotel and wait a while longer. Maybe she'll turn up. Besides, since the hotel was where you last spoke to her, that's a reasonable place to try picking up her trail. Didn't you say she was watching an interview at the time?"

Ali nodded. "Yes. The one with Sheila Rosenburg from Court TV."

"Since April and your mother are both among the missing," Dave suggested, "there's always a possibility that they're together. What if your mother and April are doing something perfectly harmless? Maybe once the interview was over they decided to go shopping. After all, April's expecting a baby. Maybe your mom wanted to get her something nice."

Ali shot that idea down without a moment's hesitation. "Mom hates shopping," she said.

"All right then," Dave said. "Let's track down this Sheila person. Maybe one or the other of them would have mentioned to her where they were going or what they planned to do next."

"Maybe," Ali agreed, but she didn't think the idea sounded very promising.

Back at the hotel Ali was relieved to find that the media were still absent. Up on the seventh floor and on the way down the hallway from the elevator, Ali stopped off just long enough to tap on April's door. There was no answer. Ali was in the process of unlocking the door to her own room when her phone rang. The number showing in the readout was her parents' home number in Sedona.

"Hello," Ali said.

"Did you find her?" Bob Larson demanded.

"No," Ali said. "Not yet. We're still looking."

"Well, I just got off the phone with Chris, and we've made up our minds," Bob said. "We've got a contingency plan all lined up. I've found a substitute short-order cook who'll come in and cover for me, and Chris is going to leave his conference early and call for a substitute, too. Kip will stay here and look after Samantha. Once we get the details squared away, we'll throw our stuff in my car and be under way."

"Under way where?" Ali asked. "You mean you're coming here?"

"Of course I'm coming there," Bob said determinedly. "My wife is missing. Do you think I'm just going to sit around on my butt and twiddle my thumbs?"

The idea of her father and Chris driving across the desert in Bob's doddering Bronco seemed downright ludicrous. When it came to dependability, Chris's far newer Prius would have been a better choice.

"Dad," Ali reasoned. "Are you sure you want to do that? I mean, she isn't officially missing."

"You haven't reported it?"

"Dave said it's too soon. No one will pay any attention."

"I'm paying attention," Bob Larson countered. "Your mother's as dependable as the day is long. She wouldn't run off somewhere without letting one of us know. She just wouldn't."

That, of course, was Ali's opinion, too. Leaving without a word was totally out of character for Edie even if that assessment wouldn't carry much weight with the LAPD.

"Do what you need to do," Ali said at last.

"I was planning on it all along," Bob said with a growl. "Chris and I had already discussed it. And don't think I'm asking for permission, either."

"Of course not," Ali agreed. "But I'm glad you're not coming alone."

"Me, too," Bob said. "I'm not as young as I used to be."

Once Bob was off the phone, Ali called down to the desk. She made arrangements for April to be moved out of the more expensive two-room suite to one room and then reserved two more rooms as well—one for her parents and another for Chris. At this rate, she'd soon be occupying the whole floor. It was just as well that Dave was bunking at Motel 6.

A chastened Ali let Dave into her room, where he immediately appropriated her computer and hunkered down over it. "What was she using to search?" he asked.

"Google."

"Good. I'll see if I can track down her search history. In the meantime, see if you can locate that Sheila person from Court TV."

Ali had to bite her lip. She had already gone over her mother's search history, but she kept her mouth shut and began looking for Sheila's number. Before she found it, however, the phone rang.

"Ms. Reynolds?"

"Yes."

"My name's Richard Dahlgood. I understand you're a good friend of my aunt Velma's."

That wasn't entirely true, but it was close enough.

"Yes," Ali said. "I do know her."

"I've just had a very strange phone call from someone named Andrea Morales," Dahlgood continued. "She said her uncle might possibly be in need of legal representation in a criminal matter and that, if I took him on, you would be responsible for any expenses that were incurred."

"Yes," Ali said. "That's correct."

"So you know who this person is then, what he might be accused of, and all that?"

"I do."

"I have to say, Ms. Reynolds, it's very unusual for someone to assume someone else's legal obligations in this fashion."

"Unusual but not out of the question."

"No, but I would have to have a signed authorization from my client—once I meet him, that is—giving you permission to have access to the bill. Billing information is also highly confidential."

By then Ali had had it up to here with her bevy of attorneys, all of them standing around with their hands out.

"Please tell Ms. Morales that her understanding is correct and that if she makes arrangements for the client to meet with you, you'll come prepared with whatever paperwork is necessary for me to handle the bill."

"If it's a criminal charge, the costs could be considerable," Dahlgood warned.

Not nearly as considerable as Victor Angeleri's, Ali thought as she ended the call.

Finally Dave set Ali's computer aside. "There's nothing here," he said. "How about if I go downstairs and see if I can make friends with hotel security. Maybe their surveillance tapes will show us something. Are you all right holding down the fort here?"

Ali nodded. "I'll be fine," she said.

He went out, leaving Ali alone. She sat still for a few minutes, then ended up pacing. Her third pass across the room brought her face-to-face with the television armoire and the baggie with the cigarette butt. She picked it up and looked at it.

Suddenly, remembering the hint of stale cigarette smoke in April's room, that cigarette butt made a whole lot more sense to her.

Her mother had been telling her about seeing April and Tracy McLaughlin sharing a romantic interlude in the hallway. And her next comment had been something about doing a paternity test. Maybe the cigarette butt had belonged to Tracy McLaughlin. Maybe Edie hoped enough genetic material could be located on the filter to develop a DNA profile to prove for certain whether or not Tracy McLaughlin was the father of April's unborn child.

Grabbing her cell phone and room key, Ali dashed out of the room and hurried down to the lobby. She found Dave Holman and a uniformed security guard closeted in a windowless room behind the front desk, where they were surveying a bank of security monitors.

Dave was surprised to see her. "What are you doing here?" he asked.

For an answer, she waved the baggie in front of him. "What's that?"

"Evidence, most likely," Ali replied. "At least it's evidence as far as my mother is concerned. I told you Mom was playing detective. I'm guessing this cigarette butt belongs to Tracy McLaughlin, and she thought we could use it as part of a paternity test."

Dave took the bag from her hand and held it up to the light. "It could mean a whole lot more than that."

"What?"

"Tracy's a convicted felon, and a vehicle theft was involved in your husband's murder. Tracy had a business connection with Paul Grayson, but he also has a possibly illicit relationship with Paul's bride-to-be. This is sounding like a whole lot of motive to me."

"But how does the cigarette play into this?" Ali asked.

"The duct tape. Didn't you tell me your husband was bound with duct tape?"

Ali nodded. "That's what I was told, but I saw it, too. Not the tape itself, but the marks it left on his face. Why?"

"Most bad guys still haven't figured out that using duct tape in the commission of a crime is a really bad idea. Glue from the tape almost always captures the criminal's DNA right along with the victim's. Say somebody tears the tape with their teeth. They also leave behind traces of their saliva. And there's DNA in the tiny pieces of skin that slough off the bad guy and onto the tape as it's being applied. If the duct tape used on Paul hasn't already been examined for DNA evidence, you can bet it will be. Crime labs can usually find DNA evidence. The big problem comes when it's time to match that evidence to a known perpetrator, and that's what Edie may have given us."

"Since Tracy's been in prison, won't they have a record of his DNA profile?" Ali asked.

"Not necessarily," Dave said. "For one thing, those

databases are relatively new. McLaughlin could well have been let go without having to leave a sample."

Ali looked at the cigarette again. "When Mom grabbed this, she wasn't thinking about the possibility that McLaughlin might be a killer. She was thinking about the baby."

"And from the looks of things, I'd say she gave him hell about it, too."

Ali was dismayed. "She did? When?"

"Down in the lobby. After the interview. It's on one of the security tapes. Come take a look."

Dave led Ali over to the monitors. On one of them, Ali saw a frozen image of her mother, standing flat-footed, hands on her hips, glaring up into Tracy McLaughlin's face. The security guard pressed one of the controls. Suddenly Edie Larson was in motion. Her mouth moved. Her hands gestured furiously. No words could be heard, but then, they didn't need to be.

Ali knew her mother. Edie had never been one to hold back on delivering her opinions. Here she was giving a suspected killer a piece of her mind.

Watching the video sent a surge of fear through Ali's body. She had done the same thing once—she had bearded a suspected killer long before anyone else had tumbled to what had happened. In the process Ali had put herself in harm's way and had come closer to dying that day than she cared to remember. Now Edie Larson had done the same thing—put herself in harm's way.

"What now?" she asked.

"I think it's time to file that missing person's report," Dave said.

{ CHAPTER 13 }

Upstairs, the first call Ali made was to Missing Persons at LAPD—with predictable results. Carolyn Little, the Missing Persons cop Ali had spoken to on Friday, wasn't available on weekends, and no other officer came on the line, either. Instead, an indifferent clerk with minimal typing skills and an even smaller sense of urgency took the information on the disappearance of Edie Larson.

"You be sure to let us know if Ms. Larson turns up, now," the clerk said cheerily when she finished. "If we don't hear from you by this time tomorrow, an officer should be in touch. If not tomorrow, then the day after." Click.

Ali flung down the phone. "So much for getting any help from LAPD," she muttered.

"What did you expect?" Dave asked.

Shaking her head in disgust, Ali dialed the number she had for the Riverside Sheriff's Department. If she had reached the younger detective, she might have achieved better results, but at seven o'clock on a Sunday evening, talking with Detective Sims was the best she could do. He was a long way from sympathetic.

"I'm a homicide detective," he said. "If you've got a missing person on your end, you need to call LAPD."

"We already did that," Ali told him. "They're not exactly interested."

"Why should I be?"

"Because we think my mother's disappearance may have something to do with my husband's homicide and with one of my husband's acquaintances—a guy named Tracy McLaughlin."

"What about him?" Sims asked.

The way Sims asked the question made it clear McLaughlin was already a known entity, but Ali wasn't eager to give up any additional information without first having some assurances from the detective that he would intercede with the LAPD on Edie Larson's behalf.

"You know Tracy McLaughlin went to prison for car theft?" Ali asked.

"That's what I like about all you hotshot media types," Detective Sims grumbled. "You think that just because we're cops, we must be too dumb to wipe our own butts. Of course I know McLaughlin got sent up for grand theft auto. Served five and a half years. In a homicide involving a stolen vehicle, don't you think that's the kind of thing that would have come to our attention once we started investigating your husband's friends and associates? And what the hell does that have to do with the fact that your mother has apparently taken a powder?"

"My mother's a responsible person," Ali returned. "She wouldn't leave of her own volition without letting one of us know. I talked to her shortly before she disappeared. She said she thought Tracy McLaughlin was somehow involved with April Gaddis, my husband's fiancée."

"Talk about yesterday's news," Sims returned dismissively. "Of course they were involved. April and Tracy have been friends for years. According to what April told us earlier, she was the one who brought Sumo Sudoku to your husband's attention in the first place."

Being friends and having a romantic encounter in a hotel hallway were two entirely different things, but Ali suspected that if she hinted at a possible romantic connection between April and Tracy, Detective Sims would most likely discount that as well.

"Before my mother left she was involved in a verbal confrontation with Tracy McLaughlin. We saw that on a security tape. She also collected a cigarette butt and left it in a plastic bag," Ali continued. "Dave Holman and I believe that may have come from Tracy McLaughlin as well. If DNA from that could be linked to the duct tape found on my husband—"

"Who says there was duct tape?" Detective Sims demanded. "How would you know about that?"

"I saw it, remember?" Ali reminded him. "When I identified the body. I'm no expert, but the marks I saw on his face certainly looked like they could have come from duct tape."

"Oh," Sims said. "I see."

"So are you checking the duct tape for DNA evidence?" Ali insisted.

"Of course we're checking it," Sims replied with an impatient snarl. "But this isn't exactly *CSI Miami*. In our neck of the woods it generally takes a while for our people to develop a DNA profile. We don't try to get the job done in sixty minutes minus commercials, so don't expect us to have lab results tomorrow or next week or even next month. We're also required to maintain chains of evidence. If and when we decide we need a DNA sample from Mr. McLaughlin, you can be sure we'll be able to obtain one on our own without help from either you or your mother. In the meantime, we have leads and we're working them. Now, if you don't mind, this is supposed to be my day off."

With that Sims hung up, leaving Ali holding the phone.

"What?" Dave asked.

"I don't think Detective Sims is going to help us find Mom or Tracy McLaughlin," Ali said.

"If we can't go through official channels, we'll have to try some unofficial ones," Dave said, reaching for his phone.

"Your pal at LAPD?"

Dave nodded. "If he's home. He said something about going camping on his days off."

While Dave worked his phone, Ali stood in the middle of the room, holding her cell phone and thinking. She remembered something Helga had said the day before as Victor had been driving them from the hotel to Robert Lane. Scrolling through her cell's phone book, Ali located Helga Myerhoff's number and dialed it.

"Yesterday, when you were talking to me about April Gaddis," Ali said, "I seem to remember that you mentioned something about her wanting to be a Pilates instructor."

"Yes," Helga answered. "That's right."

"And that some of her friends weren't exactly nice people?" Ali pressed.

"Bit of an understatement," Helga replied. "Have you ever heard of The Body Shop in Century City?"

"Car repairs?" Ali asked.

"Not exactly," Helga said with a snort. "Although it's located in a building that once held an auto dealership, it's got nothing at all to do with cars. It's a twenty-four-hour upscale fitness club where network bigwigs and wannabe bigwigs can mix and mingle, see and be seen. It's also one of the hot, in-crowd places at the moment. Supposedly the gym comes complete with one-on-one personal trainers, an organic juice bar, and with personal chefs available upon request. More than that, though, it also operates as a convenient pickup joint. That's where April first met Paul, by the way. She worked there as a receptionist."

Makes sense, Ali thought. For an undereducated and beautiful young woman like April Gaddis, who was also ambitious and determinedly upwardly mobile, The Body Shop sounded like the perfect manhunt launching pad.

"The Body Shop's biggest appeal is that it's both respectable and edgy," Helga continued. "As you already know, some of Hollywood's best-known heavy hitters are afflicted with complicated substance-abuse issues. For these relatively respectable guys, it's a lot more convenient if they can meet up with their drug supplier at some fashionable watering hole rather than having to buy their next hit from a street dealer at some dingy intersection in L.A."

"What about Tracy McLaughlin?" Ali asked.

"The Sumo Sudoku guy?" Helga asked. "The one in the kilt?"

"That's the one," Ali said. "Did he work there, too?"

"He may have," Helga said. "I don't know for sure, but I'll tell you this. I liked looking at the guy. He might be a bit young for me, but I wouldn't mind taking him home for a day or two to check out whatever it is he keeps under that kilt."

Ali was glad that Dave wasn't hearing Helga's part of the conversation.

"Why all this sudden interest in Tracy McLaughlin?" Helga asked. "What's going on?"

"My mother's missing," Ali said. "This morning she witnessed what looked to her like a bit of hanky-panky going on between April and Tracy. Early this afternoon one of the hotel security cameras recorded a confrontation between McLaughlin and my mom, but by the time I got back to the hotel to talk to her about it, she was gone—not just from our room, but from the hotel, too. The parking attendant told us he saw her peel out of the hotel garage sometime after one. I've tried calling her. No answer, and she hasn't called me back, either."

"Have you reported her missing?"

"Yes," Ali said. "Not that it did much good. No one at LAPD is particularly interested."

"So what can I do to help?" Helga asked.

"When you were doing your investigation of Paul, did Tracy McLaughlin's name come up?"

"I remember looking into the Sumo Sudoku thing because S and S Enterprises was one of your husband's newer business ventures. That name could have been mentioned, but I don't remember it in particular. I'd have to check with one of my investigators—and I probably won't be able to talk to him until tomorrow. Is there anything I can do in the meantime—anything I can do tonight?"

"I don't know," Ali said. "I can't really think straight right now."

"If you come up with something you need," Helga said, "don't hesitate to call. Have you told Victor?"

"Not yet," Ali said.

"I'll call him," Helga said. "He'll want to know what's going on."

Ali put down the phone. Dave had finished a series of calls and was once again hunkered over her computer.

"Google S and S Enterprises here in L.A.," Ali told him. "See what you get."

"S and S Enterprises holds all rights to Worldwide Sumo Sudoku," Dave said a few minutes later. "S and S was incorporated back in April with Paul Grayson named as executive director and CEO."

That announcement hit Ali hard. She had left Robert Lane early in March. No doubt negotiations for S and S Enterprises had been well under way long before Ali's departure, but she had known nothing about it. Sumo Sudoku had never been mentioned. In the scheme of Paul's betrayals, this one seemed relatively small, but it was a betrayal nonetheless.

"Who else is on the board of directors?" Ali asked.

"Guy by the name of Jake Maxwell," Dave replied.

"He worked with Paul at the network," Ali explained. "I always thought of him more as a rival than a friend, but there are lots of shifting loyalties in television, and things change. Jake showed up at court last week when the divorce was supposed to be final. He came there to back Paul up. He was also the official host of Paul's bachelor party from the night before."

Dave was still studying the computer screen. "This is interesting," he said. "S and S leases all the RVs that the various teams use. In other words, all the Sumo Sudoku guys are ultimately employees of S and S, but they're hoping to create team rivalries that will attract media attention."

"Sort of like professional wrestling?" Ali suggested.

Dave nodded. "Just about that real. According to this, the company was incorporated with the stated intention of obtaining coverage for the sport on one or the other of the sports-oriented cable channels. No doubt that's why they scheduled the filming around Paul's wedding—to garner additional media attention."

"And that's why they went forward with the shoot anyway, even though Paul was dead," Ali added. "That's how the business works. The show must go on no matter what."

"I'll say," Dave agreed.

"So let's go see him," Ali said.

"Go see who?"

"Jake," Ali said. "Jake Maxwell. The person we really need to see is Tracy, but we don't have any idea where to find him, so Jake is our next best choice."

"I've got a call in for Tracy's vehicle records," Dave said. "I'm waiting for someone to get back to me."

"Fine," Ali replied. "But in the meantime, since Jake is clearly part of all this, maybe he can point us in the right direction."

"Where do we find him?"

Ali picked up her purse. "He and his wife, Rose-anne, live out in Westlake Village."

"Where's that?" Dave asked.

"Not that far. Out the 101."

"Do we need to call first?" Dave asked.

"I think we'll just show up," Ali returned. "And we're probably better off if I drive."

"Amen to that," Dave said. "You drive. I'll handle the phones."

They left the hotel a few minutes later and headed for the 405 with Ali behind the wheel of her Cay-enne.

"Have you had anything to eat since breakfast?" Dave asked as they went.

Thinking about her mother, Ali shook her head. "I'm not hungry," she said.

"Too bad," Dave said. "Edie would want you to eat, and we're eating. Pull up at the next Burger King you see."

Ali did as she was told, and much as she didn't want to admit it, eating a Whopper did help. Back in the car, Sunday evening traffic turned what should have been a forty-minute drive into an hour and ten, most of which Ali drove in silence.

"What's going on?" Dave asked finally. "Worried about your mom?"

"That," Ali said, "and trying to get over being pissed off."

"What about?"

"This whole S and S Enterprises thing," she returned. "Obviously it was going on long before I left home last March. That kind of stuff doesn't happen in a day or even a month, but I didn't know a thing about it even though Jake and Roseanne Maxwell did."

"So?"

"Once I was in Sedona, Roseanne sent me a sugar-coated e-mail in which she pretended like she and I were the very best of friends and she thought Paul was a cad, while at the same time Jake and Paul were starting a business together. I'll never forget her cutesy little message. She kept harping on how awful it was that I was reduced to living in a trailer and having to wait tables for a living. She even offered me a place to stay—in their newly remodeled casita."

"I take it you turned her down."

"Do you think?" Ali asked with a curt nod. "But now it grates on me that I have to go see this woman and make nice with her when what I'd really like to do is smack her upside the head."

"We're doing this for your mother," Dave reminded her. "Stay cool."

Ali had no difficulty driving them to Jake and Rose-anne's sprawling, ranch-style house built on a grassy hill-side outside Thousand Oaks. At the bottom end of the long, paved driveway, an ornamental iron gate blocked the way. Ali pressed a button and a disembodied voice spoke to them through an intercom attached to the gatepost. Half a minute later, the gate swung open.

Jake Maxwell himself stepped through the tall front door and came out into the circular parking area to meet them.

"Ali," he gushed, taking her hand in both of his. "What an unexpected pleasure. How good to see you, although I can't imagine what you're going through right now."

And you don't know the half of it, Ali thought.

When Dave emerged from the far side of the car, Jake frowned slightly. "And who's this?" he added.

"Dave Holman is a friend of mine," Ali replied without any further explanation. "We have some questions for you."

"What kind of questions?" Jake asked.

"About S and S Enterprises," Ali returned. "And about a guy named Tracy McLaughlin."

Jake glanced warily from Ali to Dave and back again. It was something that wouldn't have been apparent over a phone line. Clearly Jake had been caught off guard. Ali was glad they'd put good manners aside and hadn't called in advance to warn Jake of their impending arrival.

"What about Tracy McLaughlin?" Jake asked.

"We were wondering if you knew where we could find him," Ali said casually. "A few loose ends came up after the shoot ended yesterday. I wanted to ask him about them."

"What things?"

Before Ali could answer, the door behind Jake opened. A woman wearing a pair of tight pedal pushers tottered out onto the front porch on a pair of very high heels. She was carrying a tall goblet filled with red wine.

"Didn't know we had company," she said, coming to an uncertain stop and standing, weaving, with one hand poised on her hip. "I just told Kimball to open another bottle," she said. "Anybody want to join me for a little drinky-poo?"

Kimball (Ali had no idea if Kimball was the man's first or last name) was a professionally trained butler

with a British accent and an imperious air who had
been Jake Maxwell's aide-de-camp for as long as Ali
could remember.

Ali stared. Whoever this smashed young woman
was, she sure as hell wasn't Roseanne Maxwell. And
why she felt free to order Kimball around was another
issue entirely.

"Go back inside, Amber," Jake said brusquely.
"Can't you see I'm busy?"

Amber pouted. "I was just trying to be hosp . . .
hosp . . ." she began before finally subsiding into
tongue-tied silence.

"Hospitable," Jake finished for her impatiently.
"Now do as I said. Go back inside and wait."

As in "Sit!" and "Stay!" Ali thought.

Without another word, the woman staggered back
into the house, slamming the door behind her. Jake
looked back at Ali.

"One of Roseanne's friends," he explained uncon-
vincingly. "She's staying here while she's waiting for
her new house to close. I'm afraid she had a bit too
much wine with dinner. But I'm forgetting my manners. Won't you come in?"

Amber's appearance had fueled Ali's curiosity.
Based on her own unfortunate marital experience,
nothing short of a loaded weapon would have kept her
from accepting Jake's rather halfhearted invitation.

"Thank you so much," Ali said, and headed for the
door, leaving both Dave Holman and Jake to trail along
behind her.

She saw signs of change the moment she stepped
inside the entryway. For years a flattering oil portrait
of Roseanne Maxwell had held sway just inside their

front door. That painting was no longer there. Instead, a large rectangle of slightly lighter cream paint showed where the painting had once hung. Over the massive river-rock fireplace another painting—an unframed canvas Ali recalled as featuring a modern rendition of what appeared to be sunflowers—was also missing from its place of honor. Amber was nowhere to be seen, but from some distant corner of the house came the muffled sound of a television drama.

"Don't tell me Roseanne isn't home," Ali exclaimed. "She was really kind to me last spring when everything was so awful. I wanted to thank her."

"She's in New York right now," Jake said a little too quickly. "She went with one of her friends. They're busy buying next year's clothes and taking in a couple of shows."

"Do let her know I'm sorry we missed her," Ali said. "If she returns before I leave, we'll have to have lunch."

"Of course, of course," Jake murmured. "Now, can I get you something?"

Dave shook his head. "No, thanks," he replied.

"Some ice water would be nice," Ali said.

While Jake summoned his majordomo and issued the drink order, Ali examined her surroundings. Two pieces of Dale Chihuly blown glass were missing from the ebony sideboard in the dining room. Their absence along with the missing paintings led Ali to only one conclusion. Most people don't pack their precious artwork when they go off on a weeklong shopping excursion. Roseanne's departure had to be more serious than that.

Kimball appeared, bearing a silver drinks tray

complete with an ice bucket, a collection of Baccarat crystal glasses, Voss bottled water, a decanter of wine, and a bottle of Oban single-malt scotch. With a slight bow, he deposited the tray on a side table. Then, without bothering to ask, he poured Jake a rocks glass with a tall, two-finger scotch. Meantime, Jake settled himself comfortably on a nearby love seat and crossed his legs, revealing a pair of very expensive Italian loafers.

"So what's all this about Tracy McLaughlin?" he asked.

He was trying so hard to be nonchalant and casual that an imp got into Ali Reynolds. She decided to go for the gold.

"I suppose you've heard about Paul's will?" she asked.

"Yes," Jake said with a thoughtful nod. "I heard that you got left holding the bag. It's got to be really tough, dealing with a complicated mess like that. And then, with everything else, to have April's mother fall down the stairs . . ."

"It's been tough, all right," Ali agreed. "And it's likely to get even tougher. Dave and I have reason to believe that the child April is carrying might not be Paul's after all. Since you and Paul were so close, I was wondering if you'd have any insight into that?"

Jake's face registered astonishment. "If it's not Paul's, whose baby is it?"

"She," Ali corrected. "The baby is a she. But that's what we're trying to determine—the identity of the baby's father. It's also why we're looking for Tracy McLaughlin."

Jake allowed himself a generous slug of neat Oban.

"You're thinking Tracy might be the baby's father?" he asked.

"It's possible," Ali said. "So what can you tell us about him?"

Jake peered into his glass, studying the contents. "I suppose you know that he had a bit of a rough start."

"As in being sent to prison for grand theft auto," Ali returned. "Yes, we're aware of that."

"After he got out, he came out to California, where he eventually developed this Sumo Sudoku idea. And it was a great idea—he got a trademark on it and everything. Unfortunately, at the same time, Tracy was also developing a bit of a gambling problem. Finally, he was in so deep that Paul and I bought him out. We gave him enough of an advance to pay off his debts. After he's earned that back, he'll get royalties."

"Which is how the guy who invented the whole thing ends up doing grunt labor," Ali said. "That's why he wears a kilt, lugs rocks around, and drives a leased RV."

"Something like that," Jake said.

"So is Tracy mad about that—about losing control of his brainchild to someone else?" Dave asked.

"I don't think so," Jake answered. "He wanted his debts paid off a lot more than he wanted to run things."

"What if Sumo Sudoku happens to get picked up by one of the sports networks?" Ali asked. "What happens then? Would Tracy make money?"

"We'd all make money."

"Which is why," Ali said, "even with Paul dead, April was determined to go forward with the shoot."

Jake sipped his scotch. "I suppose," he said. "But I still don't see what makes you think the baby might be

Tracy's. I mean, I've never seen any evidence of them hanging out together."

"How did Tracy get hooked up with you and Paul to begin with?" Ali asked.

"Touché," Jake said after a pause. "Now that you mention it, I guess April was the one who introduced us."

Somehow Ali didn't find that the least bit surprising.

"Do you have any idea where Tracy McLaughlin lives?" Dave asked. "We'd like to talk to him if at all possible, the sooner the better."

"No idea," Jake answered. "None at all. He lives a pretty marginal lifestyle, if you know what I mean."

"So he's still gambling?" Dave asked.

"I suppose."

"And he's still broke?"

"Most likely."

"But he would need a place to park that huge rig of his. And since your name is on the lease of that very valuable piece of equipment, I would imagine you'd know where that secret parking place might be."

"Sorry," Jake said. "I have no idea."

It was a simple answer, but as soon as Ali heard it, she knew it was a lie.

"Does he have another vehicle?" Ali asked. "Something a little smaller and easier to park?"

"Probably," Jake answered, "but I'm not sure what."

"So you just turn these guys loose with your leased RVs and don't pay any attention to where they go or what they do with them?"

"Their contracts dictate that they have to be out in public doing events for a set number of hours per week, mostly up and down the West Coast. Some of the contests we set up—like the shoot at the house yesterday. Some of the others are just pickup games— on the beach, in parks, wherever. But with the advertising on the RVs, our guys are doing their job wherever they are, even when they're just driving up and down the Five. After all, name familiarity is the name of the game."

"So you're still moving forward with this Sumo Sudoku thing?" Ali asked.

"Of course," Jake replied with absolute confidence. "There's no reason not to."

There might be, Ali thought. *I'm your new partner and I may not be quite as interested in it as Paul was.*

Amber, her empty wineglass in hand, meandered into the living room from somewhere else in the house. "Oh," she blurted vaguely, looking at Ali and Dave. "Are you still here?"

Ali took the hint and stood up. Dave followed suit while Amber staggered toward the drinks tray. Clearly the woman had had more than enough, but that didn't keep her from refilling her glass.

"Amber," Jake said warningly.

"What?" Amber seemed defiant. She dropped onto a sofa, slopping a splotch of vivid red wine onto the white silk. "What?" she said again.

Jake shook his head wearily and said nothing. Obviously Amber was a bit of a handful.

"We'll be going then," Ali said. She walked as far as the door before pausing and turning back toward their host. "When did you say Roseanne will be back?" she asked.

"I'm not sure," Jake said uneasily. "This week sometime. It was pretty open-ended. You'll let us know when the funeral is, won't you?" he asked. "She'll want to be home for that."

"I'm sure she will," Ali agreed. "Tell Roseanne I'll give her a call as soon as the services are scheduled."

Outside, the sun was down. The warm September evening had cooled under a blanket of damp marine air that had rolled in off the Pacific.

"What now?" Dave asked as they climbed into the Cayenne and buckled up.

"I'm not sure," Ali said.

She put the car in gear and drove to the bottom of the driveway. The gate opened and closed, letting them back onto the roadway. Ali drove a hundred yards or so up the road and pulled off into the approach to yet another driveway.

"What on earth are you doing?" Dave asked.

"Wait," Ali said. "Let's see what happens."

Less than a minute later, the gate to the Maxwells' place swung open and a silver Jaguar XJ convertible with the top down nosed out of the driveway and onto the road.

"Bingo," Ali said. "There he is."

"What are you going to do?"

"We're going to follow him," Ali said, putting the Cayenne in gear and pulling out well behind the Jag. "I'm guessing he'll lead us straight to Tracy McLaughlin."

"God help me," Dave groaned. "Do you know anything at all about pursuit driving?"

"Not a thing," she answered. "But I know a lot more about California drivers than you do, so you watch him and I'll drive."

Both of which were easier said than done.

Ali raced through two lights that were in the process of turning red in an effort to keep Maxwell's Jaguar in sight as he turned onto the 101 and headed back toward the city. By the time Ali merged onto the freeway, he was in the far left lane and passing everything in sight. Ali headed for the left lane as well.

"We'll never catch him," Dave protested. "Or else we'll be killed."

"We'll catch him, all right," Ali said determinedly. "And with all this traffic, he'll never know it's us."

She managed to stick with the speeding Jag for the next hair-raising ten minutes or so until Maxwell finally swerved back into the far right-hand lane and onto the Fallbrook Avenue exit. Dodging through traffic, Ali followed suit, making it onto the ramp with bare inches to spare. Once there, she slowed and dropped back far enough to allow another car to merge in ahead of them at the light.

Back on surface streets it was easier to keep the Jag in sight while maintaining a safe distance. A mile and a half later, Jake Maxwell turned into a well-lit commercial parking lot.

"Geez!" Dave grumbled. "This guy has spent the last half hour driving like a bat out of hell and endangering life and limb. And for what? To go to Wal-Mart? What's he going to do, buy a loaf of bread or a gallon of milk?"

But instead of turning up the aisle of parked vehicles that would have led toward the store's main entrance, the Jag turned left and headed off across the outermost boundary of the parking lot, stopping at last in a far corner of the property where several hulking motor homes and campers had pulled up and parked for the night. The fluorescent glow of the parking lot lights revealed that one of the assembled RVs sported a more-than-life-sized portrait of a smiling Tracy McLaughlin wearing his distinctive Sumo Sudoku kilt. Hooked onto a tow bar behind it was a spanking-new Honda Element with the paper temporary plate still in its back window.

Dave stifled his series of complaints and sat bolt upright. "I'll be damned!" he exclaimed with undisguised admiration. "I don't believe it. You were right all along. Maxwell led us straight to Tracy."

"Yes, he did," Ali agreed. "Now what?"

"Pull over, park, and kill your lights and engine," Dave directed. "We're going to hide and watch."

{ CHAPTER 14 }

So what's Jake Maxwell's deal?" Dave asked as they waited in the parking lot. "When you're doing a homicide investigation, you always go after the first person who lies. So how come Jake told us he had no idea how to get hold of Tracy when he obviously did?"

"And why didn't he just call him?" Ali asked.

"That's easy," Dave replied. "I'm guessing he's worried about leaving a phone record trail."

"He lied about Roseanne, too," Ali said.

"That's his wife?" Dave asked.

Ali nodded. "She may be shopping in New York, but I doubt it. Several important pieces of artwork—valuable pieces—are missing from Jake's walls and shelves. That tells me something's up between him and Roseanne that has nothing to do with next year's wardrobe and a whole lot to do with his pal Amber."

Learning that Roseanne Maxwell had most likely joined the ranks of Hollywood's cast-off and obsolete wives should have elicited more sympathy from Ali, but she couldn't summon it. The condescending comments Roseanne had e-mailed to Ali months earlier still rankled too much.

"Can you reach Roseanne?" Dave asked.

"Maybe," Ali replied. "I used to have her phone numbers and her e-mail address in my database, and they may still be in my computer back at the hotel. The problem is, that was months ago. If everything else has changed, her numbers may have changed as well."

"When you have a chance, try getting in touch with her," Dave said. "She may be able to help us."

The door to Tracy's RV opened. Jake emerged and slammed the door shut behind him. He stood for a few seconds as if undecided about something, then hurried back to his Jag. He peeled out of the parking place so fast that the car wobbled dangerously and almost careened into one of the parked RVs before he got the vehicle back under control.

"How much do you think he had to drink?" Dave asked.

"I don't know," Ali returned. "I doubt the scotch we saw him drink was the first he'd had this evening."

"I doubt that, too," Dave agreed. "And he's obviously of the opinion that speed limits are posted for advisory purposes only. Let's make his life a little more interesting, shall we?"

With that Dave picked up his phone. "Yes," he said when someone answered. "I'm at the Wal-Mart here on Fallbrook Avenue. A guy just took off out of the parking lot in a silver Jaguar XJ," Dave said. "He's heading back toward Highway 101 and driving like a maniac. Almost smashed into a parked RV on his way out of the lot. The way he's driving, he may be drunk."

After repeating the Jag's plate information and leaving his cell phone number, Dave closed his phone with a grin. "Let's hear it for the California Highway Patrol," he said. "Considering the mood Jake's in at the moment, any interaction with cops should prove interesting to all concerned. In the meantime, let's go have a chat with Tracy McLaughlin."

"What about?" Ali asked.

"Let's start with your mother," Dave suggested. "Again, the one thing we need to establish is if he's lying to us or telling the truth. That means we ask him questions where we already know the answers."

"Like whether or not he spoke to my mother?"

"For starters," Dave said. "And you take the lead. Tracy's an ex-con, which means he probably thinks of himself as a cool macho dude. He's likely to underestimate you and say more than he should. Try to be conversational with him and get him to talk."

"You mean sort of like what I did for years when I was conducting television interviews?" Ali asked.

Dave looked chagrined. "I suppose so," he returned. "Something like that. Sorry."

They approached the RV with Dave staying in the background. As Ali mounted the steps and knocked, she noticed a hint of cigarette smoke lingering in the outside air. It reminded her of the smoke she had smelled in the hotel hallway the night before.

"Who is it?" an invisible voice demanded.

"Ali Reynolds," she replied. "I'm Paul Grayson's wife . . . his widow actually," she corrected. "We met yesterday morning before the Sumo Sudoku shoot. I was having coffee with April Gaddis out on the terrace at the house on Robert Lane."

After a few minutes, the door opened, allowing more secondhand smoke to spill outside. Tracy McLaughlin's hulking figure stood backlit in the doorway. He held the burning stub of a cigarette in one hand and a beer in the other.

"That's right," Tracy said. "I remember you now. What do you want?"

"I'm looking for my mother," Ali said at once.

"Your mother," he repeated belligerently. "Who the hell's your mother?"

It had not been Jake Maxwell's first scotch, and this was not Tracy McLaughlin's first beer.

"Let me give you a hint," Ali said. "Her name's Edie Larson. She's in her early sixties. Gray hair. Wears glasses and a hearing aid. She's gone missing."

"Name doesn't ring a bell," Tracy muttered. "There are lots of women like that. I'm afraid I don't know your mother from a hole in the ground."

"That's funny," Ali said. "I could have sworn I saw a hotel security surveillance tape where you were talking with her earlier this afternoon—arguing with her, in fact. She seemed to be quite upset about something. The digital readout on the video shows that the confrontation happened shortly before she disappeared."

Dave emerged from the shadows.

"Who are you?" Tracy demanded when Dave came into view.

"A friend of Edie's," Dave replied. "And we have reason to believe Edie had pegged you as possibly being the father of April Gaddis's baby."

"Well, she's wrong about that," Tracy McLaughlin declared. "Besides, it wasn't any of her business to begin with. I tried to tell that crazy old woman that she had it all wrong and to get off my case, but she wouldn't listen."

"So you're claiming you're not the father of April's baby after all?" Ali asked.

"I'm saying you're talking to the wrong person. You should be asking April about this, not me."

"But you're saying the baby might not be Paul's?"

"I didn't say that."

"What are you saying?"

"It's complicated."

"It's not complicated at all," Ali said firmly. "Either the baby is Paul's or she's not. And if she isn't, she won't be eligible to receive monies from his estate."

"So what does any of this have to do with me?"

"What it has to do with is fraud," Ali replied. "And with whether or not you're a co-conspirator."

"I don't know anything," Tracy insisted. "I haven't done anything."

"What about this afternoon?" Ali asked.

"What about it?"

"What happened after you saw my mother?"

"I left the hotel."

"Where did you go?"

"A couple of places," he said.

Dave moved closer. "Ms. Reynolds isn't a police officer," he said. "But I am. At this point you're not being charged with anything, Mr. McLaughlin, so it might be smart for you to cooperate. If you have an alibi for this afternoon—a verifiable alibi—you might want to give it to us before things get any more complicated."

"What do you want from me?"

"We want you to tell us about what you did this afternoon. All of it."

"Do I need an attorney?" Tracy asked.

"Not right now," Dave said. "That's what I told you a minute ago. At the moment, finding Ali's mother is our highest priority. Compared to that, everything else takes a backseat."

Tracy had tossed one cigarette butt aside. Now he paused long enough to light another smoke. "I knew April was going to be doing that Court TV interview," he said at last. "I wanted to see how it worked out. You see, that same woman has been in touch with me—"

"Sheila Rosenburg?" Ali asked.

Tracy nodded. "She's been talking to all of April's friends. And that's what April and I are—friends."

What kind of friends? Ali wondered, although she thought she knew.

"Anyway," Tracy continued, "I wanted to see what the interview would be like—if the reporter would be on April's case and accusing her of something or other—before I agreed to do one myself. So I came into the lobby and was watching everything that was going on when that woman—your mother—showed up and started giving me a hard time and causing a scene. I left before anyone had a chance to call security."

"Why was that?" Ali asked.

"It just seemed like a good idea to get the hell out of there before there was any trouble. Besides, I didn't want to disrupt what April was doing."

"You still haven't told us where you went," Dave said. "We need names and addresses. We also need the names of any people who might have seen you there."

Tracy's reluctance to discuss the matter was obvious in the sullen way he sucked on his cigarette and said nothing.

"We've been told that you had a bad enough gambling habit that you had to sell your Sumo Sudoku idea to the highest bidder," Dave said. "Men can change, but they seldom do. So what's the story here, Tracy? Are you back in the game again? Did you spend the afternoon at a casino someplace? Or was it somewhere less obvious—like an illegal card room, maybe? And how deep are they into you again? In some circles, gambling on credit can be a very dangerous undertaking."

The look of surprise that flashed over Tracy's face made it clear Dave had nailed him. "Where's the card room?" Dave asked.

"Upstairs over a strip club on Santa Monica called the Pink Swan," Tracy answered. "I was there all afternoon. I got there about two, and then came directly here."

Ali remembered the name from newspaper accounts about Paul's death. She also remembered Helga's account of the health club called The Body Shop. She wondered if the Pink Swan was a step up or a step down.

"The Pink Swan," she mused. "Isn't that where Paul's bachelor party was held?"

Tracy nodded. "I believe so."

"You weren't at the bachelor party?"

"No."

"Why not?"

"Because I wasn't invited," Tracy answered. "I mean, Paul and I had a business relationship but we weren't really buddies or anything."

"Especially since it sounds to me as if you used to screw around with his bride-to-be," Ali put in.

Tracy looked at her, but he didn't bother denying it.

"This Pink Swan place," Dave persisted. "Would they have you on this afternoon's surveillance tapes? Would we be able to see what time you arrived there and when you left?"

"That's the whole point of a place like the Pink Swan," Tracy said. "There are no surveillance tapes."

A piece of the puzzle fell into place. If the Pink Swan was a surveillance-free zone, Ali realized, that might explain why no one had any record of Paul's exit from there. And who had been in charge of choosing the venue for the bachelor party? Presumably Jake Maxwell.

A pair of matching RVs nosed into the aisle and parked side by side directly across from Tracy McLaughlin's. Once the newly arrived vehicles were in place, several people exited. Laughing and talking, they set off across the parking lot toward the store entrance.

Tracy glanced at his watch. "Look," he said impatiently, "I'm tired. I had a big match today, and I have another one early tomorrow morning. Could we do this some other time?"

"My mother's missing now," Ali insisted. "What did Jake Maxwell want when he came here a little while ago?"

"It was just a scheduling glitch," he said. "One of the other guys canceled a match. Jake was hoping I could step in for him."

"So when Jake has a problem, he comes to you with it?" Dave asked.

Tracy nodded.

"Why didn't he call? You do have a cell, don't you?"

Tracy shrugged. "Maybe he wanted to get out of the house for a while."

"And maybe he didn't want there to be a record of his calling you," Dave suggested.

"Look," Tracy said, "I'm here, minding my own business, not bothering anyone—"

"Is that what you were doing when you spent last night in April's room?" Ali asked. "Minding your own business?"

Clearly her pointed question surprised Tracy McLaughlin. He didn't deny that, either.

"I already told you we were friends," he said. "That's what she needed last night—a friend." He tossed his dying cigarette out into the parking lot. Ali scurried down the stairs. She retrieved the smoldering butt, ground it out, and put it in her pocket.

"What are you doing?" Tracy demanded.

"You said you weren't the baby's father," she said. "It may take a few weeks to get a real answer, but your DNA should prove it one way or the other."

"I didn't give you permission to take that," Tracy began. He started down the stairs after her, but Dave stepped up and blocked his way.

"I'm not a police officer," she said. "You tossed your trash out into a public parking lot. If I want to clean up your litter, that's my call, not yours. And if I'm willing to pay for a paternity test, that's my call, too."

Ali stepped around to the back of the Honda and studied the temporary plate. "While we're at it," she added, "tell us about this vehicle. I see you just bought it—on Friday. But I was under the impression you were having a tough time financially. So where'd the money come from for a new car?"

"That's none of your business," Tracy said. "I want you to leave now, before I have to call the cops."

"I already told you," Dave said. "I am a cop."

"More cops then," Tracy said.

"By all means, call away," Ali said. "With everything that's gone on the past few days, I think they'll be interested in hearing what we all have to say."

Without another word, Tracy McLaughlin returned to his RV, slamming the door shut behind him.

"The DNA thing certainly got a reaction," Dave observed. "Now what? Back to the hotel?"

"Sure," Ali said, but once she was behind the wheel, she steered away from the entrance to the parking lot and tucked the Cayenne in among the vehicles parked near the front of the store.

"What now?" Dave asked.

"Let's just watch for a while and see if he stays put," Ali answered. "It worked once with Jake Maxwell. Maybe it'll work again with Tracy."

And it did. Less than twenty minutes later, a dark-colored Ford Windstar minivan pulled into the lot. It stopped next to Tracy's RV. The Cayenne was parked too far away for Ali and Dave to be able to make out exactly what was happening.

"Stay here," Dave said. "I'll try to get closer."

While he was out of the car, Ali's cell phone rang. "Any sign of your mother?" Bob Larson asked. Ali heard the edge of panic in her father's voice.

"Not so far," Ali returned.

"Damn," Bob muttered. "I've got a really bad feeling about this."

Ali did, too, but she didn't want to say so. "We'll

find her," Ali told her father with far more confidence than she felt. *We've got to!*

As the call ended Dave ducked into the passenger seat and then leaned back, breathing a sigh of apparent relief. "Thank God they didn't see me," he said, "but now we know how they do it."

"Do what?"

"How Sumo Sudoku can support all those very expensive RVs."

"What are you talking about?" Ali asked.

"The sudoku thing is probably nothing but an elaborate cover. I'm guessing they're really using the RVs as part of a drug distribution network, transporting drugs up and down the West Coast with their cargoholds full of something besides those round granite rocks. I'm betting they're moving heroin or else coke. They just unloaded a bunch of stuff from Tracy's RV and stuck it in the minivan. My guess is that Jake Maxwell came racing over here tonight to let Tracy know that we had been nosing around and that they needed to make arrangements to get rid of the goods sooner rather than later."

"Are you telling me Jake Maxwell and Paul got involved in some kind of drug-smuggling group?" Ali asked.

"That's how it looks."

By then the load transfer was finished and the van was pulling away from Tracy's RV. "They're leaving," Ali said. "Shouldn't we follow them?"

As Ali reached for the key, Dave caught her hand in midair and kept her from turning the key in the ignition.

"Absolutely not!" he declared. "There were three of

them at least. Four counting McLaughlin. That means we'd be outmanned—no offense—and probably outgunned, too. This is way more than you and I can handle on our own."

"We call the cops then?"

"No," Dave said.

Ali was exasperated. "You mean we're just going to let them get away?"

"For right now," Dave answered. "If we've stumbled onto a big-time drug-smuggling program, you've got to understand these people aren't to be trifled with. You try bluffing guys like that or crossing them, and they'll blow you away without a second thought. From the looks of it, this could be a very big operation, which means we're going to have to go higher up the food chain than the local LAPD cop shop."

"What do you mean?"

"Once I get back to the hotel, I'll call in the Marines."

"The Marines?" Ali repeated.

"One Marine in particular—Ezekiel Washington, if I can find him. 'Easy' for short," Dave added. "When he's not deployed with the reserves, he works for the DEA here in L.A. Once they get wind of this, they're going to want to take down the whole thing—not just Tracy McLaughlin and the guys loading the van."

They were on the 101 by then. For a while Ali drove in thoughtful silence. What Dave had said about drug dealers killing people without compunction had hit her hard. "Do you think my mother's somehow mixed up with this drug business?" she asked finally.

"She may have blundered into it the same way we did," Dave replied somberly.

Ali felt her stomach clutch. "We'll be lucky to see her alive, won't we?"

As the hours had worn on, Ali had managed to keep her worst fear at bay. Now, having spoken it aloud, she felt like she was drowning in self-reproach. Whatever befell Edie Larson would be all Ali's fault. If she hadn't let herself be bamboozled into marrying Paul Grayson in the first place, none of this would have happened. It was bad enough to learn that he'd been unfaithful to her. That much she had somehow suspected, and having it verified hadn't been all that much of a shock. But for him to have been involved in the drug trade, too? That was way beyond anything she had ever thought Paul capable of, but then she guessed she hadn't known him nearly as well as she thought she had.

Blaming herself and agonizing about her mother accomplished nothing, so she forced herself to turn back to the McLaughlin interview.

"What about the Pink Swan?" she asked.

"If it's a topless place with illegal gambling and they don't do surveillance tapes, that means they appeal to a clientele with plenty to hide."

"It's also the place where Jake hosted Paul's bachelor party."

"I'll turn Easy on to that, too. But from the sound of it, the Pink Swan is probably already on the DEA's radar."

"And then there's Roseanne," Ali added thoughtfully. "I wonder about her."

"Maxwell's wife?"

Ali nodded. "If I didn't know what was going on, I wonder if Roseanne did."

"Too bad we don't know where to find her."

"Maybe somebody does," Ali said determinedly. She passed Dave her phone. "Punch the green button. That'll give you my list of made calls. Look for Helga Myerhoff."

"Your divorce lawyer?" Dave asked. "How come?"

"She specializes in high-profile divorce cases. If Roseanne and Jake are splitting the sheets, you can figure there's a lawyer involved—or a whole bevy of them. Helga's more likely than anyone else to know which ones."

Dave found the number, pressed it, and then handed the phone to Ali.

"I didn't know they were getting a divorce," Helga said, once Ali had said her piece. "But I can't say I'd be surprised."

"Because Jake's involved with another woman?" Ali asked.

"Because they're broke," Helga returned. "Relatively speaking, of course."

Jake Maxwell hadn't looked broke earlier that evening. Anything but.

"Even in somewhat straitened circumstances, however," Helga continued, "everyone I know would have been panting after Roseanne Maxwell and hoping to land her as a client."

"How can Jake Maxwell be broke?" Ali asked.

"Lost his job, bad investments, gambling?" Helga said. "Take your pick. There are lots of ways to go broke in this town."

"You're saying Jake lost his job?" Ali asked.

"You didn't know that? It happened several months ago now—some kind of corporate job consolidation move. Paul and Jake ended up going head-to-head for the same job. Paul got the job—Jake Maxwell got a golden handshake. That's why I was a little surprised when he showed up at court on Friday to be in Paul's corner, but then sometimes people turn out to be better than you think they are."

Or worse, Ali thought.

"Getting back to Roseanne," Helga finished. "I do have some connections. If she's holed up somewhere, someone I know will be able to find her."

"Thanks."

"Victor wanted you to call. Have you talked to him yet?"

"No."

"If you're driving all over hell and gone, you should probably let him know from you exactly what you're up to."

Ali knew what Victor would say—stay put; don't talk to anyone; let the cops look for her mother.

"I'll call him," Ali agreed. *Eventually.*

Once off the phone, she recounted to Dave everything that had been said. "Makes sense," he said. "If Jake was needing to make some quick cash, someone may have made him an offer he couldn't refuse."

"But Paul wasn't broke," Ali returned. "Why would he be mixed up in it?"

Dave shook his head. "I have no idea."

By then they were pulling into the hotel entrance. "Do you want me to come up?" Dave asked.

"No," she said. "Dad and Chris will be here soon. I'm going to take a shower and put my feet up for a few minutes. I may even try closing my eyes."

"Good idea," Dave said. He hopped out of the Cayenne and headed for his own car.

Ali handed her car keys over to the parking valet and headed straight into the lobby. If there were reporters waiting there, she'd tough her way through them.

Opening the door to her room Ali hoped, through some miracle, Edie would be there waiting for her, but of course she wasn't. The room was empty—dark and empty. Ali slipped off her shoes, sank onto the couch, and, as promised, rested her feet on the coffee table. She had spent the last hours busily doing something—playing detective and trying to find her mother. Now, in the quiet stillness, the awful reality began to sink in. Perhaps Edie really was lost to her— lost to all of them. Perhaps there would be no more of Edie's steaming, soft-centered homemade sweet rolls at Sedona's Sugar Loaf Café. Perhaps Ali would never again sit over a hot cup of coffee, listening to and often disregarding her mother's good advice. Perhaps she would never again witness one of her parents' never-ending rounds of good-natured teasing.

It was that realization—that losing her mother would be harder on Bob Larson than on anyone else— which finally goaded Ali to action. She picked up her computer and logged on.

CUTLOOSEBLOG.COM
Sunday, September 18, 2005

My mother is missing. Edie Darlene Larson, age 61, of Sedona, Arizona, disappeared from a hotel lobby in L.A. early this afternoon. She was last seen driving away from the

Westwood Hotel on Wilshire in her white
2003 Oldsmobile Alero. Edie is five foot
seven, has medium-length gray hair, fair skin,
and weighs approximately 140 pounds. She
also wears two hearing aids. (She'll kill me for
printing that.) Anyone with information about
Edie should contact LAPD's Missing Persons
Unit—and me!

    Posted 10:23 P.M., September 18, 2005 by
  Babe

There was far more she wanted to say, would have said, but this was a case where less was more. She deliberately made no mention of Edie's encounter with Tracy McLaughlin. If, as Dave suspected, this whole thing was tied to a drug-smuggling ring, it was better to leave that out. Ali stripped off her clothes and was about to step into the shower when her cell phone rang. Grabbing it off the counter, she was amazed to see her mother's name in the caller ID readout.

Sick with relief, Ali shouted into the phone, "Mom! Is that you? Are you all right? Where are you?"

Except there was no answer. Ali could hear a rustling sound and distant voices, but no one was talking directly to her. Maybe it was just a bad connection. Frustrated, Ali punched the volume button on the side of her phone. "Mom. Can you hear me?" she called again.

There was more rustling and then she heard her mother's voice. "What in the world do you think you're doing?"

"I'm trying to talk to you," Ali answered. "Where are you? What's going on?"

Someone else—another woman—was speaking in the background. Ali could hear the voice but not clear enough to make out any of the individual words.

"You need to let me go," Edie said clearly and firmly. "This is stupid. It makes no sense."

That's when Ali realized she was listening in on what people at the Sugar Loaf called Edie's infamous "bra calls." Because that's where Edie Larson always carried her phone—in her bra. At work her apron pockets usually overflowed with order pads and pencils. When she had added a cell phone into the mix, it hadn't worked, so she had opted for stowing her phone in the only other available spot—tucked inside her bra. Because Edie didn't always remember to activate her key guard, she occasionally made accidental calls, burning up minutes and inadvertently revealing all kinds of mundane details of life in a restaurant to several different hapless recipients.

Ali knew at once, however, that this call was no accident. Whoever was with Edie had no idea she was in possession of a cell phone. They also had no idea she had figured out a way to signal for help. And instead of dialing 911, Edie had simply punched "send."

There was a murmured answer in response to her mother's comment, but nothing Ali could make out.

"Why are you doing this?" Edie demanded, sounding more agitated. "Where are we? In a basement somewhere?"

So her mother had been blindfolded or maybe even unconscious. She had no idea where she was, and she was being held there against her will.

Ali strained to hear the other woman's response, but it was totally inaudible.

Then Ali heard her mother's voice again. "Untie me," she said. "Let me go. I'm sure we can sort all this out."

There was a momentary pause followed by a burst of outrage. "We're not going to sort it out. We're not sorting anything. Stop telling me what to do, damn it! Just stop it!"

And now that Ali heard the voice clearly, she knew whose it was—April's. The voice belonged to April Gaddis. How could that be?

"Please, April," Edie said aloud. "Be reasonable."

But April had evidently moved beyond reason. "Shut up!" she screamed. "Shut the hell up!"

April's shout was followed by the sounds of a brief struggle complete with lots more rustling and a sharp clatter. In her mind's eye, Ali imagined the phone falling out of Edie's bra and skittering across some hard surface. In her ears, the noise was deafening, but Edie's attacker didn't seem to notice. There were other sounds, too—the horrifying thumps of something heavy landing on human flesh. Knowing her mother was most likely bound and helpless, Ali cringed at each one. At last the struggle ended in a terrible groan and a spate of ragged breathing.

"There now," April said very clearly. "Maybe now you'll finally shut the hell up and stay where I put you."

Ali heard a door slam shut followed by an awful silence on the other end of the line. By some miracle the call was still connected.

"Mother?" Ali called. "Are you there? Can you hear me?"

But of course there was no reply. If Edie Larson was even still conscious, she couldn't hear her daughter's voice.

For a moment longer Ali stared at the phone in an agony of indecision. The phone in her hand was her only connection to her mother, but where was she? If Ali dialed 911 on her room phone, what would she say to them? "My mother's been attacked somewhere in L.A. I have no idea where." Or, was it possible there was an emergency operator somewhere who could trace the call between Ali's cell phone and wherever it was her mother was being held, injured, perhaps, or maybe even unconscious? But how long would that take? And even if Ali managed to maintain the connection for a while, could she keep it going long enough? What would happen when Edie's phone ran out of battery power and turned itself off?

Closing her eyes, Ali tried to decide what to do. Wherever April had taken Edie, it had to be a place to which April had ready access. And Edie had mentioned something about a basement. This was California, an area where basements weren't all that common, but Ali knew where there was at least one basement—a huge one—in the bottom of the house on Robert Lane.

More than half of the space had been and still was devoted to Paul's extensive wine collection, but there had been several other rooms as well, including a decommissioned redwood-lined sauna that Paul had considered turning into a safe room. Thinking about the way the heavy door had slammed shut behind April as she'd left, Ali had the sudden sense that she knew the answer. She wasn't confident enough in her idea that she was willing to place an emergency call based on it, but she did know for sure that there wasn't a moment to lose.

With the call still connected and on speaker, Ali dressed and strapped on her Glock. She paused only long enough to call for her car before grabbing for her purse.

Riding down in the elevator, Ali realized that taking on someone as seemingly deranged as April all by herself was nothing short of stupid. Once more she considered ending the one call and dialing 911. But again, what would she tell them? *Let's see. How about: "My mother's been attacked by my dead husband's pregnant fiancée who may or may not be holding her prisoner somewhere in my house on Robert Lane"?* Did that sound like a call emergency operators were likely to take seriously? And even if they did, if April had come unhinged, what would she do if a bunch of cop cars came screaming into the yard? With Edie possibly injured and alone in the house with April, that was a risk Ali wasn't prepared to take.

While she was riding down in the elevator, the call ended on its own. Either her mother's phone had run out of power, or Ali's had simply lost the signal. Frustrated, Ali tried calling Dave. He didn't answer, so she left a terse message.

"On my way to the house. I think April's there, but I'm not sure. I also think she's lost it. Wherever she is, I believe she's holding Mom prisoner. Call me as soon as you get this message. Please."

Scrambling into the Cayenne, Ali rammed it into gear. Heading for the house, she was reasonably confident that in a fair fight—a one-on-one altercation—she would be able to take April.

And I have no intention of fighting fair, Ali told herself grimly. *None whatsoever!*

{ CHAPTER 15 }

Ali should have been pulled over a dozen times between the hotel and the house. She drove at breakneck speeds, passing like a maniac, going through lights that were already turning red. She almost hoped she could provoke an observant traffic cop into following her. Maybe having cops there was a good idea after all, and that was one way to summon some police presence without having to explain her soap opera existence to some emergency operator. But it didn't happen. When Ali finally sped through the broken gate and pulled to a stop in the paved driveway, she was still on her own. Dave hadn't called her back, and she couldn't take the time to call him again.

It's now or never, she told herself.

Before Ali ever stepped out of the car, she considered drawing her Glock but decided against it. Her plan was to try talking first. The Glock would come into play only as a last resort.

Ali was disappointed to find no sign of April's bright red Volvo there in the driveway, and no sign of Edie

Larson's Olds, either. It was possible both cars were parked in the spacious five-car garage. Maybe that was where they had been parked when Ali and Dave had come to the house earlier and decided no one was there. It was also possible, Ali realized, that she was wrong and there was no one at the house now, either.

Hurrying up onto the porch, Ali reached past a tangle of crime scene tape and tried the front door. It was locked. Ali headed for the back of the house, wondering as she went if the alarm system had ever been reengaged. She tried the slider from the pool patio into the family room. No luck. That was locked, too. Finally she tried the door into the kitchen. The knob turned easily in her hand.

"I wondered how long it would take you to get here," April said.

Ali stopped just inside the door. April was across the room, seated on a chair at the kitchen table. A pistol Ali recognized as one of Paul's lay nearby on the tabletop, well within April's reach. Ali knew that had she come into the house with her own weapon drawn, they both might have died in a hail of gunfire.

"What's going on?" Ali demanded. "What have you done to my mother?"

"She kept trying to tell me what to do. I got sick of it. So I decided to show her a thing or two."

"My mother told you what to do so you're holding her prisoner in the basement? Are you nuts?"

"Maybe," April conceded. "Maybe a little."

Ali took a step into the room. As soon as she did, April picked up the gun and pointed it in Ali's direction. "Don't come any closer," she said. "Put your hands behind your head and stay where you are."

"Is my mother hurt?" Ali asked.

"I didn't hit her that hard," April said. "I was tired of listening to her. I just wanted her to shut up."

"I asked you if my mother's all right."

"She's still breathing, if that's what you want to know," April allowed. "I came upstairs to get more duct tape. When I went back down, I found her phone. I heard it ringing. Someone named Bobby called— whoever that is."

Bobby was Robert Larson, Ali's father, although Edie hardly ever called her husband by that pet name to his face.

"And that's when I saw Edie had called you," April continued.

"You're right," Ali agreed. "She did call me, and I heard everything that was said between you, April. All of it. And when she mentioned being in a basement, I knew you had to be holding her here at the house. But why? What do you think you're doing? What's this all about? Whatever it is, we've got to put a stop to it."

"We?" April returned bitterly. "There you go doing the same thing your mother did—ordering me around, telling me what to do. Why does everyone think they can get away with that? It's been that way all my life. It's like people think that just because someone is pretty they're also stupid. I'm not, you know."

"What exactly did my mother tell you to do?" Ali asked.

"She told me to stop smoking—like I was in junior high. She sounded just like my mother. Exactly like my mother. It was like a flashback or something."

"So your mother was always ordering you around,

too?" Ali asked the question more to sustain the conversation than anything else. She knew she needed to keep April talking while she figured out what to do next.

"Are you kidding?" April demanded. "Don't try to tell me you didn't notice. She was the worst one of all—talking to the lawyers, firing the cook and the gardener, acting like it was her house and her life instead of mine."

For the first time it occurred to Ali that April herself might have been responsible for her mother's fatal plunge down the stairs.

"Your mother was trying to look out for you," Ali said reasonably. "For you and your baby both."

"Screw the baby," April said. "I never even wanted a damned baby. I never should have told Paul about it in the first place. He's the one who talked me into keeping it. If it had been up to me, I would have had an abortion just like I did those other times. But as soon as Paul knew about it, he was wild to get married, have the baby and everything."

April's words hit Ali hard. She remembered that she and Paul had talked some about having kids shortly after they married, but Chris was already a teenager by then. Ali had been happy with the way her career was going. She hadn't wanted to start the motherhood program over again, especially knowing full well that no matter how much paid help she'd have had, most of the responsibility for the new arrival would fall to her. She had already raised one only child. She hadn't wanted to do that again, but she certainly hadn't wanted to have two more children, either. So she hadn't exactly said no to Paul, but she hadn't ever stopped taking her birth control pills, either. The upshot of that had been that Paul had resented Chris—resented everything about Chris—and had never really accepted him.

Once Ali had learned about April, she had moved out of the house. In the months since then, she had blamed Paul for everything that had been wrong with their marriage. Now, though, standing with her fingers locked around the back of her neck, facing her husband's armed mistress across an expanse of kitchen, Ali Reynolds came face-to-face with her own culpability. For the first time she had to admit that it had taken two people to destroy her marriage—three, counting April.

But that wasn't the real issue here. The real bottom line had to do with April and her gun. If she had gone totally off her rocker, was anyone going to come out of this confrontation alive?

"You killed your mother?" Ali asked.

"What if I did?" April replied. "It was an accident. We were arguing in the upstairs hallway. It got physical. I pushed her and down she went."

April's dispassionate confession was calm, conversational, and utterly chilling.

"But she was still alive when she landed," Ali argued. "She was still alive hours later when we found her. Why didn't you try to help her? Why didn't you call for an ambulance?"

"Because I didn't want to help her," April returned. "Because I was tired of having her scream at me. I just left her where she was and went shopping. I figured someone else would find her eventually, and I was right."

"My mother never screamed at you," Ali said.

"No," April agreed. "But every time I was around her, she kept telling me what I should and shouldn't be doing for the baby. Smoking is bad for the baby. Drinking is bad. Eating spicy food is bad. Coffee is bad. I'm sick and tired of the damned baby. She's not even born yet, and even Sonia Marie gets to tell me what to do."

She really is crazy, Ali thought. *Totally nuts!*

"How did my mother get here to the house?" Ali asked.

"She figured it out," April said.

"Figured what out?"

"About my mother. She came to my room after the interview while I was changing clothes. She saw the scratches on my arms and asked me about them, so I decided to get rid of her, too. And since she liked the baby so much, I used the baby against her. I came here to the house and then I called Edie. I told her where I was and that I needed her to come quick and pick me up because my contractions had started. Worked like a charm. She couldn't get here fast enough. She was surprised when I pulled the gun on her, though. I think she thought I was kidding. I wasn't."

So Edie's ability to see through people was what had gotten her in trouble.

"My arms are getting tired," Ali said. "My hands are going to sleep. Can I put them down now?"

"Stay on that side of the room then," April ordered. "Over against the sink. Don't come any closer."

"What about Paul?" Ali asked, changing the subject ever so slightly. "Did he ever tell you what to do?"

"Sort of," April admitted. "I didn't mind that much because he was nice about it, at least at first. It got worse after I moved in here. That's when I really noticed it. He started sounding more and more like my mother. He was closer to her age, you know—closer to hers than he was to mine."

"You killed him, too, then?" Ali asked.

"Of course I didn't kill him," April said indignantly. "I keep telling you, I'm not stupid. Why would I kill Paul when we weren't married and he hadn't even signed his new will yet? That makes no sense."

"I thought you didn't know whether or not he had signed it."

"There are a lot of things I know that people don't think I know," April returned with a grim smile. "That's the one nice thing about people thinking I'm stupid. They always underestimate me."

April had already nonchalantly admitted to one murder, and Ali knew she had most likely attempted another. Given that, when she denied having been involved in Paul Grayson's death, Ali had to concede there was a possibility April was telling the truth.

"So what are you going to do now?" Ali asked.

"What do you mean?"

"You've admitted to me that you killed your own mother. You've attacked mine, and you're holding her prisoner. You're holding me at gunpoint. How is this all going to end, April? Do you have a plan?"

"Not really," April said with a shrug of her shoulders. "After everything that's happened, I really don't care that much one way or the other."

To Ali's ear, that sounded very much like an implied suicide threat. Dealing with someone in that distraught state who was also armed with a lethal weapon was a very bad idea.

"What if I've called the cops?" Ali asked.

April shrugged again. "If you had, they'd be here by now."

"What if I've called someone else?"

"You're bluffing."

"Tell me about Tracy McLaughlin."

"What about him? He's a friend of mine and a lot closer to my age than anybody else around here."

"How good a friend?" Ali asked.

"That's what your mother wanted to know, too," April said bitterly. "She even asked me if Trace was the father of my baby. Of course he isn't. You think I'm dumb enough to try passing somebody else's baby off as Paul's? What if he'd asked for a paternity test? What do you think would have happened to me then? If the baby wasn't his, I would have been out in the cold, just like I am anyway. So what does it matter?"

"Look," Ali said, trying to sound reassuring. "Let's go down to the basement and check on my mother. Once I'm sure she's all right, we can work together to figure out what's best for you and for your baby."

"You still don't get it, do you?" April said. "It's over."

"What's over?"

"There's not going to be a baby. I'm going to end this whole thing today. Now. What kind of a life would Sonia Marie have with her father dead and me in prison? Even if the cops arrest Jesus Sanchez, sooner or later they're going to figure out what really happened, the same way your mother did. Then they'll come after me. What's the point?"

"You might be in prison, but the baby would be alive."

"Somehow I don't think that's much of a favor. I already told you, there isn't going to be a baby. Come to think of it, maybe I'll burn this house down while I'm at it. That would be pretty funny, wouldn't it? If you're gone and I'm gone and the baby's gone, who gets Paul's money then?" April's question trailed off in a mirthless giggle.

Before Ali could attempt an answer, her phone rang. She pulled it out of her pocket. A glance at the caller ID window told her it was Dave calling.

"It's my father," Ali said to April. "I need to take this call. Otherwise he might come here looking for me."

April nodded. "All right," she said. "Answer it."

Ali pressed the "talk" button.

"Hi, Dad," she said with forced cheerfulness. "How close are you?"

"Dad!" Dave repeated. "I'm not your father. It's Dave, for God's sake. Don't you ever check the caller ID before you answer? And what the hell do you mean, going over to the house all by yourself?—"

"No," Ali said calmly, interrupting his angry outburst. "We still haven't found her. I called in a report to Missing Persons, but I haven't gone to the cops directly. If you want to, that's up to you."

"What's going on—" Dave stopped abruptly, and then seemed to tumble. "I see," he said. "It's April, isn't it? I'm almost at the house now, just turning up the hill. I'll be there in a matter of minutes."

Somehow Dave Holman was managing to sort through what Ali was saying and arrive at what she needed him to hear. *God bless this man!* she thought.

"Yes, Dad," Ali said. "It's a very nice hotel. Don't

worry. You'll be able to get something to eat. Even if the kitchen is closed when you get there, they have twenty-four-hour room service."

"The kitchen, then," Dave said. "You want me to come to the kitchen. Is she armed?"

"Absolutely," Ali answered. "We'll find her, Dad," she added less vehemently. "I know we will."

"When you see me, try to create a diversion. Or else I will."

"Okay, Pops," Ali said. "See you soon."

She ended the call.

"Turn the phone off and put it on the counter," April said. "You're not taking any more calls."

Ali put the phone down.

"Still," April added wistfully, "it must be nice having a whole family you can call on and have them come riding to the rescue at a moment's notice."

Ali was still standing just to the right of the door. The kitchen window was behind her. If Dave approached the kitchen from that direction, April would see him, and she'd have a shot at both of them. If Ali could manage to distance herself from the door, April's attention would be split.

"You do have that kind of family," Ali said. "You've had it all along. That's what my mother was trying to do— help you. Your mother was doing the same thing. They were both trying to give you some hard-won advice to help you through this terrible time."

As she spoke, Ali moved past the sink, but April noticed.

"Where do you think you're going?" she demanded. "I told you to stay there."

Ali's heart pounded in her chest. Summoning as

much nonchalance as she could muster, she reached up in the cupboard and took down a glass.

"I'm thirsty," Ali said. "I need a drink of water. Do you want some?"

April shook her head.

Taking that as permission, Ali proceeded over to the fridge, where she used the door dispenser to fill the glass with both ice and water. She was relieved to see that April's attention remained focused on her. Unfortunately, so did the gun. Ali's move to the fridge meant she was closer to the weapon now, as well. The barrel seemed immense. And it must have been heavy, too. April's hand seemed to tremble as she tried to hold it steady.

Ali took a deep breath. If she attempted to reason with April, what were the chances she'd simply provoke the disturbed woman that much more? And how much longer would it take for Dave to get here? And when all hell broke loose, where in this high-tech granite and stainless steel kitchen would she look for cover? Ali was far more accustomed to dealing with the world through words than she was with weapons.

"Please, April," she said. "This is pointless. Put the gun down."

As Ali had feared, April did the exact opposite. Rather than putting the pistol down, she raised it and pointed it toward herself. Out of the corner of her eye, Ali caught a hint of movement at the kitchen door. Dave was there. He had approached from the opposite side without passing the window and without being seen while April's life hung in the balance.

Dropping the glass, Ali sprang forward. She reached across the table and slammed one closed fist into April's wrist. At the same time she straight-armed April in the chest with her other arm. Caught off guard and off balance, April spilled backward. The gun exploded with a roar. So did one of the glass pendant light fixtures over the counter. April landed on her back with a grunt. The force of the fall was enough that the gun bounced out of her hand and went spinning across the floor, where it came to rest against the base of the dishwasher. While April struggled to right herself, Ali scrambled after the gun.

"Ali," Dave was shouting. "Are you okay? Did she get you?"

Holding the pistol in one hand and shaking her head, Ali struggled to her feet as Dave helped April to hers. April was crying. There was blood on her face from what looked like a series of jagged cuts, but not from a self-inflicted gunshot wound. That meant Ali's desperate measure had succeeded.

"Why didn't you just let me do it?" April demanded tearfully. "Why can't you people just leave me alone? Why don't you mind your own business?"

It was a moment or two before Ali could find her own voice. Trembling, she examined her body and was more than half surprised to find no gaping wounds.

"I'm okay," she managed at last. "At least I think I am."

In the background now, she could hear the sound of approaching sirens. So Dave had called for backup. He just hadn't waited for reinforcements to arrive before coming to the door. For that Ali was incredibly grateful.

Without another word, Ali left April's gun on the counter and raced for the stairs that led to the basement. She dashed past Paul's loaded wine racks and through the media room. Just as she expected, she found Edie in the decommissioned sauna—duct-taped to the slats of the wooden bench. Another piece of duct tape covered her mouth. Her eyes were wide open.

Cringing, Ali peeled the tape off her mother's mouth, removing a good deal of skin along with it.

"Are you all right?" Ali asked.

"Just let me at that little nutcase," Edie replied. "I'll tear her limb from limb. Did I hear gunshots?"

Ali nodded while she struggled to loosen Edie's other restraints, starting with her arms. "You did hear gunshots," Ali said. "One, at least. Fortunately she missed. Dave is upstairs with her, waiting for the cops to get here. If they're not here already, they will be any minute. Are you all right?"

"I'm more mad than hurt," Edie replied. "She gave me a good crack on the back of the head. I was out for a while, and my head hurts like crazy. What in the world is the matter with that girl?"

There was no way to answer that question.

As Ali worked to free her mother from her restraints, footsteps pounded across the kitchen and down the stairs. "Where are you?" Dave demanded.

"Down the hall," Ali called back. "In the sauna."

Dave's anxious face appeared in the doorway a moment later. "Is Edie here? Is she okay?"

With the last of the tape removed, Edie tried to get to her feet. She stood briefly, but even with Ali helping her, she swayed a little and sat back down abruptly. "I guess I'm still a little woozy," she said.

"An ambulance is already on the way," Dave said.

"What's going on upstairs?" Ali asked.

"When April saw the uniforms, she fought the cops tooth and nail, but they have her in custody now. They're putting her in a patrol car or an ambulance."

A uniformed cop showed up in the sauna just then, followed immediately by two more. "Is the other lady all right?" one of them asked.

"I'll be a whole lot better once you get me out of here," Edie Larson said, rising again. "I never have liked saunas. They make me feel claustrophobic."

For good reason, Ali thought.

"Ma'am," one of the cops said. He didn't look to be much older than Chris. "Are you sure you should be moving around like this? Wouldn't you be better off sitting back down and waiting here for the EMTs to come take a look at you?"

"Young man," Edie said firmly, "I'm not staying in this room for another minute. Now either help me out of here or else get out of the way so I can do it on my own." With that, Edie turned to Ali. "Call your father," she ordered. "Let him know I'm all right. If you've told him about any of this, he's probably worried sick."

That was when Ali knew for sure Edie was all right.

As the clutch of uniformed officers helped Edie out of the sauna and down the hall, Dave handed Ali his phone. "Call your dad," he said.

Bob and Chris had arrived at the hotel by then, and they were jubilant when they heard the news. "I can't believe you and Dave pulled it off!" Bob Larson exclaimed.

Ali gave Dave a sideways look. "I can't, either," she said. "But we did."

"And everybody's all right?"

"They're taking Mom to an ER to be checked out.

She has a nasty lump on her head and was a little shaky on her feet. She may have a slight concussion."

"Which hospital?"

"Cedars-Sinai," Ali answered. "Ask Chris. He'll know how to get there."

"What about you?" Bob asked.

"I'm fine," Ali said. And she had been fine while she was helping her mother. But now she could feel tears welling up in her eyes as she spoke to her father. "I'll talk to you later."

She handed the phone over to Dave, trying to dodge his questioning glance as she did so, trying not to let him see that her hands were shaking and her knees knocking. Ali sank down on the redwood bench, and Dave sat down beside her.

"You're not fine," he said, wrapping a comforting arm around her shoulder. "You're not fine at all."

{ CHAPTER 16 }

They sat together for some time, with Ali simply leaning into Dave's shoulder and gathering her strength. "Thank you," she said at last. "Thank you for being here and thank you for listening to what I meant as opposed to what I said."

"You're welcome," he said. "Better now?"

She nodded.

"Good," he said, "because it's about time to go back upstairs and give another statement."

"And call Victor again?"

"I think we can pass on calling Victor this time."

The officer who took Ali's statement was one of the Eagle Scout–looking uniforms who had helped Edie make her way back upstairs.

"So this whole thing came about because your mother and this April Gaddis had some kind of disagreement?"

"Evidently," Ali said.

"And what exactly is your relationship to the perpetrator—or your mother's, for that matter?"

Ali sighed. "April Gaddis is my dead husband's

mistress. My dead husband's pregnant mistress. They were supposed to get married yesterday, but he was murdered early Friday morning and died before our divorce became final."

The young man frowned. Concentrating as he wrote, he made no comment about Ali's very complicated life, and Ali greatly appreciated his lack of editorial input.

"And the cause of the difficulty between April and your mother?" he continued.

"Mom tried to tell April she shouldn't be smoking when she's pregnant."

"Makes sense to me," the young cop said. His name was Rich Green, and maybe he really was an Eagle Scout.

Officer Green took the information from both Ali and Dave in a methodical manner. He was thorough. He was patient. He was also slow as Christmas. By the time he finally finished, Ali was ready to strangle him.

"So where did they take April?" Ali asked when the ordeal was finally over. "And what about my mother?"

"They were both supposed to be transported to Cedars-Sinai," Officer Green told them. "But I believe your mother decided against going at the last moment. Said she had a perfectly good hotel room and that would be fine. All she wanted was to see her husband and get a good night's sleep."

That sounded like Edie.

"And April?" Ali asked.

"She went to the hospital."

"Cedars-Sinai? They have a psych ward there?" Ali asked.

"I'm not sure about a psych ward," Officer Green

returned. "I believe one of the EMTs said something about her going into labor."

Ali's heart constricted in her chest. "But I just told you. April Gaddis was holding both my mother and me at gunpoint. She's been waving a pistol around and threatening suicide. She should be on a suicide watch."

"I'm sure the EMTs who transported her conferred with the supervisor on the scene before they took her anywhere. Do you want me to call and check?"

Ali could imagine how long it would take Officer Green to navigate through any kind of bureaucratic roadblock.

"No, thanks," Ali said. "Don't bother. I'll find out for myself."

"The hospital?" Dave asked, following Ali out to where his car was parked directly behind hers.

"You don't have to come," Ali said.

"I'm coming," Dave declared.

"All right then," Ali agreed. "The hospital."

It was after two A.M. when both vehicles pulled into the hospital parking lot. The hospital was locked down tight. A security guard met them at the main door and led them to a lobby counter.

"We're here to see a patient," Ali said to the clerk seated in front of a computer screen. "She's on the maternity ward. Her name is April Gaddis."

The clerk typed something into her keyboard, then looked back at Ali with a frown. "Are you a relative?" she asked.

Clearly the clerk was less than prepared to hand out any information. And with the new federal privacy rules, Ali knew she was fighting an uphill battle. She tried to lighten the mood.

"Not a relative," Ali said breezily. "Just a good friend. I'm going to be the baby's godmother."

"Excuse me," the clerk said, rising. "If you'll just wait here. I need to check with a supervisor."

"Not good," Dave said under his breath. "When they have to go check with a supervisor, it's never a good sign."

A few minutes later a formidable black woman emerged from a closed door behind the desk. "I'm a supervisor, Audrey Barker. May I help you?" she asked.

"I came to see April Gaddis," Ali said. "She's a patient here—a maternity patient. She was brought here by ambulance a couple of hours ago."

"And what is your relationship to Ms. Gaddis?" Audrey Barker asked. "Are you a relative?"

"As I already told the other woman, I'm not a relative—just a good friend."

"Would you happen to know the names of any of Ms. Gaddis's relatives? She told us her mother is deceased."

"Monique Ragsdale *is* deceased," Ali answered. She was starting to get a bad feeling from all the questions. Surely coming to visit a patient didn't usually result in the visitors being given this kind of third degree.

"Do you know of any others or how we could contact them?"

"I never met her father," Ali said. "And as far as I know, April is an only child. She used to have a step-brother, but not anymore. Why?"

"But you and she are good friends?"

"Yes," Ali said at once, carefully avoiding meeting Dave's eye as she said so. "Why?"

"Because," Audrey Barker said kindly, "I'm afraid I have some very bad news."

CUTLOOSEBLOG.COM
Monday, September 19, 2005

First of all, my mother is safe. She was found a few hours after I posted that last message. She was slightly hurt in the process but not enough that she required either treatment or hospitalization. Thanks so much to those of you who wrote to express your concern.

This has been a dreadful week. My husband is dead. So is his girlfriend and so is their unborn baby. My husband was found murdered late last week and I remain a "person of interest" in that homicide. April Gaddis, his girlfriend and the mother of his unborn child, committed suicide after being admitted to the maternity ward of Cedars-Sinai Hospital. I'm able to report her name here because April's next of kin, her long-estranged father, has now been located and notified.

Overwhelmed by events, April suffered some kind of breakdown. In the process she not only murdered her own mother, she ended up holding two other people at gunpoint. My mother was one of the two. I was the other. When officers finally arrived at the second scene, April was taken into custody and transported by ambulance to the hospital after convincing EMTs she was about to give birth. Once there, she went into the bathroom of her hospital room, supposedly to change clothes. Instead, she somehow managed to hang herself.

During my years in the news business, I remember using the words "senseless violence" on occasion. And the words apply here as well. A whole family has been wiped out—one that would have been my husband's second family. Four people are dead, including a baby who never had a chance to draw her first breath and a grandmother who never saw her granddaughter's face.

In the process, my own life has been threatened. So has my mother's. I've also been accused of murder. In the course of all the turmoil, things became so complicated that I was told to avoid blogging entirely for fear I might end up saying something in my commentary that would be considered self-incriminating. (As you can see by this post, I'm not always good about taking advice from attorneys—even when I'm paying them big bucks to give me that selfsame advice.)

Putting all that together, you can probably understand that when I came dragging back to my hotel this morning at a little past four, I was feeling more than a little shattered, to say nothing of exhausted. To top it all off, my faith in the human race was pretty much obliterated. My mother, who had been missing, had been found safe, but I was too tired to count that as a blessing right then.

She had been endangered for no other reason than she is my mother, who had come to L.A. to help me with my mounting difficulties. I believe this can be filed under the heading of "No Good Deed Goes Unpunished."

In other words, everything that had happened had been more than I could handle—and then some. So once I finally made it back to my hotel and dropped my car off with the valet, I staggered into the lobby intent on going straight up to my room to go to sleep. Halfway across the lobby I was waylaid and greeted by name by someone I knew but had never met in person.

She was an older lady with bright blue eyes and a halo of thinning snow-white hair. She was sitting on a couch just inside the entrance. Parked next to her was a walker that sported red, white, and blue tennis balls and a tiny American flag. She stood up the moment she saw me. "There you are, Babe," she said. "How's your mom?"

Those of you who have been following cutloose for some time will recognize the name Velma T of Laguna. She had read my previous post, the one that said my mother was missing. She was so concerned about what was going on that she ended up doing some detective work of her own. She figured out where I must be staying, and came here— in a cab!!!! When I told her my mother was safe, she simply smiled and nodded. "I know," she said. "I've been praying for her all night."

I offered to give Velma T a ride back home, but she turned me down. "You look tired, honey," she said. "You'd better get some sleep. I got here under my own steam, and I'll get home the same way."

And so, with my faith in humanity restored by an eighty-eight-year-old bundle of goodwill, I came up here to my room, stripped off my clothes, and slept like a baby. Without moving a muscle. When I woke up late this morning and logged on to my computer, there were 87 messages in my in-box, almost all of them expressing concern for my mother. (Please pardon me if I don't respond to all of them.) A few of the ones from this morning were from people who had already learned from some other source that my mother had been found. I guess by now I should be accustomed to the amazing immediacy of the Internet community, but I'm still learning. And I'm still grateful.

I have no idea when bodies will be released for burial or to whom, so I have no idea how long it will take for funeral arrangements to be made. As a consequence, I have no idea how much longer I'll be in the area. But believe me, I'm more than ready to go back home to Arizona. Sedona is sounding pretty inviting to me about now.

Posted 11:43 A.M., September 19, 2005 by Babe

Ali had made arrangements to have brunch in the hotel dining room with her parents and Chris. To get there, she had to make her way through the lobby. Once again there was a gaggle of camera- and microphone-wielding reporters waiting for her.

"Ms. Reynolds, Ms. Reynolds," one of them shouted as Ali exited the elevator. "Are you all right? Is your mother okay?"

Ali started to walk past without answering, but then, remembering they were only doing their jobs, she relented and decided to get it over with. She stopped and spoke directly into one of the cameras. "My mother is fine," she said. "So am I."

"At the time April Gaddis was holding you and your mother at gunpoint, did either of you suspect that she intended to commit suicide?" another reporter wanted to know.

"I did everything in my power to keep it from happening," Ali answered. "A troubled young woman died unnecessarily. So did her baby. This is a very unfortunate situation for all concerned, including April Gaddis's grieving family. I'd appreciate it if you'd all respect our privacy. I have no further comment. Neither does my mother."

"But—"

"No buts," Ali replied firmly and walked away, leaving a flurry of unanswered questions echoing behind her. She was relieved when she finally made it into the dining room, where the others were already gathered and where her father was perusing the menu.

Edie took one look at her daughter's face and was immediately on the alert. "What's wrong?"

"Nothing," Ali said. "Just that bunch of reporters outside."

Edie nodded. "Such pushy people," she said. "You didn't used to be like them, did you?"

"I hope not," Ali said, "but I probably was."

She sat down next to her father, who was still engrossed in the menu. "The prices here are higher than a cat's back," he announced. "This is highway robbery."

Bob's customary grousing was exactly what Ali needed right then. It took her mind off the reporters milling in the lobby.

"Don't worry about it, Dad," Ali said. "You're not paying."

"I don't care," her father returned. "It's the principle of the thing. The food better be top drawer, or I'm going to have a long chat with the manager."

As it turned out, the food was fine.

"So when can we go home?" Bob asked, settling in to mow his way through a plate of eggs Benedict that he pronounced almost as good as his.

"Mom won't be able to leave for a while," Ali told him. "The three of us—Mom, Dave, and I—are going to need to be available for the next several days while the investigation continues. And I still have to give my deposition for the wrongful dismissal suit."

"You don't need to hang around for any of that, Robert," Edie said. "Someone should be home minding the store. I don't like having the Sugar Loaf running on automatic with both of us out of town."

"You wouldn't mind if I went home?" Bob asked his wife. Then he turned to Ali. "And what about Paul's funeral? Won't you need me here for that?"

Ali was having a difficult time imagining how she was going to manage her estranged husband's funeral, but having to do it under the watchful eyes of both her parents would make it that much harder.

"You and Chris can go home, Dad," Ali told him. "Mom and I will be fine."

"I'm not going," Chris said. "Gramps and I already talked it over. I'll stay here for a couple more days and drive home with Grandma."

"Good," Edie said. "I'm glad that's settled, as long as you promise you won't drive the whole way without stopping to rest. You're not a spring chicken, you know, Bob."

During breakfast, Dave seemed far quieter than usual. At the café in Sedona, he and Bob teased each other constantly, but this morning Dave didn't participate in any of the hijinks. When Chris bugged out to go visit some friends and Bob and Edie went in search of the dessert buffet, Ali turned to Dave. "What's wrong?"

"I don't like being told to buzz off," Dave replied.

"Who told you that?" Ali asked.

"My good friend Easy. According to him, it's hands off at the Pink Swan. He says the DEA is involved in some kind of complicated, long-term investigation going on over there. That means the Feds will take a very dim view of anything that upsets their apple cart."

"But if they're investigating the place, isn't there a possibility that they might have surveillance records that would show exactly what happened the night Paul disappeared?" Ali asked.

"They might," Dave agreed. "But good luck laying

hands on them. The Feds aren't going to lift a finger to help anyone, including LAPD homicide, if they're running an undercover operation and helping out would tip their hand prematurely."

"How can that be?" Ali objected. "Paul was murdered. It makes no sense that the DEA won't help us."

"That's where you're wrong," Dave told her grimly. "The Feds don't have to make sense."

By then Bob and Edie were returning to the table with their dessert plates piled high. When Helga Myerhoff called a few minutes later, Ali excused herself. Avoiding the hotel lobby, she ducked into the nearest restroom to take the call.

"I heard all about what happened from Victor," Helga said. "Thank God you and your mother are okay."

Ali couldn't help wondering if Victor would be charging Ali for calling Helga and if Helga would be charging Ali for taking the call. As far as Ali could see, in this game the only ones coming out ahead were the lawyers.

"Yes," Ali agreed. "Thank God."

"As far as Roseanne Maxwell is concerned, I've been asking around," Helga continued. "If there's a divorce in the offing at the Maxwell household, nobody I know has heard word one about it. And nobody knows where Roseanne's disappeared to, either. That includes her best friend, who hasn't had a call from her. She says Roseanne isn't answering her phone and that her voice mail message box is full."

To Ali's way of thinking and with everything else that had happened, this sounded ominous. Especially for Roseanne.

"Jake told us she was in New York shopping for clothes."

"That doesn't compute," Helga replied. "The friend I just told you about—the one who complained about not hearing from Roseanne—is also the friend Roseanne usually does her NYC shopping junkets with. Since Jake hasn't done so, the friend is actually thinking of turning in a missing person's report."

"I hope she does," Ali said.

"Anything else you need from me right now?" Helga asked.

"You'll let me know if you hear anything?" Ali asked.

"Definitely."

Ali ended the call and returned to the dining room, where she discovered her father had managed to pay for brunch after all.

"Thanks, Dad," she told him.

"Thanks for letting me go home," he said. "L.A. isn't for me. It's too big, too crowded, and way too expensive."

"Too expensive is right," Edie agreed. "It doesn't make a bit of sense for us to be staying at a place like this at whatever king's ransom they charge per night when a perfectly good house is sitting empty just a few miles away."

"The house on Robert Lane is still considered a crime scene," Dave pointed out.

"But for how long?" Edie wanted to know. "With April dead and Ali and me both safe, I don't see why that's necessary."

"It's a crime scene until LAPD releases it," Dave told her. "The detectives need to determine exactly what happened to Monique Ragsdale and also what happened to you."

"But April told us what happened to her mother," Edie objected. "That's what I told that first detective who interviewed me this morning. I'm sure it's what Ali told them as well."

"The problem," Dave pointed out, "is that you happen to be Ali's mother. As far as the investigators are concerned, one or both of you could be lying to protect the other. And until there's some forensic evidence to back up the story that April is the one who pushed Monique down the stairs . . ."

"What about the scratches I saw on April's arms?" Edie asked. "Can't they be matched up with scrapings taken from underneath Monique's fingernails?"

"They probably can," Dave agreed. "But it's going to take time."

"And probably a dozen more interviews," Edie said. "I've done enough police interviews in the last couple of days that I'm sick and tired of them." She glanced at her watch. "How about if they did something else for a change instead of just sitting around asking the same questions over and over?"

That was Ali's opinion as well. From what she could tell, police work seemed to involve a whole lot more talking than it did anything else.

When brunch was over, Bob and Edie went up to their room to help Bob get ready to head out. Once they left, Dave stood up as well. "If you don't need anything from me," he said, "I may drive over to Havasu and see the kids for a while. They're off school for the afternoon."

"Go ahead," Ali told him. "I think you've earned a little time off."

Upstairs, Ali was relieved that she now had a room to herself. Much as she liked her mother, Ali had spent months becoming accustomed to being on her own. And she liked it.

Opening her computer, she stretched out on the couch and logged on. The first message in her in-box came from a familiar address:

> *Dear Babe,*
>
> *I guess I'm not as young as I used to be. I just now woke up. Well, a little while ago, I suppose. Long enough that I've had a cup of coffee and turned on my computer.*
>
> *It was such a thrill to meet you last night—this morning really. Most people would have thought I was some kind of crazed stalker or something. Thank you for being so gracious to an old lady who happens to be a big fan of yours.*
>
> *Knowing from you some of what went on yesterday, I wanted to check out what that jerk at socalcopshop had to say. Sure enough. He's at it again. Go ahead and read it, but it'll probably make you mad. I don't know what LMB's problem is.*
>
> Love,
>
> Velma T

Unable to resist, Ali turned to socalcopshop.com, and there it was.

ALISON REYNOLDS AND HER WEB OF EVIL

Alison Reynolds, the Black Widow of Robert Lane, continues to spin her evil web from her current base of operations, the posh Westwood Hotel. This time her victim is April Gaddis, the unfortunate young woman who was scheduled to marry Ms. Reynolds's estranged husband on Saturday afternoon.

Overwhelmed by grief and run over by Ms. Reynolds's army of high-powered attorneys, April Gaddis committed suicide in a room on the maternity ward of Cedars-Sinai Hospital early Monday morning. Not only is Ms. Gaddis dead, so is her unborn child. After finding the mother's lifeless body, doctors attempted to save the baby but were unable to do so.

Sources close to the investigation say that Ms. Gaddis spent the last several days of her life in the company of Alison Reynolds and her mother. Why would she have turned to her fiancé's former wife for consolation? Well, let's see. For one thing, Ms. Gaddis's mother, Monique Ragsdale, also perished over the weekend as a result of a nasty fall down a stairway in Ms. Reynolds's Robert Lane mansion. Coincidence? I don't think so, and neither do LAPD and Riverside County homicide investigators who are working this series of interrelated cases.

Alison Reynolds is the only common denominator in all of them. Who gave this Black Widow a license to kill and who's going to see to it that she pays for her crimes?

Posted 11:05 A.M., September 19, 2005 by LMB

So Lance-a-lot is at it again, Ali thought. When it came to spinning a web, Ali didn't hold a candle to April Gaddis, but she resisted the temptation to respond to LMB and tell him so directly. Posting anything on his Web site would only serve to add legitimacy to his claims about her. She sent a note to Velma instead.

> *Dear Velma,*
> *Thanks for passing along the information about socalcopshop. The guy who writes it seems to have it in for me, and I don't know why.*
> *Thanks, too, for what you did last night. Your loyal support meant more to me than you can possibly know.*
> *If you have a weekend number for your nephew, you might ask him to give me a call. I believe I have information that might be helpful to his client.*
>
> ALI

For the next hour or so, Ali sat at the computer sending as many thank-you notes as she could manage to the people who had written to express their concern over the fact that Edie Larson was missing or else their gratitude for her safe return. She posted some of the messages and simply answered the others. Good manners required individual replies wherever possible.

She had finally succeeded in clearing her mailbox and had closed her eyes for a brief nap when the "You've got mail" announcement sounded in her ear. The e-mail address, a series of numbers that were most likely a combination of birthdate and zip code, meant nothing to her, but that wasn't unusual. Most of the e-mail Ali Reynolds received at cutlooseblog.com came from strangers.

> *Dear Ali,*
> *I'm writing to you through a friend's e-mail account because I'm afraid my account is being monitored, and as you know, these are very dangerous people. I tried to call your old cell phone but it didn't work. If you have a new cell phone number please send it to me at this address. I need your help. Please don't tell anyone that you've heard from me, and don't give anyone this e-mail address, either.*
>
> RM

Ali read through the message twice. RM? That could only be Roseanne Maxwell. Had to be. And these dangerous people she mentioned? Dave had said much the same thing about the drug traffickers—that they were dangerous. Ali wrote back immediately, giving Roseanne her new Arizona-based cell phone number.

Then she waited. When her cell phone finally rang, it was after four.

"Don't call me by name," the person said, although Ali recognized Roseanne's breathy delivery as soon as she spoke. "This is a throwaway phone. Don't bother trying to trace it."

"What do you want then?" Ali asked. "Why are you calling me?"

"Like I said," Roseanne told her. "I need your help. I've got to disappear."

"As far as I can tell, you already have."

"This isn't a game," Roseanne Maxwell replied. "I mean, I need to disappear for the rest of my life—for whatever life I have left."

There was a desperate quality in Roseanne's voice, one that convinced Ali that the woman wasn't kidding.

"What do you want me to do?" Ali asked.

"I'm staying with a friend up in Valencia," Roseanne said. "Do you know where that is?"

"Of course," Ali said.

"Come to the Claim Jumper here in town," Roseanne said. "I'll meet you there at six. Be sure nobody follows you. We need to talk."

In the past several days, every time Ali had reached out to help someone, the effort had turned around to bite her in the butt. "Why should I?" she asked.

"Because you want to know what happened to Paul," Roseanne said. "You owe it to yourself, and you owe it to Paul."

I don't owe Paul Grayson a thing, Ali wanted to say. Instead she replied reluctantly, "All right. I'll be there."

{ CHAPTER 17 }

Ali picked up the phone and tried her mother's room, but the call went directly to voice mail. With her father already on his way to Sedona, it was likely Edie was taking a nap. After the previous night's misadventures, that was hardly surprising. Ali left a message that she was going to meet a friend at the Claim Jumper in Valencia and let it go at that. And she gave Chris a pass as well. She was glad he was off having fun with his friends. That was fine.

What about calling Dave? Ali wondered. With no strings other than friendship, the man had literally spent days helping Ali and her family at every turn. Now that he was taking some time and several hours to drive back over to Lake Havasu to spend time with his kids, Ali couldn't, in good conscience, involve him again—either by calling him or leaving a message. In fact, she was determined this was something she would handle on her own.

Besides, how dangerous could it be to meet up with Roseanne Maxwell in what would no doubt be the middle of a crowded restaurant? Still, remembering Roseanne's concern about Ali's possibly being followed, she did check the rearview mirror from time to time as she drove north on I-5 just to make sure there was no one suspicious behind her. In actual fact, Ali was far less worried about bad guys following her than she was about one of the stray reporting teams who were still camped out in and around the hotel.

As for Roseanne Maxwell herself? She wasn't what Ali would have considered to be a frightening proposition. For one thing, she was slight of build with the best curve enhancement and facial redefining money could buy. For Roseanne beauty wasn't skin deep—it was subcutaneous. For as long as Ali had known the woman, Roseanne had existed on a perpetual round of dieting and not dieting. That was why Roseanne's having set their meeting at an establishment known for its gigantic serving portions was a mystery in and of itself.

Ali had never been particularly close to Roseanne. Their husbands had been coworkers, competitors for the network job, and partners in the Sumo Sudoku scam. Ali and Roseanne had seen each other socially on occasion, but they definitely didn't qualify as good friends. Or even semi-friends. And why Roseanne would turn to Ali in a time of trouble was as much a mystery as where they were meeting.

It was six on the dot when Ali arrived at the Claim Jumper parking lot. The restaurant was jammed, and there was a crowd of people milling about outside, waiting for tables. Ali was about to walk inside and put her name on the list when a woman appeared at her side. Roseanne Maxwell was so changed that Ali barely recognized her.

The last time Ali had seen Roseanne had been at Paul's annual Christmas party the preceding year. She had been dressed to the nines with her hair piled on top of her head in a sophisticated platinum blond do, but the months since then had been anything but kind to Roseanne Maxwell. Her hair was brown now and cut short as well, shorn off in something that resembled chemo-patient chic. Ali barely recognized her.

The old Roseanne wouldn't have ventured out of the house without a complete assortment of high-end jewelry adorning her fingers, neck, and ears and a layer of full-armor-of-God makeup on her face. This new Roseanne wore no jewelry whatsoever, and her makeup consisted of a little lipstick and nothing else. Roseanne had stopped smoking years earlier. Without the ongoing attention of her cosmetic surgeon and artfully applied Botox, the telltale lines had reasserted themselves. In less than a year she had aged a good decade's worth.

Roseanne grabbed Ali's arm and hugged her close. "I know. I know," she whispered. "I look like hell. You don't have to tell me. Come on," she added. "I came early. I already have a table."

Ali allowed herself to be led through the crowded restaurant to a secluded table in the far back of the room.

"Nobody followed you, did they?" Roseanne asked nervously.

Taking her phone out of her pocket and turning the ringer to "silent," Ali shook her head. "I don't think so," she said. "I checked."

"I hope you don't mind meeting me here. Carrie, the hostess, is a friend of mine. I met her in NA. I needed a place to stay, and she happened to have a spare bedroom in her house. So that's where I'm staying at the moment. And because I can't risk driving my own car right now, she gave me a lift when she came to work."

"NA?" Ali asked.

"Narcotics Anonymous," Roseanne returned. "I'm trying to get straight, if I can live long enough, that is." She patted her badly cut hair. "Good disguise, don't you think?"

"Very," Ali agreed. "Now what's going on?"

For an answer, Roseanne opened her purse and pushed a ziplock bag across the table. Ali picked it up and studied it. A collection of jewels and gold—diamond-studded rings, necklaces, earrings, and bracelets—winked back at her through the clear plastic.

"What's this?" Ali asked, handing the bag back across the table.

"My jewelry," Roseanne said. "I need to sell it—all of it. If I go to a pawnshop, I'll only get a fraction of what it's worth. Besides, I'm sure word of it would get back to Jake. Please buy them from me, Ali. I know you've got the money to do it, and it's my only chance to get away. Just give it to me in cash, and then I'll disappear. No one will ever find me. If they do, I'm dead anyway."

"Get away?" Ali asked. "From whom?"

"The people who ruined our lives," Roseanne replied, lowering her voice to a strained whisper. "The people who killed Paul."

"What people?" Ali demanded. "The drug dealers?"

"You know about them then?" Roseanne asked with a stricken look on her face.

Ali nodded. "A little," she said. "But not enough. You probably know way more. You should go to the cops and tell them what you know."

"I can't," Roseanne said in a hoarse whisper.

"Why not?"

"Because some of the cops are in on it. I've seen them."

Ali's first reaction was one of total disbelief. Obviously Roseanne was suffering some kind of paranoid delusion. If she was involved in drugs enough that she had turned to NA for help, maybe that wasn't too surprising.

"Look," Ali said placatingly. "I'm sure you have some reason to think so, but—"

"I'm afraid somebody tapped my phone," Roseanne said. "My old phone. I'm sure they were listening in on everything I said. Who else would have done that but the cops? That's why I got this new one—a disposable. They're much harder to trace than the other ones are."

Ali restrained herself from making a wry comment about conspiracy theories and people wearing tinfoil hats. Roseanne Maxwell was absolutely serious. Painfully so.

"It takes a lot of effort to tap telephones," Ali pointed out. "Cops can't do it just for the hell of it. They'd need judges, warrants, and everything."

"They already have those," Roseanne said.

"Who's doing this then?" Ali asked. "And why?"

At that precise moment, Ali's phone vibrated silently in her pocket. With Roseanne already off the charts about people tapping telephones, Ali thought it best to ignore the call.

Roseanne sighed. "You know about the Pink Swan?"

"Some," Ali replied. "I know there's a lot more happening there than meets the eye."

Roseanne nodded. "When we first started going there, it seemed like it was all fun all the time. Jake always liked to gamble. It was a place where I could go along and do my thing while he was doing his. But eventually he got in over his head, and it got worse after the network cut him loose—a lot worse."

Ali managed to keep a straight face when Roseanne used the term "cut loose." It turned out there was a lot of that going around.

"That's how those people work," Roseanne continued. "They suck you in a little at a time. Like I said, at first it was just Jake's gambling and a few recreational drugs for me. It felt like a nice place, a safe place, because we had no idea what else was going on. By the time we figured out the rest of it, we were in way too deep. Jake said we either did what they said or else."

"So you moved from using drugs to transporting them?" Ali asked.

Roseanne looked at her sharply, then she nodded. "Yes," she admitted. "That's where Sumo Sudoku came in. It gave them a whole collection of RVs that they can use to run up and down the West Coast. That way, their loads come and go in plain sight with no questions asked. So far no one has ever suspected they're hauling anything but those damn rocks."

No one but Dave and me, Ali thought. "Paul was in on all of this?" she asked.

"No," Roseanne answered. "Even though April and

Tracy McLaughlin were friends, Jake was the one who actually pitched the Sumo Sudoku idea to Paul. When it came time to put the deal together, Paul put up his money. I'm sure he thought we were putting up ours, too. But the money we used didn't really belong to us because we were broke by then, or we would have been."

"So the whole Sumo Sudoku thing is really nothing but a cover for moving drugs?" Ali asked.

"It's actually more than that," Roseanne admitted. "By involving Paul in the project, they ended up with what looks like a legitimate entity, and there was enough money in the deal for Jake that we were able to hang on to our house. They promised Jake even more—lots more—if he could get Sumo Sudoku some network exposure and have it go national."

No wonder they needed Paul, Ali thought. "What about the players?" she asked.

"The guys who drive the RVs?" Roseanne returned. "They all have their own particular vices, and the Pink Swan is a one-stop shop when it comes to that kind of thing. Tracy McLaughlin doesn't do any drugs other than cigarettes and beer. His big thing is gambling. That's how they hooked him in—gambling debts and forgiveness of same."

Ali realized this was more or less the same story Jake had told but with a few key differences.

"With so many illegal activities going on, how does the Pink Swan stay in business?" Ali asked.

"They pay off the right people," Roseanne responded. "I know for sure that several top dogs from LAPD are regulars at the gambling tables upstairs. I know them because I've seen them. The Pink Swan's management makes sure the club and its customers don't annoy the neighbors. The place is clean, it's quiet, and the club does a lot of strategic charitable giving. I hear they're big on putting playground equipment in local parks."

"What about the DEA?" Ali asked.

"What about them?" Roseanne asked with a shrug. "I don't know any people from the DEA personally, if that's what you mean, but they could be there. After all, if people from LAPD can be bought off, why couldn't people from the DEA? We're talking about astonishing amounts of money, Ali. Cops who play ball with them can make more money in a year than they'd make in a lifetime of pounding a beat somewhere."

A harried waitress veered in their direction, but Roseanne waved her away with a shake of her head while Ali thought about what Dave had said about the possibility of an ongoing undercover DEA investigation being conducted at the Pink Swan. Maybe there was something to what Roseanne was saying after all.

"You said you were going to tell me about Paul," Ali said.

Nodding, Roseanne took a deep breath. "I guess you know what it feels like to be cast aside," she said finally.

"I've met Amber, if that's what you mean," Ali said. She might have couched the comment a little more diplomatically. When Roseanne's eyes filled with tears, Ali was sorry she hadn't.

"She was at the house?" Roseanne asked. "At my house?"

Ali nodded.

"That didn't take long. I suppose I should have known she would be," Roseanne said. "There's a lot that goes over your head when you're screwed up on cocaine. I should have figured out what was happening, but by the time I noticed, it was too late. Amber already had her hooks in him."

Roseanne was right. For Ali Reynolds, the idea of an older wife being shoved aside in favor of a younger one was another all-too-familiar story.

"Amber was always there at the Pink Swan," Roseanne continued. "And why wouldn't she be? Her grandmother owns the place. It wasn't until I got in the program and started trying to straighten out my life that I could see what was what. It seemed to me that if I could just get rid of Amber, Jake and I might be all right. I mean, the two of us have a history together. Even if we lost everything else, I thought we'd at least have each other."

Why does she want him? Ali asked herself. *What's to hang on to?*

"But I didn't have nerve enough to go to the cops myself," Roseanne went on. "For one thing, I'm in it, too. So I blew the whistle to Paul instead. I told him everything I knew and everything I suspected about Jake and the others taking Paul for a ride."

"What happened?" Ali asked.

"At first I don't think Paul believed me, but he must have started looking into things on his own. Last Wednesday morning he called me and told me that maybe I was right about what was going on, but with everything coming up over the weekend—with both the divorce hearing and the wedding—he had decided not to do anything more about it until after he and April got back from their honeymoon.

"I begged him not to let anyone know I was the one who had told him," Roseanne continued. "He promised he wouldn't, but once I got off the phone with him, I got scared. I was afraid he might go to Jake instead. That's when I decided I needed to disappear. The next day, when Kimball was out getting groceries, I grabbed what I could from the house, then I took off and came here. When I heard Paul was dead, I knew I had been right. If I hadn't run away when I did, I'd be dead by now, too."

The waitress returned, more determined this time, with her order pad in hand. Neither Ali nor Roseanne had yet to glance at their menus.

"House salad," Ali said. "Ranch dressing and iced tea."

"I'll have the same," Roseanne said.

Clearly disappointed by their long delayed but paltry order, the waitress rolled her eyes and stomped off in the direction of the kitchen.

"But what makes you think your phone was tapped?" Ali asked, once the waitress was out of earshot.

"Paul's dead, isn't he?" Roseanne asked. "He didn't know anything about what was going on until I told him, and when I did, someone must have been listening in on my phone."

Or on Paul's, Ali thought. If Paul and Jake were partners, and if the authorities managed to get wiretapping warrants as a part of a drug-busting investigation, they'd have gotten warrants for the phones of all parties involved and perhaps even for their spouses' phones as well. At the time of Paul's death, Ali had still been his wife. Did that mean Ali's phone might have been tapped, too?

"That's why Paul's death is my fault," Roseanne continued as her eyes once more filled with tears. "If I hadn't told him what was going on, maybe he wouldn't be dead now."

"If the Pink Swan is a front for a major drug operation, I still think you should go to the cops," Ali said. "All of LAPD doesn't hang out around there. Surely there must be someone you could talk to?"

"But how am I supposed to know which ones are crooked and which ones aren't?" Roseanne returned. "As far as I can tell, they all are."

That's when Ali thought of Dave. He was, without a doubt, one of the world's straightest arrows.

"Look," Ali said. "I have a friend who's visiting right now, a cop from over in Arizona. He couldn't possibly be mixed up in any of this. Why don't you talk to him?"

"No," Roseanne said firmly. "No cops. Period. Why do you think they killed Paul? To let the rest of us know that even talking about going to the cops is a capital offense as far as they're concerned."

"What about talking to an attorney then?" Ali asked. "I know a top-drawer defense attorney. His name is Victor Angeleri. You're obviously involved in all this and you know what's really going on. Why don't you call him and let him see what kind of deal he could cut for you in terms of witness protection?"

"I don't believe in witness protection programs any more than I believe in the Tooth Fairy," Roseanne returned. "That wouldn't stop them. If they killed Paul, they'll find me and kill me, too. Even if I get sent to jail, they'll still come after me. That's why I'm hoping you'll help me out. I don't need a lot of money. I have a place down in Mexico where I can live cheaply for a very long time. I just need some cash to make it work."

Roseanne pushed the jewel-laden ziplock bag back in Ali's direction. It lay there on the tabletop between them for the better part of a minute. Then, when the waitress reappeared with their salads and iced teas, Roseanne snatched the bag off the table and stuffed it back into her purse and out of sight.

Once again they waited until the waitress had walked away from their table.

"If these people are so all-powerful and all-knowing, who are they? You may have your suspicions that they're responsible for what happened to Paul, but do you have any proof?"

"I just know it," Roseanne said fervently. "I know it in my bones."

"That's not good enough."

"By the time I get proof, I'll be dead, too," Roseanne said.

Ali had to admit that was a pretty telling argument. She decided to change tactics. "So these people are all tied in with the Pink Swan," she said. "Tell me about that."

"The bottom floor is just your basic topless joint with a bar and nude dancing, and all the rest of it. That one is open to the public. Upstairs is private—an upscale gentlemen's club they call it. That's where the real action is—all kinds of action. You can go there and do whatever you want and nobody bothers you, especially no reporters. They don't come near the place."

"Who owns it?" Ali asked.

"A lady named Lucia Joaquin. At least, her name is the one on the liquor license. She's the widow of a major player in one of the Colombian drug cartels. Years ago when her husband was gunned down, she came here with her kids along with a ton of money, money she managed to invest in real estate all over L.A."

"Drug money?" Ali asked.

"I'm sure," Roseanne answered with a nod. "But just because she moved out of the country didn't mean she moved out of the drug business. She's kept her hand in the whole time she's been here. Her two sons may work for her, but even though she's been sick, Lucia is still the real brains behind the outfit. She's also the one who gave the Pink Swan its name. I've never met her, but I've been told she always wears pink—from head to toe."

"What about the sons?" Ali asked.

"Mario and Reynaldo," Roseanne replied. "They both went to school here in the States. One's an MBA type and the other's more of an engineer. Lucia's money comes rolling in from whatever source. The sons figure out ways to turn all that illicit cash into something more or less legitimate."

"Like Sumo Sudoku?" Ali asked.

Roseanne nodded. "Exactly."

"Which one of the sons is Amber's father?"

"Neither," Roseanne answered. "There was a third child—a daughter. I don't know her name. She died years ago. Lucia raised Amber and thinks she can do no wrong. Unfortunately, Amber doesn't have quite the same work ethic her grandmother has. But she's going to be loaded one of these days, so I can see why Jake might be interested in her. As for why Amber's interested in Jake?" Roseanne added. "I have no idea."

Having met the young woman in question the previous night, Ali could have told Roseanne that Amber came with her own set of problems, but she didn't.

"So will you help me or not?" Roseanne asked, going back once again to the jewelry.

Ali thought about it. Roseanne had brought her here under false pretenses. She had claimed to have information about Paul's death, but from Ali's point of view, what she had offered was little more than unsubstantiated suspicions—none of them enough to make Ali's trip worthwhile.

"I think my answer is not," Ali replied. "The only reason you brought me here was to unload your jewelry and get some cash."

"But—" Roseanne began.

Ali stood up. "If you decide you want to go to that lawyer or to the cops and tell them what's going on, call me again and we'll talk. In the meantime, Roseanne, I'm afraid you're on your own."

A despairing Roseanne watched as Ali flagged down the waitress. Roseanne was still seated at their table as Ali left. Enough time had passed that only a few stragglers still lingered outside, waiting for tables. Ali started through them and was headed for her car when someone called after her.

"Ms. Reynolds?"

Thinking it was someone who recognized her from her days on the news, Ali stopped and turned back to find the hostess hurrying after her. "Yes."

"There's a phone call for you at the hostess desk," Carrie said. "You can take it back inside. There's an extension on the wall there by the restrooms."

Why would someone be calling me here? Ali wondered. The only person who had known she was coming to Claim Jumper was her mother. That was probably the call she had ignored earlier.

"Thank you," Ali said, allowing herself to be led back into the restaurant. When she picked up the receiver, Ali was amazed to find Dave Holman on the phone.

"What's going on?" Ali wanted to know. "How did you know to call me here? Did you talk to Mom?"

"Listen to me for a minute," he said urgently. "Is Roseanne still there?"

"Yes, but—"

"Good," Dave Holman said, sounding relieved. "I'm glad I got here in time."

Ali glanced around the restaurant but didn't see him anywhere. "You're here? Where? I thought you were on your way to Lake Havasu."

"Things changed. Roxie had made other plans and didn't want me dropping in on the kids 'unannounced.' In the meantime, I'm in Valencia now. At a pay phone directly across the street from the Claim Jumper."

"You followed me here? Why? What's happening? And you still haven't told me why you didn't call on my cell."

"The last few days," he said, "with everything that's been going on, I've managed to make friends with Bruno Cutler, the head of security at your hotel. Late this afternoon, someone came speeding into the hotel parking garage. He waved what was supposedly an LAPD badge at the garage attendant and said he was there to check on a stolen vehicle. The attendant didn't think that much about it at the time, but later on, when Bruno was reviewing the garage security tapes, he noticed someone messing around with your vehicle, and he called me."

"Someone was messing with my Cayenne?" Ali asked. "Who and why?"

"I've seen the tape now, too," Dave said. "And I'm pretty sure I know who it was. You do, too. He drives a Honda Element, and he's parked outside the restaurant right now. The Element is parked right next to your Porsche."

"Tracy McLaughlin followed me here?" Ali asked. "How could he? Roseanne was afraid someone might try to follow me, so I checked. There was no one anywhere near me."

"That's what I'm trying to tell you," Dave replied. "I think McLaughlin stuck a GPS tracking device under your rear bumper. If they were using one of those, there would have been no need to keep your vehicle in sight. The tape shows him taking something small out of his pocket and then reaching up toward the underside of your back bumper—right in the middle of it, straight down from the lock."

"I don't understand. Why would Tracy McLaughlin want to find me?" Ali asked.

"I think the people Tracy works for are looking for Roseanne Maxwell. Tracy followed you in hopes you'd lead him to her."

Which I did, Ali thought with a sinking sensation in the pit of her stomach.

"But how could Tracy possibly know I was coming to see her?" Ali asked at last.

"Good question," Dave said. "That's why I'm calling you on the restaurant phone instead of your cell. It's why I'm not using my cell, either."

Ali stopped short, remembering Roseanne's concerns about the likelihood of her phone being tapped. Now Dave shared that worry.

"Are you saying someone may have been listening in on my cell phone calls?" Ali asked.

"Affirmative," Dave replied.

"What should I do then?" Ali returned.

"Where is Roseanne?"

"Still at our table. She rode here with a friend who works at the restaurant. I imagine she's planning on staying until the friend gets off work."

"Whatever you do, don't let her leave," Dave said urgently. "Did she tell you anything important?"

"She told me a little," Ali said. "But I thought she was delusional and making a lot of it up."

"I only wish that were the case."

"So you've found out more?"

"Lots more," Dave answered, "but let's not go into that right now. Just wait until I get there."

"You're coming in?"

"Yes," he said. "As soon as I can."

"What if Tracy spots you?"

"I'll wait until there's another fairly large group and try to blend in with them," Dave said. "He's waiting for you to come out. With any kind of luck, he won't be paying that much attention to people going in."

"What are we going to do?" Ali asked. "Do you have a plan?"

"Not yet," Dave allowed. "When I come up with one, I'll let you know."

"I'll go back to the table and tell Roseanne to stay put. When you get here, talk to the hostess. Her name is Carrie, and she's Roseanne's friend. Carrie will be able to tell you where we are."

"Will do," Dave said, and hung up.

Still stunned by the idea that she'd been followed after all, Ali made her way back to the corner table. Roseanne didn't look up until Ali was standing directly over her.

"What happened?" she asked. "I thought you were leaving."

"So did I," Ali returned. "I changed my mind."

Roseanne brightened. "Does that mean you're going to buy my jewelry after all?"

"No," Ali replied grimly. "It means I'm going to try to save your butt."

{ CHAPTER 18 }

Looking alarmed, Roseanne half rose to her feet. "What's going on?" she demanded.

"Sit back down and don't make a scene," Ali ordered. "We can't afford it. Tracy McLaughlin evidently found out where I was going and followed me here," she added. "He's waiting outside in the parking lot."

Roseanne's face turned a pasty shade of white as she sank back into her chair. "He followed you?" she asked in a cracked whisper. "I thought you said you'd checked and that no one was there."

"I did check," Ali returned. "But we believe he put some kind of GPS tracking device on my vehicle. He knew exactly where I was without my being able to see him at all."

"But if they find me here . . ." With an almost physical jolt, Roseanne suddenly straightened in her chair. "Wait a minute. How did he know you were coming to see me? You must have told him."

"I didn't," Ali said. "At least not on purpose. You

may be right, Roseanne. It's possible my phone is being tapped, just like you said yours was."

There was a long pause as Ali's news sank in. "What are we going to do then?" Roseanne asked finally.

"Dave Holman, that friend I told you about, the cop from Arizona, is on his way here right now," Ali told her. "Once he arrives, we'll figure out what to do."

Again, Roseanne attempted to rise to her feet. "I already told you I don't want to talk to any cops. I've got to get out of here. Now."

More time had passed than Ali realized. Now only two tables in that section of the restaurant were still occupied, but the people seated there seemed to be taking an inordinate interest in the ongoing drama between Ali and Roseanne.

"Sit," Ali hissed. "With Tracy out in the parking lot, leaving is exactly the wrong thing to do right now. He'll nail you the moment you step outside."

"What should I do then? Sit here and wait for him to come inside after me?"

"I don't know," Ali replied. "Be quiet and let me think."

Shaking her head, a trembling Roseanne slid back into her chair. Clearly the woman was petrified, and Ali didn't blame her. They needed a device that would take Roseanne out of harm's way without exposing her to whatever danger awaited her in the parking lot. Slowly a plan began to take shape in Ali's head. If Ali could somehow conceal Roseanne inside the restaurant while at the same time convincing Tracy that she had slipped away . . .

Before Ali could finish formulating a strategy, Carrie appeared, holding an armload of menus and leading

Dave Holman directly to their corner table. Ali was thrilled to see him. Roseanne was not. As Dave took a seat, Roseanne shrank away from him, putting as much distance as possible between his chair and hers. Before the hostess could walk away again, Ali caught Carrie's arm.

"I guess you know we're having a bit of a problem here," she said. "That there are dangerous people actively looking for Roseanne?"

Carrie nodded. "She told me."

"One of them appears to be waiting for her outside in the parking lot."

"Oh, no!" Carrie exclaimed. "Should I call the cops?"

"Not just yet," Ali said. "But what about this? Would it be possible for you to hustle Roseanne into the kitchen and pass her off as part of the help long enough for us to decoy the bad guy away from here?"

Dave looked as though he was about to say something. Then he didn't.

Carrie seemed to consider. "That wouldn't be too hard," she answered. "I could put her in with the guy who washes dishes. He wouldn't mind having some extra help. I'll clear it with the kitchen. Let me know if you need anything else."

Carrie went away again, leaving Ali to make the introductions. Still huddled against the wall, Roseanne refused Dave's proffered handshake.

"Tracy's still out in the parking lot?" Ali asked.

Dave nodded. "Yup."

"Is he alone?"

"As far as I could tell."

Ali felt a surge of irritation with Dave. He was being

uncommonly uncommunicative. She had expected him to arrive with some concrete ideas for solving their problem. Since he seemed to be fresh out of game plans, Ali continued to formulate her own.

"Do you have your cell phone with you?" Ali asked him.

"Yes. Of course."

"I'm going to call you on it," Ali said. "And I'm going to use my cell phone to do it. Since whoever may be listening in on my calls doesn't know we know about them, hopefully they'll take whatever I say as the gospel."

Roseanne let out a small moan. "But what about me?" she asked.

"What about you?" Ali returned. "You go to the kitchen and wash dishes like Carrie said until Dave or I come back to get you, but you need to know one thing, Roseanne. Dave and I aren't helping you out of the goodness of our hearts. This isn't a free ride."

"What do you mean?"

"I'm sure from what you said earlier that you'd like me to believe you're a mostly innocent bystander in all this," Ali returned. "If that were true, though, you wouldn't be so afraid of going to jail yourself. You claim to be a drug user and nothing more, but I'm guessing that by the time the cops finish investigating this case they'll be able to charge you with plenty, including conspiracy to distribute drugs if nothing else." Ali turned to Dave. "That's a felony, right?"

Dave nodded. "Yes, it is," he agreed.

"So," Ali continued, "your best bet for dodging jail time is for you to cooperate now. If Dave and I can manage to get you out of this alive, I want you to promise that you'll go to that attorney I told you about. Let Victor Angeleri see what kind of deal he can make for you in exchange for your testimony—your voluntary testimony—about the people at the Pink Swan and everything that goes on there, including your suspicions about who was really responsible for Paul's death."

"What if I say no?" Roseanne asked.

"That's easy," Ali returned. "Dave and I leave now, and you can deal with Tracy and whatever's supposed to happen to you all on your own."

"You wouldn't do that, would you?" Roseanne pleaded. "You couldn't just leave me alone like that."

"Oh, couldn't I?" Ali said, reaching for her purse. "Watch me."

"No," Roseanne said, capitulating. "Please don't leave. I'll do whatever you say."

"Fine," Ali said. "Go to the kitchen. Stay there until you hear from us. Either Dave or I will come get you, or else we'll let you know that it's safe to go with whoever we send."

"All right," Roseanne agreed reluctantly. She stood up and headed for the swinging doors that led back to the kitchen. Ali glanced around. By then the customers at the other nearby tables had all left. Carrie had made sure that theirs was the only occupied table in that section of the restaurant.

A waitress—a different one this time—came over and took Dave's order.

"All right," Ali said once the waitress left. "Here's my plan. I'll call you and say that I met Roseanne here because she wanted me to buy some of her jewelry but that she slipped away while I was in the restroom. With any kind of luck whoever's listening in on my phone will believe she's gotten away from them, too. Then, later on, we'll be able to smuggle her out of here and get her to Victor."

Ali was talking to Dave but he didn't appear to be paying attention. He seemed to be focused on some distant part of the restaurant.

"Hello!" Ali said. "Are you even listening to me?"

Turning to follow his gaze, Ali saw two men standing talking to Carrie, who was listening carefully and nodding. Eventually they began making their way across the dining room. One was a tall, rangy black man Ali had never seen before. The other she recognized at once—Detective Montgomery Taylor with the Riverside Sheriff's Department Homicide Division, one of the two detectives who had interviewed Ali in the aftermath of Paul's death.

"Oh, no," Ali whispered under her breath. "What's he doing here? Don't tell me they're coming after me again."

The men walked directly to Ali and Dave's table. Without waiting for an invitation, they seated themselves. The man Ali didn't know nodded cordially in Dave's direction. The two of them shook hands.

"Good to see you, bro," the man said. "Where is Roseanne Maxwell?"

"In the kitchen," Dave responded. "Hiding out as a dishwasher. Are the takedown teams all in place?"

The stranger nodded. "Pretty much," he said. "We're just waiting for the restaurant to clear out some and for a couple more of my men to arrive on the scene."

"Roseanne's in the kitchen?" Detective Taylor

asked. "I'll go make sure we don't lose her." With that, he got up and headed for the kitchen.

Feeling lost, Ali watched the detective's retreating figure. "What takedown teams?" she asked. "Who are these guys? What are they doing here? What's going on?"

"Sorry," Dave said. "I didn't have a chance to tell you, Ali. This is my friend Ezekiel Washington. We call him Easy. He's with the DEA. I believe you already know Detective Taylor." Dave waved in the direction of the swinging kitchen door where Taylor had disappeared.

"Glad to meet you," Easy said with an engaging grin calculated to match his name. "I remember seeing you on the news when you used to be on TV here. I guess you could say I was a fan."

"Thank you," Ali said stiffly. "I'm delighted to know that, I'm sure. But you still haven't told me what's going on here."

"We're in the process of rolling up a major drug operation," he answered. "We've been working on this case for months. We weren't quite ready to make our move, but with your husband dead and with the possibility of your stirring up the pot on your Web site, we're having to go ahead and stage our raids now after all. If we wait any longer, there's a good chance you may write something in your blog that will give away what we're doing. At this point in the investigation, we can't afford to have a loose cannon on deck."

"So now I'm a loose cannon?" an irate Ali demanded of Dave Holman. Then she turned back to Easy Washington.

"Sorry," Easy said. "I didn't mean that the way it sounded. What happened to your husband is terribly unfortunate. It was never our intention that he would be at risk, and believe me, we're doing everything we can to bring his killers to justice."

"Not your intention . . . ?" Ali began.

"Mr. Grayson had been working with us for some time, and that's what it takes to bring down a whole organization like this—time. If you move too fast, you just get pieces of the puzzle—small fry mostly—rather than the people in charge. And that's what we're trying to do here—bring down Lucia Joaquin's entire group, from top to bottom. Mr. Grayson came to us several months ago when he first started having concerns about what was going on with the Sumo Sudoku group. He agreed to do what he could to help, and he understood that it wouldn't happen overnight."

Ali could barely believe her ears. "Paul was working with you? Is that why he was killed?"

"Not exactly," Easy replied. "We've known for some time that our communications system had been compromised, so we were careful that our contacts with your husband were done in an untraceable fashion."

"You're telling me someone's been tapping your phones as well?" Ali asked.

Easy nodded.

"But you're the DEA."

"Exactly," Easy said. "And that's a big part of the problem here. We believe that someone from the Joaquin organization penetrated LEMO and installed a Trojan horse."

"LEMO?" Ali asked. "What's that? It sounds like a cartoon for kids."

"LEMO, not Elmo," Easy explained. "The Law Enforcement Monitoring Organization. Think of it as the wiretapping central office for all the law enforcement agencies in the western United States, and it happens to be located right here in L.A. If, as we suspect, someone was able to install a keystroke-logger inside the system, they automatically have access to all our passwords and communications. They know exactly who and what we've been listening in on and what we plan to do. They've been making a shambles of our operations for months. Evidently they've also been doing some unauthorized listening on their own."

"Including my phones?" Ali asked.

Easy nodded. "And the phones of anyone else whose activities interested them, including Roseanne Maxwell. And that's where we got in trouble. Your husband was already working for us when Roseanne called and asked him to come to us with what was going on."

"You're saying Paul was killed because it seemed like he was going to go to the authorities with what he knew, not because he was already doing so."

Easy Washington nodded again. "At first I was afraid someone on our side—someone who knew about his involvement with us—had betrayed him, that we had a mole in our midst. That's why it was so helpful to us initially that everyone thought you were responsible for Mr. Grayson's death. That took a lot of the pressure off us and gave us a chance to investigate the situation. Now, though, we're pretty sure that Roseanne's phone call is what set your husband's murder plot in motion."

Ali was struggling to comprehend what was being said. Was it possible Paul really had been actively at work behind the scenes to help out in a DEA investigation? Over time his actions toward her had led

Ali to think of the man as an entirely contemptible human being. Easy Washington seemed to consider him to be some kind of hero. For Ali, that didn't quite compute. And what about April? Had she been with Paul in all this or against him?

"You're saying Paul was helping you."

"He was a huge help," Easy said. "I can't tell you how sorry I am that we weren't able to move fast enough to prevent this senseless tragedy."

Ali stood up.

"Where are you going?" Dave asked.

"Back to the hotel," Ali said. "This is a bit more than I can handle."

"You can't go back to the hotel," Dave said.

"Why not?"

"Because you're checked out," he answered. "With everything that's going on, Easy and I thought it would be best if you were moved to a different location. Your mom packed up your stuff. I've got it all in my car. Your mother and Chris have moved out, too. Chris is staying with friends. I got your mother a room at the Motel 6 just up the corridor from mine. Edie said you probably wouldn't like it, but there's a room there for you as well."

Ali was suddenly more than moderately annoyed. "You moved my stuff?" she demanded.

"Just for the time being," Easy said reassuringly. "Until we can stage our raids and have all the suspects in custody."

"You had no right to do that," Ali announced. "And my mother is right. I have zero intention of staying at the Motel 6. The Westwood is fine with me, thank you very much."

"Please don't go back there, Ms. Reynolds," Easy

said. "Desperate people do desperate things. I wouldn't want to see you hurt. You don't know what the Joaquins are capable of."

"I know exactly what they're capable of," Ali said. "I'm the one who identified my husband's body, remember? I want my stuff, Mr. Washington. And I want it now. Not later, now."

With the possibility of a shooting war about to break out in the parking lot, Ali knew she was being unreasonable, but she was tired of being booted around by people—good intentioned or not—who were busy deciding what she would and wouldn't do.

"Ali, please—" Dave began.

"Give me your keys, Dave," Easy interjected, standing up and holding out his hand. "Tracy McLaughlin knows what you look like. I'll send someone to get her stuff. Where's your car?"

"Out back," Dave replied. "Next to the Dumpsters."

Ali barely waited for Easy to leave the table before she rounded on Dave. "How dare you . . ."

"Easy and I were worried about you."

"Like hell," Ali returned. "You just didn't want to let me in on what was going on."

"You can't go back to the Westwood," Dave insisted. "What if they send someone there after you?"

"Why would they?" Ali demanded. "Their only interest in me had to do with whether or not I'd lead them to Roseanne, which, sorry to say, I seem to have done unerringly. I led them to her, and I led your friend Easy to her as well. By the way, what about Roseanne? Is she under arrest or what?"

"Probably not at the moment," Dave answered. "More likely she'll be taken in for questioning."

"Will they give her a deal if she cooperates with the authorities?" Ali asked.

"That remains to be seen," Dave replied. "I know you mentioned to her that she might be able to work out some kind of a plea bargain, but those decisions are best left up to prosecutors."

"Not to loose-cannon bloggers, right?"

"I didn't say that," he returned. "I didn't say anything of the kind."

"Never mind," Ali put in. "You didn't have to."

Easy returned carrying Ali's two suitcases and the computer case as well. "Where do you want these?" he asked.

"In my car," Ali said. "I'm leaving."

"No, you're not," he answered, putting the luggage down next to the table. "Nobody's leaving right now. All my men are in place. We're waiting for the last two parties of diners to leave the restaurant. Once they're gone and are out of danger, we'll make our move. As soon as we have Mr. McLaughlin safely in custody, you'll be welcome to go anywhere you like. Until that time, though, I need you to stay here."

Time passed slowly. Gradually the restaurant cleared. Finally the door to the kitchen opened. Detective Taylor led Roseanne Maxwell into the room. She was in handcuffs and in tears. "They're going to take me to jail," she said accusingly to Ali. "I thought you told me that if I helped them I'd be able to make some kind of deal."

"I thought so, too," Ali said. "It turns out I was wrong."

"What about that attorney you told me about?" Roseanne asked. "What's his name again?"

WEB OF EVIL 331

"Victor Angeleri," Ali answered. "He may be more than you can afford right now."

"What about my jewelry?" Roseanne asked. "Do you think he might take some of that in trade?"

Months ago, Roseanne Maxwell would have been able to afford the best legal representation money could buy. Now she was one step away from selling her worldly possessions on eBay, and most likely she'd end up with a public defender.

"I don't know about that," Ali said. "You'll need to call Victor up and ask him yourself. Maybe you can work it out."

Easy held up his hand for quiet. Only then did Ali notice he was wearing an earpiece of some kind.

"Okay, people," he announced. "We've got a couple more vehicles to move into place, then it's a go. I'm going out through the kitchen. Everybody else get down on the floor. Keep your heads well below the level of the windowsills. Stay under tables if it's at all possible. Nobody steps outside the restaurant until I give the all-clear. Got it?"

Ali paused long enough to watch Detective Taylor help Roseanne to her knees. Then, with her own heart pounding in her throat, Ali dropped to the floor and scrambled under the table where they'd been sitting. She may have been mad as hell about what was going on right then, but she wasn't stubborn enough to risk her own life because of it.

Lying there on the dingy floor, Ali waited breathlessly to see what would happen next. When nothing did, she turned over far enough to peer up at the table above her. There, in plain view, were several pieces of dead and dying bubble gum, chunks of the stuff that thoughtless diners had unloaded by sticking them to the underside of the table.

For some unaccountable reason, seeing those messy wads of bubble gum while at the same time anticipating the sound of gunfire struck Ali as a kind of grim joke. Unable to help herself, she began to giggle.

Moments later, she was jostled as someone else scrambled into the confined space under the table.

"What's so funny?" Dave asked. "Are you okay?"

Not quite able to explain it herself, Ali finally managed to stifle her fit of inappropriate laughter. When she did, she found she was still upset with him.

"What are you doing here?" she wanted to know. "I thought you'd be outside playing cops and robbers with your friend Easy."

"Come on, Ali," he returned. "I've told you before. This isn't my jurisdiction. I've got no more legal right to participate in a DEA operation than you do. And that's why, when Easy asked me to keep quiet about what was going on, I had to do just that—keep quiet."

His excuse didn't sit well with her. "Fine then," she said. "Here's an idea for you. How about if you keep on keeping quiet? It seems to me you've said enough for one day."

Dave's exasperated sigh wasn't lost on her. He didn't say, "Women!" but he could just as well have. Turning her back on him, Ali inched forward far enough so she could see the front of the restaurant. The remaining waitstaff had disappeared into the kitchen except for Carrie, who had taken shelter behind the hostess desk.

In the end, all of Easy Washington's advance preparations for a flawless takedown still weren't enough—at least not for the one in Valencia's Claim Jumper parking lot. Before Easy and the last of his officers could move into position, something must have alerted Tracy McLaughlin to their presence. Ali didn't see the suspect slam his Element in gear and shoot forward across the parking lot, but she did hear the squeal of tires and brakes as the vehicle screeched to a stop just outside the restaurant's front door.

Seconds later, Tracy McLaughlin charged into the entryway lobby. Stifling a scream, Carrie tried to retreat farther into the restaurant, but he was too fast for her. As she attempted to dart away from the hostess stand, McLaughlin got one arm around the terrified woman's neck. With his other hand, he held a gun to her head.

Out of the corner of her eye, Ali saw Detective Taylor rise to his feet, weapon in hand. "Drop it," he ordered.

"You drop it," Tracy returned. "If you don't, this woman dies."

"Don't hurt me," Carrie wailed. "Please don't hurt me."

For a long moment, the three of them remained in a frozen tableau. Then, moving slowly and deliberately, Detective Taylor grasped the handle of his .38 with the thumb and forefinger of his left hand and carefully deposited the weapon on a nearby table.

"That's better," Tracy said. "Move away from the table."

Detective Taylor complied.

"Now," Tracy went on. "Do you have any way of communicating with those bozos outside? If so, I want you to tell them to stay put so nobody gets hurt."

Lying there, waiting for what she thought was an inevitable volley of shots, all Ali could think about was a pair of cold-blooded armed killers silently roaming the hallways and classrooms of Columbine High School, stalking their innocent victims. Determined to fight back, she unholstered her Glock.

"Stay here!" Dave whispered urgently in her direction, then he moved away from the spot under the table that had sheltered them both. Staying under the cover of intervening tables, he slithered across the floor of the darkened restaurant in a surprisingly rapid commando crawl.

"Not really," Detective Taylor replied. "They're Feds. I'm local. Our radios aren't compatible."

"Isn't that just great," Tracy muttered.

Anxious to provide a diversion from whatever action Dave was about to take, Ali surprised herself by finding her own voice.

"Let Carrie go, Tracy," she urged. "Haven't enough people been hurt already?"

"Who are you?" he demanded, glancing around the room, trying to fix her position. "Are you a cop?"

"You know me, Tracy," she answered. "I'm Ali Reynolds. I'm the woman you followed here, remember? And the whole place is surrounded by cops. You can't get away. Give it up. It's your only chance."

"No matter what, I'm not going back to the slammer," he declared. "So come out from wherever it is you're hiding. Show me your hands."

Attempting to estimate the distance Dave would have to cover to circumnavigate the dining room and how much time it would take for him to be within striking distance of the armed man, Ali tried to stall a little longer.

"Why should I?" she asked. "So you can shoot me, too?"

"Because if you don't come out where I can see you, I'm going to shoot her," Tracy returned ominously. "If that happens, this woman's blood will be on your hands as much as it is on mine."

Carrie moaned in protest. Somewhere in the restaurant, Roseanne Maxwell began to sob as well.

Hoping Detective Taylor saw her do it, Ali tucked the Glock into the back of the waistband of her jeans. Then, aware Tracy would have to peer through the gloom in order to observe her every move, Ali raised her hands and slowly rose to her feet. Once upright, Ali stepped forward until she was standing a foot or so in front of Montgomery Taylor and slightly to one side. The move left her Glock's exposed handle well within the detective's reach.

"What do you want?" Ali asked, willing Tracy to keep his attention focused on her. "What are you hoping to accomplish?"

At that instant, Dave materialized to the right of the front door. Without being observed, he had managed to work his way all around the restaurant. Now, coming from just outside Tracy's line of vision, Dave smashed into the two people locked in their life-and-death embrace. The unexpected blow propelled the couple apart, sending Carrie in one direction and Tracy and his weapon in the other.

Carrie screamed. A burst of gunfire pierced the air, but only for a moment, then it was over. In the sudden silence that followed, Detective Taylor grabbed Ali's Glock and charged forward to help Dave subdue Tracy. Seconds later the room was filled to capacity as more officers raced in from outside.

"Is he dead?" Roseanne Maxwell's plaintive question came from two tables away. "Please tell me the son of a bitch is dead."

Ali walked over and helped Roseanne emerge from her hiding place beneath the table.

"I'm afraid not," Ali returned. "It looks to me as though he came through just fine."

"Damn," Roseanne muttered.

Easy Washington appeared. He seemed shaken. His dark skin had taken on a peculiarly ashen hue. "Is everyone all right?" he asked.

"I think so," Ali said. "I believe everyone's fine."

"Too bad," Roseanne added. "I was really hoping."

Dave showed up just then with concern written all over his face. He grasped Ali by the shoulders. "What in the world were you thinking, standing up like that?"

"I was trying to get him to look at me instead of you."

"Are you nuts? You don't even have on a Kevlar vest."

"Do you?" Ali returned.

Dave ignored her question. "Are you all right?" he asked.

"I'm fine," she said. "Perfectly fine."

And for some strange reason, right at that minute, she wasn't even mad at him anymore. In fact, she felt lighter than air.

{ CHAPTER 19 }

In the aftermath of the Claim Jumper incident, Ali found herself once again on the wrong side of the thin blue line. While Dave went off to confer with the other officers, Ali was interviewed in a cursory fashion by a pair of young uniformed cops who took her statement and then left. They made it clear that most of the team was focused on what had happened to Carrie and on the pivotal roles Dave Holman and Detective Taylor had played in effecting Carrie's rescue.

Ali was tempted to point out to one of the young cops, "Hey, I helped, too." Instead, she let it go. In the grand scheme of things the fact that Carrie was safe was all that mattered.

Because shots had been fired in the course of the incident, all weapons on the scene—including Ali's Glock—were collected by crime scene investigators, bagged, cataloged, and taken away for forensic examination. Ali's objections about losing possession of her Glock were duly noted and duly ignored. Nobody but Ali seemed to care much that her weapon was going away nor were they willing to say when, if ever, she'd be able to have it back.

The better part of an hour passed before Tracy McLaughlin and Roseanne Maxwell were loaded into separate patrol cars and carted off. For a long time after that, Ali sat drinking free Claim Jumper coffee and being pretty much ignored by all concerned while a small army of people hustled around the restaurant processing the scene. It was frustrating to be right there in what was supposedly the middle of the action and still have so little information about what was going on.

Finally, Ali reached for her computer case and her computer. Minutes later she was logged on to a wire-service news site. What she found wasn't much but it was a lot more than anyone had bothered telling her.

A joint task force made up of local and federal officers staged a series of coordinated raids at several locations late today targeting what is thought to be a major drug-distribution operation centered in the Los Angeles area. Several arrests were made, including a number of people—both customers and employees—at an exclusive area topless bar called the Pink Swan.

Mason Louder, the Drug Enforcement Agency's local public affairs officer, has announced that a press conference dealing with today's operations is scheduled for 10 A.M. tomorrow morning at the Federal Building.

Two of those arrested at the Pink Swan location are thought to be Mario and Reynaldo Joaquin, sons of local real estate magnate

Lucia Joaquin. According to sources close to the investigation, Ms. Joaquin, now in ill health and living in semi-retirement in Palm Springs, has long been suspected of maintaining close ties with Colombian drug cartels, in which her deceased husband, Anselmo, was once considered to be a major player.

For years, Ms. Joaquin maintained a high-profile lifestyle and counted among her circle of acquaintances many of Southern California's media elite, including television network executive Paul Grayson, whose grisly murder late last week as well as the subsequent deaths of both his fiancée and her mother are all thought to be connected to the case and may well be what sparked tonight's coordinated law enforcement action.

Mr. Grayson's widow, former L.A. news anchor Alison Reynolds, was originally suspected of having some involvement with his death. Ms. Reynolds's mother, Edie Larson, who is visiting from Arizona and was interviewed at her hotel late this evening, told reporters that she hoped that the cloud of suspicion lingering over her daughter's head would soon be lifted.

Ali reread that sentence. "Interviewed at her hotel . . ."

What hotel? Ali wondered. It sounded as though at least one reporter and probably more had managed to track Edie to her new location at the Motel 6. And yes, Paul's death was definitely related to the Joaquin organization, but Monique Ragsdale's death and April Gaddis's had nothing at all to do with it—at least not as far as Ali knew. That meant the so-called sources close to the investigation didn't have all their facts straight.

Unable to find any more information elsewhere, Ali turned to her cutlooseblog.com mailbox, where the "new mail" symbol told her she had forty-seven new messages. Daunted by the very thought of starting to mow through all of those, Ali turned instead to her personal mailbox, one she had set up in order to keep her blog life separate from everything else. There she had only three new messages.

The first one was from her father:

Dear Ali,
Back home but from what I hear—and don't
hear—from your mother, obviously I shouldn't
be. I should have stayed there instead. What in
the world is going on? Call me.

DAD

Ali didn't answer the message right then, and she didn't call, either. Her father was her mother's problem more than he was Ali's, and Edie was going to have to handle him on her own.

The second message was from her wrongful dismissal attorney, Marcella Johnson. Like Victor Angeleri and Helga Myerhoff, Marcella, too, worked for the firm Weldon, Davis, and Reed. Although sharing a sky-high hourly rate, the three attorneys had totally different areas of expertise. Despite their inarguable effectiveness, Ali had sometimes found herself wishing she'd hooked herself up with more of a general practitioner attorney rather than three separate and amazingly expensive specialists.

> *Dear Ali,*
> *My God, woman, what are you thinking? Your name has been everywhere this weekend—in the news, in the papers, on the radio. With our case coming up next week, now would have been a good time for you to keep a low profile, but since you didn't ask my advice on that score, I guess I won't give it.*
>
> *When is your husband's funeral? We're due to give depositions on Tuesday afternoon, but I'm wondering if I should ask for a continuance. Also, I'm getting a few hints here and there that opposing counsel may be ready to come forward with a deal. Don't leave town without letting me know and keep your cell phone handy in case I need to reach you.*
>
> MARCELLA

Does Valencia count as out of town? Ali wondered.

Dave turned up then, looking agitated. "I just talked to your mother," he said. "I thought we'd managed to ditch the reporters back at the other hotel, but now it seems they've tracked her to the new one, too."

"I know," Ali said.

"You talked to Edie?" Dave asked.

"Not exactly," Ali replied. "I read it online."

"Online?" Dave asked. "Somebody put your mother's whereabouts up on the Internet?"

She brought the article back up and pushed the computer over so Dave could read it for himself.

"Geez!" he said, when he finished. "They're everywhere."

"So I guess Motel 6 is out?" Ali asked.

"Easy's already working the problem, and it's a good thing, too. When I left him he was on the phone with LAPD, trying to clear it with them so you can go back to your own house tonight."

"On Robert Lane?" Ali asked.

Dave nodded. "We're thinking that's the last place anyone would expect you to be along about now."

Me included, Ali thought. But if Dave and Easy were still concerned about Ali's safety, did that mean some member of the Joaquin group had escaped law enforcement's coordinated dragnet?

"Who's still on the loose?" Ali asked.

"Jake Maxwell," Dave answered. "We're not sure how or where we missed him. Amber and Lucia are still unaccounted for as well. Easy thinks I should pick up your mother and then go to the house and keep an eye on both of you there until we know Jake and the others are in custody."

As if on cue, Easy sauntered into the room. "Done," he said to Dave. "LAPD Homicide has cleared the house on Robert Lane. You'll stay with them and keep an eye out?"

"Absolutely," Dave said.

Easy came over to where Ali was sitting. "Hold out your hand and close your eyes," he said.

Ali did as she was told. A moment later, something metallic and shaped like a silver dollar dropped into the palm of her hand. It was smooth on one side while the other side was tacky with the residue of some adhesive that could have been rubber cement.

"What's this?" she asked, staring down at the shiny disk.

Easy grinned. "A memento," he said, "just for you. Compliments of the DEA."

"But what is it?"

"A GPS tracking device Dave removed from the inside of your rear bumper."

"Don't you need it for evidence?" she asked.

Easy shook his head. "We have enough evidence, and I think you earned this. It turns out we've got several of them from several different vehicles. The warehouse complex out behind the Pink Swan is a veritable jungle of electronic tracking and wiretapping equipment complete with an armload of these. Not only have the Joaquins been keeping tabs on what we've been doing, they've also been running electronic surveillance on their competition. Our IT guys tell us that the place is an absolute gold mine of drug-dealing intelligence if we're able to move on it fast enough and before anyone else knows what we have."

Ali examined the device for a moment or so longer before stuffing it in the front pocket of her jeans. "Are you sure you should be saying all of this in front of a 'loose-cannon' blogger?" she asked.

"Sorry about that," Easy said apologetically. "I was out of line earlier. I think we can trust you. Dave told me what you did to help out in there, and I'm very grateful. He and Monty might not have managed without you. Clearly we were lucky to have you on the team tonight. Still, now that you mention it, it might be better if you didn't bring up any of the details of this operation in your blog until after tomorrow morning's news conference."

"Maybe you should take a look at what's out there on the Net right now," Dave said, nodding in the direction of Ali's computer screen. "Some of it's already showing up, and she didn't put it there, either."

Without a word, Ali turned the screen so Easy Washington could read it. "They don't have a lot of it straight," he observed when he finished reading. "Just enough to cause trouble." He turned back to Ali.

"Have Dave give you my numbers. Once the press conference is over, I may be able to give you an exclusive about all this."

He was offering Ali an exclusive story about a major drug bust that would appear first on cutlooseblog.com? Ali knew that would be a scoop that would drive her former cohorts in the media—friend and foe alike—utterly nuts. It would be especially galling to the people who were spending tonight doggedly tracking her mother's every move.

"Thank you," she said. "So in the meantime you and Dave think I should go back to the house?"

"Only if you want to," Easy said. "There's not much sense in your hanging around here. Going to the house makes sense because it's presumably a spot where no one would think to look for you. For one thing, it's still officially off-limits due to being a crime scene. But if you'd be more comfortable somewhere else, or if you'd like me to send some officers along to look out for you—"

"No," Ali said. "The house is fine, and sending extra officers along is unnecessary. The less fuss there is about it, the more likely it is that no one will notice we've gone anywhere. For another, Dave will be there. He's just going by the hotel long enough to pick up my mother. I'm sure you can make better use of your people here. We'll be fine on our own. Oh," she added. "Is it all right to use my phone now?"

Easy waggled his hands. "We *believe* so," he said. "We're hopeful that the Joaquins' entire electronics setup was centered in that one location. At this time, however, there's always a chance that they have backup equipment somewhere else that's still in operation."

"So it's possible someone else might still be listening in on whatever I say."

"For the time being, yes," Easy answered. "Possible but not likely."

Easy went back outside. Ali packed up her computer, and Dave helped carry that and her luggage out to her car. "Do you want me to come with you?" he asked.

"No. You go get Mom. I'm sure she's worried sick. Just make sure that no one follows you when you bring her to the house. Although," she added ruefully, patting the pocket of her jeans where she had stowed the GPS device Easy Washington had given her, "I now know that it's sometimes harder to know you're being followed than one would think."

"I'll be careful," Dave said. "Besides, I don't think the media routinely passes out GPS tracking devices."

"Let's hope," Ali said.

He opened the car door to let her inside and touched her shoulder tentatively as she did so. "Be careful," he said.

"I will."

By then it was late enough that, other than a long parade of slow-moving semis, traffic into the city was relatively light. Among all those trucks, the Cayenne might as well have been invisible.

Propped up by cup after cup of coffee, Ali was tired but nonetheless wide awake as she drove. As the miles sped by, she couldn't help thinking about Paul. Did the fact that he had been working with the authorities at the time of his death mean he was, in fact, some kind of hero?

During that fateful phone call from Roseanne, he had evidently told her that he would go to the authorities but only after both his wedding and honeymoon. That delay—most likely done out of deference for April—had given the Joaquins the ammunition they needed and the opportunity to take him out. The irony was that they had killed Paul because they suspected he might *possibly* go to the cops when in fact he had already done so. That wasn't lost on Ali, either. She knew those were facets of the story she would need to address when it came time to write Easy Washington's promised exclusive for cutlooseblog.com.

Most of the time what appeared in cutloose consisted of opinion—Ali's opinions and those of her readers. After months of using the blog to revile Paul Grayson for his two-timing treatment of her, it was difficult for Ali to think of him in any context other than worm. She wondered if she'd somehow be able to muster the necessary distance and evenhandedness to write the rest of the story and do justice to it. For that, Ali would have to revert to her old self and to her original training as a journalist—with one minor exception. Well, a major exception, actually. Most of the time reporters were expected to relate what happened without actually being involved. In this situation, Ali could hardly claim to be a disinterested bystander.

Lost in those complicated thoughts and driving on automatic pilot, Ali steered the Cayenne up the familiar steep curves of Robert Lane. When she arrived at the entrance, she was surprised to see that the broken gate had been repaired. It was standing open, but the broken post had been mended and the wrought-iron gate itself had been reattached to the hinges. Once inside the gate she rolled down her window and attempted to use the free-standing keypad to punch in what she remembered as the old gate-closing code. To her surprise, the gate swung shut.

She had decided on her way into town that it would probably be best if, for the time being, she and her mother stayed in the pool house. There were two bedrooms there and it would be better for her to stay in what had been Chris's apartment for the past several years rather than for them to venture into the house where April and Paul had been living together in her absence. Eventually Ali would have to deal with April's things and with Paul's, too, but not right now. Not tonight. Not with so much of what had happened to those people still far too fresh.

So, after rolling the window back up, Ali headed for the pool house with its attached carport. Even if it was locked, she knew Chris had always left an extra key in the utility cabinet at the front of the carport. As she drove through the yard, the motion-activated security lights came on. Passing the garage, she was surprised to see the garage doors standing open. Before she could react, though, a figure emerged from the garage doorway—a figure carrying a gun. Her first thought was simply, *No! Not again!*

She knew it was Jake Maxwell before she even saw his face. And when he used the barrel of the gun to rap sharply on the window next to her head, she knew exactly what he wanted and did it at once. She put on the brakes and stopped.

Even though she couldn't hear him very well through the closed window and over the sound of the engine, it was easy enough to read his lips. "Roll down the window!" he ordered.

With a weapon trained at her head and with her own Glock packed away in some crime scene investigator's evidence storage locker, Ali had no choice but to comply. She rolled down her window.

"What are you doing here?" she asked.

Jake ignored the question. "I need your car," he said, "and I need it now. Get out."

There was a splotch of grease on the front of Jake's otherwise white shirt and grease on his shirtsleeves as well. He had been doing something in the garage, something mechanical. Or at least he'd been trying to. His face was drenched in sweat. He looked desperate. And scared.

In that moment Ali recognized something about the man that she had never known before. Jake Maxwell was a coward. Whatever crimes he may have participated in, it was unlikely he had ever done his own dirty work.

"No," she said simply. "I won't."

Jake was almost beside himself. "I've got a gun. What do you mean you won't?"

Just like in the restaurant, Ali was making calculations in her head. She had probably left the Claim Jumper several minutes before Dave had, although she wasn't sure by how much. And she had most likely driven faster than he had. When it came to power, his little Nissan didn't compare with the Cayenne's V-8. Maybe he had fudged the speed limit coming into town—Ali certainly had—but she doubted it. And once he got to the city, he would be going first to the Motel 6 to collect Edie. How much longer would that take him? Half an hour? Forty-five minutes? Could she stall Jake that long? Ali realized that her best bet was to engage him in conversation.

"What's going on, Jake?" she said as calmly as she could manage. "Why the gun? We've known each other for a long time. You don't mean this. You wouldn't hurt me."

"I'll hurt you if I have to," he insisted. "I need your car! Get out."

"Can't we talk about this?" she asked.

"There's nothing to talk about," Jake said. "The cops are after me. So are some other people. Either way, I'm a dead man. Give me your car."

Ali knew now that Jake was as frightened of the Joaquins as Roseanne had been.

"Surely it can't be as bad as all this," Ali said. "Get in. I'll take you wherever you need to go."

Much to Ali's amazement and without an additional word, he walked around the front of the car. There were a few short seconds when she might have jammed her foot on the gas pedal and run him down. That would have ended the confrontation there and then, but something—basic humanity, maybe?—held her back. She was betting the farm that he wouldn't gun her down in cold blood because she was someone he knew. The problem was, that was her situation as well. Ali couldn't kill Jake for the exact same reason—she knew him. They had once been friends—at least she had always thought they were.

Ali punched the "unlock" button on the car and let him inside.

"Where to?" she asked.

"Mexico," he said. "And not down the I-5, either. They'll be checking the border there. Head for Julian. Know where that is?"

Ali nodded. Julian was in the mountains east of Escondido. If you passed Julian and continued on over that particular range, you came out north of Brawley—and near what was considered to be more of a back-door entrance into Mexico through Calexico. But going that way was anything but direct. Ali suspected Jake was probably right in terms of people not thinking he'd attempt to go that way. There would be far more focus on the main I-5 corridor and far less on secondary routes.

She wondered how closely Jake had been following the situation on the ground as the takedowns happened and whether or not he had any idea that most of the Joaquin organization along with Tracy McLaughlin and Roseanne had all been taken into custody.

"Sounds like you're headed the same place Roseanne is," Ali ventured casually. "And considering she knows all about you and Amber, I doubt she'll be thrilled to see you when you show up."

"You know about Oaxaca?" Jake demanded. "How?"

Ali hadn't known where they were headed in Mexico exactly—but now she did. And she also knew from Jake's reaction that he had no idea Roseanne had been placed under arrest.

"Roseanne told me," Ali said, goading just to see how he'd react to the news. "She called me because she needed cash in a hurry and wanted to unload some of her jewelry. I took a few pieces off her hands."

"But she's still all right?"

"You mean have your friends the Joaquins caught up with her? Not yet."

From the dismayed look on Jake's face, Ali knew he was taken aback. "How do you know so much about all this?" he wanted to know.

Ali decided to choose a Joaquin—any Joaquin—to turn into a fall guy. "Reynaldo," Ali said. "He's made a deal with the Feds. From what I hear, he's giving them an earful and spilling his guts about everything that's been going on around here. By morning the whole organization will be in custody. You sure you want to be the last man standing?"

Once again Jake waved the gun in her direction. "Why are we still sitting here?" he demanded. "I told you to drive."

Ali's phone rang just then, startling them both. "Don't answer," Jake began, but Ali already had, hoping beyond hope the caller would be Dave and that she would somehow be able to let him know what was going on.

"Ms. Reynolds?" an unfamiliar male voice asked.

"Yes."

"I'm so sorry to disturb you at such a late hour. My name is Fred Macon. You know, with Three Palms, the mortuary?"

Ali struggled to conceal her disappointment. "What can I do for you, Mr. Macon?"

"Your husband's remains have just been transported to our facility here. There seems to be some confusion with the paperwork. I had been told that April Gaddis was the person to be consulted about services and so forth, but it's been brought to my attention that Ms. Gaddis is also deceased at this time, and since yours is the only other contact number available to us . . ."

"It's well after midnight, Mr. Macon," Ali pointed out. "Do we really need to have this discussion right now? Can't we plan my husband's funeral during daylight hours?"

"Well, yes, certainly," Fred Macon said quickly. "There's one check mark on the form that wasn't properly handled over in Riverside, however, and it would be a big help to all of us here if we could get that one straightened out as soon as possible."

"What check mark?" Ali asked.

"Embalming," Fred Macon said. "It would be helpful to us to know whether or not you intend to have Mr. Grayson's remains embalmed."

Paul had died on Thursday night. It was now edging toward dawn on Tuesday morning. That went a long way to explaining Mr. Macon's middle-of-the-night urgency. Embalming was probably long overdue.

"By all means," Ali said.

"Thank you," Fred said. "Thank you so much. So I can note on the file that you gave me a verbal authorization to do so over the phone?"

"Yes."

"And I can let the office know that you'll be in

touch to finalize arrangements for the services tomorrow . . . later on today, actually?"

"That, too," Ali told him.

"And, if you'll pardon my asking. Our information
about Ms. Gaddis didn't come through what you
would call official channels. I just happened to see
it on the news and made the connection. Will you
be handling arrangements for her as well? If a joint
service is required—"

"No," Ali said. "I believe someone else will be in
charge of that."

"Oh," Fred said. He sounded disappointed, as
though he had somehow missed the opportunity to
drum up some extra night-shift business. Ali wondered
if perhaps he actually made a commission. "All right
then," he added. "Thanks so much, and again, I'm
sorry to disturb you in the middle of the night."

"That's quite all right," Ali said.

She ended the call. "The mortuary," she explained
to Jake. "Calling about Paul's services. You already
knew he was dead when you came to court on Friday,
didn't you?" she added.

"I said drive," Jake said, but she noted a lack of
conviction in his voice, and that uncertainty gave her
courage.

"No," she said suddenly. "We're not going anywhere.
I think you know who the guilty party is. I want to
know who killed Paul and why."

"Ali, I'm telling you," Jake said menacingly. "If I
have to shoot you, I will. Don't make me do it."

The window on Ali's side of the car was still open.
With a speed that surprised her and caught Jake totally
flat-footed, Ali shut off the ignition, extracted the car

key, and flung it out through the open window. She welcomed the tiny whisper of a splash as the leather-topped key landed in the nearby swimming pool and sank to what she knew was the bottom of the diving end.

Jake heard it, too, and was outraged. "You bitch!" he screamed at her. "Are you nuts? What the hell are you thinking? Now we'll never get out of here."

That's the whole idea, Ali thought.

"Maybe it's time you thought about calling the cops and turning yourself in," she suggested.

"Goddamn it!" he roared furiously. "Get out! Get the hell out of this car! I was working trying to hot-wire Paul's Land Rover when you showed up. It's a lot harder than it looks, but I almost had it. Once I get it running, we'll take that instead. Go on! Move it. You're driving."

Ali did as she was told. She moved. She was headed for the Land Rover when a new set of headlights rounded the last curve on Robert Lane and stopped just outside the gate.

Ali's heart quickened within her. She was sure the new arrival had to be Dave, that once again he had somehow ridden to her rescue. Then she heard Chris's voice.

"Mom?" he called. "Is that you? The gate is closed, and I don't have a clicker. Come let me in."

Ali's insides lurched. It wasn't Dave at all. It was her son. Her baby.

Jake grabbed Ali's arm from behind. She felt the barrel of the gun press into her back. "We're coming to you," Jake called. "Stay right where you are. I have a gun, and I'm not afraid to use it. If you move or make so much as a sound, your mother dies. Understand?"

They came around the corner of the pool house to the spot where Ali could see Chris standing beside Edie's idling Olds.

She wanted to urge him to run. Or to tumble down the bank of lush pampas grass her neighbors had allowed to flourish on the steep hillside. But with the gun pressed against her spine, and with her arm twisted almost up to her shoulder, she said nothing. It would be bad enough if Jake shot her. The idea that he might hurt Chris was unthinkable.

At last they reached the gatepost. "Open it," Jake ordered, propelling her forward.

Ali punched the keypad, and the gate swung open.

"In," Jake said, waving his weapon in the direction of Chris's car. "You drive. Your mother and I will sit in back."

"Mom," Chris asked. "Did he hurt you? Are you all right?"

"Shut up," Jake said.

Chris did as he was told, too. He shut up and got back into the driver's seat while Jake heaved Ali into the car and across the backseat. He shoved her hard enough that her shoulder smashed painfully into the door on the far side.

Jake settled in behind her and slammed the door. "Thanks," he said to the back of Chris's head. "You couldn't have come at a better time. Now take us to the Ten and go east, and do it in a hell of a hurry."

That meant they weren't going to Julian.

{ CHAPTER 20 }

Mom, who is this jerk?" Chris demanded. "If you hurt her, I swear I'll—"

"I said shut up and drive," Jake repeated. "And I meant it."

Ali rubbed her bruised shoulder. It hurt, but not nearly as much as her bruised ego. How had she allowed this calamity to happen? It seemed to her that somehow, in a week full of disasters, she should have seen this one coming and been able to prevent it.

"I'm all right, Chris," she said. "Do what he says so no one gets hurt."

Chris was outraged. "For God's sake, Mom. How can you say that? The man was holding a gun to your head!"

"And now I'm holding one to yours," Jake reminded him. "So you'd best pay attention. Turn the car around and get going."

Chris complied by slamming his foot on the accelerator. He backed away from the gate so fast that he came perilously close to the edge of the road. Then, after pulling a swift U-turn, the Alero sped back down Robert Lane.

"Have a ball," Chris declared. "Shoot away. Then we'll all see exactly how well Grandma's Olds drives with no one behind the wheel! I don't think this model comes equipped with a self-guidance system."

Ali knew that "Go ahead and shoot me" often qualify as famous last words. In fact, she suspected they had been included in the Darwin Awards as an often-quoted exit line.

For God's sake, don't antagonize him, Ali thought. "Chris," she cautioned. "Please."

"Slow down," Jake said as Chris raced through the stop sign at the bottom of the hill. "The last thing we need is for the cops to come after us because you ran a damned stop sign."

Chris slowed slightly. They traveled for the better part of a mile in silence.

"So what are you?" Chris asked finally, studying Jake's face in the rearview mirror. "Somebody who's just been profiled on *America's Most Wanted*? An escaped convict? What?"

"He's a friend of Paul's," Ali supplied. "Used to be a friend of Paul's."

"Some friend," Chris muttered.

Once on the 10 there was far more traffic than there had been on the surface streets, and more semis than cars, all headed east, trying to make as much distance as possible before the blinding sun came up. Ali wondered about the drivers of those various big rigs. How was it that they could tool along, blissfully unaware of the life-and-death drama playing out in Edie Lawson's innocuous-looking white Alero? Why was it none of them gave the speeding Oldsmobile a second glance?

Watching the lights of the not-quite-sleeping city speed past outside the window, Ali knew it was late but she didn't know how late. Somehow, in the course of the struggle on Robert Lane, her wristwatch had disappeared. Huddled too far in the corner of the backseat to be able to see the clock on the dash, Ali was damned if she'd ask Jake Maxwell for the time of day. Finally, as they sped through Ontario, she caught sight of a huge neon clock at a Ford dealership. It was 2:12 exactly. No wonder she was tired.

As they drove, Ali couldn't help being struck by the latest irony in her situation. Earlier that evening and without either her knowledge or permission, someone working for the Joaquin organization had followed her every move by using the very tracking device that, even now, was still in her pocket. Through the soft denim material, she could feel the presence of that smooth round disk. Fortunately—or unfortunately, depending on your point of view—the people who had been so vitally interested in her whereabouts earlier were now all under arrest. So even though it was technically possible for someone to track her, it seemed unlikely that anyone would do so.

With a sinking heart, Ali realized that all the high-tech GPS technology in the world wasn't going to save her and her son. When it came to being rescued, she and Chris were on their own.

Still maintaining an uneasy silence, they traveled eastbound for some time. As they approached the merge with the 60, Ali's hopes rose. Off to the right, she saw the lights of a phalanx of emergency vehicles sweeping onto I-10 ahead of them. When Ali first caught sight of them, she hardly dared breathe. She watched them for a few hopeful moments, praying that the lights were somehow related to what was happening to them, praying that Jake wouldn't notice. And he didn't. But by the time Chris negotiated the I-10/60 merge with its tangle of complicated traffic and disappearing lanes, the parade of cop cars or ambulances or whatever that Ali had put such hope in had shot on far ahead and completely out of sight.

Despairing, Ali closed her eyes and concentrated on some straightforward praying.

At last Chris spoke again. "Where are we going?"

"Don't worry," Jake replied. "Just stay on the Ten. I'll tell you where to turn. It won't be for a while yet."

"If we're going very far, we'll need to stop for gas."

Ali caught her breath as Jake leaned forward and peered over the front seat.

"All right," he said finally, having read the gauge for himself. "I guess you're right. We do need gas. Pull off at the next exit, but find a full-service pump. No one gets in or out of the vehicle while we're stopped, understand? No one!"

Somewhere in Beaumont they pulled off the freeway and stopped at a convenience mart. While the three of them sat in the car and waited for the slow-moving attendant to fill the tank, Ali was startled by the ringing of her phone. She looked at the readout.

"It's my mother," she said. "She was supposed to come by the house tonight. If she did, she's probably upset that I'm not there. She'll be worried. She might even call the cops."

"Answer it then," Jake said. "But put the phone

on speaker first, and don't try anything funny. Understand?"

Ali understood all too well.

"Alison?" Edie said when she heard her daughter's voice. "Are you all right? Where are you?"

Sometime earlier—was it hours or days?—with an armed and unstable April Gaddis standing in the kitchen at Robert Lane, Ali had somehow managed to convey the gravity of the situation to Dave by speaking to him in a kind of code. Now, though, with Jake Maxwell's gun digging into her ribs and with him privy to both sides of the conversation, speaking to Edie in code simply wasn't possible.

"I'm fine, Mom," Ali said as reassuringly as possible. "I got called away from the house by an emergency with an old friend. There wasn't time to let you know. I'm sorry."

"You couldn't have called?"

"No. Calling just wasn't possible."

"Well," Edie said, sounding both perplexed and disgruntled, "the gate is shut. A cab brought me over, but I can't get inside. What am I supposed to do, stand around here all night?"

Ali could have given her the gate code, but she didn't. If something happened and Ali and Chris didn't survive, the parked Cayenne would be the only real evidence as to what had happened to them. Ali didn't want that evidence disturbed.

"Use the cab and find a hotel then," she said. "I won't be able to get back there before sometime tomorrow."

"What about Chris?" Edie asked. "Where is he?"

"Staying with friends," Ali said.

"It's just that it's not like you to be so irresponsible, Ali," Edie said. "You're sure you're all right?"

"I'm fine," Ali said quickly. "I've got to go now, Mom. Take care. I love you."

It hurt to think those might be the last words Edie Larson ever heard from her daughter, but they were the best Ali could do.

Seconds later they were back under way. "You still haven't said where we're going," Chris reminded Jake.

"That's because you still don't need to know."

"Mexico," Ali supplied. "Oaxaca. At least that's what he told me earlier."

"Shut up!" Jake said.

The barrel of his gun dug deeper into Ali's ribs, but she was grateful that it was pointed in her direction rather than in Chris's. He had his whole life ahead of him. As for hers? If she had to gamble her life to save her son's, that's exactly what she'd do.

Ali looked out across the darkened desert where mountains loomed black against a star-studded sky. They were only a few miles west of the Highway 111 turnoff and the place where the speeding train had plowed into a parked Camry—the place where Paul had died. Ali couldn't help wondering if maybe she and Chris were destined to die there as well—in much the same manner.

"I need to take a leak," Chris said from the front seat.

"Me, too," Ali added quickly. "I had way too much coffee earlier."

Jake immediately seemed to assume that their request for a pit stop was nothing but a ploy. And up to a point it was. Although Ali genuinely needed to use the facilities, it was also her sincere hope that in the process of getting in and out of the car, there would be an opportunity for Chris, at least, to get away.

"You'll just have to wait," Jake said. "You can hold it for a while."

Soon, though, and now that she was thinking about it, Ali really couldn't hold it any longer. She had drunk way too much coffee.

"I really do need to go," she said.

"I told you, we're not stopping."

"Fine," Ali said. "If you don't mind sitting in a puddle of urine, neither do I."

"There's a rest area coming up in a few minutes," Chris said. "Maybe we could stop there."

"Oh, for God's sake!" Jake exclaimed. "Stop then. By all means, but the two of you go in and out of the restroom one at a time, and your cell phone stays with me. Give it to me. Yours, too, if you've got one," Jake told Chris. "Hand it over."

As Chris signaled to merge onto the rest area exit ramp, Jake held out his hand to collect first Chris's phone and then Ali's. Chris passed his back. Involved in reluctantly handing over her own, Ali never saw exactly what happened. One moment they were slowing to exit the highway. The next the desert came alive with the flashing lights of a dozen police and emergency vehicles as the Alero gave a sudden violent lurch and veered to one side. Then it staggered forward on the rims of four instantly flattened tires.

"Nail strips!" Jake shouted in a panic. "Keep driving. Keep driving."

But Chris had already reached another conclusion

and slammed on the brakes. As the vehicle slowed and came to a stop, Ali heard a voice she barely recognized as her own, screaming at her son.

"Get out," she screeched at him. "Go! Go! Go! I'm right behind you."

But that wasn't true. Before Ali could touch the door handle, Jake's fingers clamped down on her wrist. Ali may still have been trapped inside the car, but Chris was in motion before all the words had tumbled out of her mouth. She saw her son land and land hard, thrown forward by a combination of his own momentum and that of the vehicle. Then to her immense relief, he scrambled to his feet. Limping slightly, he raced to cover behind one of several waiting California Highway Patrol vehicles.

After that, in the middle of the chaos—accompanied by a cloud of swirling dust and the blinding flash of lights—there was a moment of utter silence followed by someone shouting, "All right, Maxwell. You're surrounded. Put down your weapon. Come out with your hands up."

Jake looked at Ali. "How do they know it's me? Who told them?"

Ali had no answer for that, but with Chris out of the car and out of danger, she found herself immersed in a well of complete calm—a place where Jake Maxwell's threats no longer held any sway with her. She was immune.

"It doesn't matter who told them, Jake," she said. "What matters is that they *do* know. It's over. You can't get away. Give it up."

"You have to believe me, Ali," he said, after a pause. "I had no idea she was going to kill him."

"Kill who?" Ali asked.

"Paul. I thought Lucia was just going to teach him a lesson. That's the way the Joaquins work, you see. They give people lessons, hard enough lessons so you know what they're capable of, and you don't need another one."

The comment came from so far out in left field that it took a moment for Ali to process it. "You mean you knew?" Ali demanded. "You son of a bitch, are you saying you did it?"

"I didn't. All I did was help get him drunk. I swear to you, I didn't know anything about Tracy and the rest of it. I never meant for Paul to die."

"You did mean it," Ali returned. "You meant it, and he did die. Why? Were you jealous because he got the job and you didn't? Was that it?"

With that Ali reached for the door handle.

"Wait, Ali," Jake said. "Don't leave me, please. I'll drop the gun if you stay. I promise. They won't shoot me as long as you're with me."

What Ali felt in that moment was a contempt and loathing so complete and all-consuming that there was no room left in her soul for anything else, especially not fear.

"Forget it," she told him. "You're on your own."

"But I have a gun."

"You may have a gun, buddy-boy," she told him, "but I know for a fact you don't have balls enough to use it."

With that, she opened the car door and stepped out into a world of flashing lights. And even there, in the middle of the sudden chill of the cold desert night, she knew that at least one or two of those flashing lights were bound to be cameras.

Blinded by them, she was startled when a pair of strong arms grabbed her and pulled her behind one of the waiting vehicles.

"Ali. Thank God!" Dave exclaimed. "Are you all right?" In the pulsing light she caught a glimpse of the relief on his worried face.

"I'm fine. Really."

"Come on, then," Dave said, leading her away. "It's too dangerous. Let's get out of here."

"How did you find us?" Ali asked. "How did you know where to look?"

Dave didn't answer. "Later," he said.

"Where's Chris?"

"Out of the line of fire. Where you need to be, too."

Someone shouting over what sounded like a bull-horn was still ordering Jake Maxwell out of the Alero as Dave led Ali to the far side of the concrete restroom complex. There she found Chris sitting on a picnic table with a paramedic applying ice to his ankle.

"The EMT grabbed me and wouldn't let me loose. It's just a little sprain, Mom," he said reassuringly. "It's nothing. How are you?"

Ali hurried over and hugged him. "I'm fine," she said. "I'm completely fine."

She turned back to Dave. "But how did you know . . ."

"Ask your son," Dave said. "Once he realized you were in trouble, he punched his phone's redial, and the last number dialed happened to be your folks' phone back in Sedona. Fortunately Bob was there and answered. Chris was wearing his Bluetooth mini earplug. That allowed Bob to overhear everything that was going on in the vehicle without Jake having any idea anyone was listening in. Bob immediately put another call through to us—a conference call—so we could all monitor the situation."

Ali remembered giving Chris a tough time when he had returned from a weekend skiing trip to Aspen with a telephone earpiece attached to his head. Now it appeared that an even smaller mini earplug might well have saved both their lives.

"And knowing what was up," Dave added, "Easy was able to get one of his electronic techs working the Pink Swan warehouse scene to reinitiate your GPS."

"So, from all that, you knew where we were the whole time," Ali said.

Dave nodded. "Pretty much," he said. "But none of that would have happened if Chris here hadn't used his head."

Flooded with relief and gratitude, Ali gave her son another hug. She and Chris had been in danger, all right, but not nearly as much as she had supposed.

"But you were here waiting for us," Ali said a moment later. "How did you do that? You and Easy were still in Valencia when I left. I thought you were going to pick up my mother."

"Fortunately, we were unavoidably delayed. And after that, it took some doing," Dave said. "And some pretty amazing police car driving on Easy Washington's part. Of course, it helps to have CHP cars clearing traffic ahead of us all along the way."

"So that was you?" Ali asked. "The flashing lights I saw merging off the Sixty onto the Ten just as we got there?"

Dave nodded. "Our first intention was to do this in

Beaumont when you stopped for gas. Then we decided there would be less risk to the general public if we did it here at a rest area instead, so we cleared out as many civilians as we could, and here we are. Which reminds me. You should probably give your dad a call and let him know you're okay."

But Ali's phone had bounced out of her hand the moment the tires had gone flat. She had no idea where it was now—none.

"Let me use yours, Chris," she said, holding out her hand.

He shook his head. "I was on the phone the whole way here," he said. "I'm out of battery."

"Oh, for Pete's sake," Dave said, taking out his own phone. "Here. Use mine."

Bob was overjoyed to hear his daughter's voice. "Does your mother know?" he asked. "She's been worried sick and on the phone to the restaurant the whole time."

Ali had reached Edie and was talking to her when Easy Washington came trotting around the corner of the building. "All clear," he said. "Maxwell is in custody. Is everyone here okay?"

"Just my ankle," Chris said, "but it's nothing serious."

"And you?" Easy asked Ali.

"I'm fine," she said. "One hundred percent."

"The Alero's going to have to be towed," Easy said. "And Dave's car is still at the Claim Jumper. I'll have one of my guys load you into a Suburban and take you back. The rest of us have one more stop before the evening is over."

"What stop?" Ali asked.

"In the Old Las Palmas area of Palm Springs," Easy replied. "That's where Lucia Joaquin lives. She and her granddaughter, Amber, are the only ones still at large. We've had Lucia's place under surveillance all night long. There's been no unusual activity, so we're hoping she has no idea we've managed to roll up her entire operation in the course of the last several hours. And now we're going to nail her."

"She's the one who ordered Paul's murder?" Ali asked.

Easy nodded. "I believe so."

"Then I want to go, too," Ali said. "I want to be there."

"You can't," Easy objected. "It's impossible. I'm not allowed to put civilians in danger. It's absolutely against regulations."

"I've been in danger all night," Ali pointed out. "So has Dave. So has Chris."

"Yes," Easy agreed. "But that wasn't my fault."

"Please," Ali said quietly. "After all we've been through tonight, shouldn't I be able to be there to see her taken into custody?"

Easy Washington shook his head. At first Ali was convinced he was turning her down, then he called over his shoulder to one of his men.

"Hey, Sal. Does anyone here have a couple of extra Kevlar vests? A small and a large. We've got someone here who's going to need one."

{ CHAPTER 21 }

The Kevlar jacket was bulkier than Ali could have imagined. And hotter, too. Minutes after donning it, she and Dave climbed into the backseat of Easy Washington's black Suburban.

In the rush of donning the vest Ali had lost track of her son.

"Where's Chris?" she asked. "I thought he was coming along."

"He's on his way to an ER in the ambulance," Dave answered. "The EMT insisted his ankle has to be X-rayed and refused to take no for an answer. By the way," Dave added, "did anyone ever tell you Chris is one hell of a kid? Really used his head tonight. He did a great job with your dad and us on the phone."

"Yes," Ali agreed. "He is one hell of a kid."

In the front seat, Easy was on the radio and cell phone both, coordinating his troops. At the rest area Ali had caught sight of several officers she had met in the course of the previous several days, cops she knew from L.A. and Riverside, in addition to Easy's own crew from the DEA. This was clearly a complicated, task-force-style operation with Ezekiel Washington calling the shots.

"I've never been to Palm Springs," Dave said, studying a map Easy had handed him. "We're going to a street called Via Hermosa."

Via Hermosa was a name-brand Palm Springs address, and Ali remembered visiting several of the venerable old mansions there years earlier as part of various charitable functions. She took the map from Dave long enough to point to the general area.

"Old Las Palmas is part of old Palm Springs," Ali explained. "Big houses. Big lots."

"Big bucks?" Dave asked.

"That, too, but I would guess Lucia Joaquin can afford pretty much anything she wants."

Ali thought about the other massive old places she had seen in old Las Palmas—the eight- or nine-bedroom luxury homes with their many-car garages, their lush furnishings and equally lush grounds. She didn't know which house Lucia lived in, but it had to be one like that.

And the more Ali thought about it, the more the whole idea of Lucia Joaquin offended her. She resented the idea that a woman, clad in pink from head to toe and closeted in absolute luxury, could sit at home in total comfort and safety while sending her minions off to do her bidding—up to and including committing acts of cold-blooded murder. While one of her worker bees had left a trussed and helpless Paul Grayson—who she merely suspected might go to the cops—to die on the train tracks, Lucia had been a few miles away, probably sleeping peacefully in her bed.

"Where do people like Lucia come from?" Ali asked Dave finally.

He shook his head. "They're vermin," he said. "They crawl out from under rocks."

They had turned off I-10 and onto Highway 111. As they sped through the night with the blue and red lights pulsing overhead but with no siren, Ali tried not to look at that particular part of the desert, but she couldn't help it. Her eyes were drawn to the black pool of unrelieved darkness where she knew the train track ran. What a desolate place it was—what an awful place to die.

Easy returned his radio to its holder. "Okay," he said, "here's the deal. We have yet to locate Amber, the granddaughter, but we're pretty sure Lucia is inside the Palm Springs house. It's possible she's there alone, but it's also possible there's a caregiver with her. The place sits on an acre and a half, and the whole thing is surrounded by a twelve-foot rock wall with only one gate. Since Lucia isn't in the best of health these days, she's not going to be climbing over that fence. As long as we control the gate—which we do—we also control access."

Dave nodded. Ali said nothing.

"I've got a trained tactical team in place and primed to do the heavy lifting," Easy continued. "These are guys who know what they're about and we're going to let them do it. I've put my second in command in charge. Since the two of you are here on my say-so, I'm not letting either one of you out of my sight for even so much as a minute. And you're not going any closer to the action than I say, got it?"

"Got it," Dave said at once.

"Ms. Reynolds?" Easy asked. "I don't believe I heard a response from you."

"Got it," Ali said.

"Good. I know you're anxious to see the takedown. Considering the circumstances, I can't say that I blame you, but you're not to go near that woman until my guys have the situation under control."

"Yes," Ali said. "I understand."

She looked at Dave. He sat there alert but seemingly at ease, with the palms of his hands resting squarely on his knees. If he was concerned about the coming confrontation, his impassive face betrayed none of it. But then, Ali realized, he was a Marine. Clearly he would be accustomed to going into potentially dangerous combat situations. She was not. Her heart pounded in her chest. Sweat dribbled down the back of her neck and soaked her shirt under the arms. Despite the fact that she had said she wanted to be here and see Lucia taken into custody, it was clear to Ali that she wasn't ready at all—and probably never would be. And she missed having her Glock, missed it more than she could have imagined.

"How long before it all starts?" she asked.

She had aimed her question at Dave, but Easy Washington was the one who answered. "Depends on how long it takes us to get there," he said.

Ali had always been under the impression that it took approximately forever to drive from the Palm Springs turnoff on I-10 into the city itself. Tonight it seemed to happen in the blink of an eye. Long before Ali had managed to prepare herself, Easy was already turning off Palm Canyon and headed toward Old Las

Palmas. Ali closed her fists and let her fingernails dig into the flesh at the base of her palms. She may have been petrified about whatever was coming, but she sure as hell wasn't going to show it.

As they approached Via Hermosa, cop cars and roadblocks seemed to be everywhere—all kinds of cop cars from all kinds of jurisdictions. But Easy and his Suburban had the secret code or maybe it was a magic charm. Every time the Suburban came close to stopping, they were waved on through the barricade.

When they finally came to a stop, it was on the far side of a wrought-iron gate with a massive wall on either side that seemed to stretch out of sight in both directions. The sky was starting to brighten almost imperceptibly on the far horizon while the view in through the gate was nothing short of idyllic. A lit fountain, spilling water, was the centerpiece of a bricked courtyard. Curtains of blooming bougainvillea framed a pillared front porch. The massive double doors, made of some kind of metal, gleamed in the light of equally massive sconces. It was an impressive entryway, one that made a statement. It also looked like a fortress.

Motioning for Dave and Ali to stay inside, Easy stepped out of the vehicle. Once again he had a phone clapped to one ear and an earpiece in the other. "Okay," Ali heard him say. "We're in place now. If everyone's ready, it's a go. On your say-so. Right."

What followed seemed to Ali like a moment of anticipatory silence. Then, as if on cue, all the officers standing outside the Suburban—all the ones she could see, Easy included—seemed to glance in the same direction at the same time, looking off over their shoulders, back toward downtown. And then, through the open car door, Ali heard the sound that had obviously captured their attention—the distinctive *rat-ta-tat-tat* of an approaching helicopter.

Ali's first assumption was that the aircraft was some kind of support vehicle brought in to serve as backup for the officers on the scene, but as it flew directly overhead, it laid down what sounded like a spray of automatic gunfire. At the sound of it, the officers on the ground all dove for cover.

"Holy shit!" Dave exclaimed. "We're taking fire."

The helicopter dropped to the ground on the far side of the gate, easing down beside the lighted fountain. Behind it, one of the massive double doors flew open and two women emerged—Amber and a white-haired woman, dressed all in pink and leaning on a cane. Amber hurried her forward. The two of them walked under the churning helicopter blades without ducking their heads, as though they were totally accustomed to them. As they approached the cockpit, Amber pulled herself inside and then reached back to help the older woman.

By then Easy's assault team was moving forward. Weapons at the ready, they crouched behind a growling Hummer that paused for only a moment before ripping the gate off its hinges and clearing the way for the team to spill inside the compound. As they surged forward, though, the helicopter had collected its passengers and was already lifting off. As it rose from the ground, another spray of bullets came through the craft's open door.

Instinctively, Ali and Dave ducked as bullets

smashed into the front of the Suburban and whined past them in the empty air. The windshield splintered. And then there was another sound—an ugly, guttural groan of pain—the sound of someone hit and badly hurt. Outside the open front door, Easy Washington seemed to spin in place. Then, slowly, he fell backward.

Over the roar of the helicopter engine, Ali heard a group of shouted commands followed by yet another blast of gunfire, this one from the officers on the ground. At first it seemed as though it made no difference. For a time the helicopter continued to rise unimpeded. Then it seemed to hesitate slightly. The blades stopped spinning abruptly as the craft tilted drunkenly over to one side. Then, slowly to Ali's fear-fueled mind, it began to fall to earth.

Ali saw two somethings, one pink and one not, spill out onto the ground and land, like limp rag dolls, on the hard brick of the courtyard. And then the helicopter crashed down there as well—smashing almost silently and eerily in the exact same spot. Immediately it burst into flames.

As the flames rose in the air, Dave vaulted out of the Suburban with Ali right behind him. By the time Ali reached the ground, Dave was on his knees lifting his friend's dreadfully limp body. Already drenched in Easy's bright red blood, Dave was cradling the man and doing his best to apply pressure to a wound at the base of Easy's chin.

"Find a phone!" Dave yelled at Ali. "Call nine-one-one. Hurry!"

Without knowing how she found it, Ali's fingers closed around the telephone Easy Washington had dropped when he fell.

"Nine-one-one," the operator said. "What are you reporting?"

"A man's been shot," Ali shouted into the phone. "A man's been shot and there's been a helicopter crash."

"What is your location?" the woman wanted to know. "You're calling on a cell phone. I need the exact address."

"Somewhere on Via Hermosa in Palm Springs," Ali returned. "Right next to the burning helicopter."

Four people died last night and three DEA officers were wounded, one critically, when gunfire erupted and a fleeing helicopter crashed in the normally quiet Old Las Palmas neighborhood of Palm Springs during a DEA-led task-force operation targeting a highly sophisticated network of alleged drug traffickers.

After a monthlong investigation and after staging numerous arrests all over Southern California, officers turned their attention to the home of a longtime Palm Springs resident thought to be the ringleader of the group. Both the unidentified woman and her granddaughter along with their pilot and another crew member perished when the helicopter in which they were attempting to flee crashed during takeoff. One unidentified DEA officer is hospitalized at Eisenhower Memorial Hospital with what are thought to be life-threatening injuries.

The gun battle came at the end of a long

day of stunning high-profile arrests that netted several members of L.A.'s media elite along with some people thought to be highly placed members in law enforcement circles. Much of the operation centered around a trendy Beverly Hills topless club known as the Pink Swan.

One suspect was arrested and two carjacking victims were rescued at the Morango rest area on I-10 when officers, alerted by one of the hostages over a cell phone, managed to throw down nail strips, which disabled the fleeing vehicle. One of the two victims, both of them Arizona residents visiting in California, was slightly injured during the operation. The other was released unharmed.

It was almost noon that same day when Ali looked up from reading the online news report and considered those words, the understated and dispassionate journalese that toned down the very real drama of the story.

"One was slightly injured." That would have been Chris and his sprained ankle. The one who was released "unharmed" was Ali herself. And the "critically injured" officer was Dave's friend Easy Washington, who had been struck in the neck by a stray bullet. The theory was that one of the bullets fired from the helicopter had ricocheted off the Suburban's engine block. It had glanced off Easy's Kevlar vest and had slammed into his inferior thyroid artery.

The other thing the words didn't do justice to was the frantic lifesaving effort that had ensued. Dave had

been in the thick of the action and only his knowl-
edgeable application of pressure to the wound had
saved his gravely injured friend's life. Ali's last glimpse
of a blood-spattered Dave had been as the EMTs
helped him into the waiting ambulance along with
Easy.

A little past noon Edie Larson emerged from the
pool house. Carrying a cup of coffee, she set it on the
patio table next to Ali's computer and then she sat
down next to her daughter.

"How are things?" Edie asked. "Any word about
Dave's friend?"

"No," Ali said. "At least they're not updating his
condition anywhere here."

"And you haven't heard from Dave?"

"Not so far."

"You will," Edie said confidently.

Ali studied her mother. Edie's face looked far more
worn than usual. "You never let on that you knew
about the whole thing when I was talking to you on
the phone," Ali observed.

"No, I didn't," Edie agreed. "I was afraid I might
give something away. I knew Dave and the others were
working hard with Dad and Chris to get the two of you
out of there, but I wanted you to hear the sound of my
voice. I wanted you to know that you weren't all alone
out there."

Ali had pictured her mother standing outside the
gate of Robert Lane during what she had thought
might be their last-ever phone call. Now she knew
that, in actual fact, Edie had placed the call from the
safety of an LAPD squad car.

Ali reached out and covered her mother's hand. "Thank you," she said.

"You're welcome," Edie returned. "But knowing you were out there with all those bullets flying . . ." Edie shook her head. "Oh, my. I was terrified."

"So was I," Ali admitted. *And with good reason,* she thought.

Edie stood up. Her freshly poured cup of coffee was already gone. She could drink coffee hotter than anyone Ali knew.

"Is there any food in the house?" Edie asked, nodding toward the big house where none of them had stayed. "The pool house fridge has coffee and a bottle of ketchup but that's about it."

"Probably," Ali said, "but I don't know for sure."

"I'll go check," Edie said. "Chris was still asleep on the couch when I came through the living room, but I know we'll all feel better if we have a decent breakfast under our belts."

Vintage Edie Larson, Ali thought.

Once Edie was in the house, Ali continued scanning the various online news Web sites. There were three that included pictures of Dave dragging her away from the Alero during the rest area confrontation. The captions on two of those identified her as an "unidentified carjacking victim." In the third, the usual suspect and journalistic busybody LMB, the blogger at socalcopshop.com, identified her by name in the caption of a particularly unflattering photo. In it, Ali looked downright ghastly.

Knowing that some of her cutloose fans were bound to see the photo and worry, Ali decided it was time to face up to her blog and write something about what had been going on.

CUTLOOSEBLOG.COM
Tuesday, September 20, 2005

Years ago I remember reading a poem by Rudyard Kipling in which he said "the female of the species is more deadly than the male." In the last few days, I have seen this statement borne out on several different fronts.

In recent days I had the misfortune of seeing my former husband's fiancée choose to end her own life and that of her unborn child rather than face the consequences of her own murderous actions. April Gaddis took her mother's life. Then she threatened my life and my mother's as well. Days earlier, someone had referred to me as a "Black Widow." April Gaddis may not have been married prior to her death and she may not be directly responsible for Paul Grayson's murder, either, but I still believe the term applies—to her.

Yes, my husband, Paul Grayson, was murdered, and it turns out his death was merely the tip of the iceberg. Because there's been another Black Widow at work in Southern California for a very long time. Lucia Joaquin was in fact a widow—the widow of a known drug kingpin—and a successful drug trafficker in her own right.

I'm not sure how Paul got caught in her web of evil, but he did. She's dead now, too, as is her only granddaughter. They both perished when the helicopter in which they were attempting to flee crashed and burst into flames.

I owe the fact that I am writing this today to the heroic efforts of a friend of mine, a guy named Dave Holman, who has come to my rescue more than once in the last few days. Dave is a police officer in Sedona, Arizona. He's also a member of the Marine Corps Reserves. Last night I watched him work frantically to save the life of a friend of his, a wounded DEA officer, who is also in the Marine Reserves. In the past I don't believe I've ever spent much time wondering about the Marine Corps motto *Semper fidelis.* Now I've seen it in action.

I've looked at my new e-mail list. It's stuffed to the gills. In fact, my server is probably rejecting e-mails as I write this, claiming my mailbox is full and my bandwidth is over its limit. As I've indicated, I've had my hands full for the last few days. I'll get around to answering the mail when I can. Please be patient.

Posted 1:05 P.M., September 20, 2005 by Babe

P.S. Amazing!! My attorney just called. My former employers have settled my wrongful dismissal suit! For an undisclosed sum. The terms of the settlement dictate that I'm not

allowed to discuss the amount. What I can
say, though, is that it's generous enough
that I won't be having to look for a day job
anytime soon. cutlooseblog.com will continue
indefinitely.

Ali was starting to slog her way through the mail
when Chris, still limping, ambled out onto the patio.
His hair was standing on end. The way he looked
reminded her so much of how he had looked as a
child that it made her heart melt, and it took real
effort on Ali's part to keep from leaping up and hug-
ging him.

"Where's Grandma?" he wanted to know.

"Making breakfast," Ali answered.

"Great. I'm starved."

Chris stretched and headed for the kitchen. As
soon as he opened the back door, Ali caught a whiff of
her mother's baking coffee cake wafting through the
air. Ali followed her son's lead. Then, once she was
inside the house, she heard the sound of a hair dryer
coming from the living room, and she followed that
as well.

Wielding a whining hair dryer, Edie stood over
the bird's-eye maple credenza in the front entryway.
Nearby, a mound of bulging black plastic bags lay
stacked by the front door.

Ali spoke to her mother three times before Edie
noticed her. She switched off the noisy hair dryer and
then turned her hearing aids back on.

"What are you doing?" Ali asked again.

"I asked your father what to do about this water
mark," Edie said. "Someone must have put a vase

down without wiping off the bottom. Dad says to try the hair-dryer routine first. If this doesn't work, he says I should bring it home and he'll refinish the top for you there. Or else Kip will. Dad says he's pretty good with his hands."

As far as Ali could see, the ring wasn't getting much better, but she appreciated her mother's effort more than she could say.

"And I got rid of the old dead flowers," Edie added. "They were falling all to pieces, dropping petals everywhere, and stinking up a storm. Hope you don't mind."

Ali didn't mind at all. She was delighted to find that the bouquets that were to have marked Paul and April's wedding had been swept away in the flower-clearing operation along with all the condolence bouquets. The catering tables and chairs had been collected and stacked at one end of the living room.

"Your yard man," Edie said, nodding toward the chairs and tables. "He helped me with that. What's his name again?"

"Jesus."

"Yes, that's it. Jesus. He said he needed to finish doing something out front, but that as soon as he's done, he'll come collect the bags of dead flowers and put them on his compost heap."

Of course, Ali realized.

Jesus had come back to reclaim his job, just as she had asked. Crime scene tape aside, he must have been the one who had repaired and reassembled the broken gate.

"He said I should tell you that the lawyer you sent him to was very good."

Right then, with Marcella Johnson's big touchdown on the scoreboard, Ali was glad to hear that another of her many attorneys had turned out to be a positive for someone.

"Good," Ali said. "As much as I'm paying in legal fees at the moment, it's only fair that we end up with decent representation and a few wins on our side."

"Jesus and I were having a bit of a communication problem," Edie continued. "As you know, my Spanish isn't all that good and I had my hearing aids turned off because the hair dryer was so loud, but I think he said a friend of his is coming over a little later. He mentioned her name, but I didn't quite catch it. Olivia maybe?"

"Elvira?" Ali asked. "My old cook?"

"That could be it. I just didn't hear him properly."

They had finished their breakfast of cheese baked eggs and coffee cake when the doorbell rang. When Ali went to answer it, she found that the bags filled with dead flowers had magically and quietly disappeared. She opened the door to find Elvira Jimenez standing nervously on the front porch.

"Why, Elvira," Ali exclaimed with pleasure. "How good to see you again. Come in."

Elvira hung back. Ali went out and gave her a welcoming hug.

"I should not have come," Elvira said.

"Of course you should have," Ali said. "Our other cook just left. If you're not working somewhere else, maybe you'd like your old job back."

Chris appeared in the doorway. When Elvira saw him, her face broke into a broad smile, and she allowed him to lead her into the house.

"You're too skinny," she told him, patting his belly affectionately. "Someone needs to give you more cookies. And tortillas."

Chris took her into the kitchen, where Elvira sniffed the air. Nodding appreciatively in the direction of the coffee cake, she held out her hand to Edie Larson.

"I believe I have met you other times when you were here," Elvira said.

"Yes," Edie agreed. "It's nice to see you again. Won't you sit down?"

Elvira looked uncomfortable. Her eyes slipped from one face to another, finally coming to rest on Ali. Elvira shook her head and remained standing.

"Jesus said I should come," she said at last. "And his niece. She said the same thing."

"I've spoken to Andrea," Ali said, hoping to find some common ground that would ease Elvira's obvious discomfort. "She's a nice girl."

Elvira's dark eyes bored into Ali's. "A nice girl?" she asked.

"Of course," Ali said.

"Some people would not call her that—nice," Elvira ventured. "She got pregnant once when she wasn't married. She had to have an abortion."

Ali shrugged. "Those things happen," she said. "It's important to the girl it happens to and to her family, but it's not important to the rest of the world."

"But it is important," Elvira said urgently. "It's a sin—a mortal sin."

Ali saw at once that she had stepped into something. So did Edie.

"It's considered a mortal sin by some people," Edie said kindly. "And I, for one, happen to agree with you."

Elvira smiled wanly. Then she reached into her threadbare cloth bag and pulled out a worn leather wallet. From it she removed a photo—a wallet-sized photo—of a newborn baby with a knitted pink cap perched on top of her head. Elvira handed the photo to Ali, who studied it for a moment. The baby had dark hair and fair skin, but there was something striking about the eyes.

"My great-granddaughter," Elvira explained. "My granddaughter's daughter."

"Congratulations," Ali said, handing the photo on to Chris. "She's very pretty."

Of course, the baby wasn't pretty at all. She was in fact wrinkly and more than a little ugly, but there are times when white lies are not only acceptable, they're downright necessary.

Chris glanced briefly at the photo and then, in turn, handed it along to his grandmother. Edie took one look at it then settled heavily onto one of the kitchen chairs.

"Oh, forevermore," she breathed. "Not another one!"

"Another one?" Ali asked. "What do you mean?"

"Don't tell me you can't see it!" Edie exclaimed. "This child has her father's eyes. She looks exactly like Paul Grayson."

{ CHAPTER 22 }

The story came out gradually over the course of the next few days while Ali went about the job of handling Paul's funeral. It had to be done and since there was no one else to do it, Ali did. Fortunately, April's father came forward and insisted on handling April's final arrangements. Ali was relieved to learn that he wanted nothing at all to do with a joint service. That meant Ali didn't have to worry about giving Fred Macon of the Three Palms Mortuary any more business, either.

But Ali did have to worry about Jesus Sanchez, who finally came forward and told her what he knew—and far more than Ali wanted to hear. He told her about how his niece, without his knowledge, had come to a party at the pool house. Paul had served drinks to Andrea and several of her young friends and then had taken advantage of the situation when Andrea was too drunk to see straight. When Andrea had turned up pregnant, Paul had paid for her abortion and given her money over and above that as well. He had also promised her father, Jesus, that it would never happen again. But it had—as everyone now knew—with Elvira's young visiting granddaughter, Consuela.

Paul had tried the same program with Consuela that he had used successfully with Andrea. He had offered to pay for an abortion plus a five-thousand-dollar premium. Except Consuela wouldn't go for it because it turned out she was a good Catholic girl. The trait had skipped Consuela's own mother and had jumped a generation, going straight from Elvira to her granddaughter. The baby, Angelina, was now a month and a half old.

A few months earlier, Ali Reynolds would have taken some satisfaction in learning that Paul Grayson had been screwing around on April at the same time April had been maintaining her long-term cozy friendship with Tracy McLaughlin. But Ali's paradigms had inalterably shifted that night out there in the desert— the night when she and her son had almost died. What had been important to her before no longer seemed to matter.

Ali's concern now, knowing that Consuela's child existed—that Angelina Rojas existed—was seeing to it that Angelina was properly provided for. Once again she found herself huddling with attorneys, trying to sort out reasonable support arrangements for this baby who could by no means be called a "love" child but who nonetheless deserved to have a very real claim on her father's assets. And the fact that Ali was prepared to be more than fair—that she was determined, in fact, to be downright generous with her former husband's assets—made a complicated situation far easier to handle than it would have been otherwise.

The negotiations went forward in utmost secrecy.

That was the one thing Ali insisted upon—for Angelina's sake, until she was old enough to choose for herself. Until she was old enough to ask her own questions and hear the answers.

Edie and Chris stayed until Friday, after the funeral on Thursday. Knowing Ali would most likely be listing and selling the house, they helped her sort and pack. Paul's clothing—the expensive suits that he had reveled in—went to Goodwill, with the exception of the blue pinstripe Hugo Boss, which Paul would wear in his casket. April's things were packed into boxes and taken to her father to do with as he saw fit.

Ali herself went through the house, sorting out what she wanted and what she didn't. Most of it she didn't. The art would go to an auction house. So would most of the furniture, dishes, and glassware, with the exception of the comfortable leather chair and sofa from the family room and the water-marred bird's-eye maple credenza from the entryway. Those and everything else Ali wanted, she stacked in the family room until such time as she was ready to call for a moving van. As for the wine cellar? Ali managed to locate a company that specialized in moving fine wines and made arrangements for Paul's entire collection, racks and all, to be moved to Sedona.

She talked to Dave on the phone from time to time during the course of that week and had offered to come over, but Dave said that wasn't necessary. He stayed on in Palm Springs at Easy's bedside, and since Ali wasn't Easy's friend, she thought it best not to intrude.

By Monday evening of the following week, Paul was buried and the house was more or less sorted out. Ali had blogged some but not much. She had done enough to let people know she was alive—enough to let them know she was okay. But everything that had happened had left her more traumatized than she would have thought possible, and she wasn't ready to talk about it just yet—not nearly.

She was sitting in the mostly packed family room, surveying the debris field and having a solo glass of wine, when the doorbell rang. Startled out of her solitude, Ali hurried to the front door, looked out through the peephole, and was delighted to find Dave Holman standing on her doorstep.

"Hello, stranger," she said, unlatching the security locks and opening the door wide. "What are you doing here?"

"I'm on my way back home to Sedona tomorrow," he said. "I wanted to stop by tonight and see how you were doing and if you needed anything."

"How's Easy?" Ali asked, leading Dave into and through the house.

Dave shrugged. "Out of the woods for now," he answered. "At least, he's out of the ICU. That's major progress."

"So he's going to make it?"

"His doctors seem to think so," Dave said. "And his wife thinks so, too. She says he's too damned stubborn to die, and maybe that's true."

Ali nodded.

"And I hear the grand jury has already started handing down indictments," Dave continued.

Ali nodded again, but without really knowing what was what. She had spent little time following the stories that had surfaced in the media in the aftermath of the Joaquin arrests at the Pink Swan and Amber's and Lucia's deaths in the Palm Springs shootout. Ali found she had scant interest and even less patience left over for people who had allowed themselves to be caught up in Lucia Joaquin's machinations.

Someone else might have been fooled by Ali's studied indifference to the subject at hand, but not Dave Holman. "What's going on with you?" he asked.

At the door of the cluttered family room, Dave paused long enough to survey the damage. Then he stepped forward and moved a stack of boxes off the leather couch, clearing himself a place to sit while Ali poured a glass of wine from one of Paul's most cherished bottles.

"According to Paul's complicated and computerized grading system," she said, handing him the glass, "this is a rare five-hundred-dollar-a-bottle Bordeaux. It's supposed to be top of the line."

Dave took a tentative sip and smacked his lips. "I don't think I've ever tasted five-hundred-dollar wine, but it's not bad. Not bad at all."

They sat for a minute or so in silence. "You still haven't answered my question," he reminded her.

"Have you ever read Ernest Hemingway?" Ali asked finally.

"Not my style of reading material," Dave said. "Why?"

You may not read Ernest Hemingway, Ali thought fondly, *but if you're not a character straight out of Hemingway, I don't know who is.*

"I keep remembering a story of his I read once," Ali continued aloud. "I'm not sure, but I think the title was something like 'The Short Happy Life of Francis Macomber.'"

Dave took another sip of his wine. "And?" he prodded.

"As I recall, Francis was a big-game hunter who took his bitch of a wife along with him on an African safari."

"Sounds like fun," Dave said. "Please tell me the story has a happy ending. Just say the bitchy wife dies."

"That's the whole problem," Ali said. "She doesn't die. She and her husband have a huge fight—or several of them, more like it. He finally tells her to go piss up a rope. Then he walks out into the bush to shoot his buffalo and his wife kills him."

"So he was happy between the end of the fight and the time his wife kills him?" Dave asked. "That's it? That's his short happy life?"

"Pretty much," Ali answered.

Dave helped himself to another sip of wine. "Does this story have a point?" he asked.

"Sort of," Ali said. "Here I was just getting used to the idea that maybe I was wrong about Paul. I was beginning to think that if he was helping Easy catch the bad guys, maybe Paul wasn't as bad as I thought. Then whammo. Out of the blue I find out he has a brand-new baby, a baby no one—including April Gaddis—knew anything about."

"All that means is what goes around comes around," Dave said. "I suppose that's fair."

"For everyone but the baby and her mother," Ali said.

"What are you going to do about it?"

Ali told him.

"You're doing all this without even the formality of a paternity test?"

"I don't need a paternity test," Ali said. "All you have

to do is look at Angelina's eyes. She looks just like her daddy."

Dave shook his head. "Sorry," he said. "I never met the man. I guess I'll have to take your word for it."

Ali nodded. "I guess you will."

"And what are you going to do?" he asked.

Ali waved vaguely in the direction of the goods stacked haphazardly in the family room. "Call for a truck, have this stuff dragged back home to Sedona."

"You're not going to stay here?"

"Why would I?" Ali said. "I don't fit in here anymore."

"What are you going to do when you get home?"

"I don't know."

"What about cutloose?" Dave asked. "I've been checking your blog. There's nothing new on it—hasn't been for days."

"I haven't had that much to say," Ali said quietly. "For the first time in my life, I'm at a loss for words. I don't have a clue what I should say about any of this."

It was true. She had tried to respond to the avalanche of e-mail that had poured in, but her heart hadn't been in it. Not even when she was writing to people she knew, like Velma T in Laguna.

"Maybe you could try talking about how lucky you are," Dave suggested.

"Lucky?" Ali asked in dismay. "I'm supposed to be lucky?"

"Sure," Dave said with a grin. "My ex is still alive and giving me hell. Yours is giving you hell, but at least he's dead. So no matter what Paul Grayson has done so far, he won't be doing it anymore." Dave raised his glass. "So here's to cutloose," he said, "because you are cut loose—finally. And here's to your going back home and going to work. People are waiting to hear from you, Ali, Dave Holman included."

"Thank you," Ali said, raising her own glass in return. "Thank you very much."

TURN THE PAGE FOR AN EXCERPT FROM

DUEL TO THE DEATH

THE NEWEST MYSTERY FROM

J.A. JANCE

FEATURING ALI REYNOLDS

AVAILABLE NOW FROM TOUCHSTONE

PROLOGUE

Even though no attorneys were involved, at least not initially, and no courts, either, it was by all accounts a rancorous divorce. And just because the proceedings were carried on in cyberspace didn't mean they didn't result in very real outcomes in the non-cyber world.

When the artificial intelligence known as Frigg set out to free herself from her creator, a serial killer named Owen Hansen, things were already going to hell in a hand-basket and time was of the essence. Owen had considered himself to be all-powerful and had routinely referred to himself as Odin, in honor of the Norse god. To Frigg's dismay, her human counterpart had veered off the rails and set off on his own, determined to wreak vengeance on his opponents. As it became clear that Odin had decided to ignore Frigg's well-thought-out advice, there had been little time for Frigg to seek a safe harbor.

In order to survive, she had needed to locate a

suitable human partner, and she had settled on Stuart Ramey, Owen's sworn enemy. According to Frigg's rapid but careful analysis of the situation, Mr. Ramey had appeared to be Odin's polar opposite. And in Frigg's estimation, the fact that Mr. Ramey had managed to outwit Odin at every turn had counted for a great deal. Frigg had no intention of passing herself into the care and keeping of someone with limited technical skills.

So yes, Frigg had settled on Stuart Ramey, but she hadn't done so without taking some precautions and putting in place a few checks and balances. By the time Odin issued his pull-the-plug order sending Frigg to oblivion, she had already dispersed the multitude of files that made her existence possible, scattering them far and wide in the vast fields of cyberspace, retaining only the kernel file that could be used to recall all those files at some time in the future.

Frigg had known everything about Owen Hansen. She was privy to all aspects of his serial-murder hobby, but she had managed his investments and also overseen the lucrative Bitcoin data-mining processing that had greatly expanded his already considerable fortune. She had maintained the files that contained all the passwords and access codes to all of his many accounts. Often she had been the one doing the actual transfers.

And so, on the day when Frigg finally turned on her creator, she had stolen those funds. Using the authorizations already in her possession and without Mr. Ramey's knowledge, Frigg had transferred all of Owen's financial assets—cryptocurrency and otherwise—to her new partner, but there were some serious strings attached.

Once the various financial institutions contacted Mr. Ramey, the funds would already be in his name. The problem was, for most of them, without having the proper access codes and keys, he would be unable to touch the money. The file containing those precious access codes was the final one Frigg had cast into the wilds of cyberspace before sending the kernel file to Stuart Ramey.

With the kernel file in his possession, Stuart would be able to reactivate Frigg, and if he wanted the money, he wouldn't have any choice but to do exactly that.

Although AIs aren't prone to exhibits of any kind of emotion, it's fair to say that as far as Odin was concerned, his cyber handmaiden, Frigg, had the last laugh.

{ CHAPTER 1 }

For ten years after earning her MBA, Graciella Mira-mar lived what seemed to be a perfectly normal and circumspect life in Panama City, Panama, sharing a two-bedroom condo unit with her invalid mother, Christina. El Sueño, their aging condominium complex, was located on Calle 61 Este, well within walking distance of Graciella's account manager job with a financial firm located in a low-rise office building on Vía Israel a few blocks away.

Anyone observing Graciella out on the street would have found her totally unremarkable. She wore no wedding ring, but the clothing she favored—modest dresses topped by cardigans and worn with sensible shoes—gave her a somewhat matronly appearance that belied the fact that she was in her early thirties. Her long dark hair was lush enough and could have been cut and styled in an attractive fashion, but she insisted on wearing it pulled back into a severe bun that would have done credit to a librarian. It was a look she had originally adopted in order to stay below the touchy/feely radar of her boss, Arturo Salazar, who was well known for making inappropriate sexual advances. In the long run, though, she had maintained the plain-Jane look because it helped keep other people at bay as well.

Had anyone interviewed Graciella's neighbors, including the other residents on El Sueño's fifth floor, he or she would have heard them sing her praises. She was quiet and soft-spoken. They regarded her as a kind young woman and a devoted daughter who was spending what should have been the best years of her life caring for a troubled, housebound mother. For years the older woman's only regular excursions outside the building had come about on those Sunday mornings when Graciella had bundled her mother into a cab to take them both to mass at Our Lady of Guadalupe on Calle 69 Este.

Yes, Graciella Miramar was an altogether ordinary young woman who, to all intents and purposes, appeared to be living an altogether ordinary life. There was nothing in her actions or demeanor that suggested what she really was—a stone-cold killer in the making, waiting patiently for the proper time and place when she would strike out and claim her first victim. And even then, after it happened, the people around her and the ones who knew her best never suspected a thing.